GRACIAS
THANKS

por / by

PAT MORA

ilustraciones por / illustrations by **JOHN PARRA**

traducción por / translation by
ADRIANA DOMÍNGUEZ

LEE & LOW BOOKS INC.
New York

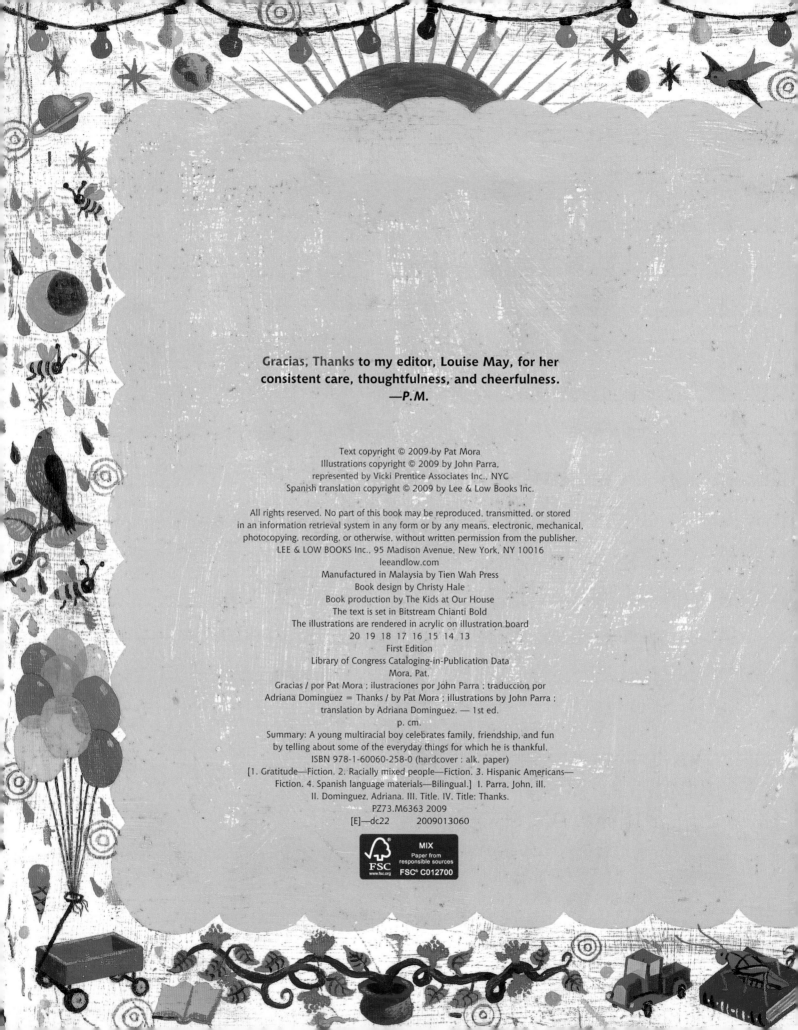

Gracias, Thanks to my editor, Louise May, for her
consistent care, thoughtfulness, and cheerfulness.
—*P.M.*

LEE & LOW BOOKS Inc., 95 Madison Avenue, New York, NY 10016
leeandlow.com
Manufactured in Malaysia by Tien Wah Press
Book design by Christy Hale
Book production by The Kids at Our House
The text is set in Bitstream Chianti Bold
The illustrations are rendered in acrylic on illustration board
20 19 18 17 16 15 14 13
First Edition
Library of Congress Cataloging-in-Publication Data
Mora, Pat.
Gracias / por Pat Mora ; ilustraciones por John Parra ; traduccion por
Adriana Dominguez = Thanks / by Pat Mora ; illustrations by John Parra ;
translation by Adriana Dominguez. — 1st ed.
p. cm.
Summary: A young multiracial boy celebrates family, friendship, and fun
by telling about some of the everyday things for which he is thankful.
ISBN 978-1-60060-258-0 (hardcover : alk. paper)
[1. Gratitude—Fiction. 2. Racially mixed people—Fiction. 3. Hispanic Americans—
Fiction. 4. Spanish language materials—Bilingual.] I. Parra, John, ill.
II. Dominguez, Adriana. III. Title. IV. Title: Thanks.
PZ73.M6363 2009
[E]—dc22   2009013060

MIX
Paper from
responsible sources
FSC® C012700

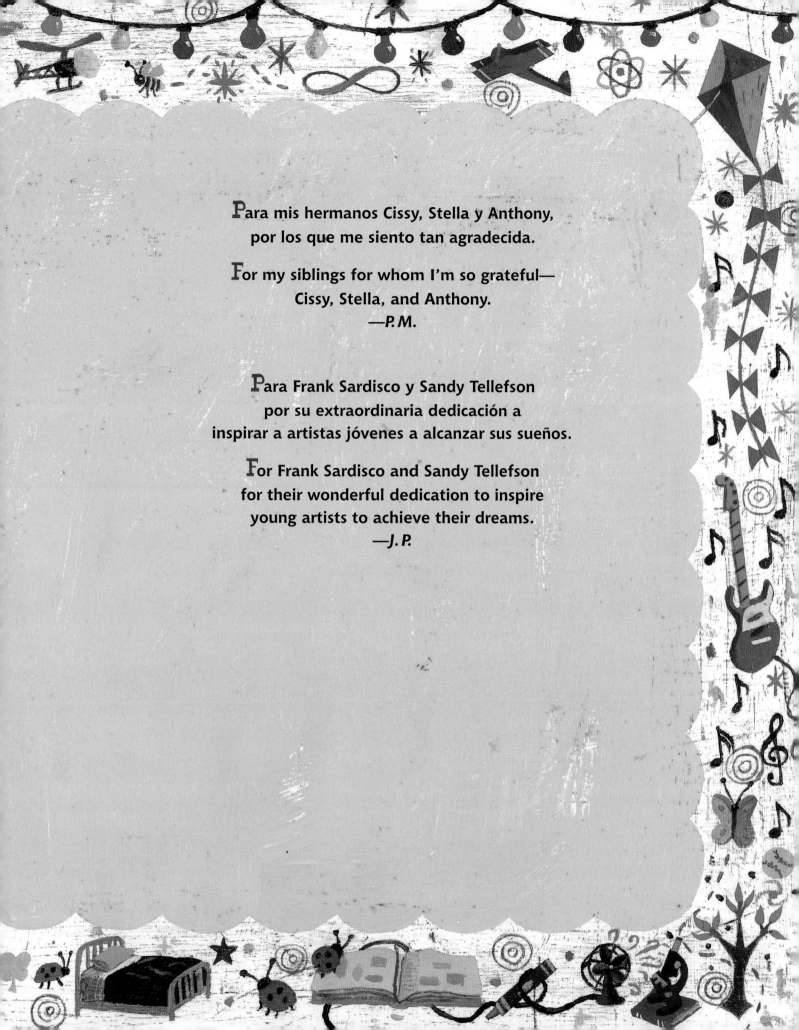

Para mis hermanos Cissy, Stella y Anthony,
por los que me siento tan agradecida.

For my siblings for whom I'm so grateful—
Cissy, Stella, and Anthony.
—*P. M.*

Para Frank Sardisco y Sandy Tellefson
por su extraordinaria dedicación a
inspirar a artistas jóvenes a alcanzar sus sueños.

For Frank Sardisco and Sandy Tellefson
for their wonderful dedication to inspire
young artists to achieve their dreams.
—*J. P.*

Por el sol que me despierta y no permite
que siga durmiendo por años y años, y que
me crezca una larga barba blanca, gracias.

For the sun that wakes me up so I don't
sleep for years and years and grow a long,
white beard, thanks.

Por la mariquita que se posó en mi dedo, una pequeña sorpresa voladora roja, gracias.

For the ladybug that landed on my finger, a little red flying surprise, thanks.

Por las olas espumosas que nos persiguen a mí y a mi hermana,
y a veces corren hacia nosotros con un rápido *¡PLAF!*, gracias.

For the foamy waves that chase my sister and me and sometimes dash after us with a fast *SPLASH*, thanks.

Por las abejas que no me picaron y convirtieron en un alfiletero, gracias.

For the bees that didn't sting me and turn me into a pincushion, thanks.

Por abuelita, que siempre me guiña y me da un dólar cuando nadie nos está mirando, gracias.

For Abuelita, who always winks and gives me
a dollar when nobody's looking, thanks.

Por mi amigo Billy, que me enseñó el libro sobre el niño
gigante que pone a sus padres pequeñitos en la cima de
un gran árbol cuando ellos se portan mal, gracias.

For my friend Billy, who showed me the book about a boy giant who puts his little parents on top of a tall tree when they misbehave, thanks.

Por los gusanos que atrajeron al gran pez
que tiró de mi hilo de pescar, gracias.

For the worms that brought the big fish
to tug on my line, thanks.

Por mi hermanito, que le lanzó su puré
de chícharos a mi hermana y me hizo reír
tanto que me caí de la silla, gracias.

For my little brother, who threw mashed peas
at my sister and made me laugh so hard I fell
off my chair, thanks.

Por mamá, que encontró mi tarea
en la basura, gracias.

For Mom, who found my homework
in the trash, thanks.

Por la música de mi tío y su guitarra, que convierte
a nuestros perros en cantantes aulladores, gracias.

For the music of my uncle and his guitar that turns our dogs into howling singers, thanks.

Por mi familia, que aplaudió y siguió aplaudiendo cuando me caí en el escenario durante nuestra obra de teatro escolar, gracias.

For my family, who clapped and clapped even when I tripped on the stage in the school play, thanks.

Por el chocolate que papá derrite hasta que se convierte
en un líquido espeso que llamamos lodo tibio cuando
lo vertemos sobre el helado de vainilla, gracias.

For the chocolate Dad melts into thick syrup
we call warm mud when we pour it on vanilla
ice cream, thanks.

Por mis piyamas viejos, tan suaves que me siento
como si me estuviera poniendo aire, gracias.

For my old pajamas, so soft they feel like
I'm putting on air, thanks.

Por el grillo escondido que nos canta una
serenata antes de dormir, ¡gracias!

For the cricket hiding when he serenades
us to sleep, **thanks!**

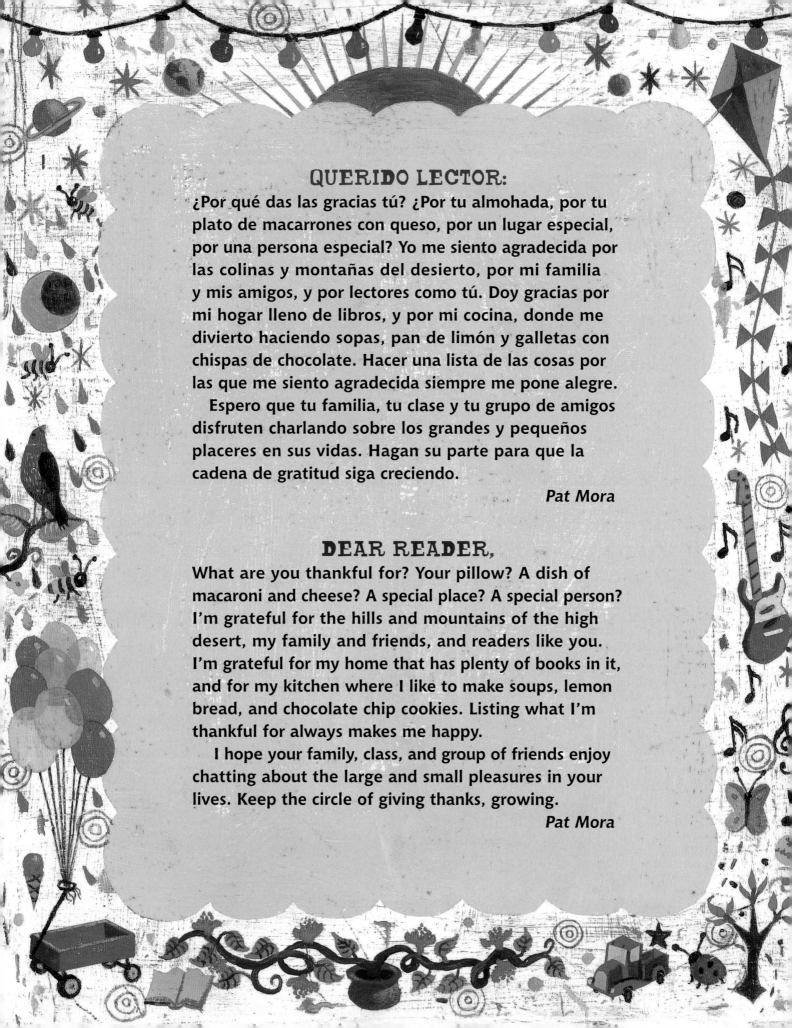

QUERIDO LECTOR:

¿Por qué das las gracias tú? ¿Por tu almohada, por tu plato de macarrones con queso, por un lugar especial, por una persona especial? Yo me siento agradecida por las colinas y montañas del desierto, por mi familia y mis amigos, y por lectores como tú. Doy gracias por mi hogar lleno de libros, y por mi cocina, donde me divierto haciendo sopas, pan de limón y galletas con chispas de chocolate. Hacer una lista de las cosas por las que me siento agradecida siempre me pone alegre.

Espero que tu familia, tu clase y tu grupo de amigos disfruten charlando sobre los grandes y pequeños placeres en sus vidas. Hagan su parte para que la cadena de gratitud siga creciendo.

Pat Mora

DEAR READER,

What are you thankful for? Your pillow? A dish of macaroni and cheese? A special place? A special person? I'm grateful for the hills and mountains of the high desert, my family and friends, and readers like you. I'm grateful for my home that has plenty of books in it, and for my kitchen where I like to make soups, lemon bread, and chocolate chip cookies. Listing what I'm thankful for always makes me happy.

I hope your family, class, and group of friends enjoy chatting about the large and small pleasures in your lives. Keep the circle of giving thanks, growing.

Pat Mora

POPULAR SONG

anhattan
Res
Will you still love me tomorrow?
Ev'ry time w
Respect
I'd do anything for love (but I w
fe (however do you
Tea for two
Blue yodel #1, 't' for Texas
Secret love
chie man
Maple leaf rag
It had
the queen
Love will tear us apart
balls of fire
Relax
he wind 9
Nothing compares 2 U
love a lassie
Brov
Ol' man
Stayin' alive
u up
My way
Summ
All along the watchtower
see
Strawberry fields foreve
Stand by me
Stardust
Ca
rlene
Melanchc
ck blues
After
oddity
Singin' in the ra
message
I still haven't found what I'm looking
Pack up your troubles
Roses of Picardy
Blue
or me
Autobahn
you (I didn't want to do it)
Heebie
Penny lane
Don't cry for me
you under my skin
cket '88'
Smoke gets in your eyes
St
bewildered
Ah! Sweet mystery of life,
Rudolph the red-nosed
my regards to Broadway
You've lost that lovin' feelin
Baby one
Sledgehammer
My heart will do
The preacher
dixie mel

alan lewens

POPULAR SONG
soundtrack of the century

Billboard Books
An imprint of Watson-Guptill Publications
New York

First published in 2001 by HarperCollins*Illustrated*, an imprint of
HarperCollins*Publishers*, under the title *Walk on By*.

First published in the U.S. in 2001 by Billboard Books
An imprint of Watson-Guptill Publications,
a division of BPI Communications, Inc.,
770 Broadway
New York
NY 10003

Editor: Julian Flanders
Designer: Liz Brown
Indexer: Susan Bosanko

ISBN 0-8230-8436-1
Library of Congress Card Number: 2001088393

First printing 2001
1 2 3 4 5 6 7 8 9/09 08 07 06 05 04 03 02 01

Printed and bound in Great Britain by Bath Press

"Writing a popular song is very, very hard to do so that it doesn't sound like hundreds of people have written that song before. I've always found that it's a tough form, if they're going to survive for a long period of time.

There have been popular songs that are big hits, that you can't stand after two, three weeks or two, three months; they overwhelm you, they inundate you, they beat you up. And then there are songs you can hear sung in a bar somewhere that are different versions of the record that you know well – and they work because there's longevity there. You've got to have some length.

But I don't know that you can sit down in a room and just say, 'I'm gonna write a song with longevity', it doesn't work that way. Lyrics have to be really strong. But I don't think a really great, great lyric could survive with a very inferior melody. Could a great, great melody with an inferior lyric survive? Yes, because people remember a tune and stick with it, and sometimes don't even listen to what the lyric is saying."

Burt Bacharach

contents

introduction

It's a well-worn cliché (but true nonetheless) that popular music has provided us with the soundtrack to our lives. Can anyone recall a day in their life without music? It is almost impossible to live in the world these days without hearing pop music on adverts, in movies, on the radio and, yes, even on TV series, all striving to manipulate our emotions with songs that resonate from our common past. The Levi's adverts in the 1980s were classic examples, dipping into a deep well of nostalgia (and, in the process, generating a new and lucrative income stream for record companies in the marketing of back-catalogue songs). So were the many teen movies that used old songs on their soundtracks. While our individual pasts obviously differ, they do tend to cross at the same junctions. Songs have a habit of clinging to those important moments (most obviously, when falling in love). They address the heightened emotions that we all feel but may not be able to articulate in any other way. They become so personal to our own lives, that we virtually assume ownership of them. For many of us these favourite songs tend to have coincided with our own rites of passage. They may also have brought us closer to each other physically since they have always also functioned as dance tunes. They stay with us forever and become touchstones for our most poignant memories. Think of 'Candle in the Wind', Elton John's 1997 elegy for Diana, Princess of Wales. It swept round the world in an instant and became the best-selling record of all time. Or 'Drive' by The Cars – can you ever dissociate that track from the film of starving children in Ethiopia and from Live Aid? Even those people who find secularized pop hymns nauseatingly sentimental cannot escape. One man's hit song is another man's turkey – 'How can you like that awful song?' Love them or loathe them, they excite strong emotions in all of us.

There is something magical about the way that words and music go together in a song and make something bigger than the sum of its two parts. We rightly revere those who are good at making music, whether they're performers or writers. Beyond the nostalgia – a century's worth of love and loss, hope and sorrow – is that perfect three-and-a-half-minute revelation that is the popular song, the 20th-century's most alluring artform. But before we get too carried away, let's not forget that making music is also a commercial enterprise. From its first stirrings in the melting pot of turn-of-the-century New York Tin Pan Alley (one tiny area in a bustling city, so called because of the clatter of pianos being played in tiny cubicles), where hungry young men like Jerome Kern and Irving Berlin would hustle sheet music round the theatres and burlesque halls, to the now global billion-dollar enterprise that has overtaken movies as a revenue earner, the music business has always been into money.

This is a book that celebrates the great songs. Of course, they have all had great performances and occasionally definitive ones. But that's not necessarily what gives a song classic status, and consequently the performance is not the priority here. In fact many of the songs have been chosen either for their ability to transcend a specific performance, for their lasting power (or 'legs' as the industry calls it), and because they have subsequently changed the path of popular music for ever; and, most importantly, because they have all been substantial hits of one sort or another. At the end of 1999, there was a rush of 'The Hundred Great This' and 'Our Best That' that picked a bunch of songs a magazine or a radio station's phone-in vote happened to dictate, but what's the use of that? The songs here have been selected on the basis of one song for each year of the century. The year in question is the year the song was published (or as close to it as possible) rather than the year it became a hit. In exceptional years two songs have been chosen and I have taken a few liberties with the first five years of the century in an effort to uncover the foundations of pop. Of course, music charts didn't really become the spectator sport they are today until the 1950s and counting sales of sheet music, records, or

radio plays (all of which generated income for writers) was open to all sorts of distortion. For the first few decades of the last century, it was impossible to accurately calculate what songs sold most. I have tried to make an estimation which balances popularity with innovation, and judge whether a song has a life beyond one good original performance. If there are several contenders, I concede in a few instances it helps to like a song, but it is by no means the case that this list represents my own personal taste. There are some songs in this collection that have been so overwhelmingly popular it would have been perverse to ignore them, but I wouldn't necessarily give them house room.

It was a tough call faced with the challenge of choosing 'Tea for Two' over 'Fascinating Rhythm'; 'Blue Suede Shoes' over 'Be Bop A Lula', 'That'll Be The Day' and 'Heartbreak Hotel'; or making a choice between 'You've Lost That Loving Feeling', 'Can't Explain', 'Satisfaction', 'Like A Rolling Stone' and 'Papa's Got A Brand New Bag', 'Tracks of My Tears' and 'Yesterday' – all written and released in the same year. There were also difficult choices to be made in the period immediately after the First World War and up to the early 1930s when George Gershwin, Irving Berlin, Jerome Kern, Richard Rodgers and Cole Porter were at the top of their game. Just as hard was the period between 1958 and the early 1970s, when Lennon and McCartney were competing with Brian Wilson, Holland, Dozier, Holland, Stevie Wonder, Paul Simon, Carole King, Bob Dylan and Smokey Robinson to write some of the greatest songs ever.

I hope the selection overall gives a sense of the sweep of the music of the 20th century and the way that one style slowly gave way to another. There were no sudden lurches from one form to another. Only evolutions. Show tunes did not start with George Gershwin or Jerome Kern any more than rock 'n' roll started with Elvis. Those of us who witnessed the early stirrings of rock 'n' roll may have felt it was unlike anything we'd heard before, but, in truth, it was because we hadn't been listening hard enough. The pop music industry is more like a rolling river with tributaries running into it, than a series of smaller and separate oceans.

There are some writers I am embarrassed to have left out: Noel Coward, Charles Trenet, Paul Simon, Smokey Robinson, Curtis Mayfield, James Brown and Queen come to mind instantly. They are clearly writers whose songs have stood the test of time. All I can say in mitigation is that the competition was too strong in the years their songs were contenders.

It used to be true that the century was split into two camps. The pre- and post-rock generation. The generation gap polarized taste on both sides, neither conceding much in terms of generosity of spirit. But since the record companies discovered the commercial value of the back-catalogue and reissues, there is so much choice to be had, the old distinctions no longer seem important. It all seems to be one enormous cavern of nostalgia. Pop music, to air another cliché, is now a global language. I'll never forget the thrill of walking into Tower Records on Sunset Boulevard in Los Angeles for the first time and finding their comprehensive catalogue of pre-Beatles British pop: Billy Fury, Cliff Richard – it's amazing what you see filed under rock 'n' roll. And for all the distaste that greeted its arrival in the 1950s, rock and its sub categories have proved to be the most resilient of styles, far outstripping any of the competition in popularity.

Of course, it's easier to pick songs that time and hindsight have accorded classic status. There are some hits that stay with you and seem to mature with age and some that 'pretty soon, beat you up' to use Burt Bacharach's phrase. The most recent hit songs have not yet had time to bed down and evolve into classics. Whether they will or not, time will sort out. I'm sure there are many readers of this book who will be infuriated by some of the choices included here. How could I leave out 'The Man I Love' or 'Imagine' for example? Well, I apologise in advance, but I hope at least to have put down a framework for animated discussion on this most serious of issues.

The 'Walk on By' team at the BBC was all that one could hope for. Music fans of conviction and enthused by the scope of this series, they dealt graciously with the demands of the programmes, the book, the affairs of the BBC, and added immensely to the project. So thanks to Susie Tassell for her unfailing good spirits, Miriam Walsh for her sharp and quirky humour, William Naylor for his peerless taste, Simon Ashley for his quiet authority, Ben Whalley for knowing, and Kate Slattery for caring so much as well as keeping the books. Thanks also to my Executive Producers Andy Batten Foster and Michael Poole for their wisdom, and to the film crew, Jane Barnet, Vinnie Besasie, and especially cameraman John Warwick who has followed me round the world filming musicians for the last 20 years, quietly tolerating my more inarticulate requests... and then doing it his way.

Finally, to the team of directors, Ian Pye, Peter Jamieson, Jeff Morgan, Andrew Graham Brown and Jeremy Marre, all warriors for the cause.

Deadlines demanded I take as much help as I could with writing this book. I am grateful to Julian Flanders for helping to put all this together. I should also like to thank Anthony Wall for his articles on 'Blue Suede Shoes' and 'No Woman No Cry', Michael Parker for 'Penny Lane'/'Strawberry Fields' and 'All Allong the Watchtower', Ian Pye for 'Strange Fruit', 'I Want to Hold Your Hand', 'Good Vibrations', 'The Message', 'Eight Miles High', 'Hotel California', 'Love Will Tear Us Apart', and 'Brown Sugar', and, for the other 30 most recent songs, Sam Kiernan Lewens. Thanks also to all the team at HarperCollins.

ALAN LEWENS

the top 100

songs 1–13

Maple leaf rag

After the ball

Sweet Adeline

Give my regards to Broadway

Jelly roll blues

The preacher and the bear

Stand by me

I love a lassie

Ah! Sweet mystery of life

Oh Danny boy

Alexander's ragtime band

You made me love you (I didn't want to do it)

Melancholy baby

1 maple leaf rag

Words and **music** Scott Joplin **1900**

Whichever way you look at it, it's the music of African-Americans that best characterizes the journey into 20th-century popular music. In the early 1900s minstrel songs (known then as 'coon songs') were immensely popular in music hall and vaudeville. They were mostly (but not exclusively) delivered by white performers with blackened faces, in a style based on stereotypes of southern blacks of the time. Blues and black gospel music flourished in areas where former slaves lived and worked and would go on to energize popular music from the 1930s onwards. Slavery had only been abolished 23 years before **Maple Leaf Rag** was written, but it was to take almost a century or so for African-Americans to achieve something approaching equal civil rights with the white population. But at the beginning of the 20th century, white America, and a little later white Europe, liked the sound of black America, even if they couldn't always bring themselves to watch it performed by 'real darkies' as they were carelessly referred to at the time.

Although **Maple Leaf Rag** was written in 1899, it qualifies as a 20th-century hit not only because it took a while to become popular, but also because it was an important influence in the development of popular music in the first two or three decades of the century. Its popularity was so great that it spawned a host of songs with the word 'rag' in the title, though most were not rags in the true sense, the most notable being 'Alexander's Ragtime Band' which launched the career of Irving Berlin. **Maple Leaf Rag**, however, is the real thing, easily identified by the steady oompah, oompah beat of the left hand while the melody, played with the right hand, is syncopated, with the emphasis on the secondary, weaker beat. This musical innovation was key to the development of jazz, and also influenced some of the more progressive European classical composers of the time, such as Claude Debussy and Eric Satie.

Scott Joplin was a classically trained black piano player. Texas born, he first had access to a piano in a white household where his mother worked as a servant. He was later given formal lessons and it was the classical repertoire that fired Joplin's ambition to join the ranks of the great composers. **Maple Leaf Rag**, named after the Maple Leaf club in Sedalia, Missouri, where Joplin played regularly, was the first rag to sell over a million copies of sheet music, earning its composer one cent per copy. It was first recorded in 1904. Joplin did not like other musicians improvising on his compositions, as he felt his work should be accorded the same respect as classical music. But it was a vain hope because it became popular with the early jazz pioneers for whom improvising was meat and drink. Ragtime became the music of choice for the genteel middle classes, and also gave a veneer of classical respectability to the lobbies of many brothels when played by talented musicians like Eubie Blake and 'Jelly Roll' Morton. If you were black, as most decent ragtime pianists were, you would have to play behind a screen to avoid laying eyes on the white girls displaying their wares. A lyric was written in 1904 in mock patois, but it is the tune that remains paramount, and when played as originally written, it is a delight to the ears.

Above Scott Joplin

trivia

★ Known as the 'King of Ragtime', Joplin had a formal music education that gave him the ability to write down much of the ragtime music he heard.

★ In 1902 Joplin wrote *The Guest of Honour*, the only known ragtime opera.

★ Ragtime enjoyed something of a revival in the 1970s with the release of the movie *The Sting*, which used Scott Joplin's 'The Entertainer' as its theme song and other Joplin rags on the soundtrack.

★ The most noted recordings of Scott Joplin's music, including the soundtrack to *The Sting*, are all performed by contemporary pianist Joshua Rifkind.

Words and music Charles K. Harris 1901

Above
Charles K. Harris

One of the great pioneers of 20th-century commercial pop music, Charles Harris had a sign in his Milwaukee shop window that said, 'Songs Written to Order. Maximum Price $20.' He would write songs for births, marriages, deaths, or even picnics – any occasion you could imagine, he would fashion a song for it. He moved to the great melting pot of New York in the late 19th century when tens of thousands of Italians, Poles, Swedes, Irish, Russians and Chinese were passing through Ellis Island on their way to the Land of the Free to feed the ravenous belly of US industrial expansion.

In the pre-recording era, sheet music was the only way to derive real income from songwriting, and not only was Harris a writer but he was also a publisher and entrepreneur. By publishing his own sheet music, he could avoid arguments over the number of copies sold, and measurably increase his own earnings; it required marketing and distribution skills, and Harris seemed to have these in abundance.

As the American nation grew more affluent, the number of pianos in American homes outstripped that of any other country. Vaudeville, or music hall, was becoming more popular in the bigger cities, and the market for songs and their sheet music was expanding at a similar rate to other industries.

After the Ball was a sentimental ballad with a memorable, tearjerking chorus in the form of a story constructed for middle-class ladies to learn on their parlour pianos. Story songs were popular as they inevitably brought a tear to the eye, and who can resist a sad song?

A little maiden climbed an old man's knee, begged for a story, 'Do, uncle please.
Why are you single; why live alone? Have you no babies; have you no home?'

While working in the theatre district of New York, Harris persuaded a Broadway producer to place the song in one of his shows entitled *A Trip To China Town*. Where a sentimental Victorian waltz fitted into a story about Chinese immigrants can only be imagined, but the show gave the song great exposure, and it allowed Harris to refer to the song as a 'hit song', later to become a 'million-selling hit song'.

In 1901 **After the Ball** was the first popular song to register sales of more than one million copies of sheet music, and by 1920 it had been translated into many languages, and had racked up sales of more than ten million. Harris was deriving an income of $25,000 a year from sales.

Such was its popularity, that Jerome Kern borrowed the song and inserted it into his first musical, *Showboat*, as an example of contemporary popular entertainment. Eventually Harris persuaded an actor, J. Aldrich Libby, to perform the song for him. (He knew every other aspect of the business, but he couldn't sing.) The actor got $500 and a cut of the royalties for his trouble.

Harris quite rightly regarded himself as an expert in the field of songwriting and publishing, and it's true to say that many of the techniques he used are still flourishing today. It seemed natural enough that he should write a manual on his field of expertise. It was called *How to Write a Popular Song*, and his advice, for the most part, still holds good today: 'Look at the newspapers for your storyline. Acquaint yourself with the style in vogue. Avoid slang. Know the copyright laws.'

trivia

★ **After the Ball** was an immediate hit but its popularity was further enhanced when the popular bandleader John Philip Sousa included it in his regular set at the Chicago World's Fair in 1893.

★ **After the Ball** was most famously performed by Al Jolson in the 1946 movie *The Jolson Story*.

★ The practice of paying performers a royalty for performing became commonplace as the stars who sang them became more powerful and Elvis Presley, among others, frequently took a cut of the composer's royalties.

3 · sweet adeline

Words Richard H. Gerard **Music** Harry Armstrong **1902**

The popularity of the vocal style of groups like The Beach Boys, Crosby, Stills & Nash, and even The Beatles on songs like 'Here, There And Everywhere', all started in the 1920s with America's passion for tight harmony singing. **Sweet Adeline** is one of the songs that set the movement going and now almost seems to define the genre. The song was named after a Spanish light opera singer called Adelina Patti, born in Madrid, but hugely popular in New York after her debut in 1859. Legendarily beautiful, she specialized in the more comic roles in operas like *The Barber of Seville* and she had an unusually rich soprano voice, perfect for the lead in four-part harmony singing. She visited New York in 1902 to work at the Metropolitan Opera. Her neighbours in Brooklyn, where she stayed during the engagement, were two young songwriters, Richard Gerard and Harry Armstrong. So impressed were they with her beauty and her talent that they renamed a song they had already written called 'You're The Flower of My Heart, Sweet Rosalie'. Now called **Sweet Adeline**, it was first sung in a tribute to her by the Quaker City Four at the Victoria Theatre, New York.

The term barbershop was first used in the 1920s and usually applied to male quartets and small choruses. *The Grove Dictionary of Music* describes it as, '…four-voice parallel part writing in thirds, fourths and fifths, with a particularly close harmony of diminished and dominant seventh chords, augmented sixth chords and triads with added sixths.'

The technique was introduced in the late 19th century as a way of orchestrating songs in a more interesting and complex way for audiences used to the straightforward delivery of the better-known popular tunes. It also meant that groups didn't need to carry instruments around, apart from the odd banjo, so they could travel lightly. Nobody knows why the style became known as 'barbershop', but there was a vogue in the 1940s for male quartets to wear handlebar moustaches and dress up in barbers' aprons to perform.

African-Americans used the same technique to sing gospel songs, and Sam Cooke, the pioneering soul singer, came out of a gospel group called The Soul Stirrers Black Gospel Quartet. Real musical instruments were frowned upon in the early gospel movement, and that allowed the singers to be more adventurous, sometimes imitating musical instruments with their voices. Secular black harmony groups like The Mills Brothers and The Ink Spots became popular in the 1930s and 1940s adapting show tunes and jazz pieces to the style. In the 1950s white quartets like The Four

Above Adelina Patti

Freshmen regularly charted, and Brian Wilson of The Beach Boys has acknowledged them as a major influence.

So entrenched is the song in the culture of barbershop singing that **Sweet Adeline** has now become a generic term for any female singer of the style. There are annual conventions of barbershop throughout America and it is still enormously popular.

4 give my regards to broadway

Words and **music** George M. Cohan **1903**

It's the shameless chutzpah of **Give My Regards to Broadway** that makes it stand out. It could only have been sung by an opinionated, cocky young man with a very high opinion of his own worth, and George Michael Cohan was that young man. He was a natural to play the lead in the show the song came from. It was that larger-than-life quality that made him such a well-known figure on the musical scene in the early years of the century.

There's a life-size statue of Cohan in the busiest part of New York's Broadway, an appropriate home for the man who virtually invented musical comedy. A forerunner of the great practitioners of musical theatre, Jerome Kern, George Gershwin and Richard Rodgers, Cohan was the dominant force on Broadway during its heyday. He pioneered shows with a proper narrative structure interspersed with songs. Taking the style of European operetta, he gave it a tub-thumping, jingoistic and sentimental style. His best work, like Irving Berlin's, synthesized the idea of American-ness, useful in a country of so many young immigrants. Oscar Hammerstein II said of him, 'Cohan's genius was to say what everyone else was subconsciously feeling', not an inconsequential skill for a songwriter to have.

Dancer, actor, songwriter and producer, George M. Cohan was that cliché of pop performers, a man of few chords. Simple to learn and simple to play, his songs had the most basic structure and a melody line that rarely exceeded four beats. His brilliance was in making them attractive and memorable. Much of his best remembered work was written in march-time, with an added hint of syncopation. Stirring military marches, by composers such as John Philip Sousa, were popular round the turn of the century, and played no small part in the creation of Dixieland jazz in New Orleans at that time. Cohan came from a family of song and dance men working in vaudeville – the equivalent of the old-style British music hall variety. Cohan began writing 'coon songs' as a teenager. Coon songs were especially popular in the first two decades of the century, an era when racial stereotyping and discrimination was prevalent. They were songs sung by white people with blacked up faces in the vernacular of black people, often with a banjo accompaniment or in a ragtime style.

Give My Regards to Broadway was written for a show called *Little Johnny Jones*. The show also contained Cohan's equally well-known 'Yankee Doodle Dandy', an adaptation of a patriotic children's song called 'Yankee Doodle'.

Above George M. Cohan

Cohan's dominance of musical theatre waned in the early 1920s when a whole wave of brilliant younger composers came on the scene. He was awarded a congressional Medal of Honour for his song 'Over There', which referred to the war in Europe, where brave and patriotic American soldiers were risking their lives, and which became the unofficial national anthem during the First World War.

But Cohan's legacy lives on. He was fortunate in having the great Hollywood actor James Cagney play him with great style and energy in one of Hollywood's better musical biographies *Yanky Doodle Dandy*, released in 1942 – the year of Cohan's death – which did much to extend the life of his songs. And more recently **Give My Regards to Broadway** was parodied by Paul McCartney, in his musical *Give My Regards to Broad Street*, some 80 years after it was first written.

5 jelly roll blues

Music Ferdinand 'Jelly Roll' Morton **1904**

Another key figure in the development of 20th-century popular music, Jelly Roll Morton, started recording around 1918, according to his own memory. However, none of those early recordings have survived and the earliest known dates from 1924. **Jelly Roll Blues** was his first published song and it's believed he wrote it sometime in 1904 or 1905. It represents an early example of ragtime developing into jazz. Jelly Roll himself said, 'Jazz is to be played sweet, soft, with plenty rhythm. You have the finest ideas from the greatest operas, symphonies, and overtures in jazz music because it comes from everything of the finest class music.' Put simply Jelly Roll Morton used the piano like an orchestra in order to add greater tonal colour to the music. On top of that he added continuous improvisation to more structured composition. He's probably best known for combining ragtime piano style with blues and jazz piano styles by loosening ragtime's rhythmic feeling and decreasing its embellishments. This reduced the adornment of ragtime style, resulting in a lighter and more swing-like feeling.

Morton was born Ferdinand La Mothe in New Orleans in the late 1880s. He was Creole by birth (a mixture of French and African) and considered himself a cut above purer blooded blacks by virtue of his European ancestry. He studied classical piano as a child which gave a great range to his compositions, drawing from a wide palette of sounds including folk, blues, spirituals, Spanish and Caribbean material, as well as ragtime and classical music. A musical prodigy, he was forced to make a living after the death of his mother by playing piano in the brothels of Storyville, New Orleans' legalized red-light district. He moved north to Chicago, where his reputation grew, and played in various trios and small bands while developing his compositional skills. Morton had a very high opinion of his worth and he was generally cantankerous and skilled at upsetting people. Bandleader George Morrison who Morton played for in Denver said, 'He couldn't stay in one band too long, because he was too eccentric and too temperamental, and he was a one-man band himself...' He famously claimed to have single-handedly 'invented jazz', and though he was certainly its most gifted early exponent, the claim has no basis in fact.

Late in 1926, Morton began recording for the Victor record label and, during the next six months, recorded with His Red Hot Peppers, a group of six New Orleans jazz musicians familiar with his work. He continued to record with this group until about 1930. Later Morton moved to New York where jazz had taken a turn towards the new big-band style of 'swing' and the music of soloists. Morton, unable to adjust his style to the new jazz style, quickly lost popularity though by then his reputation was secure. This was the era of the dance bands of Fletcher Henderson and Paul Whiteman whose music clearly showed the influence of Morton's genius.

Like Louis Armstrong, Morton should really be judged for the whole body of his work, which helped liberate music from the shackles of the European classical tradition, than from one single composition. Because quite simply, without jazz, there would be no rock 'n' roll.

Above 'Jelly Roll' Morton
Left 'Jelly Roll' Morton makes a point to His Red Hot Peppers

Words and **music** George Fairman **1905**

This is the perfect case study to illustrate how popular taste changed during the new mechanical recording era in the early years of the 20th century. **The Preacher and the Bear** is based on an old hunting tale, with several different endings, depending on who's telling the story. First copyrighted as a song by Joe Arzonia in 1904, it had been composed a few years before by George Fairman. Fairman sold the recording rights to Arzonia for $250 with the stipulation that he should share the royalties for sheet music with another songwriter, Arthur Longbrake. Arzonia owned the restaurant where Fairman was the resident piano player and Longbrake was a regular patron.

The first recording, in 1905, was by an immensely popular singer of the time, called Arthur Collins, who had previously recorded other songs by Arthur Longbrake. The recordings were made on two-minute wax cylinders which started selling in the 1890s, costing around a week's wages each, though the big money was still in sheet music sales. But Collins' version of the song turned out to be the first million-selling recording. He re-recorded it at every opportunity for different companies round the country. It was listed in the original record company catalogue as 'a comic coon song sung in the ragtime style'. It may be hard for us, at this distance in time, to understand why a white man blacked up, singing in a caricature of a negro dialect, with a banjo accompaniment, should be funny. But coon songs were all the rage in the early years of the century, and Collins himself had previously scored with a song called 'All Coons Look Alike To Me', written by the black songwriter Ernest Hogan. In fact Collins was so popular, that the contemporary publicity tells us, 'A monthly list without a coon song by Arthur Collins is like a play with a prominent actor missing. The unctuous sound of his chuckles in dialect work is unfailingly charming. His negro heroes usually were in hard luck, but they bore up bravely and saw the funny side of their own misfortunes.'

By 1908, when improving technology allowed for four-minute recordings rather than two, Collins re-recorded the song which had clearly exceeded its original sales expectations. Publicity for the new version claimed, 'This comic coon song has run second in popularity to none in the list of Edison two-minute Records... Our new Amberol Record gives an extra verse, chorus, and scene.'

Collins' recording of the song was still available in the early 1940s, where it remained popular in the rural communities.

The Big Bopper, who died in the same plane crash as Buddy Holly, recorded the song in the late 1950s.

Right J.P. Richardson, aka The Big Bopper

A preacher went out a-huntin'
'Twas on one Sunday morn
I thought it was against his religion
But he took his gun along.
He shot himself some very fine quail
And one big frizzly hare
And on his way returning home
He met a great big grizzly bear.
Well, the bear marched out in the middle of the road
And he waltzed to the coon, you see.
The coon got so excited
That he climbed a persimmon tree.
The bear sat down upon the ground
And the coon climb'd out on a limb
He cast his eyes to the Lord in the sky
And these words said to Him:
'Oh Lord, didn't you deliver Daniel from the lion's den?
Also delivered Jonah from the belly of the whale and then
Three Hebrew chillun from the fiery furnace?
So the Good Book do declare
Now Lord, if you can't help me
For goodness sakes, don't you help that bear!'

[And then spoken, to the accompaniment of growling, by the singer:]

'Now, Mr Bear, let's you and I reason this here thing out together.
Nice bear! Good old bear. Say, Mr Bear, if I should give you just one nice
big juicy bite, would you go away? Oh, you wouldn't, eh? Well, I'll stay
right here!'

[In a later ending the preacher calls on the Lord to instantly convert the bear to
Christianity in the hope that he will be spared a grizzly death. The bear stops in
his tracks, falls on his knees and thanks the Lord for the meal he is about to
consume!]

When the storms of life are raging,
Stand by me (stand by me).
When the storms of life are raging,
Stand by me (stand by me).
When the world is tossing me
Like a ship upon the sea
Thou who rulest wind and water,
Stand by me (stand by me).
In the midst of tribulation,
Stand by me (stand by me);
In the midst of tribulation,
Stand by me (stand by me);
When the hosts of hell assail,
And my strength begins to fail,
Thou who never lost a battle,
Stand by me (stand by me).
In the midst of faults and failures,
Stand by me (stand by me).
In the midst of faults and failures,
Stand by me (stand by me).
When I do the best I can,
And my friends misunderstand,
Thou who knowest all about me,
Stand by me (stand by me).
When I'm growing old and feeble,
Stand by me (stand by me).
When I'm growing old and feeble,
Stand by me (stand by me).
When my life becomes a burden,
And I'm nearing chilly Jordan,
O thou 'Lily of the Valley',
Stand by me (stand by me).

Words and **music** Charles Albert Tindley **1906**

The influence of black gospel on popular music cannot be overstated. One may have to wait till the rock era to recognize it most directly, but it permeates the whole landscape of popular song not only in its construction but also by the manner of its performance. Watch an early James Brown show and compare it to the great gospel singer Mahalia Jackson and the similarities become obvious.

Doctor Charles Tindley is credited with incorporating the sound of the blues into the English protestant-style hymns sung in black churches in the 19th century. For that, he is now regarded as one of the fathers of modern gospel music.

Tindley was born the son of slaves in the 1850s. He gained a divinity degree by a correspondence course and by the early 1900s he'd become pastor in the Calvary Methodist Episcopal church in Philadelphia where he'd previously worked as a caretaker. He wrote dozens of hymns, several of which are still very much part of the black hymnal. It is thought that Tindley's **Stand By Me** was written in the first few years of the century, but not registered until 1916.

Many in the gospel community believe that the 1962 Leiber and Stoller song of the same name (see page 113) is a direct interpretation of Tindley's hymn. Since his songs were part of the black sacred oral tradition, which included the use of improvisation, they probably have a point. Leiber and Stoller wrote a lyric that could just as easily have been sung in church by changing just one word, 'Darling', into something more appropriate to worship.

Tindley's song used the same chord structures that can be heard on Elvis Presley's first release, 'Blue Moon of Kentucky' (see page 90), which demonstrates just how far back the roots of rock travel.

Left Charles Albert Tindley

8   I love a lassie

Words and **music** Harry Lauder **1907**

Harry Lauder was the first British entertainer to sell over a million records in America. Together with his sheet music sales that would have made him a very wealthy man. Lauder was a professional Scotsman and an immensely popular performer all over the English-speaking world. Popularly known as the 'Laird of the Music Hall', he was one of Winston Churchill's favourite comic performers.

As young man, he was forced to work in the mines to support his widowed mother and seven brothers and sisters, but after 10 years he fulfilled his ambition to become an entertainer. He must have cut an odd figure in the vaudeville theatres of New York when he first arrived in 1907 with his kilt, grass green coat and trademark nobbly stick and bonnet. But his popularity was immediate and he was soon signed up by William Morris, who went on to establish himself as the most prestigious theatrical agent in the world. In all Lauder made 22 working visits to the US and his memory is as treasured there as it is in Britain. As a man who pulled himself up by his own bootstraps from unpromising beginnings, he would have admired American enterprise, as much as they would have admired him for fulfilling his own version of the American Dream. Immensely patriotic, he became Sir Harry Lauder as much for his fundraising efforts during the First World War as for his popularity as a singer and comedian.

I Love A Lassie was Lauder's most important hit and like many of his songs it is written about his wife Nance, and how he proposed marriage to her. He's also famous for 'Roamin' in the Gloamin' and 'Keep Right on to the End of the Road'. All three songs can still be heard in Glasgow pubs on wild Saturday nights. His songs are in many ways throwbacks to the Victorian music hall era – simple, irresistible, melodic songs with lyrics that implore you to sing along. But the fact that they have remained popular is a testament to Lauder's skill.

Above Harry Lauder

Words Rida Johnson Young **Music** Victor Herbert **1908**

Victor Herbert occupies a space in the history of music between the full-blown European opera of Puccini and Verdi, and the lighter, more comedic work of Jerome Kern and Richard Rodgers. Herbert composed light opera (with the emphasis on light), full of accessible, melodious tunes, but rooted in the 19th century – songs that you could play on the parlour piano at home. **Ah! Sweet Mystery of Life** (the very title resonates with Victorian pseudo gentility) was the hit song of the operetta *Naughty Marietta*, first produced on Broadway in 1910. It was turned into a movie in 1934, the first to pair Jeanette McDonald and Nelson Eddy. Another of Herbert's operettas, *Babes in Toyland*, was the inspiration for *The Wizard of Oz* and his work dominated Broadway for the period up to the First World War, when audiences began to tire of his sentimentality.

Born in Ireland in 1859, he arrived in America in 1886 with a reputation as a brilliant cellist (and composer of note). By the end of his life he had completed 54 operettas and written hundreds of popular songs. In his heyday he could knock out two or three operettas a year.

Rida Johnson Young (who also wrote the lyrics for 'When Irish Eyes Are Smiling') was, by all accounts, a beautiful actress, socialite and sometime lyricist whose work on *Naughty Marietta* is the most well known of her extended pieces.

In truth Herbert's music was overshadowed by that of his more famous contemporaries: George Gershwin, Jerome Kern, Richard Rodgers and Irving Berlin. Many critics feel that this is unfair because their work shows clear signs of his influence. But he was honoured in a posthumous Hollywood biopic in 1939 called *The Great Victor Herbert*.

Just as significant as Herbert's career as a composer, was his establishing the American Society of Composers, Authors and Publishers. In 1913 he was dining at Shanley's Restaurant in New York City, when he heard the house orchestra playing one of his songs. He considered it unfair that restaurants and other eating and drinking establishments should play a song without paying royalties to its composer. After all you paid to hear music in a theatre. So he sued the restaurant, and, after a very long case, he won. The result was that Herbert formed ASCAP, which brought together America's best composers and lyricists and others working in the music industry to protect their financial interests, and which remains the cornerstone of musical copyright in the USA today.

More recently **Ah! Sweet Mystery of Life** was adopted by the Forest Lawn Cemetery in California as its theme song and was also memorably sung by Madeline Kahn at the climax of the Mel Brooks movie *Young Frankenstein*.

Oh, and for those people who can't be bothered to read to the end of the lyrics, the answer to the sweet mystery of life is... to fall in love, of course.

> **ah! sweet mystery of life** was the hit song of the operetta *Naughty Marietta*

Left Jeanette McDonald and Nelson Eddy

Above Shane McGowan

Words Frederick Weatherly **Music** traditional **1909**

There is not one single bar in Ireland or in America that has not, late at night and in its cups, warmed to the delicious melancholy of **Oh Danny Boy**. This song is, quite simply, one of the most popular songs of the 20th century. Ironically, the lyric was actually written by an Englishman, Frederick Weatherly, who wrote song lyrics as a profitable sideline. And he wrote thousands of them – at least 1,500 were published! **Oh Danny Boy** and the equally sad 'Roses of Picardy' (see page 39) are probably the best known. Although a practising lawyer and sometime politician, he never considered giving up law or politics for music.

The song is a mother's lament for her son about to leave home and either find his fortune or fight the English. In her motherly way, she adds a bit of blackmail by suggesting that if he goes, he will never see her alive again. In his original version, Weatherly had written a tune to go with the words. The song was not successful until a relative of his in America sent him a copy of 'The Londonderry Air' which just happened to fit the words he had written. Its first publisher assumed that Weatherly had written the melody. This led to some friction when another of his clients produced two other lyrics to the same tune. Nobody knows who composed 'The Londonderry Air', but the tune can be traced back to the first half of the 19th century and has led a promiscuous existence coupled with hundreds of different lyrics.

There are 40 million Americans who claim Irish ancestry and America took the song to its Gaelic heart; in among the hundreds, there are respectable versions, recorded in the 1940s, by those well-known Irishmen Glenn Miller and Bing Crosby! Judy Garland recorded it and there's a great version by Jim Reeves. More recently Shane McGowan and Eric Clapton have recorded versions, and the melody was played at the funeral of Diana, Princess of Wales. Whenever alcohol and sentimentality are mixed in Irish bars around the world, the lovely lilting ballad **Oh Danny Boy** is for any Irishman, fake or real, forever Ireland.

❝ this song is one of the most popular songs of the 20th century ❞

Words and **music** Irving Berlin **1910**

Irving Berlin was one of the great architects of popular music in the 20th century. Composer of 1,500 songs during his career, including some of the most famous of the century, he exemplifies both the spirit of Tin Pan Alley and business acumen of commercial pop. Berlin was a genius, regarded by his contemporaries as the best there was. His reputation for writing popular songs of great quality has not diminished down the years, and his best songs are still popular in the repertoire of performers like Tony Bennett, Shirley Bassey, Harry Connick Jr, and even David Bowie's had a go.

Born Israel Barline in 1888, the son of a synagogue cantor, he and his family fled the anti-Jewish pogroms in Russia in 1893 and settled in New York City. He started his career selling sheet music for artists such as Jerome Kern. He quickly saw the potential to make big money writing songs, and learned the market from the street up. Hustling was what he did best. If there was a bandwagon, he was the first to jump on it. And so it was with ragtime.

Ragtime was a very precise form of music which was immensely popular around the turn of the century and which was a precursor to jazz. It was loosely part of the 'coon' music genre, which, in its earliest forms was written by black composers, and mostly played by whites made up to look black. Racial segregation was still rife in most of America in the early years of the century and it was deemed inappropriate for blacks to play in front of 'genteel' white audiences.

Left Irving Berlin

However, many of the later compositions labelled 'ragtime' were not ragtime at all. They were songs written by white commercial songwriters, who knew a trend when they saw one. **Alexander's Ragtime Band** was one such song. It was not Berlin's first 'rag', but it was the first to take off commercially in the USA and Europe, selling over a million copies of sheet music in the first year. As the musical historian Ian Whitcomb has noted, **Alexander's Ragtime Band** was a clarion call to the population at large to listen to the new music, its lyrics encouraging everyone to come and hear Alexander's Ragtime Band – the best band in the land.

And it worked. It was Berlin's first big hit and he made $30,000 from its sheet music sales within the first few years. The recording industry was in its infancy, and the piano in the drawing room had not yet given way to gramophone as the instrument of choice at home. It also proved popular with singers, who toured the country in vaudeville. If they sang ragtime songs they were called 'coon shouters'. They liked a song that was easy to sing, that had memorable lyrics. **Alexander's Ragtime Band** fitted the bill, hitting you with all it had within the first few bars. Perhaps the finest version is by the great Judy Garland who manages to invest the song with a pathos that was not evident in its earlier performances.

Berlin went on to achieve notable successes with Broadway shows such as *Annie Get Your Gun* and with Hollywood movies like *Top Hat*, but he is most remembered for his songwriting and with titles such as 'There's No Business Like Show Business', 'White Christmas', 'Let's Face the Music and Dance' and 'Easter Parade' to his credit it's easy to understand why Jerome Kern said, 'Irving Berlin has no place in American music. He is American music.'

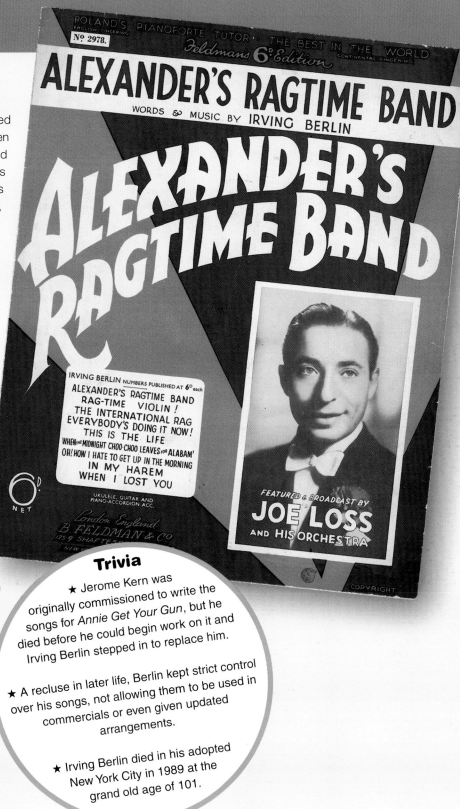

Trivia

★ Jerome Kern was originally commissioned to write the songs for *Annie Get Your Gun*, but he died before he could begin work on it and Irving Berlin stepped in to replace him.

★ A recluse in later life, Berlin kept strict control over his songs, not allowing them to be used in commercials or even given updated arrangements.

★ Irving Berlin died in his adopted New York City in 1989 at the grand old age of 101.

you made me love you
(I didn't want to do it)

Words Joe McCarthy
Music James V. Monaco **1911**

This song was the first recording featuring Al Jolson as vocalist, and helped launch his career. Though later on it was the other way round – if you could persuade Jolson to sing one of your songs, you were made. These days, the Judy Garland version, recorded for the movie *Broadway Melody of 1938*, is probably better known. It was also recorded by Jeannette MacDonald in 1948 and Harry Nilsson on his 1973 album *A Little Touch of Schmilsson in the Night*. The song clearly did a lot for James Monaco as he has the title and musical notation inscribed on his gravestone.

> **a skillfully crafted lyric that perfectly matches its bluesy melody**

Like many other European musicians, James Monaco emigrated from Italy to the USA in the 1890s and started his career as a self-taught ragtime pianist in Chicago, calling himself 'Ragtime Jimmie'. He moved to New York and became a jobbing songwriter on Tin Pan Alley. There he wrote several big hits of which the best known today are, 'Row, Row, Row', 'What Do You Want To Make Those Eyes At Me For?', which topped the British charts in 1959 sung by Emile Ford And The Checkmates, and **You Made Me Love You (I didn't want to do it)**. The latter was the first of two songs he wrote for Jolson, the other being 'Dirty Hands, Dirty Face' which was featured in *The Jazz Singer*, the world's first talking picture.

This is the only song on which Monaco collaborated with lyricist Joe McCarthy. McCarthy wrote songs for a number of Broadway shows in the 1920s and 1930s, including *Irene* which, like his other famous song, 'I'm Always Chasing Rainbows', was sung by Judy Garland in the 1942 film *Ziegfield Girl*. Perry Como, Harry

Above Patsie Cline

Nilsson, and even Alice Cooper have recorded versions of the song over the years.

If a song has some decent qualities, it will always find a new interpretation, and both the composer and the lyricist of **You Made Me Love You (I didn't want to do it)** are still drawing income from just a handful of songs more than 50 years after they both died. Somebody up there is looking after them. Like many songs of the century's first few decades, **You Made Me Love You (I didn't want to do it)** is remembered for the chorus which carries the familiar melody. Verses, which tended to carry the story of a song, often seem to be lost in the mists of time. But this is a skillfully crafted lyric that perfectly matches its bluesy melody, and suited Jolson and Garland's capacity for melodrama. There's also a memorable version by the great country and western singer Patsy Cline, recorded in the 1950s.

13 melancholy baby

Words George Norton **Music** Ernie Burnette **1912**

This song is not only one of the first ballads of the new era but also the subject of an exam question for those who study copyright law. **Melancholy Baby** is a song loved in equal measure by barroom drunks and jazz musicians. It's been covered by all the really great singers of the century from Bing Crosby and Judy Garland through Ella Fitzgerald, Frank Sinatra, Barbra Streisand and Dean Martin. It was also very popular with the swing bands of the 1940s, like The Dorsey Brothers and Benny Goodman, and was still going strong in the bebop era when reworked by Charlie Parker, Miles Davis and Thelonious Monk. It's the oldest song in this collection still popular with jazz stylists. George Norton's easy going, bluesy melody doesn't quite go where you'd expect it to but when it gets there, it feels right, and it's a great tune for improvising on, which is why jazz players love it.

If you take away the word 'Baby' the lyric still has more in common with Victorian parlour songs than songs like 'Alexander's Ragtime Band' (see pages 24–25). And it's the lyric that brings us into legal territory. Norton, who wrote the melody, registered the song with a lyric written by his then wife, Maybelle Watson. The song was then called 'Melancholy' and, as far as we know, it was never performed. Norton and Watson divorced and Norton sold the song to a publisher called Bennet, who didn't like the original words. With Norton's permission, he arranged for Ernie Burnette to write the lyrics we know today. Three years later the publisher added a chorus to the original composition with new words that he had written himself. So there were then three versions of the song. In 1939, Burnette and his former wife tried to take back ownership of the original song after the original period of copyright had expired, only to learn that the publisher has sold the song on to another publisher, which rendered all of the three original writers unable to benefit from it. All of which demonstrates what sort of income songs are capable of generating if people are prepared to spend that amount of money on lawyers to sort it all out.

However, the song has a happy ending. According to music historian Ian Whitcomb, the story goes that during the First World War Ernie Burnette was doing his patriotic duty in France when he was wounded and fell unconscious. When the stretcher-bearers finally got to him, he had lost his memory and his nametag was missing. So as far as anyone could make out, 'Ernie Burnette' had been killed in action. As the wounded were being entertained in the hospital, Burnette heard one of his companions singing **Melancholy Baby**. 'That's my song,' he not unnaturally exclaimed, only to be told that the composer had been killed in battle. Eventually, however, after recognizing his own song, Burnette was able to put his memory back together, claim authorship of the song and return to his career as a vaudeville pianist.

Right The Dorsey Brothers

Sing These Songs and Be Happy!

You Ain't Heard Nothin' Yet

Popular music was invented by people who were largely immigrants or children of immigrants in New York City. The music they made was largely for an urban audience, and its dynamism and its lyrical content reflect the American melting pot.

Jodie Rosen, writer and historian.

In 1892, the publisher and composer Charles Harris paid for a song he'd written to be inserted into a Broadway vaudeville show. The song, 'After the Ball', went on to sell seven million copies of its sheet music providing Harris with enough money to live on for the rest of his life. Thus the scene was set for the beginning of 20th-century popular music.

In the early years of the 20th century, the music listened to in America and Europe, though dominated in terms of performance by vaudeville and music hall, was a melting pot of styles. French and Italian light opera, marching bands, English music hall, minstrelsy, 'coon' songs, ragtime, gospel and blues shouting were all represented. Between them these styles set the pattern for the whole century of popular music. Everything that we think of as popular music at this end of the century has roots going back to the early 1900s. And, although today we have a sense of pop music reinventing itself every 20 or 30 years, everything is an echo of something that has gone before.

Stephen Foster (1826–1864), whose songs included, 'Camptown Races', 'Swanee River' and 'Beautiful Dreamer' (a hit for John Leyton in the 1960s), was probably the first pop composer to make a living from writing songs. His melodies incorporated campground (an abbreviation for the post-emancipation black experience) ideas. This white reinterpretation of the black sound became a constant theme throughout the century. Foster was a minstrel composer creating wonderful melodies that the public have still not tired of. His influence was pervasive and even English music hall was indebted to him; 'Daisy, Daisy, Give Me Your Answer Do' could quite easily be a Foster song. Since then there have been a line of composers, from Hoagy Carmichael to Paul McCartney, who seem to fit into a similar tradition.

From Gospel to Soul

Ben E. King's 1961 hit record 'Stand By Me' was firmly based on a song of the same name written in 1906 by Charles Albert Tindley, which was one of the earliest gospel songs. So, nothing new there. In fact, gospel was one of the most pervasive influences on music for

Left Advertisement on the back of 1913 sheet music

much of the century, and reached its peak of influence in 1960s Tamla Motown soul music, which is demonstrably secularized gospel music. While Motown is central to the emergence of soul, other artists, like Sam Cooke, also played a part. Armed with a gospel background, Cooke did little to change his style of delivery when he made his transition into popular music – instead he changed the subject matter of his songs. His 'A Change is Gonna Come', a hit in 1964, concerned the experience of living in America as a black man. His career, which included 30 US Top 40 hits between 1960 and 1964, gave the firm impression of someone in control of a career in popular music. This gave him the stature of an important role model in black music, one which influenced the careers of artists like Aretha Franklin and James Brown.

Gospel's biggest influence, however, can be seen in the manner of performance, where a line can be traced back to African ringshouts, through the holy dance and the style of so-called 'sanctified music'. This contrasted with the rather more sedate European tradition. But the tensions within the black church-going community about performing styles, the godliness (or otherwise) of musical instruments, and whether singers were allowed to improvise on a melody, are ones which resonated right up to the 1950s.

The Vaudeville Tradition

Burlesque and then vaudeville had dominated live musical entertainment in America since the late 1800s. A combination of music and comedy, that often featured scantily clad women, vaudeville became the popular entertainment for the masses. In 1919 there were some 900 theatres across the country that played vaudeville. In 1913 the Palace Theatre, situated on Broadway and 47th Street in New York, opened its doors, and became the home of vaudeville.

Al Jolson came out of the vaudeville tradition (along with Sophie Tucker, George M. Cohan and many others). At first they called themselves 'coon' singers, parodying the genuine black entertainers, many of whom found it difficult to get work within the racist environment that pervaded America at the time. Jolson was the perfect bridge between the old minstrel singers and the golden age of American song, recording material by both Stephen Foster and

George Gershwin. Appreciated more now for his energy and devotion to his audience than for his interpretative skills – which to modern ears seem raucously over sentimental – Jolson had such audience pulling power that he could command a share of the songwriter's royalties. Elvis Presley was later to use the same technique in the 1950s.

But the arrival of 'talking pictures' in 1927 signalled the end of the vaudeville tradition. Try as they might, by showing movies in conjunction with live shows, the theatre owners struggled to stay alive. They soon realized that the people came for the movies and not the shows. By 1930 many of the theatres had closed or converted to movie houses, and even the famous Palace Theatre closed its doors in 1932.

The Ragtime Rage

Ragtime was all the rage at the turn of the century. The music of its most famous composer, Scott Joplin, – for example 'Maple Leaf Rag' – can still be heard today. So great was its popularity that the then struggling song plugger Irving Berlin named his first big hit 'Alexander's Ragtime Band', apparently unconcerned that the tune bore little resemblance to a rag. Ragtime was the immediate precursor to jazz. Identified by the pianist's technique – the left hand echoing the old marching tunes (oompah, oompah) and the right hand allowed a more freewheeling rhythmic approach (syncopation) – ragtime was the foundation of the New Orleans' style of jazz music.

The first recordings were made on wax cylinders around 1876, and they were very expensive. The gramophone was invented in 1887 and the first recorded discs were available around 1897. By 1914 discs had replaced cylinders as the popular form of recorded music. Records were 10 inches wide and had two sides which played at 78 rpm. By then they were affordable to the general public.

Another battle that raged was for the respect of the composer's intentions. To improvise or not was a thorny question for many. Joplin was not alone in demanding that his tunes be played strictly as written. But ragtime made the journey south from the great industrial Midwest towns of Chicago and St Louis to infuse the culture of what later became the cradle of jazz, New Orleans. There ragtime met the irresistible force of the three greatest improvisers jazz has ever known – Louis Armstrong, Sidney Bechet and 'Jelly Roll' Morton, all born in the last decade of the 19th century. Each highly skilled on different instruments – Armstrong on trumpet, cornet and voice, Bechet on clarinet and saxophone and Morton on piano – they were excited by the new freewheeling rhythms of ragtime. Their technical expertise and feel for the music they played, freed from the constraints of playing music as written, enabled them to improvise as they chose, and they went on (with others) to make jazz and popular music indistinguishable concepts for the first half of the century.

A Cultural Renaissance

Sheet music, and the capacity to print and distribute it, was the first great leap forward in the marketing of popular music. Player pianos, which were simply pianos fitted with an apparatus enabling them to play automatically, were another key in the popularization of tunes. They were everywhere until the early 1920s. But, of course, recording was the big new idea. Edison patented his Phonograph in 1870. It was acoustic and crude. But by 1925, electronic recording and the invention of the microphone opened up a whole new world of possibilities. So when Al Jolson climbed on stage after a recital by Enrico Caruso in 1926, walked over to the microphone, and said, 'You ain't heard nothin' yet,' he could barely have been aware of the symbolism of the moment.

In the immediate aftermath of the First World War, Europeans and Americans were ready to have a good time, and the 1920s was a decade which reflected that (in many ways later echoed by the 1960s). There was a new sense of freedom. A certain loosening up of moral standards allowed even single women to be seen enjoying themselves. Perversely, prohibition (by its very avoidance) created an atmosphere in which people went out of their way to seek pleasure. Musical theatre, dance halls, record sales and, later on, movies, not to mention better mobility and increasing economic wealth, all led to greater opportunities for musicians and composers. Add to that the sense of a new age, which the First World War had merely postponed, and a cultural renaissance and you have all the ingredients for a musical explosion.

Although frowned on by the moral guardians, jazz was by now a force to be reckoned with. Turn-of-the-century immigration was yielding confident second-generation dealers and shakers who had all the cultural confidence of their motherlands. Landing in America from the anti-Jewish pogroms in Eastern Europe must have been like winning the lottery. Prominent among them were the new generation of writers and performers such as Irving Berlin, George Gershwin and Al Jolson.

American Popular Song

Musical theatre had given us the old world light opera of Franz Lehar and the sophisticated lyrics of Gilbert and Sullivan. Vaudeville found a

Right 'Jelly Roll' Morton on piano and Sidney Bechet on clarinet

COTTON

DINNER $1.50

HOSIERY
HOSIERY | HAND-BAGS | LINGERIE

Palais D'or
HAT SHOPPE

1584
De Milo
DRESSES

LEWIS
MOULIN ROUGE
HAT SHOPPE

NEVER A

new energy with George M. Cohan, and the likes of Al Jolson and Sophie Tucker. And in that mix, all of the great classic American songwriters flourished. Predominately Jewish, they harnessed (often rather crudely) the indigenous jazz and minstrel sounds to the European classical and folk traditions of their immediate forebears and created the truly distinctive sound of American popular song.

Jerome Kern started his working life as a song plugger, and went on to revolutionize musical theatre, creating a bridge from the light opera of Sigmund Romberg and Victor Herbert, to popular and daring musicals that have now become standard repertoire. Both George Gershwin and Richard Rodgers claimed Kern's influence in their work. Remarkable not only for their modern tunefulness, but for their musical sophistication, they set the standard that everyone else followed. At the other end of the scale, Irving Berlin would have loathed being thought of as sophisticated, but in his ceaseless quest for a hit song – he's credited with more than 1,500 compositions – he became the quintessential architect of American popular song. The classically trained George Gershwin hankered after more immortality than he thought the three-minute song could give him. But many of his three-minute offerings are works of sheer musical brilliance, some would say far better than his extended compositions for the concert hall. His death in 1937 robbed America of a peerless musical talent. Cole Porter, Hoagy Carmichael, Vincent Youmans and Richard Rodgers all add to the seemingly endless list of composers of what we now casually call standards or show tunes.

A Question of Race?

Up in Harlem in the 1920s, there was a black middle-class renaissance going on. Duke Ellington reigned supreme at the Cotton Club. But the Cotton Club was a venue that catered mainly for white audiences. Racial segregation was institutionalized. The classically trained black composer W.C. Handy, who became known as the 'Father of the Blues', was composing in Memphis. 'St Louis Blues', his

Left The Cotton Club, Harlem, New York

best-known piece, was written in 1916 and sold phenomenally well right through to the 1950s. Eubie Blake had developed from an accomplished ragtime composer/performer into a stride pianist ushering in the era of swing. Other black writers and arrangers, such as James P. Johnson and Noble Sissel, were spreading the messages that were picked up and interpreted by the white writers with varying degrees of sophistication. Mixed race bands were very rare so there was little direct influencing across the racial divide, but the sense of black music infusing white songwriting ideas was palpable. The relationship between blacks and Jews was a theme in the development of popular music of all styles.

During the first 50 years of the 20th century Jewish songwriters, working mostly on Tin Pan Alley, and black musicians working in all genres of music, most notably blues and jazz, held popular music in thrall. Some historians claim that Jewish people and black people were drawn together through their similar experiences of persecution and racisim. But this is to deny the influence of other musical genres like light opera, English music hall and folk. It was not simply a question of race. Rather it was that America was emerging from its racist culture. Black musicians, who had found it difficult to get paid work in the music business, were emerging on the strength of their talents. And genius led the way, whether that of Irving Berlin, Louis Armstrong, George Gershwin or Duke Ellington. As musicologist and critic Stanley Crouch points out, 'I think one of the things that we always have to understand when we discuss these matters is that we are talking about performers and composers of genius. We're not talking about the average guy. See, George Gershwin doesn't represent Jews, he represents a genius first, he's a genius who's a Jew. You know, Irving Berlin is a popular songwriting genius who's a Jew. Right? Duke Ellington is a genius who's black. They all have one thing in common, they're geniuses first and then the ethnic category comes second. That's what Duke Ellington, George Gershwin, Louis Armstrong and Irving Berlin have in common, and I think that is the American story really.'

the top 100

songs
●
14–26

St Louis blues

They didn't believe me

Pack up your troubles

Roses of Picardy

Rockabye your baby to that

Dixie melody/My mammy

Swanee

Tiger rag

Careless love

Lovesick blues

I cried for you

It had to be you

Tea for two

Manhattan

Words and music W.C. Handy **1913**

Above W.C. Handy

If they'd kept hit record charts for the first half of the century **St Louis Blues** would have been up there, with 'White Christmas', as the most played and most recorded number ever. Although it's hard to imagine these days, when it rarely gets an airing, it's impossible to overstate the popularity of this song. It is thought by some to be the most important blues song ever written.

W.C. Handy was a classically trained black musician born in Alabama in 1873. His band, which performed to mixed race audiences in the southern states of the USA, had a repertoire of popular dance tunes and marching songs. He was nicknamed Fess, short for professor, because his knowledge of music was extensive and wide-ranging. He started writing blues numbers after his white audiences kept asking him to play 'his own music'. What they were asking for was black, or 'coon', music which was gaining in popularity as the various rural black jug bands travelled round the communities. Commercial pressure drove Handy to compose blues music in a similar style. The first was called 'Memphis Blues', but it was **St Louis Blues** that caught the public's imagination. He was forced to publish his own compositions, because the publishers of sheet music were no less racially prejudiced than the general population, and **St Louis Blues** generated an annual income of $25,000 over the next 40 years, which by current earnings would have put him in the billionaire bracket.

Its popularity spread round the world. The great theatrical producer Florenz Ziegfeld credited Handy with putting black bands on the previously all-white map of Broadway in New York. It proved to be too steep a learning curve for many white musicians unfamiliar with any form of blues.

The tune itself was written in Beale Street, Memphis ('a coloured thoroughfare, where you could find the best and worst of negro life,' as Handy described it) in a bar where black musicians gathered between performances. The street now features a statue of Handy. Forty years later Elvis Presley was similarly inspired by the musicians of Beale Street. The song also contains influences of Afro-Spanish rhythms that Handy picked up and his various trips to Cuba around the turn of the century. He claimed to have written the lyrics after hearing a woman (from St Louis, Missouri) tormented by her husband's philandering complaining about his hard heart.

It was taken up by many of the popular singers of the time, like Ethel Waters and Sophie Tucker, as well as by jazz bands. But probably its most famous performance was by Bessie Smith who appeared in a dramatized version of the sad tale made in 1929 that featured Louis Armstrong on cornet. It was Smith's only film appearance and was a great showcase for her magnificent talents.

Handy's innovation in 'composed blues' were the result of his familiarity with the real blues and standard musical notation. Although a piano could not bend notes in the way a guitar or a blues singer could, Handy approximated this ambiguous major/minor sound by flattening the third note in his song – making it a minor note in a major scale. By using this effect in **St Louis Blues**, along with the occasional flattened fifth and seventh to increase the blues feel, Handy created one of the most influential and most recorded songs in the American song repertoire.

trivia

★ Handy's autobiography, *Father of the Blues*, was published in 1941.

★ Jug bands enjoyed great popularity between 1890 and the Great Depression. Music was played on 'found' instruments – empty liquor jugs, kazoos and washboards – and the craze swept up and down towns on the Ohio and Mississippi Rivers. Jug bands claim to be the missing link between the blues and the slave music of West Africa.

Words Herbert Reynolds **Music** Jerome Kern **1914**

This song is held to be the earliest on the cannon of show tunes, or standards, which have come to be known as 'American popular song'. Before this there was European light opera, Victorian music hall, or vaudeville, minstrel songs, ragtime and 'coon' songs. Although Irving Berlin had written 'Alexander's Ragtime Band' (see pages 24–25) three years earlier, it was Jerome Kern whose colloquial style both musically and lyrically, synthesized these various elements into Broadway theatre songs, something new and intrinsically American. Kern, like George Gershwin and Richard Rodgers, wrote songs exclusively in the context of musical theatre. Berlin and Cole Porter wrote pop songs as well as musicals. But all of them acknowledged Kern as their working inspiration.

Like other great songwriters, Kern served his apprenticeship by being a song plugger, and a rehearsal piano player, which must have given him a feel for what sold in the popular music of the times. Like Gershwin, he had been something of a musical prodigy as a child and by his teens was writing pop songs (against his father's wishes) as well as studying classical music. He studied composition in Heidelberg and was selling songs by the age of 17 in both the US and England where he has always been held in high esteem.

The lyric was by Herbert Reynolds, which was the pen name of Michael Rourke. Born in England, Rourke moved to the States and became a press agent. For some unknown reason he changed his name to Herbert Reynolds around the time the First World War started. Up to that point, under the name Rourke, he had supplied a dozen or so lyrics to Kern's early work. **They Didn't Believe Me** was written under his new pen name and the words work perfectly with Kern's melody, which feels tender, and natural, and still sounds fresh today. Reynolds wrote several further lyrics for Kern until replaced by the altogether classier writing partnerships both with Guy Bolton and P.G. Wodehouse.

Kern preferred the European light classical tradition of Victor Herbert, Franz Lehar and the operettas of Gilbert and Sullivan over the vulgar jingoism of George M. Cohan, the early Broadway pioneer. He quite consciously laboured to elevate American popular music of the early century which he considered 'has no class whatsoever and is mere barbaric mouthing'.

They Didn't Believe Me was inserted into a show called *The Girl from Utah* in 1914 after its London run. It did not find favour with the contemporary critics, but proved popular with the theatre going public. Not an unusual event for a composer of popular songs. It

Above Jerome Kern

proved to be Kern's first big success on both sides of the Atlantic. It was Kern who fired up and inspired the other four great composers of American song, Berlin, Rodgers, Gershwin and Porter, into a golden age. Not for another 40 years, till the 1960s, would there be so many gifted songwriters working and being inspired by each other, within the same timeframe. 'Composing is like fishing,' said Kern, 'You get a nibble, but you don't know whether it's a minnow or a marlin until you reel it in.'

After Kern's early death in 1945, President Harry Truman spoke of his 'simple, honest songs that belong to no time or fashion'. They were 'simple' only in the sense of them sounding natural, uncomplicated and rounded, but they certainly were honest, timeless and beyond fashion. He was only superseded in his gift for melody by his protégé Richard Rodgers who was inspired by Kern's early musicals. As Rodgers said later in his autobiography, 'If you were at all sensitive to music, Kern had to be your idol.'

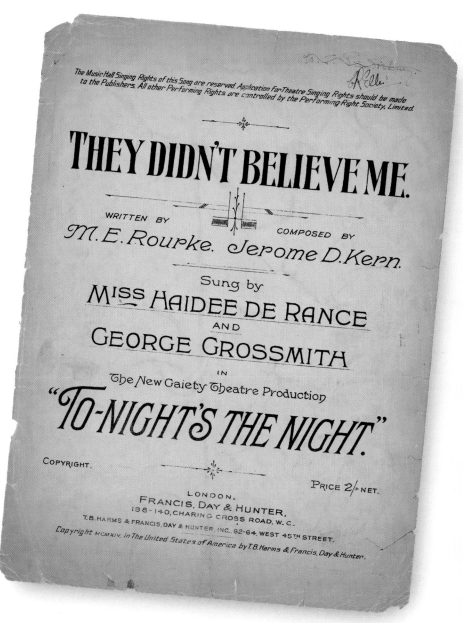

> **they didn't believe me** was Jerome Kern's first big success on both sides of the atlantic

pack up your troubles

Words George Powell **Music** Felix Powell **1915**

You don't often hear the verses of this song – perhaps they were too long to remain in the memory for the soldiers who sang it while fighting the First World War in Europe. But the chorus is still posted as the all-time second favourite song of American veterans of the Great War. George and Felix Powell were music hall performers who got lucky with this song. George had written the words in 1912, but it was a couple of years later that his brother added the melody. Neither of them had much faith in the song, but it went down well in the British music halls and it has now become indelibly associated with soldiers marching through the trenches of France.

In 1915 the Germans torpedoed and sank the British passenger ship the *Lusitania*. Of the 2,000 passengers on board, around 130 were American. Up to that point the US had remained steadfastly neutral in the conflict, but the sinking of the *Lusitania* was the turning point and public opinion turned in favour of Uncle Sam helping out. America was no slouch in helping the war effort with songs either. George M. Cohan wrote the stirring 'Over There' to stiffen the resolve of US troops with the key line: '… and we won't come back till it's over, over there'.

Cohan's song highlights the difference between the phlegmatic Brits and the enterprising just-do-it culture of the yanks. **Pack Up Your Troubles** tells us that in adversity we should smile and not worry, it's not worthwhile.

Americans must have had a little problem with English slang especially with words such as 'lucifer' and 'fag'; British soldiers were issued with cigarettes as part of their rations, immortalizing the humble packet of Woodbines as the cheapest 'fags' available. 'Lucifer' was simply a slang word for a match.

The First World War was, in many ways, the real end to the 19th century and the Victorian values that dominated fashion, morality and the popular music industry. The genteel parlour songs left over from the English music hall days were giving way to the new, brash, Broadway style of people like George M. Cohan and Irving Berlin. However, **Pack Up Your Troubles** and 'It's A Long Way to Tipperary', the two songs most associated with the Great War, were introduced to English audiences by Florrie Forde, a popular music hall performer, though this was probably the last knockings of the genre. The war also helped to make the world a smaller place; transport and travel became easier, the telephone was invented, radio became more accessible and sheet music, and then records, were easily exported.

As for the brothers Powell, they don't appear to have any other song credits to their name and Felix, presumably feeling that he had nothing to live for, shot himself in 1942.

If you're wondering what the US First World War veterans voted as their favourite song, it was called 'Mademoiselle From Armentiers' (also known as 'Inky Pinky Parley Vous'), and also written in 1915. There are several versions of the lyric, all of which contain words we don't use in front of children.

Left Pack Up Your Troubles was popular with both British and US troops during the First World War

17 roses of picardy

Words Frederick Weatherly **Music** Hayden Wood **1916**

Throughout history war has inspired good songs. Though, of course, they are often mournful, many of them have pretty melodies for those left behind to contemplate the ravages of battle. **Roses of Picardy** is one of the prettiest.

Picardy is a region of north-eastern France between Paris and Lille, which includes the coastline around Boulogne and Calais, and the Somme, where hundreds of thousands of soldiers lost their lives in the Great War. Because the song is so closely associated with the war, the roses are felt to represent the blood of fallen soldiers, which gives the song a terrible poignancy.

Frederick Weatherly, who wrote the words for 'Oh Danny Boy' (see page 23), also wrote the lyric for **Roses of Picardy**. Given his success and the skill he displayed in matching words to music, it makes you wonder why he was so reluctant to give up the legal profession and become a full-time songwriter. He originally wrote these words to fit a completely different melody by Herbert Brewer, but his music publisher liked neither the music nor the words. Clearly not one to let a decent lyric go to waste, he sent the manuscript to another composer, Hayden Wood. Wood was a prolific British classical composer, who ventured into sentimental song after marrying his wife, the singer Dorothy Court, and it is his irresistible setting of the words (dedicated to his wife) that the public has still not tired of.

The song was a hit in America where the great Irish tenor John McCormack popularized it and released it on record in 1919. McCormack, along with other operatic tenors such as Benjamino Gigli and Enrico Caruso, was the closest thing to a pop star in America in the early years of the century. Frank Sinatra was a great admirer of the technical skills of the famous operatic tenors. He studied their breathing techniques as a young man learning his craft, and regularly swam underwater to practise breath control. He would have heard McCormack's version of **Roses of Picardy**. Somebody has recently unearthed a version of Sinatra singing the same song, in what sounds like a private recording booth sometime around 1936 or 1937 after he left the Hoboken Four and before joining the Harry James Band, which makes it his first solo recording. He also recorded it in 1961 for an album of exclusively British songs. There is also a quartet version by The Platters.

Lyric writer Frederick Weatherly was also something of a minor poet in his native Somerset, and the full text of **Roses of Picardy** reads more like a poem than a song. It has the sentimentality associated with late Victoriana.

Left John McCormack

She is watching by the poplars
Colinette with the sea blue eyes,
She is watching and longing and waiting,
Where the long white roadway lies,
And a song stirs in the silence
As the wind in the boughs above
She listens and starts and trembles,
'Tis the first little song of love.
Roses are shining in Picardy
In the hush of the silver dew
Roses are flowering in Picardy
But there's never a rose like you.
And the roses will die with the summer time
And our roads may be far apart.
But there's one rose that dies not in Picardy
'Tis the rose that I keep in my heart.
And the years fly on forever,
Til the shadows veil their sighs,
But he loves to hold her little hand
And look in her sea blue eyes.
And he sees the rose by the poplars
Where they met in the bygone years
For the first little song of the roses
Is the last little song she hears
She is watching by the poplars
Colinette with the sea blue eyes
She is watching and longing and waiting,
Where the long white roadway lies,
And a song stirs in the silence
As the wind in the boughs above
She listens and starts and trembles
'Tis the first little song of love.

Words Sam Lewis and Joe Young **Music** Jean Schwartz (**Rockabaye**) Walter Donaldson (**My Mammy**) **1917**

By 1917 cylinder recordings had given way to discs, and the vaudeville/music hall craze was at its peak, with some 25,000 performers touring 4,000 US theatres. Sheet music sales were running at over two billion copies annually. So there was a great deal of money to be made in the music industry.

Sam Lewis and Joe Young were Tin Pan Alley writers who wrote for the vaudeville circuit. Lewis had been a café singer before he became a writer. Young was a singer who demoed songs for publishing houses – a real, live, walking equivalent of today's demo discs. For the audiences that filled those venues the songs had to be direct, big hearted and emotional, and if they were and the composer was lucky, they'd become showstoppers.

Lewis and Young wrote the lyrics for both of these songs. Also known for 'Five Foot Two, Eyes of Blue' and 'I'm Sitting on Top of the World', the duo were fortunate in having Al Jolson, Broadway's most charismatic performer, sing many of their compositions. It's difficult to convey the influence of Jolson in today's terms. He was as popular as any pop singer you could name. Crooner Bing Crosby, who superseded Jolson in the electronic recording era, said of him, 'Nobody could sell a song like Jolson', and when you hear recordings of Jolson today it's hard to argue with that. For the modern listener, Jolson's singing sounds over the top, but if you can imagine trying to sing to the back row of a large and packed theatre without the aid of a PA system, and still convey some emotion, you begin to get the idea. It wasn't only that he was good at selling songs, he was a genius at building his own showbiz career. Modesty was never Al Jolson's style and he coined for himself two phrases that are still reference points for his career: 'The World's Greatest Entertainer', and 'You Ain't

Heard Nothin' Yet', which he first used in 1914, but went on to symbolize the beginning of the era of talking pictures when he spoke the words in the 1927 movie *The Jazz Singer*.

These two songs, released separately but equally famous in Jolson's early repertoire, had music by different composers. The first, Jean Schwartz, who wrote **Rockabye Your Baby to that Dixie Melody**, was taught piano by his sister who had studied under Franz Liszt in their native Hungary. The song was written for the stage show *Sinbad* in which Jolson starred in his familiar black face comic character. This visceral link between the Jewish community (Jolson's father, like Irving Berlin's, was a synagogue singer) and African-Americans remains a feature of the music industry in the States. Despite early tensions it probably began through a shared sense of dispossession in the midst of the predominantly white Anglo Saxon population. Both races playing up to each other's dominant racial stereotypes.

The music to the nauseatingly sentimental **My Mammy** was written by Walter Donaldson, who went on to write 'Blue Heaven', 'Makin' Whoopee' and 'My Baby Just Cares For Me'. Both of these songs consolidated Jolson's career as a recording artist.

Right Al Jolson

19 swanee

Words Irving Caesar **Music** George Gershwin **1918**

Swanee was George Gershwin's first major hit, and the song that made both he and lyricist Irving Caesar famous. The song is named after the river that runs from Georgia through north Florida into the Gulf of Mexico.

Caesar started his working life as a mechanic for the Ford Motor Company and went on to write the lyrics for 'Tea For Two' (see page 50) and 'Animal Crackers in My Soup' among many others. He tells of meeting Gershwin in a New York restaurant and deciding to write a song in the style of 'Hindustan', a popular dance tune of the time. Gershwin suggested giving it an American setting, based on the old Stephen Foster song 'Swanee River'. They caught the bus back to Gershwin's house by which time Caesar had completed the lyrics. Legend has it that Gershwin took another 15 minutes to write the music. It is one of many songs written by urban sophisticates from the north, praising the perceived virtues of rural southern life. It sold only moderately well until Irving Caesar managed to persuade his friend Al Jolson to include it in the show *Sinbad* which had already given him the hits 'My Mammy' and 'Rockabye Your Baby to that Dixie Melody' (see pages 40–41) in the previous year. Clearly it was the Jolson touch that did the trick.

George Gershwin had two brothers and a sister, and came from a well-to-do family. It was his elder brother Ira who was thought to have the musical talent in the family. But George appropriated the piano bought for Ira by their mother. He was given music lessons and studied the European composers, and his brilliant talent quickly became apparent. He had a phenomenal musical memory and could play back complete pieces after only one hearing. Ira went on to become a celebrated lyric writer and the two brothers later combined their talents on some of the greatest songs of the century.

Gershwin started his Tin Pan Alley career making anonymous piano rolls of other composers' work. This experience gave him invaluable insights into the constituents of hit songs, and he started writing his own songs a few years later. It was a period before he took himself seriously as a composer, and Tin Pan Alley was the place to be. Gershwin was a great admirer of Irving Berlin, who was already the man to beat for writing hits. But he turned down the opportunity to work with Berlin in 1918. By 1919 Gershwin had written two Broadway reviews, one of which included the song **Swanee**. Such was Jolson's pulling power, that within a year it had sold two million records and a million copies of the sheet music.

Left George Gershwin

I've been away from you
    a long time,
I never thought I'd miss
    you so.
Somehow I feel, your
    love was real, near you
    I long to be.
The birds are singing, It
    is songtime,
The banjos strummin'
    soft and low,
I know that you, yearn for
    me too, Swanee you're
    calling me.

Swanee, how I love you
    how I love you, my
    dear old Swanee.
I'd give the world to be,
    among the folks in
    D-I-X-I-Even know my
Mammy's, waiting for
    me, praying for me,
    down by the Swanee.
The folks up north will
    see me no more, when
    I go to the Swanee
    shore.
(I'll be happy, I'll be
    happy)
Swanee, Swanee, I am
    coming back to
    Swanee.
Mammy, Mammy, I love
    the old folks at home.

20 | tiger rag

Words and **music** The Original Dixieland Jazz Band **1919**

Above The Original Dixieland Jazz Band

Tiger Rag is said to be the very first jazz standard and has been played and recorded by hundreds of New Orleans-style bands right through to the rock era. The Original Dixieland Jazz Band, who started their musical careers as members of one of the many competitive New Orleans marching bands so crucial to the development of jazz, was the first jazz outfit ever to be recorded, around 1916 or 1917, and the members of the band are the registered composers of the song. Those are the facts – much of what follows is speculation.

The common belief is that The Original Dixieland Jazz Band was the first jazz band in the recording studio because they were white and, given the prevailing views on race and segregation in early 20th-century America, that seems likely. Nick La Rocca, leader of the band, also claims that the band invented Dixieland jazz. But the vast majority of historians disagree. It is possible that he was the first to put the two words 'Dixieland' and 'jazz' together. It simply meant that they played jazz in a southern style. But there were plenty of other people playing in that style – generally referred to as 'rag music' – especially in New Orleans, between 1910 and 1920. However, the band moved north to Chicago in 1916 and became the first band to popularize the music outside the region. The records they made in those first few years sold well and the band moved on to a residency in New York and then to London where they became a sensation.

Jazz history is, by and large, the history of great players: Louis Armstrong, Jelly Roll Morton, Duke Ellington and the like. The Original Dixieland Jazz Band did not have an outstanding player. They were a good ensemble band and played with great energy and enthusiasm. There's a great sense of fun being had when you hear **Tiger Rag** but not one of great music being played. The interesting thing

about the song is that it played to the strength of a band who did *not* have an outstanding soloist. Unlike many later jazz compositions, there wasn't much scope for an extended solo break, and the minimal lyrics highlight that. For most of his life, La Rocca was bitter at the way the band seemed to have been written out of the story of jazz because of that concentration on great soloists, and also probably because he was white. It is an inescapable truth that jazz is predominately an African-American construction, but there were plenty of white and mixed race players in New Orleans in that era.

Although The Original Dixieland Jazz Band first registered **Tiger Rag**, the tune had been around for a while. Jelly Roll Morton was one of several prominent jazz musicians to claim authorship. In the 1930s, La Rocca threatened legal action in one attempt to hijack the composition. Many older musicians recall the tune being played on the streets of New Orleans under the title 'Number Two', and full of references to bowel movements! But the earliest version can be heard on a Pirogue Race Records LP, released in Louisiana in the 1980s, called *Played With Immense Success*, which carries a recording of the song on a music box disc dating from 1867.

The ever generous-spirited Louis Armstrong regarded The Original Dixieland Jazz Band's recording of **Tiger Rag** as the best.

> ❝ tiger rag is said to be the very first jazz standard ❞

Words and **music** traditional (arranged by W.C. Handy) **1920**

Above Bessie Smith

There can't be many songs recorded by such a cast list of iconic performers as **Careless Love**, aka 'Oh Careless Love' and 'Loveless Love'. Like 'Great Speckled Bird' (see page 71) and 'Stand By Me' (see page 20), **Careless Love** is mobile both lyrically and melodically in that there are dozens of variations in the lyrics and in the arrangements. The song has been part of the staple repertoire of folk, blues, country, Dixieland and rock performers, and looking back with the benefit of hindsight, it might easily have been considered by Elvis when he first visited Sun Studios in 1954 to record 'That's Alright Mama', 'Mystery Train' and 'Blue Moon of Kentucky' (see page 90). The first great performance of the song was by the classic blues singer Bessie Smith, (she called it 'Careless Love Blues'), since when it has been covered (among others too numerous to mention) by Kid Ory, Lonnie Johnson, Fats Waller, Fats Domino, Connie Francis, Ray Charles, Bob Dylan (in a duet with Johnny Cash) and Janis Joplin.

Careless Love was first registered by W.C. Handy, who also wrote 'St Louis Blues', the most commercially successful blues song of the century (see page 35). He originally called it 'Loveless Blues' and claimed to have composed the song in the early years of the century. After the great success of 'St Louis Blues', Handy was known to wander the streets of his hometown, Memphis, collecting and writing down the blues tunes of travelling musicians. In his book *Folk Songs of North America*, folk song historian Alan Lomax claimed that it started life as a blues sung by just the type of travelling black workers that Handy would have overheard. But in reality it's older than that and started life as an English folk song that somehow travelled to America and ended up being sung by black workers on the Ohio River. Its great virtue as a melody was that it was easy to turn it into a blues. Consequently there have been many rather idiosyncratic versions. Listen out for Janis Joplin's heavy rock version of the song. In the combative version Bob Dylan recorded with Johnny Cash in 1969, they traded their own made up lyrics with the rule that the end rhymes should be some make of gun.

> **66**
> **careless love** started life as an english folk song that somehow travelled to america and ended up being sung by black workers on the ohio river
> **99**

22 lovesick blues

Words Irving Mills **Music** Cliff Friend **1921**

It is the perfect irony that a song regarded as a seminal country music classic should have been composed by a Tin Pan Alley songwriter a quarter of a century before it became a hit. Hank Williams used **Lovesick Blues** to launch his career at the Grand Ole Opry in Nashville in 1947. At the time it was assumed that either Williams had written it himself or that it was traditional. In fact Williams did get royalties for his yodelling arrangement of the song, which recalled the style of Jimmie Rodgers, but the main writing credit goes back to Irving Mills, one of the major players in Tin Pan Alley.

Mills did every job there was to do in the music business, from runner to song demonstrator, from singer to lyricist (he collaborated on the lyrics for 'Stardust', see pages 60–61) and from bandleader to band-booker, the list is endless. Like so many of those working on Tin Pan Alley, he was of Russian-Jewish extraction. But perhaps his greatest contribution to popular music was in launching and managing the career of the greatest of jazz composers, Duke Ellington. Indeed his name appears as lyricist alongside Ellington on many of his compositions, most notably 'Mood Indigo', 'Sophisticated Lady' and 'It Don't Mean A Thing if it Ain't Got That Swing'. His contribution to Ellington's compositions is shrouded in controversy, but at the time it was frequently regarded as a management perk to share composing credits of artists, especially if the management were as powerful and influential as Irving Mills. They later fell out over precisely that issue of royalties.

His influence on black popular music in the 1930s as manager and publisher is undeniable. He also managed Cab Calloway and Lucky Millinder, gave Benny Goodman and Tommy Dorsey places in his band and was the first to put together a mixed race band in the recording studio in America, and in the late 1920s that was a pretty brave thing to do.

Cliff Friend was strictly a tunes-to-order man for many of the vaudeville performers of the 1920s, including Al Jolson. What is a complete mystery is what happened to the song between 1921 and 1947 and why Hank Williams ever picked up on the number and turned it into a No.1 hit. But he did and it is now regarded as a country classic, recorded by Patsy Cline, LeAnn Rimes and ZZ Top, among many others.

Above Hank Williams with his wife Audrey

❝a seminal country music classic❞

Words and **music** Arthur Freed, Abe Lyman and Gus Arnheim **1922**

Bing Crosby, Sarah Vaughan, Ray Charles, Frank Sinatra, Judy Garland, Billie Holiday and Ella Fitzgerald have all covered this song, and that's the best possible testament to its quality. Music historian Alec Wilder says of the song, 'I believe this melody ranks among the great melodic inventions… inspired, whether of American heritage or not.'

I Cried For You is obviously a singer's song, with a whole octave dive at the end of the second bar that allows the singer to show off a dramatic technique, but it has few notes, which makes life complicated for the lyric writer. However, Arthur Freed, a major player both as songwriter and producer in the era of the great Hollywood musicals, hit paydirt with this one. It is a song about survival and the lonely recuperation from a broken heart.

There is something about the lyrics of **I Cried For You** that harks back to the tradition of vaudeville rather than forward to the great American songbook, which was still very much in its infancy when the song was written. That makes some sense when you look at Arthur Freed's career. Producer of acclaimed musicals like *Babes in Arms*, *The Wizard of Oz* and *The Bells are Ringing*, Arthur Freed's greatest moment, however, was in both producing and writing all the songs for *Singin' in the Rain* in 1952.

Left Sarah Vaughan

I Cried For You was his second hit after the now less familiar 'When Buddha Smiles'. But he also wrote 'All I Do is Dream of You', 'You Are My Lucky Star' and 'Temptation', the last covered by Frankie Laine in the 1950s and The Everly Brothers in the 1960s. He did just about everything in showbusiness including touring with the Marx Brothers and writing stage material for them. He became a singer for a short time before starting his songwriting career. MGM took him on as a staff lyricist and his name became synonymous with the 'big musical'. As staff producer, he frequently put his own songs into the movies he made, thereby augmenting his income substantially.

The other two names on the credits, Abe Lyman and Gus Arnheim, both went on to become bandleaders in Los Angeles, but in the early 1920s they were joint leaders of the same outfit, The Syncopated Five. Lyman was the drummer, Arnheim the pianist. Though neither led top-flight bands, Arnheim's band featured actor Fred McMurray on saxophone in his pre-Hollywood movie career days and launched Bing Crosby on his solo career in the early 1930s after he left the Paul Whiteman Orchestra. Neither Lyman nor Arnheim was in Freed's league as a composer, so it would be interesting to find out what their respective contributions were to the song. It was common practice to share the composing royalties with bandleaders who played the songs in those days.

It is difficult to say who's version is the definitive one, but Judy Garland and Billie Holiday both excelled at survival songs, and it would be churlish to look any further, although Sarah Vaughan, with her wide vocal range and precise timing, also deserves a listen.

> " a song about survival and the lonely recuperation from a broken heart "

Words Gus Kahn **Music** by Isham Jones **1923**

It Had to be You most recently made an appearance on the soundtrack of the movie *When Harry Met Sally*, sung by Harry Connick Jr – just the latest confirmation of its evergreen status. This song was one of the earliest in a 10-year golden period of sophisticated songs, taking in George Gershwin, Richard Rodgers, Jerome Kern and Cole Porter, with grown-up, often witty lyrics that have stood the test of time, are endlessly revived and still sound as good today as they did then.

It is the combination of two great craftsmen collaborating to produce their best work. Gus Kahn was a German-born lyricist who had served his apprenticeship in Tin Pan Alley writing for vaudeville. He'd written for Gershwin and Sigmund Romberg among many others. Perhaps his best known lyric was two years later, for a Walter Donaldson tune called 'Makin' Whoopee', brilliantly arranged by Nelson Riddle for Frank Sinatra's 1956 album *Songs For Swinging Lovers*. Kahn was a man with an acerbic take on the mating game, and, like 'Makin' Whoopee', the lyric of **It Had to be You** fits the tune like a glove as if they'd been created in tandem, which is doubtful. It lacks the gushiness of so many songs of the era and marks a step forward in treating romance in a more down-to-earth way. Clearly the singer is meant to be someone breaking away from the coy values of Victorian lovemaking, the lyrics stating that for all the faults of the loved one they are still loved, still give a thrill.

Isham Jones, who wrote the music, was a popular dance bandleader based in Chicago in the 1920s. His first job, working in a coal-mine leading blind mules, was not what one would automatically think of as proper training to run a dance band. His coal-mining career came to an end when he crashed his string of coal-carrying trucks into a shaft door because he was playing the fiddle while trying to ride the lead mule. The Isham Jones Orchestra

was immensely popular and had an excellent reputation in the music industry, serving as training ground for Benny Goodman and Woody Herman who later went on to form their own bands. Isham Jones refused to label his music as jazz despite its provenance, preferring the term American dance music. Unlike many of the bandleaders of the period who took writing credits for the songs they helped to popularize, Isham Jones actually wrote very good songs of his own. His purple patch came in 1924 when he wrote two other best-sellers, 'I'll See You In My Dreams' also with Gus Kahn, and 'The One I Love (Belongs To Somebody Else)'. **It Had to be You** is a beautifully constructed variation-on-a-four-beat tune, where the accented note always falls on the first beat – thrill-/still-/you-/you – which is not only what all good dance songs should do, but induces a tension that pulls you into the next line. Listen to 'I Feel Good' by James Brown, like many of his great songs, it works the same trick, and gets you dancing.

Another of the great lyricists, Johnny Mercer, who wrote 'Moon River' and 'One For My Baby' cites **It Had to be You** as the best pop song ever written.

Left Isham Jones and his Orchestra
Right Harry Connick Jr

Words Irving Caesar **Music** Vincent Youmans **1924**

Tea For Two is a charming boy/girl duet that has had many varied lives both as a vocal and as an instrumental. It has been reworked many times by musicians as diverse as Art Tatum, the prodigiously gifted jazz pianist, and Russian classical composer Dmitri Shostakovich, who adapted the tune in 1928 and called it 'Tahiti Trot'. It is greatly favoured by jazz musicians because the complex harmonic construction of the melody gives great scope for improvisation.

    Tea For Two was written for the musical comedy *No No Nanette*, a story of three couples on a trip to Atlantic City in the 1920s. In a plot of engaging silliness, the title comes from the leading lady's need to hold off one rich suitor, who keeps trying to give her money, in favour of her chosen true love.

    Vincent Youmans, who wrote the music, was a popular composer of New York's Broadway theatre scene with several other enduring songs to his credit ('More Than You Know', 'I Want to be Happy' and 'I Know That You Know', for example). Dogged by ill health throughout his short career, he died of the effects of tuberculosis aged 48. *No No Nanette* is generally regarded as his best score.

    The boy/girl duet is a real hangover from the early days of musical comedy, but still maintains a presence in the charts with songs like Sonny and Cher's 'I Got You Babe', Frank and Nancy Sinatra's cloying 'Something Stupid' and more recently Shane McGowan and Kirsty MacColl's 'Fairytale of New York'.

    The lyrics of **Tea for Two**, by Irving Caesar, demonstrate all the hallmarks of Tin Pan Alley craftsmanship, artfully simple and pleasingly full of rhymes and alliterations. Caesar was the archetypal Tin Pan Alley cigar chomping, wisecracking showman. If you had the money, he'd write the song and it was invariably a good one. He had over 1,000 songs to his name when he died in 1996 aged 101, so he could speak with authority on popular music. And he often did. When asked the perennial question, 'Which comes first, the tune or the words?', he replied, 'The contract.' About the lyrics for **Tea For Two**, he confessed to taking as long as 15 minutes to complete them. 'Sometimes I write lousy but I always write fast.' It's widely believed that he wrote **Tea For Two** as a dummy lyric to enable him to better remember the tune. Youmans liked the dummy lyric and so it became the real lyric.

    Like many of his generation Caesar loathed the music of the rock 'n' roll generation, describing it as a form of musical juvenile delinquency. He didn't have to worry though since he'd made his fortune before Elvis was born.

    Listen to the Art Tatum solo version for a masterclass in piano virtuosity and the vocal version by Anita O'Day for her delicious and affectionate send up.

Above Art Tatum

Picture you upon my knee;
Just tea for two and two
  for tea,
Just me for you and you for
  me, alone.
Nobody near us to see us
  or hear us,
No friends or relations on
  weekend vacations.
We won't have it known,
  dear, that we have a
  telephone, dear.
Day will break and you will
  bake
A sugar cake for me to
  take for all the boys to
  see.
We will raise a family. A
  boy for you, a girl for me.
Oh, can't you see how
  happy life will be?

I'm discontented with
  homes that are rented,
So I have invented my own;
Darling this place is a
  lover's oasis,
Where life's weary chase is
  unknown.
Far from the cry of the city
Where the flowers pretty
  caress the streams,
Cosy to hide in,
To live side by side in
Don't let it abide in my
  dreams.

Words Lorenz Hart **Music** Richard Rodgers **1925**

Rodgers and Hart were never pop writers in the strictest sense, since they wrote exclusively for musical theatre. But many of their songs have become part of the repertoire of pop singers down the years. Songs like 'My Funny Valentine', 'With A Song in My Heart', 'Dancing on the Ceiling', 'Little Girl Blue', 'There's A Small Hotel', 'The Lady is A Tramp', 'This Can't Be Love', 'Bewitched' and 'I Could Write A Book', have all stood the test of time.

Rodgers wrote his first song aged nine, and there was never any doubt about what he wanted to do with his life. His career fits into two broad sections, writing with two very different lyricists, Lorenz Hart and Oscar Hammerstein II. With Hammerstein he wrote *Oklahoma!*, *Carousel* and *The Sound of Music*. But his most inventive and sophisticated songs are those for which Hart wrote the lyrics. If ever there was a song that can be said to have made Rodgers and Hart, it was surely **Manhattan**. 'We were… kids who had worked like hell, and were now enjoying the almost unbearable ecstasy of having everything turn out just right,' confessed Rodgers later in life. It was an immediate hit (despite an early rejection by a tone-deaf producer), and generated 10 curtain calls when first sung in public. A light-hearted ode to the joys of living in Manhattan, it was a boy/girl duet for singing in front of the curtains while the scenery behind was being changed. They wrote the song originally for a show with the unpromising title of *Winkle Town*. But it was first aired in a later show called *The Garrick Gaieties*. Its easygoing melody is supported by Hart's literate and sophisticated lyrics, showing a wide range of writer's tricks: internal rhymes, feminine endings and familiar place names.

Unlike Hammerstein, Hart was not concerned with the placing of a song in a narrative – his interest was in exploring the single moment of pure emotion in what he called, rhythmic dialogue. In spite of the self-conscious cleverness of the lyric (which one critic described as 'rich but unsingable') when the words of **Manhattan** come from a singer with the gifts of Ella Fitzgerald it becomes a timeless evocation of the charms of New York.

The relationship between the composer and the lyricist has traditionally been difficult, with both fighting for supremacy. There have been some spectacular fallings out down the years. In this case, Rodgers was the disciplined and professional grafter, driven to despair by Hart, the late riser with an emotional life complicated by his homosexuality and alcoholism, in an era not inclined to be tolerant. It didn't end well with Rodgers starting his new partnership with Oscar Hammerstein on the groundbreaking *Oklahoma!* before telling Hart of his intentions. But Hart was already in trouble and he died in 1943 of pneumonia brought on after a huge alcoholic binge. He was just 48 years old. But the pain in his life is not evident when you listen to his deft and witty lyrics.

Right Lorenz Hart (left) and Richard Rodgers

"You've Changed" demonstrates the power of the record. On that song you have Billie Holiday really stripped down to the minimum. You can hear the slurs, the way she breaks notes, the way she bends even one-syllable words. You can hear her, how she phrases, you can hear the liberty she takes with the melody, how she sings above and behind it. Jazz critic and poet A.B. Spellman on Billie Holiday's album *Lady in Satin*, released in 1958.

Until the 1920s, songs were by and large distributed by sheet music or word of mouth. The new era, known today as the 'Jazz Age', was an era when mechanical recordings were available and gaining on sheet music as earners for composers and publishers. Dance bands became popular in the wake of the loosening grip of Victorian morality; unmarried girls were now flocking to 10-cent dancehalls with their beaux. Prohibition proved a great boost to the smaller dancing establishments where they could sell illegal drinks. The smaller jazz combos of what came to be known as Dixieland jazz were the musical draw in the clubs. Frequently it was the liquor-pedalling gangsters who decided which musicians should play where. And they often had better taste than the customers. So the black (and occasionally white) New Orleans' bands played the smaller venues. With the closing down of the Storyville red light district in the city, the lure of other big cities and the potential money they offered drew the unemployed southerners north to Chicago and Kansas, and the jazz bands followed.

Although jazz had started in New Orleans, Chicago took over as its mecca in the early 1920s. Entertainers, such as 'Jelly Roll' Morton, Scott Joplin, King Oliver and Louis Armstrong, played in the city regularly. They were joined by

Right Fletcher Henderson's Orchestra, featuring Henderson at the piano and Louis Armstrong on trumpet, centre back

white bands, like The Original Dixieland Jazz Band, and by blues musicians from the Mississippi Delta. It was a city full of music, with clubs and dancehalls, such as the Royal Gardens, hosting both black and white bands playing for mixed audiences.

From Swinging to Singing
In the event it was white bandleader Paul Whiteman, the self-styled 'King of Jazz', who was the harbinger of the big band swing era. His recording of 'Three O'Clock in the Morning' sold 3.5 million copies in 1923. As a white bandleader he was more acceptable to the race-conscious mass market. Whiteman was among the first bandleaders to hire specialist singers (not musicians who also happened to sing) as part of his band. The most famous of his singers was Bing Crosby. Crosby had built his career singing in the small Chicago speakeasies run by people like Al Capone, and his casual intimacy became massively popular in a city steeped in jazz and blues. Whiteman took Crosby to see Armstrong perform in one of the Chicago dives, and it was a revelation to Crosby. As well as playing the horn brilliantly, Armstrong used his singing voice like another instrument in the band, improvising on the melody and making up sounds as he went along, a technique known as scat singing. Crosby was hooked and immediately changed his singing style from the old *bel canto* European tradition to the looser, jazz idiom. Just like Elvis 30 years later, his popularity grew because he was a white man who

could sing in a black manner.

Since stepping out from Paul Whiteman's band, Bing Crosby had pioneered pop singing as we know it, becoming the model for almost all who followed. Crosby's enormous success proved that there was clearly a market for the solo pop vocalist, and with record companies looking for a new way to capitalize on the talent of their 'crooners and songbirds' it was only a matter of time before singers would become an attraction in their own right. Mildred Bailey, another Whiteman singer, influenced greats like Billie Holiday, Ella Fitzgerald and Peggy Lee.

Although the band vocalist had been a popular feature of the swing era, and some, like Crosby, had recorded as soloists, it was the bands that dominated the scene and the start of the 'vocal era' can be pinpointed to 19 January 1941, the date that Frank Sinatra, still singing with The Dorsey Band, walked into Victor Studios in New York to make his first record as a soloist. Many of the early 'vocadence' recordings were issued on the lower priced labels because it was thought people wouldn't be prepared to pay as much for a record by a solo singer as for one featuring a singer and a band.

The Arrival of the Microphone

It could be argued that Crosby and Louis Armstrong between them invented modern pop singing. The combination of intimacy, made possible by the use of electric microphones in performance, and the new, more freewheeling 'Dixieland' style of interpretation, both became major features of their styles. Microphones had a huge impact on music performance, particularly for vocalists. Until their introduction, in about 1920, there was little difference between classical and popular singing. With the introduction of this new device singers were suddenly able to vary their range, wherever they performed. Slight inflections and changes of tone in their voices were able to be heard by audiences in small clubs and larger halls. The new popular singers no longer had to concentrate on voice projection, rather they were able to develop melody and pitch, concentrating more on the words of the songs. For Crosby and Armstrong fame grew, everyone heard them and finally the megaphone technique of singers like Al Jolson and Rudy Vallee gave way to the new night-club singers and a new era was born.

Right Bing Crosby poses with an early microphone

John Hammond (1910–1987) is one of the most important talent scouts ever in popular music. Initially a jazz fan, Hammond played a key role in the careers of many artists in jazz, blues, folk and rock music during a career spanning 50 years. A white man, born into a wealthy family, he is particularly noted for developing the careers of black artists, and served for many years on the board of the National Association for the Advancement of Colored People. His influence on popular music of the 20th century is incalculable.

Like many popular performers of the period, Crosby's career moved to new heights after the Wall Street Crash and the subsequent Depression. His performance of 'Buddy Can You Spare A Dime?' was a massive hit in the 1930s. Pop music was taking its inspiration from the lives that the audience lived and that song went right to the heart of the millions of Americans in the soup kitchens across the length and breadth of the country, confirming his iconic status across several genres of American music. Both Hank Williams and Jimmie Rodgers were admirers and Presley went on to cover 23 tracks that Crosby had previously recorded. Country musicians were especially fond of Crosby, whose songs were a major part of the output of the burgeoning radio network.

Radio was another important factor in the growing popularity of personality singers. Crosby built a huge following with his intimate, easy-going style, which would also influence the hillbilly singers of the 1930s and 1940s, like Will Rogers.

There were, of course, plenty of female singers, too. Bessie Smith was one of the very earliest interpreters of colloquial song. Her powerful and emotional interpretations, which were to become known as torch songs, could only have happened with microphones. Mildred Bailey and Connee Boswell (who watched Caruso to learn his breathing technique, as did Frank Sinatra in a later era) were popular recording stars along with Ruth Etting and Fanny Brice. These were the predecessors of Billie Holiday and Ella Fitzgerald, both band singers (who by the way, loathed each other) before they went solo.

The best black performers were achieving some success with white audiences by sheer force of talent and because they sang songs from the American songbook. But few performers would have had the moral authority to sing 'Strange Fruit', about the racial lynching of a black man in the deep south. Milt Gabler tells how Billie Holiday recorded it for his Commodore label when the major companies refused to touch it. The song didn't become a hit immediately but certainly played its part in drawing attention to the indignities of racial oppression in the 1940s. It's now regarded as a landmark, and Holiday is regarded as one of the very top song stylists of the century and someone who has had an enormous effect on the careers of other singers.

Vocal groups like The Mills Brothers and The Ink Spots learnt their techniques from the myriad gospel quartets that were touring the south in the 1920s and 1930s. The gospel groups frowned upon musical instruments which they thought to be creations of the devil, so they became adept at creating tight harmonies and rhythm using nothing but the human voice.

Is It Black or Is It White?

In general it was the black bands of the 1920s and 1930s, led by Fletcher Henderson, Duke Ellington and others, who provided the innovations, and the white bands that copied them. Henderson's arranger was the first to put a vocal group round the back of the vocalist using a call-and response-technique (listen to 'Marie' by The Dorsey Band and The Pied Pipers for fine examples of this). Coleman Hawkins, who also played with Henderson, is said to have invented modern saxophone technique, encouraged by his bandleader.

It took some progressive white managers to make sure the black talent was exposed. John Hammond, who had produced recordings by Fletcher Henderson, and made records with Bessie Smith and Billie Holiday for the Columbia label, led the way. He later went on to record Woody Guthrie, Bob Dylan and Bruce Springsteen. Not a bad haul for a talent spotter!

Songs of the 1920s

Some of the greatest songs of the century were written in the 1920s. Hoagy Carmichael's 'Stardust' started life as bouncy, uptempo instrumental dance number recorded by Isham Jones in 1929. But it was its appeal to both vocalists and bandleaders that led to the song's extraordinary longevity. The Bing Crosby recording of 1931 set the pattern. He had led the exodus away from unnamed band singer to soloist with orchestral accompaniment. Louis Armstrong recorded 'Stardust' later in the same year, and his version demonstrated how much freedom singers could have with material once they moved away from the performance of songs as written. Immensely popular till the early 1940s, Crosby was eclipsed only by Frank Sinatra.

After starting his career as a dance band vocalist, Sinatra was persuaded to record songs as a soloist. His solo debut at the Paramount in New York in 1943 generated a response from the so-called 'bobby-soxers' that bears comparison with Beatlemania more than 20 years later. It is because of this that Sinatra is so significant in the history of popular music. Up to the point that he went solo the real power in music was with the bandleaders, like Glenn Miller, Tommy Dorsey and Harry James. They made the bookings, hired and fired the musicians and the singers, chose the material and reaped the benefits. Of course, they were not going to relinquish their power easily. It is said that Tommy Dorsey was very unhappy at the prospect of Sinatra recording as a solo artist and that he pointed out, in no uncertain terms, that Sinatra was contracted to his band for another 20 years of so. Stories vary as to how that contract was broken, but it is surely true that the split was acrimonious.

Sinatra was the first teeny-bopper pop star who bears any comparison to the pop stars we know so well today. He wielded enough clout commercially to have his own arrangements and pick his own material, but he didn't write songs. It may have been Sinatra who ended the big band domination of popular music, but it is no coincidence that there was always an element of nostalgia in his output. Though his popularity was from the modern era, his best material came from the pens of George Gershwin, Irving Berlin, Cole Porter and Jerome Kern.

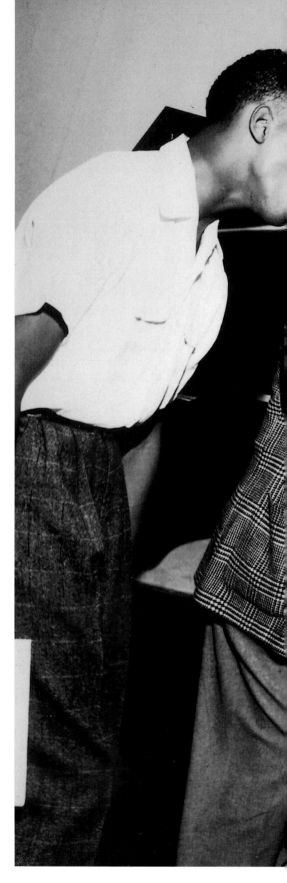

Right The Ink Spots recording in Decca's studios

the top 100

songs

27–38

Heebie jeebies

Stardust

Ol' man river

Singin' in the rain

But not for me

Blue yodel #1, 't' for Texas

Brother can you spare a dime?

Smoke gets in your eyes

Night and day

Summertime

I've got you under my skin

Great speckled bird

Words and **music** Boyd Atkins **1926**

The single most important thing about **Heebie Jeebies** is that it was recorded by virtuoso trumpet player Louis Armstrong in 1925 when he was at the peak of his powers. One could have picked any of a dozen tracks to demonstrate Armstrong's domination of popular music (or, more correctly, the sound and style of popular music, as composition was of secondary importance to his interpretations). If we were to judge by record sales, his version of 'What A Wonderful World' recorded in 1968, would probably take the prize. In that song, even though he was at the end of his career, he managed to transform a trite and sentimental song into a heartfelt and dignified epitaph.

Armstrong is one of a trio of New Orleans jazzmen who define Dixieland jazz, the other two being pianist Ferdinand 'Jelly Roll' Morton and Sidney Bechet, who played clarinet and soprano saxophone. All three were musicans of genius, but what separated Armstrong from the others was his singing voice. It is often said that he played his trumpet like a human voice and that he used his voice like an instrument of the orchestra. All the major popular singers that followed – Bing Crosby, Ella Fitzgerald, Billie Holliday, Frank Sinatra, Tony Bennett, Elvis Presley and Marvin Gaye – are indebted to him.

In its most simple definition, jazz is music that allows improvisation on a composed melody. Dixieland jazz is played in the style common to the American cities of the southern states, most notably New Orleans, where Armstrong was born. Dixieland jazz was as popular in the 1920s, as pop is today.

Before jazz, performers were respectful of composers, and for the most part played songs as written. Jazz was an organized way of allowing musicians to interpret material, often (but not always) spontaneously. This way of dealing with material is taken for granted these days, and the principal has spread to other areas of artistic endeavour, but in the first few decades of the century it was a revolutionary idea.

Armstrong did not invent the idea of improvisation, he just happened to be brilliant at it. He also had wider horizons than most of his peer group, and considered all forms of popular music to be equally interesting. He guested on all manner of musical oddities, most notably on the country song 'Blue Yodel #9' by Jimmie Rodgers, the Singing Brakeman. His eccentric vocal interpretations of Broadway show tunes set him apart from some of his fellow jazz performers who later accused him of diluting the purity of the genre. But it earned him the respect of the new generation of dance band

Above Louis Armstrong

singers, beginning with his great friend Bing Crosby who travelled the country to see Armstrong perform in order to pick up tricks on vocal technique.

Heebie Jeebies is the earliest recording to feature scat singing. The story goes that Armstrong had to make up the words when the sheet of music he was reading fell from the music stand during a recording. But more likely Armstrong was simply making up wordless sounds to fit the melody as he conceived it. However it came about, this simple notion freed singers from the sometimes terrible constrictions of the song as composed. It was also his phrasing of lyrics, utterly his own, but groundbreaking in interpretation, that leaves a legacy that nobody has equalled.

The composer of **Heebie Jeebies**, Boyd Atkins, was a bandleader, clarinettist and saxophonist who played the Chicago clubs in the 1920s, most notably the Sunset Café. **Heebie Jeebies** appears to be his only registered composition. If this is true, that's quite a legacy to leave.

Words and **music** Hoagy Carmichael (words rewritten by Mitchell Parish in 1931) **1927**

What is there left to say about **Stardust**? It's made enough money to sustain the economy of a middling Third World country, and it ranks as one of the handful of popular songs that is still being recorded (over 2,000 versions at the last count) 70 years after it was written. It is there by popular acclaim. Singers love to sing it, and audiences love to hear it.

It was originally conceived in the grounds of Carmichael's old university in Indiana, as an instrumental for dancing, and called 'Star Dust'. So strong was the melodic inspiration that came to him, that he was unsure if he had really composed it himself, or merely recalled a song written by someone else. Carmichael's son, Hoagy Jr, claims that Mitchell Parish, who wrote the familiar lyric, based it on words already written by his father. The first recognizable version was by Bing Crosby in 1931 (during his fashionably hip period). But when Louis Armstrong recorded it later the same year, he demonstrated not only its perennial appeal for jazz musicians, but also that it was a song that could have many lives. As Tony Bennett has said, '… for vocalists, all roads lead back to Armstrong'. He opened up the phrasing and taught everybody how to do things with melody and timing. He appropriated **Stardust** and, to use Stanley Crouch's words, '… gorilla-ed the lyrics, compressed that wonderful melody and made it irresistibly his own song'. People just didn't *do* that to composer's material in those days. History does not record what Carmichael felt about Armstrong's treatment of the song. One can only assume he would have been flattered by his old friend's attentions, since Carmichael was, by inclination, a jazz player. Very much influenced by another trumpeter, Bix Beiderbecke, Carmichael claims there are phrases in the melody that recall riffs from Beiderbecke's material.

Throughout the 1930s and 1940s **Stardust** led a double life, both as an instrumental covered by all the major bands (notably by Artie Shaw), and as a straightforward romantic ballad, covered by just about any vocalist you can name. Sinatra recorded it four times, once interestingly, as a cappella version during the Petrillo ban in the 1940s, when the Musician's Union forbade its members to make recordings.

Although a contemporary of the great practitioners of American song, Kern, Gershwin, Berlin, Rodgers and so on, Carmichael never felt part of that illustrious circle. He never wrote for Broadway. His songs were all one-off originals that never strayed far from his

Above Hoagy Carmichael

Bloomington, Indiana roots. His lyrics dealt with downhome issues, old rocking chairs, lazy rivers, sleeping in the sun, moonlight through the pines. They were the antithesis of the seemingly more sophisticated Cole Porter, who was also born in Indiana but went on to write lyrics of a more metropolitan bent.

Where Carmichael really scored was in his capacity for melodic invention. **Stardust**, like many of his other compositions, does not do musically what you expect it to do. It is not built in the A-B-A-B structure so beloved of Tin Pan Alley songwriters. Any lesser composer would have used the two melodies that comprise the verse and the chorus, as two separate songs. It all hangs together because Carmichael was the most inventive, sophisticated and jazz-oriented of all the great craftsmen of American song.

Its most interesting recent incarnation was in a recording by Willie Nelson, which was still in the country charts after 137 weeks in 1981. As Willie recalls after his first rather radical venture out of mainstream country and western in the opera house in Austin, Texas, in front of a notoriously conservative country audience, 'there was a kind of stunned silence in the crowd for a moment, and then they exploded with cheering and whistling and applauding. The kids thought **Stardust** was a new song I'd just written...' Willie cites the song as his all-time favourite, and it's still part of his concert set.

But perhaps the greatest version is by the incomparable Nat 'King' Cole who recorded it in 1961 at Capitol Studios in Hollywood with a string arrangement by Gordon Jenkins – it's a masterly performance that lets the song speak for itself.

Above Nat 'King' Cole

trivia

★ Bette Midler has the lyrics of *Stardust* carved in the stone of her fireplace.

★ In 1953 US DJs voted *Stardust* the greatest song of all time, and you'd be hard put to find a jukebox without one version or another.

★ A latin tinged version featured as background music in Orson Welles classic radio version of *War of the Worlds*.

> 66 there were over 2,000 versions of **stardust** at the last count 99

Music Jerome Kern **Words** Oscar Hammerstein **1928**

There are several reasons for this song to be included in a list of the 100 great songs of the 20th century, quite apart from its huge popularity. It comes from Jerome Kern's best-known musical, *Showboat*, widely regarded as the first American musical to link drama and music in an integrated way. We take it for granted these days, but prior to *Showboat*, musicals (or more correctly musical comedies) were more like themed reviews with songs as interludes. There was a feeling that they lacked depth and that they should move on from fluffy boy-meets-girl routines. *Showboat* was not only the first show to do that but it also bravely dealt with realistic subjects that had up to that point, been thought of as taboo, like interracial sex and unhappy marriages. It was also spectacularly staged on a riverboat on the Mississippi River. The plot involves the mostly white people who travel on the boat and the African-American population who service it from the riverbanks.

The black actor, Paul Robeson who starred in the original Broadway production, sang the opening song, **Ol' Man River**, and it has since become forever identified with him. There was a general fascination with the lifestyle and culture of the negroes, who were only one generation from slavery and were still for the most part treated as second-class citizens. Hammerstein's lyrics were written in the style of the black minstrel or 'coon' song, a caricature of a black southern dialect. Though by today's standards it was liberal in its sentiments, it sounds rather grating today, but in its time just to include black performers in a Broadway show with predominantly white performers was regarded as daring. It seemed the province of the mainly Jewish songwriters (who probably shared a sense of disenfranchisement from the protestant white majority) to put words and music into the mouths of black artists, that would have been less acceptable if written by African-Americans themselves. It was only a few years later that George Gershwin wrote *Porgy and Bess*, a totally black opera. Robeson, a professional American footballer and a lawyer who had felt the sting of racial prejudice in America (aggravated by his higher education) had moved to England by the time *Showboat* was written. He may have considered it beneath him to play the role of Joe, the lazy dock worker with only a marginal piece of the plot, but he must have recognized that a song of that quality, whatever its linguistic shortcomings, would do him little harm. In fact it launched his acting and singing career.

In the 1940s, Frank Sinatra scored an unlikely hit with the same song, and although his doesn't really compare with Robeson's version, it shows Sinatra's technical skills to perfection.

For his part, with *Showboat* Kern scored a second first in American musical history. Not only had he written what later became the first of the genre of American popular song with 'They Didn't Believe Me' (see page 36), but he also reinvented the American musical.

Above Paul Robeson in *Showboat*

> hammerstein's lyrics were written in the style of the black minstrel or 'coon' song, a caricature of a black southern dialect

Words Arthur Freed **Music** Herb Nacio Brown **1929**

Although immortalized in the 1952 musical of the same name, **Singin' in the Rain** was originally written in 1929 for a different show, MGM's *All Star Review*, in which it got no less than three showings (front and end titles and one in the middle). In the late 1920s many of the best known silent stars of Hollywood were anxious to show they could adapt to the new talking pictures, and no less than 70 musicals were produced that year as a sort of public audition. MGM's *All Star Review* featured Joan Crawford, Jack Benny, Buster Keaton and Laurel and Hardy, among others. It was given to a performer called Ukulele Ike to render **Singin' in the Rain**. Benny referred to the number as 'an optimistic song written by an optimist', and that's about right. The big performance in the middle of the film is taken at a faster pace than the Kelly version, and is a bit of a treat. It involves Ike, and, of course, his ukulele, playing with full studio orchestra and the MGM chorus, thoughtfully dressed in see-through plastic macs, in a cheerful dance routine with stage rain and even the occasional flash of lightning. The film's other big hit was 'You Were Meant For Me' which was also revived by Gene Kelly to less effect in the 1952 movie.

Arthur Freed, who wrote the lyrics for all the songs in MGM's *All Star Review*, went on to produce the movie *Singin' in the Rain*. What more efficient way of earning extra bucks than making a movie using your own songs? It was left to Betty Comden and Adolph Green to give a disparate bunch of 20-year-old songs a worthy setting which they did with amazing success. This was all the more remarkable as few of the songs had the lasting charm of **Singin' in the Rain**. If ever there was

an example of triumph over thin pickings, this was it. The notion of putting the songs back into the context of the era they were written for and turning it into a spoof, was brilliant, but maybe not quite as brilliant as having Gene Kelly, Debbie Reynolds and Donald O'Connor as your lead characters. They positively wrenched the film out of mediocrity. Nothing of which detracts from Kelly's version of the title song.

Above A poster advertising the film *Singin' in the Rain*
Left Arthur Freed (left) and Herb Nacio Brown (right)

Everybody's favourite film clip – the Gene Kelly routine with the song – is a joyous and unbridled declaration of his love for the Debbie Reynolds character, and it would be churlish to suggest that the song's appeal can be separated from Kelly's brilliant choreography. Here is not the place to go into too much detail about the filming of the sequence, but it all helped. The sound of Kelly's feet stomping through puddles is as important as the more conventional lyrics. One may contemplate what might have happened to this song had Kelly not revived it, but it is one of a number of decent songs tipped over into brilliance by a single, defining performance. Kelly was never the world's greatest singer, but he invests a song with honesty and truth and he could convey sense of ecstasy, which is a rare skill that only a handful of performers (Aretha Franklin and Stevie Wonder come to mind) can express.

31 but not for me

Words Ira Gershwin **Music** George Gershwin **1930**

To pick the best of George Gershwin's classic show tunes is an invidious task. In a list that includes 'Someone to Watch Over Me', 'I've Got A Crush On You', 'Fascinating Rhythm', 'S'Wonderful' and 'The Man I Love', the choice is impossible. There are eloquent apologies for all of them, especially 'The Man I Love', which musician and critic Benny Green thought was the most accomplished pop song ever written. Of course, Gershwin has always been regarded as a brilliant pianist. But brilliant musicianship and brilliant pop songs are not necessarily the same animal. Even when he was alive, people though of Gershwin's music as 'arty'. He aspired to be taken seriously in the same way as Ravel or Debussy, and his extended compositions, like *Rhapsody In Blue* and *Porgy And Bess*, will last the course. But it is for his show tunes that he is best remembered. Of course, like Jerome Kern and Richard Rodgers, and later Cole Porter, he wrote whole shows and not individual pop songs. There was always a narrative implication, and for the individual songs to have lives separate from the shows they came from was a secondary consideration.

Girl Crazy was written in 1930 and there are three killer songs in it, 'I Got Rhythm', 'Embraceable You' and **But Not For Me**. 'I Got Rhythm', like Gershwin's later song 'Summertime' (see page 69), is pentatonic – played only on the black notes – and is beloved of flashy pianists who can improvise around it. 'Embraceable You' is a lovely song, but unless you are a very skilled singer, it is one to avoid. For the perfect version listen to Sarah Vaughan.

Gershwin's elder brother Ira wrote most of the lyrics to George's tunes. Given the mortality rates of songwriting partnerships, it was a brave undertaking. In an effort not to appear to be cashing in on his brother's fame he started writing lyrics under the pseudonym Arthur Francis (after his other brother and sister). By the time they wrote *Girl Crazy* they had completed 30 shows together and Ira turned out to be one of the greatest lyricists in showbusiness, and the first to be awarded a Pulitzer Prize.

But Not For Me is a pretty straightforward song about rejection, of the type that has kept Nashville a thriving industry from Hank Williams to the present day. Ira, in a typically literate style, keeps it simple, mostly monosyllabic, with just a hint of showiness:

With love to lead the way
I've found more skies of gray
Than any Russian play
Could guarantee.

You won't find any allusions to Russian literature in an Irving Berlin lyric.

Songs of rejection always give more scope for poignancy than songs about being loved. Writing about being in love is harder. Sad songs seem to hang around longer in the imagination. That's one of the qualities that keeps **But Not For Me** popular at the end of the century, still sounding fresh and part of our everyday emotional landscape. We've all been through it. It isn't the most sophisticated of George's tunes, but it lends itself to heartfelt interpretation by singers with the gift of sincerity like Judy Garland, Frank Sinatra, and supremely, Ella Fitzgerald.

Left Ira (left) and George Gershwin

Words and **music** Jimmie Rodgers **1931**

On the statue of Jimmie Rodgers, erected in his hometown of Meridian, Mississippi, after his death in 1933, is written:

'His is the music of America. He sang the songs of the people he loved, of a young nation growing strong. His was an America of glistening rails, thundering boxcars and rain-swept night, of lonesome prairies, great mountains and a high blue sky. He sang of the bayous and the wheated plains, of the little towns, the cities and the winding rivers of America.'

An eloquent and appropriate eulogy to the man known as the 'Father of Country Music', who died of tuberculosis aged 37. Today it's hard to imagine that Jimmie Rodgers was more popular that Bing Crosby, or that Louis Armstrong played on one of his records. So embedded was he in the culture of rural America, shop customers would ask for the latest Jimmie Rodgers record to be added to their list of groceries.

Blue Yodel #1, 'T' for Texas was the first of several songs in the numbered 'Blue Yodel' series, all featuring Rodgers' unique, trademark yodelling. Executives at Victor, his record company, were so mystified by the mixture of blues and country, that they were reluctant to record the song at all. It was marketed as 'a popular song for a comedian with a guitar'. It was a novelty to hear a white man singing in a black blues style, and this marriage of blues and country is the essence of Rodgers' contribution to popular music.

One reviewer wrote that Rodgers was a 'white man gone black' and described his song as, 'engaging, melodious and bloodthirsty'. With his strong baritone voice, he articulated the day-to-day concerns of rural America, of love, loss and hardship, in a way that most Tin Pan Alley writers could not hope to emulate.

His father worked on the railroads and his own career as a railway brakeman was cut short by his illness, but not before he absorbed the sound of poor black America from his fellow workers. His illness was not only responsible for his career in music but infused much of his songwriting. He knew as soon as he was diagnosed that he would die of his condition, as his mother had before him. It was probably that knowledge that gave his voice its mournful edge.

His six-year recording career took off after **Blue Yodel #1, 'T' for Texas** sold a million copies in record time, easily outselling the popular crooners like Crosby. Country music was suddenly a force to be

Above Jimmie Rodgers, 'The Singing Brakeman'

reckoned with, and Jimmie Rodgers set the benchmark. He went on to record prolifically until the week before his death. Whether recording at home, or accompanied by a Dixieland-style jazz band or a waltzing dance orchestra, his sound always remained uniquely his own.

Words E.Y. 'Yip' Harburg **Music** J. Gorney **1932**

There have been worse stockmarket crashes than the one in 1929. On Black Tuesday in 1987 almost 25 per cent was wiped off the value of shares in one day. In 1929, it was around 15 per cent, but the ripple effect on the American economy was infinitely more serious. By 1932, when **Brother Can You Spare A Dime?** was first released, 13 million people – a quarter of the working population in the USA – had been put out of a job. Most people earned their living from the land. The banks had all but collapsed, so nobody could get at their savings. Some of those who had speculated with other people's money, and lost fortunes in the fall, committed suicide.

This song exactly captures the spirit of that bleak period in American history, when most ordinary people could only look on helplessly, and reflect on an event that they had played no part in creating. Yip Harburg, who went on to write the words to 'Over the Rainbow' (see pages 80-81), wore his heart on his sleeve with this lyric:

They used to tell me I was
building a dream,
And so I followed the mob,
When there was earth to
plough, or guns to bear,
I was always there.

It's a bitter lyric that captured the rage of the working man and his sudden inability to support himself:

Why should I be standing in
line
Just waiting for bread?

The singer is anyone who has worked the railroads, built the skyscrapers, farmed or fought in the Great War. There's even a swipe at the hollow jingoism of 'Yankee Doodle Dandy' by fellow composer George M. Cohan, the father of Broadway, who wrote the stirring march 'Over There' in praise of the patriots fighting in Europe. Harburg writes:

Once in khaki boots, gee we all looked swell,
Full of Yankee-doodle-dom.
Half a million boots went sloggin' through hell,
And I was the kid with the drum.

Harburg was one of a small group of exceptionally gifted lyricists, alongside Ira Gershwin, Oscar Hammerstein and Lorenz Hart, who were born around the turn of the century and took as their point of reference the light operettas of Gilbert and Sullivan. 'Words make you think thoughts and music makes you feel feelings and a song makes you feel a thought. Words give meaning, purpose and destination. Music gives wings and together they take off and fly as a song,' explained Harburg.

It was Ira Gershwin who encouraged Harburg to become a full-time lyricist. Unlike other lyricists, his work spoke to the underprivileged, rural workers, blacks and women, in American society, those who hadn't benefited from the American Dream. In fact he was accused of being anti-capitalist by the Republican Party in the US some of whom tried to have this song banned.

Jay Gorney wrote the score for the show *Americana* from which this song was the big hit. He went on to work in movies and television while continuing to compose, although he never repeated the success he had with **Brother Can You Spare A Dime?**.

Two versions became hits in 1932, but it was Bing Crosby's pleading baritone that takes the honours from Rudy Vallee's version.

Words Otto Harbach **Music** Jerome Kern
1933

There are many who regard Jerome Kern as the greatest writer of show tunes ever, even though his work does not have the showiness of George Gershwin or the directness of Irving Berlin. It has also been suggested that he doesn't sound as 'American' as his illustrious peers, and that there is still a whiff of old Europe in his work. But for his ability to write sublime melodies that stay in your head, he is unsurpassed. Judy Garland, who knew her way round a song, said his were, '…melodious, poignant, wistful, tender and utterly enchanting. Jerome Kern has brought to the treasury of American song the wealth of his own great talent.'

The black American doo-wop group The Platters scored a big hit with **Smoke Gets in Your Eyes** in 1958, and many people still think they wrote it. By adding a hint of black church gospel, it worked perfectly as a 1950s' composition. Former Roxy Music singer Brian Ferry also had a hit with it in 1974. It is the song's ability to both transcend time and lend itself to varied interpretations and still remain fresh that makes Garland's words so appropriate.

Lyricist Otto Harbach said that Kern originally wrote the tune for his pioneering musical *Showboat*, which premiered in 1927. It was intended as an uptempo instrumental to accompany a tap dance routine while the scenery was being changed. But on hearing it for the first time Harbach suggested turning the short notes (necessary to highlight the sound of the tap dancing) into long notes, and recreating it as a ballad. As a result of this change the song was not included in *Showboat*. It appeared for the first time in the 1933 Kern/Harbach show *Roberta*. It appeared again in 1935 in the Fred Astaire/Ginger Rogers movie of the show sung by Irene Dunne. It was not one of their best movies, but the song became a hit several times in the next few years with versions by Paul Whiteman, Ruth Etting and Artie Shaw. The show was reworked in the 1950s and renamed *Lovely To Look At*. That too was made into a movie in 1952 when Kathryn Grayson had another big hit with the song. Her crystal soprano voice was more suited to light opera than Hollywood musicals, which underscores the perception of Kern as more European than American. But her version of the song is gorgeous, helped immeasurably by the marvellous lyrics which describe the sad end of a love affair.

> " the marvellous lyrics describe the sad end of a love affair "

Right The Platters

Words and music Cole Porter 1934

The name Cole Porter has become almost a generic term for witty show songs, but it was **Night and Day**, not as witty as 'Anything Goes' or 'Let's Do It', for example, that became his best-selling song. But it was a daring composition for a straightforward love song. Since he was the best educated of all his peers one might have expected Porter to be good with words. But, like Irving Berlin in that small group of genius, his real skill was in matching words to a melody.

With the exception of his songs for the show *Kiss Me Kate*, Porter mostly wrote stand-alone review songs. More often than not his songs were the stars of the show. **Night and Day** was written for what became the Fred Astaire and Ginger Rogers musical *The Gay Divorce*. (It was called *The Gay Divorcee* in the UK, as morality dictated that a 'divorce should never be gay'.) What makes it stand out is not so much the witty lyric but the compelling melody and the way the words fit into it. One of Porter's early music teachers taught him a golden rule, one to which he remained true throughout his career, 'Words and music must be so inseparably wedded to each other that they are like one.'

The first note of the song is repeated 32 times over the words:

Like the beat, beat, beat of the tom tom when the jungle shadow fall,
Like the tick, tick, tock of the stately clock as it stands against the wall...

Then another 16 repeated notes half a tone higher:

Like the drip, drip, drip, of the raindrops when the summer show'r is through...

Before returning to the original note with yet another 16 repeated notes:

So a voice within me keeps repeating you, you, you...

And then the song moves seamlessly and into that familiar melody, which by then seem like a longed for, natural release:

Night and day, you are the one.
Only you beneath the stars and under the sun.

The tune sets up a sense of relentless, repetitive, obsessive passion, one that perfectly matches the lyrical idea. But Porter's publisher was less than enthusiastic when he first heard the song, probably feeling he wasn't getting enough variety for his money. Most of the great songwriters kept their melodies within a fairly limited range of notes (around an octave and a half) so that the untrained singer (like Fred Astaire, for example) could accommodate them. Astaire was frequently the singer of choice for the great practitioners of Tin Pan Alley, not only because he was good box-office, but because he sang the songs as written, without appearing to add his own interpretation to them.

Rumour has it that Porter got the idea for **Night and Day** from a visit to north Africa, where he heard a wailing Muslim priest calling his followers to prayer from the minaret of the local mosque. True or not, Porter was certainly a more adventurous traveller than most of his peer group, and New York's Tin Pan Alley was never his natural habitat. Though he is rightly remembered for his clever lyrics, Cole Porter's real skill was in his blending of words and music, and it's that that keeps him up there with the greats.

Left Cole Porter

Words Dubose Heyward **Music** George Gershwin **1935**

There is still some controversy about the staging of the folk opera *Porgy and Bess* and whether it confirms to white stereotypes of African-American life at the end of the slave era. It fell out of favour during the battle for equal civil rights in the 1950s. What is beyond dispute is the beauty of the songs in the opera, many of which have become part of the standard repertoire of jazz musicians and singers down the years; and after languishing unperformed for decades the show has more recently been revived in the operatic setting for which it was conceived.

Of all the songs in the piece, **Summertime** is the most played and surely one of the most recorded songs of the century. While researching the song George Gershwin went to Folly Island, off the coast of South Carolina, where the opera is set and where some of the slaves from West Africa lived after moving north to find work. He observed the customs of the local people and listened to their music and spoken idioms. He joined in their 'shouting', creating rhythms with his hands and feet as accompaniment to the spirituals that they sang for him.

Summertime does invoke the sound of the popular spiritual, 'Sometimes I Feel Like A Motherless Child'. It is sung as a lullaby and the melody is predominantly pentatonic – played mostly on the black notes of the piano. Almost all blues, early black gospel and many jazz compositions are written in pentatonic scales. The melody only uses six notes and that may be why it feels like the traditional folk song many people think it is, and why Gershwin said of it, 'The music is so marvellous, I don't believe I wrote it.'

Above Ella Fitzgerald

The opera was always intended as a vehicle for black performers. That was one reason why Dubose Heyward, who wrote the novel *Porgy* on which the show was based, chose to work with George Gershwin and not Jerome Kern, who also pitched for the show with his producer Al Jolson. Many of the original criticisms rejected it, saying that it may as well have had a white cast for all the light it shed on the race issue at the time.

The criticisms stung Gershwin who had approached the enterprise in all sincerity. He had always wanted to be taken seriously as a composer and the work that he thought of as the peak of his achievement seemed to lie in ruins. He died two years later of a brain haemorrhage.

There is a marvellous version by Ella Fitzgerald and Louis Armstrong and an intriguing instrumental by Miles Davis in absolutely top form with orchestration by Gil Evans, but perhaps the best-remembered version is by the great Billie Holiday.

Words and music Cole Porter 1936

With hundreds of recorded versions, **I've Got You Under My Skin** is simply one of the most popular songs of all time. Introduced to the world by Virginia Bruce in the movie *Born To Dance*, this well-known standard has been repeatedly recorded by the best singers and performers. Perhaps the classic interpretation is Frank Sinatra's 1956 version, arranged by the peerless Nelson Riddle. They simply made the song swing. Sinatra's timing and ability to find the exact metre of each lyric he sings are well known. But in **I've Got You Under My Skin**, he does it so effortlessly it feels like he is writing the song as he goes along.

Porter, born in 1892, was persuaded to turn professional after a brilliant series of college songs. After a few early Broadway flops, Porter joined the French Foreign Legion before deserting to become a fixture in Europe's élite where he was the guest of choice for the more extravagant upper-class soirees. Gradually his genius for songwriting emerged and, rare among the cream of America's popular songsmiths, Porter wrote both music and lyrics. Perhaps it was his legal training that endowed him with the gift of finding the right word for the right song. Or maybe he just learnt a lot from a liaison with British songwriter and playwright Noel Coward. Indeed Porter's humour and cheekiness, combined with his use of double entendres and popular cultural references as well as borrowing from famous literature, does bear more than a passing resemblance to the skills of Coward.

Lyrically, **I've Got You Under My Skin** is assumed to be about unrequited love, perhaps even gay love as, although Porter

Above Frank Sinatra

was married to a rich society lady, it is now common knowledge that he had affairs with men throughout his life. However, another interpretation suggests that the song is about drug taking. References to sacrificing everything, and trying to resist, bear this out although it is not thought that Porter himself was a prolific user of drugs, more that the society functions at which he performed would at that time have involved widespread cocaine use. But whatever the song is about, **I've Got You Under My Skin** illustrates Porter's skill at making the lyric dictate the rhythm of the melody. The way he constructs whole sentences to fall across two or more lines of a melody shows that with Porter, at least, words and music are indelibly linked.

Porter wrote this song early on in his career, alongside others such as 'Easy To Love', 'In The Still of the Night', 'It's De-Lovely', 'My Heart Belongs to Daddy' and 'Well Did You Evah?'. Later on he added to this already impressive list with such classics as 'Who Wants To Be A Millionaire', 'So In Love', 'Night and Day', 'I Love Paris', 'I Get A Kick' and many, many others.

Not all of the great interpreters of song could deal with a Cole Porter lyric. Frank Sinatra had no trouble dealing with the irony and cleverness of the words, but other luminaries couldn't quite handle them.

Words The Reverend Guy Smith **Music** traditional **1937**

Left Roy Acuff and The Smoky Mountain Boys

There are three separate points of interest in this song: the music, the lyrics and the classic performance by country artist Roy Acuff.

The Reverend Guy Smith was briefly a member of The Good Will Trio, an Ozark band who sang inspirational music. Their best-remembered song is 'Keep on the Sunny Side of Life'.

The lyrics of **Great Speckled Bird** are based on a text from the Bible:

Mine heritage is unto me as a speckled bird, the birds round about are against her: come ye, assemble all the beasts of the field, come to devour.

9 Jeremiah XII.

Religious texts are common enough in country music, and the message within this song, which fits in with a fundamentalist belief strongly embedded in American Pentecostal communities, is that the speckled bird represents the only true religion and is therefore despised by non-believers.

There will be many country artists, past and present, who consider country music to be the 'one true path' in popular music and who **are unmoved** by the mockers and modernizers. Roy Acuff had converted to Christianity when he appeared for the second time on the *Grand Ole Opry* radio show. He had recorded **Great Speckled Bird** in 1937 with his group, The Tennessee Crackerjacks, and on his first appearance had sung it in a crooning style made popular by the likes of Bing Crosby. The WSN radio show the *Grand Ole Opry* had been broadcasting from the Ryman Auditorium in Nashville since 1925, featuring live country acts every Saturday night. In Acuff's second more successful broadcast, he performed the

piece in a fiddle-based hillbilly style that also first introduced the dobro guitar to country fans. 'Everything was dark, until I found the fiddle. If it had not come along I don't know what I would have become,' he later explained.

The future was clear. He became Opry's resident act and changed the name of his band to the more dignified Smoky Mountain Boys. It put him in the front rank of country performers, and only Jimmie Rodgers had a higher standing. Acuff (known as 'The Backwoods Hillbilly' and 'The Caruso of Country') was the man to pull together the disparate elements of country music into one piece. It was Acuff who quite deliberately moved Opry into hillbilly territory and made a fortune in the process. Everybody knows that Nashville is the home of country music, but it was Acuff's personality and astute sense of business that helped turn The Opry into the venue all country music acts aspired to.

The simple three-chord (G, C, D7) tune on **Great Speckled Bird** has had many lives. Its provenance is lost in the mists of time, but was most famously used in 1952 by another celebrated country artist, Kitty Wells, in her signature song 'It Wasn't God Who Made Honky Tonk Angels'. Hers was an answer song to another country tune by Hank Thompson called 'Wild Side of Life' which used the same melody.

> **"** the lyrics of **great speckled bird** are based on a text from the bible **"**

" If I could find a white singer with the negro sound and the negro feel, I could make a million dollars. **"**

Sam Phillips, owner of the Sun Record Company in Memphis, Tennessee. In Elvis Presley, Phillips found everything he was looking for.

Sam C. Phillips had started his own Sun Records label in 1952, scoring a national r&b hit the following year with Rufus Thomas's 'Bear Cat', an answer record to Big Mama Thornton's 'Hound Dog'. For a couple of years, with the only studio in Memphis, Phillips had the field to himself recording local blues and country artists. When northern record companies, alerted by his success, moved in to Memphis to record the new generation of Beale Street bluesmen, Phillips knew he had to look for something new. Something 'he could have all to himself'.

There was, of course, nothing new about white artists covering black music, but what was unique about Elvis Presley was that he did it so convincingly. The Memphis teenager was steeped in gospel, rhythm and blues and country music. His first single, recorded on 7 June 1954 at Sun Studios on Union Street, was a coupling of a country-blues song, 'That's All Right' (originally recorded by Arthur 'Big Boy' Crudup in 1947), and a bluegrass song, 'Blue Moon of Kentucky'. Both songs were worked up and performed with a style and urgency that became the hallmark of a new fusion called rockabilly.

Rockabilly, and subsequently rock 'n' roll, was just the latest in a long line of cross pollination between black and white music – a process which had been going on since the beginnings of popular music. Despite the racism and segregation that divided the continent during these years, white hillbilly country music and black blues had never been very far from each other. Southern blacks and whites had much in common, not least the poverty and isolation of a hand-to-mouth rural existence.

Rural Roots

Country music – as we now know it – began to take shape in the 19th century in the Appalachian Mountain region which stretched as far north as the Ohio River and as far west as Arkansas and Texas. Scraps of ancient British folk songs and airs, minstrel songs, hymns, contemporary popular songs and, later, jazz and blues, was passed back and forth between travelling entertainers and medicine shows to townsfolk, between friends and neighbours, and between parents

Left Elvis Presley

and their children. Early settlers from the British Isles, who had arrived between 1725 and 1750, had made their way through the Cumberland Gap to find cheap land in Virginia, West Virginia, North Carolina and Kentucky, taking with them fiddles, lutes and other instruments and songs, ballads and attitudes which, in some cases, could be traced back to Elizabethan England. Like blues, this music reflected the Appalachian people's often devout spirituality and the stark, poverty-ridden living conditions. As blues represents the roots of most black American music, the tunes of the Appalachian Mountains are the most primal form of white American music.

Although the exact origins of the blues continue to be the subject of scholarly debate, there is general agreement that it was music born out of the oppression of slavery. The work songs, field hollers and spirituals, which helped bind the slaves together, paved a musical path to the blues; a new music which grew out of the African tradition but with lyrics which would relate to the new experiences of a notionally free life.

Blues and Appalachian music remained largely within the rural communities, hidden from wider society. Before the advent of radio, few Americans outside the rural south knew such music existed. While the north had become increasingly obsessed with progress and modernity, the south remained insular, innovation was avoided and outsiders treated with suspicion. Black people kept blues music to themselves as part of their culture, and it was never presented to whites for their approval. When eventually the blues was recorded, the records were sold as 'race' records, released through outlets in black communities and made available only on special order to those in the know.

Early recordings by white rural musicians show they actually drew their repertoire from a wide circle of sources. Apart from the traditional folk songs and ballads they brought with them, they tapped into gospel, vaudeville and the blues. Black and white rural music was harder to separate stylistically before the recording industry had created different markets for them. Black and white performers often drew from the same song lists, and folk tunes, like 'John Henry' and 'House of the Rising Sun', were covered by both country and blues artists.

Moving To The City

There were two types of blues, the result of two distinct lifestyles: country (or rural) blues and urban blues. Country blues, mostly from the Mississippi Delta, is considered the purest form – a spontaneous individual expression played by itinerant musicians on the street, in juke-joints and on the front porch. Bukka White, Big Bill Broonzy, Blind Lemon Jefferson and Robert Johnson are the prime examples of this category.

Urban blues – the second style – was more disciplined and less raw than country blues. This type of playing, where the musicians were essentially performing for an audience rather than in isolation, developed partly on Beale Street, in Memphis, where there were numerous places for the blues performer to make a living playing music. Almost everyone who is anyone in blues history played in Memphis and on Beale Street.

There were a number of contributory factors for the emergence of the blues at the turn of the century. Improved communications, like the telegraph and telephone, brought the potential for instant awareness across the continent. Greater mobility, via an expanded rail network, not only introduced the music to people in the cities, where many rural blacks had moved in search of a better life, but helped with the cross fertilization of the various regional styles, from Texas, Piedmont and Mississippi.

In 1914, William Charles Handy – the musician and bandleader from Alabama – published 'Memphis Blues' and 'St Louis Blues', which are claimed to be the first blues songs to be published and to achieve wide popularity. Handy was hardly a real bluesman – he had a classical musical education, and 'St Louis Blues' doesn't sound much like an authentic blues piece these days, but by the 1950s, it had become the song recorded by more artists than any other song in American history.

W.C. Handy had begun his career as a cornetist with a brass band and went on to tour the vaudeville circuit as musical director of a minstrel troupe. During his travels around the south, he listened to richly varied music among which were early examples of the blues. Handy carefully noted down these songs, worked on them and adapted them into a more commercially acceptable form.

The worldwide commercial success of his compositions led him (inaccurately) to be called the 'Father of the Blues'. But it is fair to say that he was instrumental in the popularization of the tradition of the 12-bar style; he transformed the raw, rural styles into a more disciplined form, so that the blues could easily be played by others.

The Rise of the Record

As the phonograph became an affordable household item and the demand for recordings increased, the fledgling but sharp-eyed music business began to look around for new markets. Record companies, like Okeh and Victor, sent talent scouts to scour the southern states for performers. One of those scouts, Ralph Peer, is credited with discovering the real market potential for country music. At the time a regular band playing country music (as we now call it, but then still unnamed) at country dances, social gatherings and fiddlers' contests would have featured a banjo, which had crossed over from black music to white in the 1860s (the guitar would follow the same path 30 years later) and fiddle. At the same time, black railroad workers were popularizing the guitar in mountain areas, and bright, church-inspired harmonies were springing up alongside the doleful tones of traditional folk music.

In 1927, Peer travelled to Bristol, Tennessee, and advertised for local players to come forward and audition for some recording sessions. There, in a vacant hat warehouse on State Street, he recorded a range of country performers including the two most influential of the century: Jimmie Rodgers, America's 'Blue Yodeller', and the Carter Family, the 'patron saints of traditional music'.

Jimmie Rodgers was a more modern performer than his Bristol sessions' peers, in that he assimilated influences outside the realm of mountain music, including pop, jazz and, most crucially, blues. He is known, above all, for his 'blue yodelling' or winding scats that he would pull out at the end of many phrases. When Rodgers first appeared on the scene, the music – then becoming known as 'hillbilly' – was mostly string band instrumentals and maudlin old stage ballads. By adding authentic blues lyrics, from Afro-American folk song, jazzy dance band accompaniments and a cool, catchy vocal style, he helped set the model for the solo country singing star, a model still evident today in Nashville.

The more traditional, God-fearing Carter Family influenced the music in ways that were subtle, but no less significant. They

The Carter Family are the 'first family' of country music. Started by A.P Carter and his wife Sara in the 1920s, their legacy of close harmony singing has lasted through three generations. They were joined by A.P.'s sister Maybelle in 1926. Her daughter, June, kept the tradition going, and married Johnny Cash in 1968. June had a daughter called Carlene whose 1993 album Little Love Letters is regarded as a fine example of contemporary country music.

Right Maybelle (left), Alvin P. and his wife, Sara – the Carter Family

delivered, with the most pure and simple close harmonies, a vast repertoire of true Anglo-American folk music, gathered from across the folkland and saved from oblivion by their interest.

Peer had earlier worked with blues artists like Mamie Smith – whose 1920 recording 'Crazy Blues' (more pop than blues) is regarded as the first genuine blues recording. 'Crazy Blues' was an enormous success. This opened the floodgates and released a clutch of 'classical' blues singers, like Bessie Smith, Ma Rainey, Trixie Smith and Alberta Hunter, most of whom had a background in vaudeville and were all-round performers who included blues numbers in their acts. Bessie Smith would go on to reign supreme for most of the 1920s and at her peak was earning $3,000 for a recording session.

Radio, Radio

During the 1920s, sales of blues records continued to rise, with each new release eagerly consumed by all levels of the black community. But the 1929 Stock Market Crash seriously curtailed all recording. In 1927 the record industry had enjoyed total sales of 140 million units, but by 1932, this had reduced to only 6 million for the whole year. The enormous slump in record sales was not helped by the mass appeal of radio broadcasting which held millions in its spell, and probably nowhere more powerfully than in the countryside. By 1938, 9.4 million, about 70 per cent, of all rural families in the US owned radio sets. On average, families tuned in for five and a half hours a day. During the 1920s a string of 'barn dance' type radio shows had sprung up. The most successful, the *Grand Ole Opry*, brought performers like Uncle Dave Macon and Roy Acuff to the entire eastern half of the United States every weekend.

Shows like the *Grand Ole Opry* and the *Louisiana Hayride* helped open new markets, creating a demand for new musical forms such as Western swing (embodied by Bob Wills), bluegrass (by Bill Monroe) and honky-tonk (by Hank Williams).

The blues, like country, rode out the Depression on radio. Sponsored shows like *King Biscuit Time* (King Biscuit was a brand of flour) kept musicians working and created and maintained an audience for the music. *King Biscuit Time* – the blues version (without dancing) of the *Grand Ole Opry* – became an institution, and some of its featured musicians, like Sonny Boy Williamson II, went on to become big names in the blues world.

Getting Louder

In the late 1940s and early 1950s, there was a sudden desire in the black ghettos of America's largest cities for updated and amplified blues. In Chicago, the sound of amplified slide guitar played by Muddy Waters, brought the vitality of Mississippi Delta blues to the city. Labels like Chess, Chance, Parrott and United discovered a host of talent playing this new sound which was then sweeping through the clubs and bars of the city's South Side. Chess, and its subsidiary Checker, became the leading labels with a roster that included Muddy Waters, Sonny Boy Williamson and Howlin' Wolf.

Country music was also moving out of the ghetto via the success of performers like Hank Williams. Signed in 1946 to Nashville's first publishing company, Acuff-Rose, Williams became the genre's first superstar. Via Acuff-Rose contacts, Hank Williams' songs were covered by pop performers like Tony Bennett and Jo Stafford, enlarging American appreciation for songs like 'Your Cheatin' Heart' and 'I'm So Lonesome I Could Cry'. Country was moving into the mainstream.

Throughout the 1930s and 1940s, white and black performers continued to influence each other. The Delmore Brothers had recorded folk-country-gospel fusions in the 1930s and early 1940s. By the end of that decade they went full tilt into boogie with rhythmic, bluesy thumps that verged on rockabilly.

The R&B Boom

Just as the blues came out of gospel music and field songs, r&b came out of the blues. It had started to surface around 1950 with the Chess recordings of Muddy Waters and Howlin' Wolf in Chicago, and became more evident in the work of Chicago-based performers like Etta James, Chuck Berry and Bo Diddley. These new sounds, with altered chords and progressions and up-tempo rhythms, spread across the United States, influencing other artists and songwriters.

Labels sprung up, specializing in recording this new black music: Aladdin in Los Angeles (which featured Shirley & Lee, Amos Milburn and Charles Brown), Imperial (who had Fats Domino), King Records (with Ivory Joe Hunter and Wynonie Harris), Duke (with Bobby Bland and Johnny Ace) and Atlantic (with Ruth Brown, LaVern Baker and Ray Charles).

After Elvis Presley's first single, all subsequent Sun releases followed the same pattern, coupling a cover of a black r&b song with a country song. But the success of rock 'n' roll – ignited by country-boy Presley – only served to marginalize country music again. As he moved from Sun to RCA and from Memphis to Hollywood, so Presley left country music behind. However, it would later enjoy a long-lasting renaissance, beginning with the singer-songwriters of the late 1960s.

Left Fats Domino

the top 100

songs

• 39–51

Strange fruit

Over the rainbow

Bewitched, bothered and bewildered

How about you?

White Christmas

One for my baby

Lili Marlene

Ev'ry time we say goodbye

Route 66

That's all right/Blue moon
of Kentucky

Tennessee waltz

Rudolph the red-nosed reindeer

Cold, cold heart

39 strange fruit

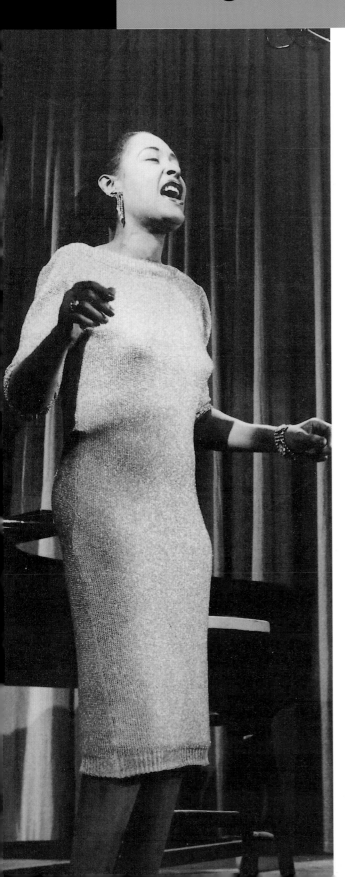

Words and **music** Lewis Allen (pen name of Abel Meeropol) **1938**

By the time Billie Holiday took up her residency at New York's Café Society nightclub in 1938 she was already a revered jazz singer of some experience. Having toured the deep south of America she knew the score on race only too well – in fact many of the hotels she played were off limits for her when it came to finding a place to stay. At the time this was just the tip of black oppression in the USA. So when a Jewish schoolteacher and poet called Abel Meeropol brought her the lyrics to a song he had written about a lynch mob she immediately felt something stirring. 'Some guy's brought me a hell of a damn song, and I'm going to do it,' she told her band when he'd left the club.

Although the poem would become her signature song, at the time it was a huge leap from the kind of unrequited love songs she was more used to. Yet Billie Holiday was one of the finest interpreters in popular music and this was a piece on which she could truly excel – turning something relatively minor into a sublime cry of pain and disgust. 'I worked like the devil on it,' she recalled in her autobiography *Lady Sings The Blues*, 'because I was never sure I could get across to a plush night-club audience the things that it meant to me.'

Her accompanist, Sonny White, helped her turn the poem into a piece of music, but her record company were less helpful. Columbia didn't want to put it out. In desperation she turned to Milt Gabler, who ran both a record shop and a small label called Commodore. Amazingly, Columbia agreed for her to record four tracks with Milt Gabler producing. Together they cut what would become the B-side, the far more traditional blues 'Fine and Mellow', and **Strange Fruit**, done as a deeply moving lament. The lyrics of the song, which depict the gruesome aftermath of a lynching, are still some of the most powerful ever committed to vinyl, describing black bodies swaying in the breeze.

Sung as if the singer were a witness to the event itself, the piece proceeds at a solemn, funereal pace. Milt Gabler said of Billie Holiday, 'She liked to sing slow, I guess she could get more feeling in that way.' And feeling is just what this song is all about. Low on melody and dynamics, this poem set to music relies massively on the performance, which was, of course, exactly what Holiday was about. Here we find her interpretative powers at their absolute peak.

Of course, it was widely banned by radio, including the BBC. Yet despite costing a whole dollar (25 cents more than usual) the record sold well and made No.16 in the *Billboard* Top 20.

The song became the centrepiece of the set she performed at Café Society. When the lights were down, the waiters were forbidden to move. 'When I sing it, it affects me so much I get sick, it takes all the strength out of me,' she said.

Left Billie Holiday

40 over the rainbow

Words E.Y. 'Yip' Harburg **Music** Harold Arlen **1939**

Over the Rainbow is the ultimate aspirational song. As with many truly great pop songs, it is about dreaming: dreaming to be with someone or somewhere else. In this case it was a place that only existed in the imagination of a little girl named Dorothy. *The Wizard of Oz*, the movie for which the song was written, was based on an allegorical fairy tale written by L. Frank Baum at the beginning of the century, about one of America's famous gold rushes (for Oz, read ounce). He wanted to address the extent to which greed had destroyed the fabric of American society, sending farmers (the Scarecrow), industrialists (the Tin Man) and others lacking in moral courage (the Lion) in search of the holy grail of personal wealth. Like most fairy tales, the actual truth is represented by innocence, and thus Dorothy, a young, dreamy girl, follows the yellow (gold) brick road to discover the hollow nature of such a selfish dream. In the 1939 film, Dorothy was played by Judy Garland, a 16-year-old nearly star with, as the *New York Times* stated at the time, 'a special style of vocalizing'. Special indeed. Not only did the film and its Oscar-winning song transform Garland into a Hollywood movie star, it also gave her a theme song around which she constructed her career.

The song itself was almost cut from the film, it was thought to slow down the narrative and be much too dreary. On one occasion, movie executives decided that it was not appropriate for the audience to see their future star singing in a farmyard!

Written by Harold Arlen and 'Yip' Harburg, together responsible for most of the songs from the movie, as well as 'It's Only A Paper Moon' (and individually, 'Ac-cent-tchu-ate the Positive', 'April in Paris', 'Brother Can You Spare A Dime?' (see page 66), 'Californ-i-ay', 'Come Rain or Shine', 'Look To The Rainbow', 'One For My Baby', 'Old Devil Moon' and 'Stormy Weather'), the song is a perfect example of the 32-bar song-form known as an A-A-B-A. That is to say there are two different sections to the song, the first of which is repeated, until a new melody (and lyrical idea) is unveiled before returning to the original. In this instance, the A-section contains a large amount of movement from note to note, gliding about between them creating a beautiful smooth and dreamy feel to the song, perfectly elegiac for the subject matter – describing a place once heard of in a lullaby. This is repeated musically, but lyrically we find out more about this wondrous place – the skies are blue and it's a place where dreams can come true. Then on to the B-section, which sounds very much like a nursery rhyme – the tempo quickens and we discover what it is that we want from such a place – troubles melting away like sweets etc. Now that we've determined what happens in this magical place, the return to the A-section isn't just descriptive, it shows the yearning to actually visit the place, asking why we can't be there.

This song form also includes a little prelude, which sets up the subject matter, often very simple melodically and greatly different from the main tune. More than anything it is used to allow the transition from speech to singing in as gentle a way as possible (or in the theatre, to allow the star to reach centre-stage before the recognizable bit of the song). **Over the Rainbow** is no different, setting up the dream scenario perfectly by stating that the world is all jumbled up, with storm clouds darkening the skies. It's odd to think that Arlen himself was so insecure about the song, that he sought the approval of his pal Ira Gershwin before offering it up.

Just about every major balladeer of the last 60 years has sung **Over the Rainbow**, from Frank Sinatra to Sarah Vaughan, and just about every great bandleader has performed it, from Count Basie to Glen Miller. And concerts or compilation CDs dedicated to great songs from the movies would be incomplete without it.

Judy Garland's daughter Liza Minnelli, herself a very fine singer, is naturally often asked to sing it at her concerts. Famously she once replied, ' …it's already been sung', and it has. The original was very much the best version. Many have sung the beautiful melody with the same dreamy quality as the 16-year-old Garland, but nobody has combined it with that same tragic subtext that seemed to imbue her best songs. It helped that the song become popular at the start of the Second World War when its rendition (like 'White Christmas') would remind fighting soldiers of better times back home. Garland, of course, has iconic status, and is every bit as important as the movie *The Wizard of Oz*. Only a real star could have sung that song in that farmyard scene and not be upstaged by Toto the dog!

bewitched, bothered and bewildered

Words Lorenz Hart **Music** Richard Rodgers **1940**

Bewitched, Bothered and Bewildered is the best-known song from the Rodgers and Hart stage show *Pal Joey*. Based on a novella by John O'Hara about a night-club singer, the stage show was true to the spirit of the elegiac book but changed the singer into a chorus line dancer. The book seemed like a natural vehicle for Frank Sinatra, who bought the movie rights and restored the lead character to a crooner. Unfortunately it was made early in the Ratpack era, and with other matters to occupy the minds of the cast, the film was a travesty of the original idea. But even a bad movie can't take away from the brilliance of its songs. As well as **Bewitched, Bothered and Bewildered**, the movie features, 'I Could Write A Book', 'My Funny Valentine', 'There's A Small Hotel', 'I Didn't Know What Time it Was' and 'The Lady is A Tramp', the last four of which were not part of the original stage show.

 Bewitched, Bothered and Bewildered has a trademark Lorenz Hart lyric. Full of proper and literate rhymes, it explores a single moment of pure emotion without offering any psychological insight into the singer's character:

I'm wild again,
Beguiled again,
A simpering, whimpering child again.

Hart knew the value of making a lyric portable enough to allow the song to work outside the context of the show for which it was written. This intimate love song about unrequited love would work anywhere. A dwarf-like man, gay in an unforgiving era, Hart had plenty of real-life practice of unrequited love. In the end he drove the infinitely more disciplined Richard Rodgers to despair. During the writing of *Pal Joey*, Rodgers made plans to replace Hart with a new collaborator, Oscar Hammerstein.

 Though Rodgers and Hammerstein had massive hits with the more rousing *Oklahoma!*, *Carousel* and *The Sound of Music* during the 1940s, the intimate love song was more the domain of Lorenz Hart. All the grace in Hart's life made its way into his work, and as a body it serves as the truest, if not factual, of autobiographies.

 Ella Fitzgerald, always at her best with a Rodgers and Hart lyric, sings this song beautifully, without overdoing the pathos of the unrequited love stuff.

Left Lorenz Hart

After one whole quart of
 brandy,
Like a daisy I awake.
With no Bromo Seltzer
 handy,
I don't even shake.

Men are not a new
 sensation,
I've done pretty well, I think.
But this half-pint imitation,
Put me on the blink.

Bewitched, bothered and
 bewildered am I.

Couldn't sleep,
And wouldn't sleep,
Until I could sleep where I
 shouldn't sleep.
Bewitched, bothered and
 bewildered am I.

how about you?

Words Ralph Freed **Music** Burton Lane **1941**

There's a sub-genre of pop songs in which the lyrics are nothing more than lists of things... reasons to fall in love, reasons to do things or just things you like, and **How About You?** is one of the greatest of these. It first made an appearance in the Judy Garland/Mickey Rooney film *Babes on Broadway* for which it got an Academy Award nomination. Written by two Tin Pan Alley stalwarts, Burton Lane and lyricist Ralph Freed, it remains Freed's best-known song and even bears comparison with the great list song 'Let's Do It' by Cole Porter.

The chorus of **How About You?** – describing the thrill of Franklin Roosevelt's looks – has been infinitely adapted to suit the singer or some special occasion, Roosevelt being modified to Ava Gardner, Lana Turner, Frank Sinatra, Marilyn Monroe and even Louis Armstrong, depending on the taste of the singer.

Ralph Freed – brother of Arthur, one of the great producers of Hollywood musicals who wrote 'Singin' in the Rain' (see page 63) and several other great songs – ended up writing incidental music for the *Flash Gordon* TV serial.

Burton Lane is said to have approached songwriting 'the way a carpenter approaches cabinet making'. Well, if that's true, then some of his 'cabinets' turned out to be very fine pieces of furniture. He's also responsible for, 'That Old Devil Moon', 'How Are Things in Gloccamorra', 'On A Clear Day You Can See For Ever', as well as the song bearing the longest title registered by ASCAP, 'How Could You Believe Me When I Said I Love You, When You Know I've Been A Liar All My Life'. This song was later dedicated to Colonel Oliver North of the Iran Contra scandal.

The story goes that having dropped out of school at the age of 15, Lane was playing the piano in an Atlantic City hotel where he was heard by George Gershwin's mother, Rose. The tune he was playing at the time was 'S'wonderful' by George Gershwin. Rose allegedly said to him, 'Not only do you play like George, you look like him.' Lane idiolized Gershwin, so that was praise indeed.

Lane later claimed that it was George who had encouraged him to start writing popular songs. They remained close friends for the rest of George's short life. Lane went on to work with several great lyric writers including George's brother, Ira, 'Yip' Harbug and Alan Jay Lerner of *My Fair Lady* fame. He also took the credit for introducing the 11-year-old Francis Gumm to Broadway and Hollywood. Frances Gumm later changed her name to Judy Garland and was the first to sing **How About You?** in public.

Above Judy Garland

> "
> judy garland was the first singer to sing **how about you?** in public
> "

Words and **music** Irving Berlin **1942**

Above Bing Crosby

'You don't have to worry about this one, Irving,' was Bing Crosby's response on hearing **White Christmas** for the first time. It didn't stop Berlin fretting about the song in the first few months of its life. The often brash and always insecure Irving Berlin approached each new song as if his life depended upon it. He insisted on being in the room with Crosby to hear it for himself. But to make sure he got a genuine reaction, he stayed out of sight until he heard Crosby's favourable comments.

It certainly needed to be a showstopper, since it was written as the big song in his new musical, *Holiday Inn*. Between bouts of paranoia, Berlin described the song not only as the best song *he'd* written, but the best song *anybody* had written.

Modesty apart, the tune has an unforced and appropriately hymn-like quality about it given the subject matter of the lyrics. For those who worry about these things, it's not thought to be the most inventive of Berlin's songs and its sentimentality is not to everyone's taste, but it's a lucky song. It's lucky because, like 'Over the Rainbow', it immediately hit a nerve with soldiers fighting in the Second World War, reminding them of their families back home. It is, of course, a song about the yearning for better times, old-fashioned values and the way things used to be. It was immediately successful, staying top of the hit parade for three months. It repeated that success 16 times in the following years to become the biggest-selling song of all time, until Elton John's 'Candle in the Wind' swept round the world in 1997 following the death of Princess Diana.

Berlin had originally based **White Christmas** on his own memories of spending Christmas in the Beverly Hills' sunshine, among the palm trees, longing to be with his family in snowy New York. In the original draft, the song dealt with that yearning in its first two verses. But noting its success with the troops and the folks back home during the darkest years of the war, Berlin, always the shrewd businessman, had those verses removed, creating a subtle shift of emphasis from the particular to the universal.

Berlin saw no irony in the fact that the son of an immigrant Jewish cantor should write a song celebrating one of the most important dates in the Christian calendar. After all he'd already had a hit with a song called 'Easter Parade'. He was married to a Catholic and his daughters were brought up as Protestants. The Berlin family was a shining example of religious tolerance. As far as he was concerned, Christmas was an *American* holiday, and *everybody* wanted a white one, whatever their religious leanings.

There are several other versions of the song apart from Crosby's original, including an intriguing one sung by Darlene Love and produced by Phil Spector, but one version that invoked the wrath of Berlin was by Elvis Presley. Berlin hated rock 'n' roll, and he instructed radio stations round the country not to play the Presley version. Unfortunately for him, they took no notice, and you're just as likely to hear Presley's version as you are Bing Crosby's in high street shops during December.

Words Johnny Mercer **Music** Harold Arlen **1943**

Arguably the best-known saloon bar song of all time, most of the honours on **One For My Baby** go to the lyricist, Johnny Mercer. Lesser songs than this have had whole screenplays built around them. The definitive version has to be by the greatest, self-styled saloon bar singer, Frank Sinatra. Once he stopped playing the bars of his home town, Hoboken, New Jersey in his late teens, Sinatra was hardly known for his small venue performances, but he had the skill to make you believe, as you were sitting among an audience of several thousand fellow travellers, that you *might* be in that small cocktail bar with a pianist tinkling away in the corner. He could *live* a song, and that set him apart from most of his peers, and also gave him his edge as an actor.

In Harold Arlen and Johnny Mercer, he reaped the benefit of two of the great craftsmen of popular song. It's a simple enough idea… a man goes to a bar to get drunk after being dumped by his lover, and tells the barman the story of the end of his affair.

It's the narrative sweep of the lyric that makes it so good. Starting off reasonably coherently, the singer gets more maudlin as the song progresses, giving us enough information to build a picture of his romantic angst, and only repeating himself to ask for another drink – one for his baby and one for the road. Sinatra lets the lyric trail off halfway through the last sentence, highlighting the sense of a drunk dozing off in his cups.

The song has a country and western feel to it in its idea, but not in its execution. It would be an interesting song for Willie Nelson, who moves effortlessly through different genres. The lyric scans in a more sophisticated way than most country songs and the music reflects that sophistication in an unshowy, offbeat, bluesy way. Arlen clearly let the lyric take centre-stage and did nothing to disturb it.

Mercer was a prolific lyricist, with more than 1,000 song credits to his name over 60 years. He was one of a handful of people whose output approached that of Irving Berlin's. As well as writing for Arlen, he wrote words for Jerome Kern, Hoagy Carmichael, Harry Warren, James Van Heusen, Michel Legrand and Henry Mancini, among many others. His lyrics won him an unprecedented four Oscars, the last two with Henry Mancini for the song 'Moon River' and the score for the film *The Days of Wine and Roses*.

In the 1940s Mercer set up the phenomenally successful Capitol record label with two colleagues. Such was the respect for his talent and ability, that he was able to gather many of the top singers of the era under the Capitol banner, including Sinatra, Nat 'King' Cole, Peggy Lee and Ella Fitzgerald. The company also had the foresight to recognize and sign up the talent of The Beatles and the Beach Boys in the 1960s.

Right Johnny Mercer

45 lili marlene

Words Tommie Connor **Music** Norbert Schultze **1944**

Above Marlene Dietrich and friends

A haunting reminiscence of love for a soldier fighting in some unspecified, distant land, **Lili Marlene** reached the peak of its popularity towards the end of the Second World War. What sets it apart from many of its contemporaries is its universal appeal. It transcended the barriers of conflict, and was sung by soldiers from all the nations involved in the war. A rather mysterious lilting melody over a gentle marching rhythm, it was especially popular with the infantry. The original version was sung in German by Lale Anderson. She recorded it in 1939, shortly after Norbert Schultze had set the original German poem by Hans Liep to music. (Shultze also wrote 'Bombs on England' in case you wonder which side he was on.) It's amazing the song took off at all, as Joseph Goebbels, head of the German propaganda machine, didn't much like it, preferring something a little more stirring. Anderson was reluctant to record it and did so under pressure. But as we know now, there's nothing better for the life of a song than to have it banned by someone. Goebbels banned it in Germany until one of his own generals, Field Marshal Rommel, ordered the song to be broadcast regularly in the nightly German radio propaganda broadcasts from Yugoslavia in 1941. It was heard over the lines by the Allied army in North Africa, and there are now versions in 48 different languages. Anne Shelton's was the first English version, translated fairly approximately from the original German by Tommie Connor in 1944.

The most played version of **Lily Marlene** these days is by Marlene Dietrich, the German-born Hollywood star who hated the Nazis. Hitler had banned all her films from German cinemas after her refusal to go back to her homeland in the late 1930s. Dietrich took American citizenship and delighted in entertaining the Allies to underscore her dislike of Hitler's regime.

46 ev'ry time we say goodbye

Words and **music** Cole Porter **1945**

Cole Porter's songs are some of the most autobiographical ever written, and **Ev'ry Time We Say Goodbye** is no different. Written in the middle of a rather lean and unsuccessful period of his life, the song proved popular by virtue of its theme of departure and longing, an all too familiar one during the Second World War. The lyrics are rather simple, unlike much of Porter's verbally dextrous and witty output, but the tenderness evident in most of his work is here in spades, as is the sexually charged nature of his writing, although in this particular song it is more evident in the music than the lyrics. The melody reaches a swooping climax, before being tragically stripped of its triumphant ending by a change into a minor key, bringing us back down to earth with a bump as we are reminded of the song's central theme.

Porter had a propensity to change from a major key, with a straight, happy feel, to a minor one, which is sad and more bluesy. He once said to fellow tunesmith Richard Rodgers that all his most successful songs were Jewish. This shift in key is certainly a common trait in Jewish music, but unlike almost all of the great American songwriters of his generation, Porter was not Jewish. In **Ev'ry Time We Say Goodbye** the change has extra significance, however, displaying once again his knowledge of musical history. As with Handel and Purcell, and other 17th-century Baroque composers, where the music would often mirror the words, Porter's lyrics follow the musical lead by mourning…

There's no love song finer,
But how strange the change
From major to minor.

Other examples of this include 'I Get A Kick', where the melody keeps rising as he states: *'I get no kick in a plane, Flying too high with some guy in the sky…'*

Ev'ry Time We Say Goodbye was written for the musical revue *Seven Lively Arts*, which ran in New York for some 200 performances. Despite boasting a score written by classical composer Igor Stravinsky, and a cast which included the great jazz clarinetist Benny Goodman, it was considered a flop, with many critics gleefully announcing Porter's fall from grace. While it is true that most of his greatest individual songs were behind him, later works included the likes of *Kiss Me Kate*, his (loosely based) musical version of Shakespeare's play *The Taming of the Shrew*, considered by many to be his greatest achievement.

Ev'ry Time We Say Goodbye is quite simply a great love song. As with 'Night and Day' (see page 68), Porter utilizes the hypnotic effect of a continuous, repetitive note throughout the song, making the triumphant sweep near the end all the more dramatic. Perhaps Ella Fitzgerald recorded the definitive version of the song during her *Songbooks* sessions, but this particular tune has been covered by just about everyone with even a passing interest in the great American standards. One thing that sets it apart from some of his other songs is the way that each artist is able to adapt it to suit their particular strengths (listen to Simply Red's soul version as a great example). Being neither lyrically clever, nor musically complex, it is almost a blank sheet from which each singer can emote. Whoever the performer, Porter's genius always shines through, as yet again he adds another contribution to the portfolio of greatest ever songs. Another multiple contributor of songs to this book, Irving Berlin once wrote a letter to Porter applauding him by inverting one of his own song lyrics, 'Anything I can do, you can do better.'

Above Cole Porter

Ev'ry time we say goodbye, I die a little.
Ev'ry time we say goodbye, I wonder why a little,
Why the gods above me, who must be in the know,
Think so little of me, they allow you to go.
When you're near, there's such an air of spring about it,
I can hear a lark somewhere, begin to sing about it.
There's no love song finer,
But how strange the change
From major to minor,
Ev'ry time we say goodbye.

Words and **music** Bobby Troupe **1946**

Travel – by foot, bus, motorbike, car or plane – is a theme of elemental symbolism in American popular music. **Route 66** is probably the most played song of its genre and holds up as a metaphor for the way Americans have felt about themselves during the 50 years since the 1920s. So potent is it that the song has become part of the history of America.

Bobby Troupe wrote **Route 66** in 1946 for his favourite artist Nat 'King' Cole. Troupe had been a pianist with The Tommy Dorsey Band briefly before he was called up in 1941. But he was only putting into song what everybody already knew – the road went from Chicago to Los Angeles (L.A.), a distance of some 2,000 miles all the way.

Troupe wasn't the first person to mythologize the road. John Steinbeck first wrote about it in his novel *The Grapes of Wrath*. He called it the 'Mother Road', because it carried poor bankrupt workers away from the rain-starved plains of the Midwest to the promised land of California. It also gave employment to thousands of young men who worked as labourers on road gangs paving the last stretches of its surface. '66 is the path of a people in flight, refugees from dust and shrinking land, from the thunder of

Above The Rolling Stones
Right: Bobby Troupe

tractors and shrinking ownership… they come into 66 from the tributary side roads, from the wagon trucks and the rutted country roads. 66 is the mother road, the road of flight,' explained Steinbeck.

Construction started on the road in 1925 and it was given its number a year later. Fully operational by 1932, it ran from the northeast to the southwest, linking rural communities with the opportunities of industrial Chicago and the temperate West Coast. They called it 'Main Street, America' and it gave rise to a host of business opportunities, not only at its extremes, but also along the route. Motels sprung up, providing a cheaper form of lodging for itinerant workers, petrol forecourts **grew from** small two-pump services operated in front of private homes, advertising hoardings appeared and all manner of shops opened up along the way.

Bobby Troupe would have travelled the road during his time with The Dorsey Band and as a serving marine. All the major military training camps were based on the West Coast, because the weather allowed more efficient field training and air manoeuvres. It was Route 66 that allowed the US to mobilize large numbers of soldiers for the Second World War.

So popular was it that in the 1960s the road gave its name to a popular TV series. But by the 1970s Route 66 had to give way to the demand for multi-lane highways and a more sophisticated arterial system. Now, at the turn of the century, it has become a heritage road and much of it has fallen into disuse. However, its fame is long-lasting, it has become a tourist attraction and you can still see the old Route 66 signs here and there along the way.

As for the song, the original cool jazz version by Nat 'King' Cole still sounds as fresh as ever, but it has given way to countless covers in every conceivable style. There's also a great country version by Asleep at the Wheel. But because of Mick Jagger's ability to reinvent songs and give them new meaning, the most memorable version has to be by The Rolling Stones.

> **66**
> so potent
> a song is
> it that **route
> 66** has
> become
> part of the
> history of
> america
> **99**

trivia

★ Route 66 is 2,448 miles long. It starts in Chicago and passes through Illinois, Missouri, Kansas, Oklahoma, Texas, New Mexico, Arizona and ends in Santa Monica, California.

★ Among the thousands of versions of the song are recordings by Paul Anka, Asleep at the Wheel, Chuck Berry, Buckwheat Zydeco, Rosemary Clooney, Nat 'King' Cole, Perry Como, The Cramps, Depeche Mode, Bob Dylan, Dr Feelgood, Johnny Mathis, Patti Page, Buddy Rich, Frank Sinatra, Them and Bob Wills.

that's all right/blue moon of kentucky

Words and **music** Arthur 'Big Boy' Crudup (**That's All Right**) Bill Monroe (**Blue Moon of Kentucky**) **1947**

These two songs were written in 1947, a full seven years before Elvis walked into Sun Studios in Memphis to record them and change not only popular music, but the culture of the whole planet, forever. At the time, however, Arthur 'Big Boy' Crudup and Bill Monroe were at the peak of their form, working in their respective genres that were later to combine and become the constituent parts of the Elvis sound.

Arthur Crudup was a Mississippi-born delta bluesman who waited till he was 32 to learn to play the guitar. His sound was essentially country-blues. But when he moved to Chicago around 1939, he became one of the pioneers of electric guitar blues, alongside Muddy Waters and Elmore James. He started recording around 1941, but became disenchanted when he, like many black performers, realized he was not being paid royalties for his work. By the early 1950s he had built up a fair roster of compositions covered by the likes of B.B. King, Bobby 'Blue' Bland and Big Mama Thornton. Most significant of these were three songs covered by Elvis in Sam Philips' Memphis Recording Facility for which Crudup probably never got paid. 'I'm So Glad You're Mine', 'My Baby Left Me' and the sublime **That's All Right** were recorded in August 1954. 'That's All Right Mama' was one side of the first Presley single released originally only for local consumption in the Memphis area. By the time Elvis was gaining public acclaim, Crudup had quit the music business, bitter at being cheated out of his royalties. It must have galled him to see such a spectacular career built partly on the edifice of his labours. After a period of farm labouring, he surfaced again during the 1960s' blues boom and finally made some money on the lucrative folk and blues festivals doing the rounds in Europe and America.

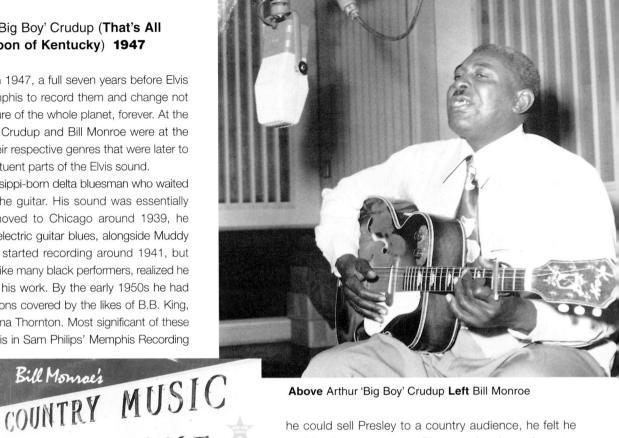

Above Arthur 'Big Boy' Crudup **Left** Bill Monroe

If **That's All Right** was the perfect country-blues song, Sam Phillips hedged his bets in releasing **Blue Moon of Kentucky**, written by Bill Monroe, the 'Father of Bluegrass', as the other side. If he could sell Presley to a country audience, he felt he could make some money. Bluegrass is a form of country music which combines harmony singing with the banjo and the fiddle. Monroe was its chief architect and it earned him a permanent place in the history of The Grand Ole Opry. Country music was a more secure and organized occupation than the blues music played by the likes of Arthur Crudup, and Monroe was hugely successful at it. **Blue Moon of Kentucky** was composed in waltz time for one of the many barn dances at which Bill Monroe and His Bluegrass Boys played. The Presley recording was done in 4/4-time and sounded like rock 'n' roll. When Presley played it his way at The Grand Ole Opry, it didn't go down very well. But that didn't stop Monroe re-recording the song using 4/4-time later on.

The rock revolution took its toll on Bill Monroe's style of country music, but unlike Crudup he was sustained by his royalties. In Crudup and Monroe we see two writer-performers of different styles and contrasting fortunes brought together by an explosive act of chance that would send popular music on to a new and enduring path.

49 | tennessee waltz

Words and **music** Pee Wee King and Redd Stewart **1948**

This song represents a key moment in the history of popular music, when country music crossed over into the mainstream. Country music sung by country singers had been popular since the early 1930s and there were plenty of famous stage cowboys making a decent living singing country songs more than a decade later. But **Tennessee Waltz** went through the roof.

Pee Wee King was born Julius Frank Anthony Kuczynski of Polish-Jewish extraction. He played in a Western swing band – a hybrid mixture of country and jazz – called The Golden West Cowboys with Redd Stewart. They wrote **Tennessee Waltz** on an unfolded matchbox as they were riding in Stewart's truck one day in 1947. The song was first released in 1948 and topped the country charts, and it was later recorded successfully by Tennessee Ernie Ford, Eddie Arnold, Les Paul and Mary Ford.

At the time something was changing in the recording industry. Up to that point, it had been either the artist or more often the bandleader who chose what songs they would record, but a new era was dawning after the end of the Second World War and singers were no longer regarded as reliable pickers of hit songs. In an effort to stem falling sales of their major artists (even Frank Sinatra's career was in steep decline in the late 1940s) record companies appointed Artist and Repertoire men to find the right artist for the right song. One such A&R man was Jerry Wexler, later to become famous as Aretha Franklin's producer, and he suggested that Patti Page, a dance band singer with a beautiful voice reminiscent of Ella Fitzgerald, record **Tennessee Waltz**.

Above Pee Wee King and his Band
Below left Patti Page

The original A-side of this release was 'Boogie Woogie Santa Claus'. There was a big vogue for novelty songs and most of the studio time at this recording session was spent on the track they expected to be the hit. That left only 30 minutes for **Tennessee Waltz**, but the public preferred the slightly hick sentiments of **Tennessee Waltz**. And how! It sold an unbelievable 65 million copies after its release in 1950, and needless to say, became her signature tune.

Pee Wee King (Pee Wee because he was short) was something of an innovator on the country music scene. It was he who broadened the instrumental range of the music both by playing the accordion and by adding brass to the line up. He was also famous for his clothing, and it's claimed he was the first to introduce dazzling western costumes to the bandstand.

In covering this song, Patti Page opened up the possibilities for many singers who were happier, both by training and inclination, with the songs of Irving Berlin or George Gershwin. It was difficult to argue with sales of 65 million, and where she trod many would soon follow, among them Tony Bennett and Rosemary Clooney. It was the first foot in the door for the real revolution that would happen five years later – rock 'n' roll.

trivia

★ Fiddler Bob Wills is the most famous exponent of Western swing. He led his band, The Texas Playboys, to fame and fortune during the music's heyday before the Second World War.

★ Patti Page's other big hit was 'How Much is That Doggie in the Window?' in 1953.

★ The state of Tennessee adopted **Tennessee Waltz** as its official anthem in 1965.

Words and **music** Johnny Marks **1949**

If you stopped counting record sales and radio plays in 1950, just before Patti Page released 'Tennessee Waltz' (see page 92), **Rudolph The Red-Nosed Reindeer**, sung by yodelling cowboy Gene Autry, would have been the second most popular song in recording history (Bing Crosby's 'White Christmas', see page 84, would have been top). The song was the beneficiary of a combination of circumstances. The end of the Second World War led to an increase in the general wealth of many Americans, more money to spend on records, a new younger record-buying public, better recording technology, a vogue for novelty records, and most important of all Gene Autry's own popularity.

The story behind the song is not well known. Rudolph was actually created in 1939 and featured in a booklet that Father Christmas could give to kids who came to visit the Montgomery Ward general store in Chicago. The idea came from a copywriter called Robert May who based it on a story called 'Rollo the Reindeer'. He had originally made up the story to help his daughter come to terms with her mother's terminal cancer. Charged by Sewill Avery, the store's owner, to come up with a marketing idea to attract customers, May visited the Lincoln Park Zoo with company artist Denver Gillen. They noticed how cute the reindeer were. May wrote up the story and Gillen did some illustrations. Rollo's name was changed to Rudolph, and they gave him a red nose that would set him apart from the other reindeer, which, while turning him into something of a reject, enabled Santa to pick him out of the crowd and offer him the job of a lifetime – driving the sleigh. The moral of the story? There's nothing wrong in looking a little bit different! Ahhhh!

It was an immediate success and the store gave away nearly two and a half million copies of the booklet in 1939. Paper being in short supply, the Second World War put paid to the idea till 1946 when it was revived, and three and a half million booklets were printed. The marketing possibilities were endless and the store copyrighted Rudolph.

Like all good children's stories, there is a sad bit. May's wife died around the same time as the first booklet was being prepared, and he was left with enormous medical bills. Luckily Sewill Avery returned the copyright to him.

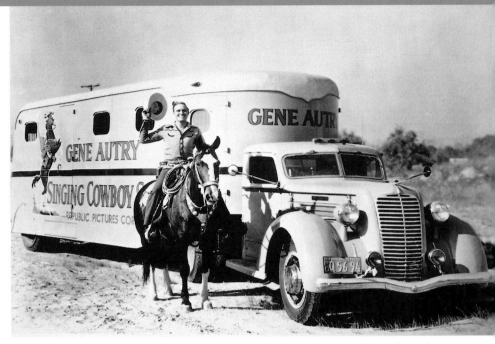

Above Gene Autry

A song was written about Rudolph in 1949 by May's brother-in-law Johnny Marks. It was rejected by everybody except Gene Autry, who recorded it because his wife, Ina, liked it. Two million copies were sold that year, and it quickly notched up a total of 15 million.

Autry had begun his career as a Hollywood cowboy in the 1920s around the same time as John Wayne. More inclined to pull out his $5 guitar than his Colt .45, he had a string of western hits, and a neat line in modesty, 'I'm not a great actor, great singer or great rider, but what the hell is my opinion when 50 million people think I do pretty good?'

It was his ability to make his audience feel good about themselves that turned Autry into one of America's best-loved entertainers. He was also one of the wealthiest, appearing regularly in the Fortune 400 list of the richest people in the USA. Rudolph was very lucky to find him.

51 cold, cold heart

Words and **music** Hank Williams **1950**

Occasionally, an early death gives a second-rate career the kind of boost the public relations industry can only drool over. Hank Williams died in the back of his new Cadillac, on his way to a performance, a bottle of whiskey in his hand, and too much medically administered morphine in his blood. He was 29 years old. But he was the real thing, one of a handful of performers who have shaped the music of the century. Louis Armstrong, Elvis Presley and Muddy Waters periodically earned writers credits, but Williams was as good a writer as he was passionate a performer. A master of the three-chord song he is the spirit and the look of country music, all cowboy hat and rhinestones. Over his short composing life he wrote more than 100 songs that have crossed over into the mainstream American songbook, including: 'Your Cheatin' Heart', 'Hey, Good Looking', 'Wedding Bells', 'Move it on Over', 'Jambalaya' and 'My Son Calls Another Man Daddy'. The song that catapulted him to stardom in 1949 was in fact a Tin Pan Alley song called 'Lovesick Blues' (see page 45). He had a gift of sounding as though he lived in his songs, and in truth he probably did.

His best work is simplest in form and direct in performance. His lyrics were mostly of one or two syllable words that gave his songs clarity and universality.

In the early 1950s record companies were scrabbling around looking for material that would replace the fading fortunes of dance bands. Songs like 'How Much is That Doggie in the Window?' and 'Rudolph the Red-Nosed Reindeer' were competing for honours in the national hit parades. Country music seemed to be the answer. It had always been popular outside the big cities. Jimmie Rodgers had sold more records

Above Hank Williams and The Drifting Cowboys

than Bing Crosby in the 1930s, but his music was still thought of as hillbilly music for the unsophisticated. After Tony Bennett (rather reluctantly) recorded **Cold, Cold Heart** in 1951, both he *and* Williams became stars with mainstream audiences. Real country music by real country performers had crossed over.

In the four years of his national fame, Williams' drinking and erratic behaviour increased. Touring constantly with his band, The Drifting Cowboys, despite a back injury for which he took morphine, he missed some performances altogether because he was too drunk. Still in his 20s, he could have passed for 50. By 1952 his life was coming apart at the seams. Around midnight on New Year's Day 1953, on his way to Canton, Ohio, for a concert, he was found dead in the back of his car.

Williams set the parameters of country music and his bequest to popular music is that the country music industry is as big as it is today. He lived a country and western life, and he died a rock 'n' roll death. The last track Hank Williams released in the weeks before his death was, 'I'll Never Get Out of This World Alive'. The irony of this wouldn't have been wasted on him.

trivia

★ In October 1952 Hank Williams married Billie Jean Jones Eshlimar, his second wife, in New Orleans at a ceremony open to the public, 28,000 people are said to have attended.

★ His funeral, in Montgomery, Alabama, was attended by 25,000 people.

★ Between 1953, the year of his death, and 1964 Hank Williams is said to have sold twenty million records.

> **If you want to sell your song, you go to the Brill Building; that's on 49th Street and Broadway, and it has 11 floors and they're all filled with music publishers, and you have two ways to sell your song. You go up to the 11th floor and you go from publisher to publisher until you get to the 1st floor, or you start on the 1st floor and go from publisher to publisher until you get to the 11th.**
>
> Hal David's brother's advice on how to sell a song.

From 1930, for a dozen or so years, swing ruled as the popular music. During the early 1940s the *Billboard* charts were dominated by the big swing bands, among them Glenn Miller, Benny Goodman, The Dorseys, Artie Shaw and Kay Kyser. Miller alone had 36 Top 10 hits between 1940 and 1943 and his 'Chattanooga Choo Choo' was the first record to be formally certified as a million seller. We can think of the period roughly between 1930 and 1943 as the era of the big band.

But between 1940 and 1946, a number of changes took place behind the scenes which would revolutionize popular music. A war between the two trades unions for songwriters (ASCAP and BMI) introduced (via BMI) new songwriters and new types of music (like country and r&b) to radio listeners; the burgeoning of the independent record label, the emergence of teen culture and, correspondingly, a whole new market, all led to the fall of the big band and the rise of the solo singer.

The Singer As Star

By the end of the Second World War the big bands were on their way out, to be replaced by the solo singer, most of whom had paid their dues in the bands. The biggest recordings stars of the 1950s all got their start as a member of a band – Sinatra, Fitzgerald, Peggy Lee, Doris Day, Lena Horne, Jo Stafford, Mel Torme, Rosemary Clooney, Dick Haymes, Perry Como and Kay Starr…

The big band era may have been coming to a close naturally but one event – the American Federation of Musicians strike of 1942–43 – hastened its demise and helped prepare the way for the emergence of the popular solo singer.

The AFM, led by its president James Petrillo, called a strike in protest at radio stations playing recorded music for which, the AFM argued, their members should collect a fee. From August 1942 AFM members were forbidden to enter recording studios. During the strike – which dragged on for over a year – the record companies recorded

Left Patti Page

the only musicians who were not members of the union – the singers. Vocal trios and quartets, like The Andrews Sisters, The Ink Spots and The Mills Brothers, made their mark helping to create a demand for the vocal sound on record and the big band vocalists emerged from their relative obscurity. By the end of the war, all the major singers – Fitzgerald, Sinatra, Lee and Day – had record contracts as solo artists.

Those big bands that survived the strike clung on for a few more years. By 1946 The Goodman, Dorsey, Harry James, Les Brown and Woody Herman Bands had all but disintegrated.

The A&R Man

Another consequence of the AFM strike was that it opened the doors for the A&R men to become the frontrunners of the industry. Previously, the bandleaders and musicians had largely chosen the material they would record. During the strike, they lost control to the A&R men, until then merely responsible for the everyday tasks of working out dates and details of studios and musicians. While musicians were concerned with music and musical values, the new Artists & Repertoire managers were concerned with business, power and money. Within 10 years of the strike, the A&R men had changed the face of the record business by replacing the bands with pop singers.

In 1945 the record industry was still dominated by three major companies – Columbia, Decca and RCA, all based in New York. Those three majors were joined by three from the regions, Mercury in Chicago, and MGM and Capitol in Los Angeles. By the early 1950s these majors would be joined by a host of independents – well over 400 record labels, of which the most important and influential were Atlantic and Chess.

By the early 1950s, Columbia Records held the top position, helped in a large part by its A&R chief, Mitch Miller. Miller, a classically trained musician who had his own successful recording career during the early 1950s, had come to Columbia from Mercury records, where he had steered Frankie Laine's career, notching up several million sellers with big sentimental popular ballads like 'That's My Desire'. As an A&R director, Miller was all-powerful, choosing the song, making the arrangements and musicians – the voice and who exactly would sing the songs were almost peripheral. He had seen what Jerry Wexler had done with 'Tennessee Waltz', turning a genuine country record into an ersatz pop tune that had sold a million for Patti Page. He did the same with 'Cold, Cold Heart' for Tony Bennett, 'Jambalaya' for Rosemary Clooney and 'Singing the Blues' for Guy Mitchell.

What was new about Miller was that he was making records for their own sake. Previously artists had simply reproduced on wax what they performed in concert. Miller knew that his records had to be distinctive, exciting, gimmicky – music that, most importantly, should grab the listener in the first few seconds. This approach – where the production and the producer were more important than the material and the artist – would be embraced by Phil Spector and Berry Gordy. Gordy, in particular, knew the value of those first 10 seconds and how they should sound on the radio.

Miller has been accused of exemplifying the worst in American pop and for almost sabotaging the careers of talented artists like Sinatra, Rosemary Clooney and Tony Bennett. With his mixture of eccentric exotica (Latin, Israeli, Hawaiian and pseudo-African music) and novelty songs (like 'How Much is That Doggie in the Window' and 'She Wears Red Feathers') backed with ear-grabbing unusual instruments, he managed at Columbia in just over a year to produce 22 hit singles and set the tone for pre-rock 'n' roll American pop which was relentlessly copied by British pop artists like Alma Cogan, Lita Roza and Michael Holliday. During Miller's time at Columbia, his success helped to re-establish the company as one of the all-time biggest multimedia superpowers. Other record companies followed suit – at Capitol Nat 'King' Cole, and Peggy Lee and Ella Fitzgerald at Decca, were saddled with inappropriate material which, nonetheless, charted. It has been said that Miller proved that no one would go broke underestimating the taste of the American public.

Despite his distaste for rock 'n' roll and 'teen' music, Miller had helped create a 'pop' music business mentality in which rock 'n' roll could operate. The impending rock 'n' roll invasion worried the music business establishment to such an extent that, in 1953, the pressure group 'Songwriters of America' had filed an anti-trust action accusing BMI (the publishers of most r&b and country songs) of a

The pop charts began in 1936 when radio stations, alarmed at the growing threat from TV, asked the trade magazine *Billboard* to track songs with the most radio plays. In the early days charts tended to be genre based or regional in nature. In 1958 *Billboard* started its first national chart, The Hot 100, which was based on record sales. Two years later its credibility was shattered by the Payola Scandal, when DJ Alan Freed was accused of hyping records into the charts to make more money.

conspiracy. Tin Pan Alley songwriters – mostly administered by ASCAP – felt under threat from BMI. Alleyman songwriter Billy Rose made a statement in which he said that the BMI were publishing obscene junk and creating a climate '…which makes Elvis Presley and his animal posturings possible'.

The Birth of Rock 'n' Roll

With the first wave of rock 'n' roll, established artists thought the end of the world was nigh. Sinatra had escaped from Mitch Miller to sign with Capitol records where, via the new LP medium, he proceeded to record a series of themed albums which would showcase the great American songbook writers. Tin Pan Alley and the Broadway songwriters – who, although still writing for the theatre, appeared to have merged into the background – would be tackled by Ella Fitzgerald. Finally free of Decca, where she had recorded her fair share of novelty singles, Ella signed with the newly established jazz label Verve. Her first album for them, *The Cole Porter Songbook*, was surprisingly well received. Over the next seven years, Fitzgerald recorded the work of the most important songwriters: Berlin, Rodgers and Hart, Gershwin, Arlen and Jerome Kern, in a series of *Songbook* albums. As we entered the second half of the 20th century, these albums were important in re-assessing the work of the greatest American popular song composers by forcing the American public to acknowledge their rich musical heritage. It has been said that the real impact of these LPs was to change the way we hear music today. By honouring popular tunes in this way – specifically, by treating the songwriters as composers and their music as a canon – they made us think about songs in a different way. Popular music could now be taken seriously. It was very much music for grown ups. It is also interesting to speculate as to whether this was the first indication of the value of a back catalogue in music, when the recycling of old material first made sense, both to the artists and to the record companies.

Whereas young people had previously been a younger version of their parents, they now had their own identity with their own music. This youth market was eagerly seized upon by the record business while they still held on to the adult market that was being catered for by the Sinatras and Fitzgeralds. The popular music scene so successfully established by Mitch Miller and his contemporaries was still active; its main players – singers like Patti Page, Perry Como, Dean Martin and Rosemary Clooney – still appeared on

Above Mitch Miller signing autographs for fans in Palisades Park, New Jersey

network big business-sponsored television shows and performed at swanky supper clubs and in Las Vegas.

In 1956, as Ella recorded her first *Songbook*, American grown ups eagerly awaited the opening of *My Fair Lady*. Although the great age of the Hollywood musical and the Broadway show appeared to be over, the post-war period was one of great innovation and great success for the musical theatre. Broadway, via blockbusting shows such as *Oklahoma!*, *Guys and Dolls*, *Kiss Me Kate*, *South Pacific*, *The Sound of Music* and *West Side Story*, continued to supply the 'standard' vocalists with material.

By the late 1950s it seemed that rock 'n' roll had been tamed. Presley, signed to the major label RCA, had lost his rawness and was now a regular on mainstream television shows. Soon, he would play the part of a good American and depart for Germany on military service. With Presley out of the country, Little Richard in the church, Chuck Berry in prison and Buddy Holly dead, the threat from rock 'n' roll seemed to have passed.

Over at Columbia Records, Mitch Miller was approached by a couple of young songwriters trying to sell a song. 'The Story of My Life', recorded by Columbia's 'country & western' singer Marty Robbins and backed by The Ray Conniff Orchestra, reached *Billboard*'s Top 20 in 1957 and started a 15-year run of chart success for its writers Burt Bacharach and Hal David.

The work of Bacharach and David, though not evident on this early song, had a sophistication and quality which was worlds apart from Mitch Miller and which harked back to the golden age of the great American songwriters. Bacharach, a classically trained musician, had been working as pianist and arranger for popular vocalists like Vic Damone and Steve Lawrence, when he was introduced to Hal David, a lyricist who had a few significant hits already under his belt. In the summer of 1957, Burt Bacharach and Hal David entered one of the Brill Building cubicles for the first time and one of the most important post-war songwriting partnerships was born. But it turned out that they were the exception that proved the rule.

Brill Songs

The Brill Building, situated at 49th and Broadway in New York City, had been the home for songwriters since the 1930s and was the final resting place in the gradual move uptown of both Tin Pan Alley and the theatre district. The Brill was packed with 11 floors of publishers' offices where, in small cubicles, songwriters churned out hit after hit. By the late 1950s it was the home to the more 'traditional' Broadway publishers, including Hill & Range Music who represented Elvis Presley. Across the street in another building, at 1650 Broadway, was where the action really was. There, primarily at the offices of Aldon Music, a group of young writers produced songs which would change the face of the music business forever.

Writers like Neil Sedaka and Howard Greenfield, Carole King and Gerry Goffin, Ellie Greenwich and Jeff Barry, and Cynthia Weill and Barry Mann became the in-house writers for Aldon Music, the publishing company started by Don Kirshner and Al Nevins who had been knocking around the music business for years trying to get a break. They found it with Aldon, by building a stable of first-class writers catering to the growing market for teenage songs.

The work of these writers and producers represents the bridge between the rawness of the first rock 'n' rollers and the sophisticated pop which took hold in the 1960s. The importance of the producer, heralded by Mitch Miller, would find its true flowering in the work of the Brill Building (a generic term) while the growing role of the professional songwriter in rock music has its roots in the work of Aldon's three star teams of Goffin and King, Greenwich and Barry, and Sedaka and Greenfield, who, between them, were responsible for dozens of hits. As a solo artist, Carole King would spearhead the singer songwriter genre of the late 1960s and early 1970s; her album *Tapestry*, released in 1970, is still one of the all-time top-selling albums.

For about six years, the Brill Building Sound reigned supreme in the American charts and was responsible for dictating musical trends such as the teen idol boy singers (the 'Bobbies' – Vee/Vinton/Darin/Rydell), dance records, and the girl group sound.

But the times were-a-changing. Groups and, in particular, British groups were what the teen record buyer wanted. The Beatles, who had covered Brill Building songs on their first few albums and who, on arriving in America, asked to meet their idols Carole King and Gerry Goffin, exploded all over the charts, spelling the end for the solo pop act and for the girl group sound. Some 50,000 groups were now working a circuit of teen clubs, teen fairs, and following the example of The Beatles and writing their own material.

Teen Beat

With the emergence of the teen culture, the 'easy listening' pop vocalists of the previous era had become marginalized, still recording and still performing but now for a much more defined audience – grown ups who were familiar with the songs from Broadway shows and Hollywood musicals. As rock 'n' roll had been perceived as a threat, so the emergence of the group seemed to spell the end for the solo vocalist. Sinatra's setting up of his own record label, Reprise, and gathering around him almost every important 'serious' popular vocalist could be seen as a safety-in-numbers measure. At least with rock 'n' roll and the Brill Building, it had been possible for grown up singers to have hits with sanitized versions of teen pop. The groups wrote their own material which was deemed inappropriate for the Sinatras and Nat 'King' Coles. Until, that is, they listened to The Beatles who – with songs like 'Yesterday' – were producing material that had something in common with the great American composers.

In former backing singer Dionne Warwick, Bacharach and David had found the perfect interpreter for their songs. The range of artists who hit with Bacharach/David songs reads like a Who's Who of the 1960s: Dusty Springfield, Tom Jones, Jackie DeShannon, Jack Jones, Aretha Franklin, Sandie Shaw and Cilla Black. The songs of Bacharach and David, such as 'Walk On By', 'Do You Know the Way to San Jose?', 'I Say A Little Prayer' and 'Make it Easy On Yourself', had managed to bridge (and transcend) the generation gap in that they were recorded by both middle-of-road favourite Herb Alpert, and the 'Queen of Soul', Aretha Franklin.

It was a Herb Alpert discovery – The Carpenters – who carried Bacharach and David into the 1970s by recording their song 'Close To You'. Reaching No.1 in June 1970, this song kickstarted one of the most successful recording acts of the next decade.

But there was still musical life outside the charts. Musical theatre had continued to turn up songs which would become standards for a new generation of singers. The successful partnership of Rodgers and Hammerstein had been ended by the death of Oscar Hammerstein. Among Richard Rodgers' new collaborators was Stephen Sondheim. Sondheim, via *Gypsy, A Funny Thing Happened on the Way to the Forum, Company* and *Follies* would become a major figure in the world of musical theatre.

Jule Styne's *Funny Girl*, based on the life of burlesque star Fanny Brice, launched the career of Barbra Streisand, whose first three albums for Columbia had showcased songs by the great American songbook writers, a pattern all her subsequent albums would follow. She did not record contemporary material until the end of the decade.

But in reality, the Great American Songbook was closed, popular music had become pop and rock 'n' roll had become rock. For many, the lunatics had taken over the asylum.

Right Hal David, standing, with Dionne Warwick and Burt Bacharach

the top 100

songs
52-63

Rocket '88'

High noon

Secret love

Hoochie coochie man

Rock around the clock

Blue suede shoes

Great balls of fire

Memphis Tennessee

What'd I say (parts 1 and 2)

He'll have to go

Will you still love me tomorrow?

Stand by me

Words and **music** Jackie Brenston **1951**

Above Sam Phillips

It is said that **Rocket '88'** was the first ever rock 'n' roll record and it certainly has the right pedigree. Jackie Brenston was a saxophone player from Clarksdale, Mississippi. A famous breeding ground for blues musicians, Clarksdale's drinking joints could boast of performances by Robert Johnson, Sun House and Muddy Waters; it is also regarded as the site of the crossroads where Johnson is said to have sold his soul to the devil in return for his unrivalled skills on the guitar.

In 1951 Brenston travelled to Memphis in company with a sharp-suited pianist and guitarist called Ike Turner and their band, modestly called The Kings of Rhythm. They were off to make a fortune writing songs and playing music. They hooked up with Sam Phillips who had a recording facility in the city (and who was four years away from recording the first efforts of a young Elvis Presley). Phillips specialized in recording black performers for what were then called 'race' records. The Kings of Rhythm were a good rocking outfit and Turner's boogie-woogie piano playing was in the popular r&b groove. He had been a session pianist, a DJ and a talent scout for a couple of r&b labels. They came up with **Rocket '88'**, a song that addressed three subjects that would feature in many successful rock songs: cars, women and liquor.

Rocket '88' was the name of an Oldsmobile car model that had been on the market since 1949. The lyric, which is an odd mixture of advertising jingle and sexual swagger with phallic overtones, would run into trouble in these politically correct days for its references to drinking and driving.

Brenston delivers the words in an emotionally charged rush, half a step ahead of a beat underpinned by Turner's rolling boogie-piano, which anticipated the style of Jerry Lee Lewis a few years later. The record also features a fuzzy rocking guitar riff. Ike Turner claims credit for this. The story goes that he dropped the guitar amp when unloading the car in which they drove to the studio. This loosened the speaker cone, producing a guitar sound that went on to feature heavily in later rock records.

SUN RECORDS

In the early 1950's Sun Records was a small recording studio located here at 706 Union. Owned and operated by Sam C. Phillips, Sun Records became nationally known for giving many local area artists, both black and white, their start in the recording industry. These included Elvis Presley, Johnny Cash, Jerry Lee Lewis, Roy Orbison, Carl Perkins, Charlie Rich, B. B. King, Rufus Thomas, Howlin' Wolf and others.

Brenston later admitted that the song was little different from a 1947 record by Jimmy Liggins called 'Cadillac Boogie'. Phillips sold the track to Chess records where, because the vocal was credited to Jackie Brenston, he also got the credit for the performance and the composition. Turner later claimed that he wrote the song. In being 'careless' with the credits Sam Phillips thought he could market Brenston and Turner as separate acts. But, whoever wrote it, it's a great track which reached its peak of popularity in the r&b charts in the same year Patti Page's 'How Much is That Doggie in the Window?' topped the national charts.

Sam Philips used the earnings from **Rocket '88'** to set up Sun Records and went on to launch the careers of Elvis Presley, Jerry Lee Lewis, Roy Orbison, Johnny Cash and B.B. King. When asked, as he frequently is, what was the first rock 'n' roll record, he cites **Rocket '88'**, which despite it predating the term rock 'n' roll ought to satisfy all but the most pedantic critic.

In true rock 'n' roll style, Jackie Brenston died in 1979 after a drinking binge. Tina Turner, who married Ike some years later, now has the status of legend that Ike Turner might have had for his pioneering work in rock music. After their messy break up, when she complained he had battered her, his career took a dive. Personal problems aside though, he is up there with the greats.

> " **rocket '88'** was the name of an oldsmobile car model "

Words Ned Washington **Music** Dmitri Tiomkin **1952**

Sometimes known as 'Do Not Forsake Me', **High Noon** is the theme song of one of the greatest Westerns of all time. It is a great song and deservedly won an Oscar in 1953. Without the sentimentality that usually accompanies movie theme songs it accurately charts the drama of the film. Despite the dedicated lyric, it became a huge hit for Frankie Laine and started the vogue for releasing movie title songs that the studios hoped would both chart, and attract publicity for the film.

Dmitri Tiomkin wrote the music for the film score and the title track. He was a Russian-born musical prodigy who fell in love with American music after hearing George Gershwin, and did more than most to promote Gershwin's orchestral works round the world. Tiomkin became an accomplished film composer (specializing in Westerns) of over 200 movies including: *Mr Smith Goes to Washington*, *The High and the Mighty*, *The Alamo*, and *Friendly Persuasion*. Ned Washington was another movie song specialist. He had great success with lyrics for songs like, 'When You Wish Upon A Star' and 'A Town Without Pity'. But his greatest successes came from writing lyrics for the great movie composer Victor Young.

For **High Noon** Tiomkin used Tex Ritter as the singer. Ritter, later known as the 'Voice of the Western', was one of those Hollywood cowboys who wasn't really a cowboy but an actor with a decent singing voice and a downhome ranch style. Ritter trained as a lawyer before he got the acting bug and must have been pleased to be associated with such an illustrious movie, but it was the cover version of the song by the crooning Frankie Laine that hit the charts and sold a million. However, the craggy voiced Ritter was exactly right for the song, the epitome of Gary Cooper, the leading man in the film. The pace of the music was that of a horse walking slowly through a hostile environment and the theme is whistled by other characters in other scenes. The whistling motif was

so successful, that Tiomkin used it again in his next movie and did away with the lyrics entirely. In fact, the theme song for *The High And The Mighty* was more memorable than the movie. In **High Noon**, Tiomkin's great skill was to compose a tune that satisfyingly reflected the country and western genre while still showing elements of classical composition. It was clearly the intention for the song to be integrated organically into the plot of the movie as the first words of the song 'Do not forsake me' are also the first words of the movie.

What's quite startling about **High Noon** is the way it shifts from being a song addressed to a lover in the choruses and becomes an interior monologue in the verses, where the lyrics address the dilemma between love and duty. Its very bleak last line, which describes shooting Frank Miller dead, are not words you'd expect to hear from the mouth of a lawman concerned with the niceties of the judicial system, but they exactly capture the movie's central dilemma.

Right Tex Ritter

54 secret love

Words Paul Francis Webster **Music** Sammy Fain **1953**

This song was one of the last gasps for the old craftsmen of Tin Pan Alley. In the early 1950s Jerome Kern, Irving Berlin, the Gershwins and Richard Rodgers, Lorenz Hart, Oscar Hammerstein and Cole Porter were about to yield their dominance of pop music to a new, some would say, coarser generation of writers who paid less attention to the arcane skills of matching words and music and focussed their attention on hit making. Of course, their decline coincided with the emergence of rock 'n' roll, but there were other factors too. Records had become the dominant means of drawing income from songwriting. National and international charts were co-ordinating record sales figures, and watching the hit parade had become the new sport. There was a new breed of record company scouts – A&R men – whose livelihood depended on matching performers to material. Power was ebbing away from the artists and writers towards the record companies, who were more concerned by sales figures than quality.

Secret Love bridged the gap between the traditional Tin Pan Alley song and a commercial hit. And it was a big hit, for Doris Day and later for Kathy Kirby and later still for Freddy Fender. The careers of Sammy Fain and Paul Francis Webster were inextricably linked to the old aristocracy of Tin Pan Alley. Both of them concentrated on movie songs. Both of them collaborated with other gifted writers – Fain with Al Dubin, Les Brown, 'Yip' Harburg and Mitchell Parish; Webster with Duke Ellington and Hoagy Carmichael. Among other songs, they wrote 'High Hopes', 'Love is A Many Splendoured Thing' and the score for the film *Calamity Jane*, which yielded several memorable songs including **Secret Love**. It's not only a great song, but it fulfils the criteria of the new era by hitting you with the big melodic line and lyric idea in the first 10 seconds – essential for grabbing the listener's attention.

Calamity Jane is the story of an accident prone, rough and ready cowgirl of the old Wild West, who dresses like a man and who spends her time being one of the boys, shooting guns, drinking and cussing with her old pal Wild Bill Hickok. She is looking to educate herself into the ways of modern romance so that she can lure a soldier into marriage, only to discover that she is actually in love with Wild Bill, hence the 'secret'. They were fortunate to have Doris Day in the lead role. 'When I first heard **Secret Love** I almost fainted,' she recalled, 'it was so beautiful... We lived in Toluca Lake at the time, which was just minutes from the studio. When I got there, I sang the song with the orchestra for the first time. When I'd finished, Ray Heindorf, the musical director, called me into the sound booth, grinning from ear to ear, and said, "That's it. You're never going to do it better." That was the first and only take we did.'

Fain and Webster won an Oscar for this song, as they did for their next collaboration, 'Love is A Many Splendoured Thing'. They both continued working with great success, producing high-quality material until their deaths in 1985 and 1989 respectively. Webster won another Oscar in 1965 for his lyrics to the haunting 'The Shadow of Your Smile'.

Doris Day was so spectacular in her role as Calamity, that she became the Sapphist equivalent of Judy Garland in The *Wizard of Oz* – both cult heroines of the gay community, which gives the song **Secret Love** an added layer of meaning.

Above Singer and film actress Doris Day

Once I had a secret love,
That lived within the heart of me.
All too soon my secret love,
Became impatient to be free.

So I told a friendly star,
The way that dreamers often do,
Just how wonderful you are,
And why I'm so in love with you.

Now, I shout it from the highest hills;
Even told the golden daffodils.
At last my heart's an open door,
And my secret love's
No secret anymore.

55 hoochie coochie man

Words and **music** Willie Dixon **1954**

If you've never heard this song then you might need to know that 'hoochie coochie' is blues slang for vagina. If you have heard it then you'll have been in no doubt. **Hoochie Coochie Man** is a song full of sexual pomp, about a man who has all the luck in the world he needs with the gentler sex. Willie Dixon wrote the song for Muddy Waters and, to date, his is the only version worthy of serious consideration. It is a perfect example of Chicago blues, electric and electrified. It was a hit in the race record charts in the 1950s, but its influence on rock music in general is incalculable.

Chicago blues is the name given to the urban blues music that came about as southern blacks moved north to find work in the industrial heartland of America. Adapted from the more rural delta blues of the Mississippi, it was originally played on acoustic guitars with whatever accompaniment was available. Muddy Waters was one of the first bluesmen to amplify his guitar for the simple expedient of allowing his abrasive guitar style to be heard in larger venues through the noise and general club ambience. Chicago blues was a local affair for local consumption until the Chess brothers started to export their catalogue of blues material, most significantly to England. Waters recorded two versions of the song for the fabled Chess Records in 1952 and 1954, the second with the composer on string bass. These recordings were heard by influential musicians such as traditional jazz bandleader, Chris Barber, who persuaded Muddy Waters to tour the UK in 1958. This influenced a particular group of blues enthusiasts, and in 1962 Mick Jagger, Keith Richards and Brian Jones wrote to the BBC and persuaded the corporation to give them airtime to play their version of Chicago blues. The rest is history as they say. In the USA Waters knew that white audiences were not ready for such impassioned and forthright material and he said to an American journalist in 1969, 'It was the Brits who exported blues back to mainstream audience in America. The British had to introduce you all to your own people.'

Above Writer Willie Dixon
Left Performer Muddy Waters

Willie Dixon was a writer, arranger, producer and A&R man for many years before becoming house producer for Chess Records. He wrote for many blues performers including Otis Rush, Howlin' Wolf and Little Walter as well as Muddy Waters. Perhaps his most famous song, 'You Need Love', was the subject of a lawsuit during the 1970s when he claimed, successfully, that Led Zeppelin's anthem 'Whole Lotta Love' was based on his original.

Chicago blues only affected early rock 'n' roll peripherally. Chuck Berry, who idolized Muddy Waters, adapted the excessive elements of his hero's music and became one of the first poets of rock. But Berry's music was adapted to suit a teen and mostly white audience; **Hoochie Coochie Man** is the real unvarnished thing, straight to the point. It is raw sex, with no concessions to gentility.

56 | rock around the clock

Words Max Freedman **Music** Jimmy De Knight **1955**

This song has a great burden of history on it, as it became the first major hit of the rock era. While Elvis Presley was just breaking free of his local Memphis audience, Bill Haley released **Rock Around the Clock** on the soundtrack of *Blackboard Jungle* (a film about juvenile delinquency, although not very delinquent by today's standards). It sold 25 million copies and became the first rock 'n' roll No.1. It was responsible for riots in movie houses, concert venues being trashed in the UK and raising the blood pressure of our moral guardians to boiling point in despair for the souls of godless youth. The word 'rock', like 'jazz' 50 years earlier, was black slang for sex. Rebellious youth was about to have its day. The critic Ian Whitcomb described the song, with its call to listeners to put their glad rags on and rock around the clock, as a clarion call for the new music, rock 'n' roll, bearing comparison to Irving Berlin's 1910 song 'Alexander's Ragtime Band' (see pages 24–25) calling on us all to listen and marvel at a new type of music.

Something was in the air in those first few years of the 1950s. The sense of change was palpable. The war was fading from memory, the dance bands had had their day and the new, young record-buying public was looking for novelty. The sound of rock was

everywhere; it's just that nobody had given it a name. An old blues song called 'My Daddy Rocks Me With A Steady Roll' had been around since the early 1920s. But the New York DJ Alan Freed later claimed credit for putting together the words 'rock' and 'roll', and even then nobody took it seriously.

In Memphis, Sam Phillips admitted with admirable frankness that he was looking for a white boy who could sound black. The music that was exciting post-war youth could be heard in black urban communities all over America. Sadly, it needed a white performer to cross over to the mainstream.

Haley was always an unlikely beneficiary of the rock 'n' roll revolution. He was a portly 30-year-old when **Rock Around the Clock** topped the charts, and despite the kiss curl, he never looked the part. He was a country music player by inclination, and though you can't fault his band, The Comets, for its energy in performing the song, it's still a pretty mediocre revolutionary anthem. It wasn't country, it wasn't rhythm and blues and it hovered on the edge of parody, but it did the business and it got the kids on their feet and jiving.

Max Freedman, an established Tin Pan Alley writer of such 1940s' hits as 'Heartbreaker' recorded by the Andrews Sisters, was 63 years old when he wrote **Rock Around the Clock**, and it seems unlikely that he expected teddy boys to be moved enough to slash cinema seats in appreciation of his lyrical skills. More especially as co-writer Jimmy De Knight claimed that Freedman had to be dissuaded from calling it 'Dance Around the Clock' and that it had originally been written as a quick foxtrot.

Like many seminal works, it's difficult to pick your way through to the true provenance of the song without getting snagged on the myths and vested interests. De Knight represented Haley's interests at the time and there is some controversy over his precise involvement in the composition of the song, but if all he did was change the word 'dance' to 'rock', then he earned his royalties. Somehow, in that magical way grubby commercialism sometimes has, the song transcends all those considerations, and has earned its 'honourable mention' in the rock revolution.

Left Bill Haley and The Comets

Words and **music** Carl Lee Perkins **1956**

The story of **Blue Suede Shoes** could have been so different. Sam Phillips had sold Presley's contract to Colonel Tom Parker who immediately signed him to RCA Records. A few months after 'Heartbreak Hotel' had introduced Elvis to the world at large, **Blue Suede Shoes** should have taken him to No.1. But it didn't. Nor did it have anything like the immediate success its reputation and its later significance would suggest. Even though Elvis made it a staple of his stage performances, just like 'Strawberry Fields Forever' (see page 128) and 'My Way' (see page 130), it didn't reach No.1. In fact it rose no higher than No.9 in the UK, and was never successfully released as an A-side in the USA.

But what the song did do was earn its author, Carl Perkins, a place in rock 'n' roll history. Styled the 'Rocking Guitar Man' to Elvis's 'Hillbilly Cat', Perkins recorded at Sun Studios in Memphis, also home to Johnny Cash, Jerry Lee Lewis, Roy Orbison and a galaxy of forgotten other disciples of the new music. Perkins had a Top 5 hit with **Blue Suede Shoes**, Elvis himself had to wait until 1960 when he sang it in the film *G.I. Blues*. Since then, of course, there have been hundreds of versions of the song.

Perkins is the rockabilly rival to Chuck Berry, a sardonic wordsmith apparently chronicling this new world of rock 'n' roll. In fact like Berry, most of his songs are about something else – Southern life, blues or women. He wrote **Blue Suede Shoes** after an encounter with a guy who virtually spoke the words of the song to him. Amused and bewildered, Perkins wrote a witty satire on the state of mind of one who could feel so strongly about his (novelty) clothes. His version is laid back and swings easy with a knowing smile.

Perkins' version has a purer sound, more raw than Elvis'. Looking back, on Elvis' version there is already a sense of him as a package – the tinge of cynicism in the lead guitar and the syrup of the Jordanaires' vocals softens the edge of Elvis's attack. All this is easier to see in hindsight, the differences between the two versions belie the singers' almost identical backgrounds and the place they share in musical history: poor white boys from the rural South, two architects of a devastating mixture of bluegrass and blues, called rockabilly. The term smacked faintly of contempt and indicated the position of poor Southern whites and their quaint music on America's social scale.

In 1956 rock 'n' roll conquered the American charts. In the UK it was a different story. Most of the rock 'n' rollers were still unheard of – competition in the charts that year came from Dean Martin, Winifred Atwell and Ronnie Hilton. Throughout June that year the two versions hovered around each other in the middle of the UK Top 20. Pat Boone occupied the No.1 slot for the whole month with 'I'll Be Home'. In America, Perkins reached No.4 – though he might have achieved more hits and more fame if he had been able to sing the song live. Days after its release, he was nearly killed in a car accident and remained hospitalized for months.

Though it hurts to say it, **Blue Suede Shoes**, 'Memphis Tennessee' and 'Rock Around the Clock' (see page 105) have all become as familiar as 'Roll Out the Barrel'. But it's impossible to exaggerate the power they had at the time.

But when Elvis came to visit his friend in the hospital in 1956 'Heartbreak Hotel', released in the US a week after **Blue Suede Shoes**, was on its way to No.1. He was already bound for glory on a different train. Elvis went on to 'kick the doors down' and became immortal. Perkins stayed the same, tending the rockabilly flame. For a time they shared a voice – together they unleashed the unheard and un-rated music of the South on an unsuspecting world and changed it forever.

Right Elvis Presley

> **blue suede shoes** earnt its author, carl perkins, a place in rock 'n' roll history

Words and **music** Otis Blackwell and Jack Hammer
1957

There are some songs, particularly in the rock era, where no matter who wrote the song, they are re-authored by a specific performance. Presley was one of those performers, Little Richard was another, and so was 'The Killer', Jerry Lee Lewis.

Whenever you read about rock stars trashing hotel rooms, swearing at journalists and generally behaving in antisocial ways, the career of Jerry Lee Lewis is the template, the model of bad behaviour. He is the epitome of the wild rock 'n' roller. It was never a publicity stunt, he never waited for the photographers to be present; there were no phone calls to journalists; he did it for real. He was the natural-born Killer. 'I'm a rompin', stompin', piano playin', mean son-of-a-bitch. I've been picked on, abused, sued, jailed, ridiculed, persecuted and prosecuted, but I never let it bother me,' he claimed.

If Elvis, his exact contemporary at Sun Records, had behaved as badly as Jerry Lee, it's doubtful that his career would have taken off. Elvis may have been cast as the devil incarnate, but in reality he was always respectful, he loved his mom and called his elders 'sir'.

As for talent, there wasn't a great deal to choose between them. They both started off singing country music with an r&b feel. Jerry Lee was a boogie-woogie style precision piano player and, unlike Presley, kept the faith throughout his career, doing what he did best, straddling the worlds of rock 'n' roll and country music. But like Presley he misspent his youth in low music dives learning from black musicians. Jerry Lee and his cousin would hide behind the bar and watch the plantation workers moving around to the blues. 'That place was full of those coloured folks, man... they had been pickin' cotton all day, had a 25 cent pint of wine in their back pocket, and were gittin' with it you know,' he remembered.

Above Jerry Lee Lewis at the piano

> **great balls of fire** is raw rock 'n' roll

Great Balls of Fire is virtuoso rock 'n' roll, raw, unproduced, played from the heart, deeply troubling for those of a delicate state of mind. It makes the backlash that accompanied the nursery slopes of rock 'n' roll completely understandable. Jerry Lee was deported from Great Britain in 1958 because he was accompanied by his new 14-year-old bride Myra (his cousin), and was once tried for murder. But one glance at his life story and it comes as no surprise that Jerry Lee almost became a preacher like his cousin Jimmy Swaggart, who fell from grace spectacularly for spending the money of his impoverished congregation on liquor and loose women.

Writer Otis Blackwell was a finalist in a talent contest for black performers at the Apollo Theatre in Harlem. He started doing demos for Elvis and later wrote 'All Shook Up' and 'Don't Be Cruel' for the King, 'Handy Man' for Jimmy Jones, as well as 'Fever' recorded by Peggy Lee. Jack Hammer came up with the title **Great Balls of Fire** and sold it to Otis Blackwell. That seems to have been the sum of his contribution to the record.

trivia

★ In 1952 Jerry Lee Lewis, intending to become a preacher, spent a year studying at the Waxahatchie Bible Institute in Texas.

★ In 1968 Lewis starred, successfully, as Iago in *Catch My Soul*, a rock musical based on Shakespeare's *Othello*.

Words and **music** Chuck Berry **1958**

Rock music's most truculent performer is also rock music's most eloquent poet. Never mind the demands for cash minutes before the start of his live performances, the strict time limitations of his output and the dodgy pick-up bands. Berry was the first person to create the lyrical landscape of the dreams and desires of the American teenager in songs like 'Johnny B Goode', 'Roll Over Beethoven', 'School Day', and 'Sweet Little Sixteen'.

That his lyrics should have the riffs of Chicago blues as musical counterpoint, albeit less harshly delivered than his hero, Muddy Waters, is doubly satisfying. He gave us the guitar licks that are the standard tools in the rock guitarist's repertoire.

His importance in the early development of rock 'n' roll cannot be overstated. He reached his peak of influence with the British blues bands in the early 1960s. His own influences are from a previous generation of performers, Charlie Christian for his jazz guitar, Nat 'King' Cole for his clear diction and Muddy Waters for his use of language.

There is a strong narrative edge to the best of Berry's songs, they are ambivalent, often sweet on the outside with a sting under the surface, and **Memphis Tennessee**, covered endlessly by r&b bands in the 1960s and 1970s, fits perfectly into that mould.

It opens as a normal love and loss song until later verses reveal that the 'party' is only six years old (the singer's daughter we presume).

It's written in a spare, colloquial voice of everyday English that is much harder to achieve than it appears. Berry has always taken a matter of fact attitude toward his songs, refusing to concede much in the way of biographical content.

Given the dramas of his life (he was imprisoned for taking a 14-year-old prostitute over the state line and has frequently spoken and written his experiences of racial discrimination), it's hard to think how he could avoid his life spilling over to his work. In truth most of Berry's best songs were written before his arrest for that incident. Berry himself claims to have taken the idea from an old Muddy Waters' song that starts with the line: *'Long distance operator, I want to talk to my baby.'*

If that's true, it only adds to his peerless reputation as a writer of tight little vignettes of American life. It wasn't a big hit like some of Berry's other songs, and the cover version by Elvis Presley, perhaps the best-known, doesn't really do it justice. But try 'Promised Land', a miniature Homeric Odyssey, for the real take on Chuck Berry's America. He is the man who laid down the defining imagery of rock 'n' roll that many lesser writers have subsequently reduced to clichés.

Right Chuck Berry

Words and **music** Ray Charles **1959**

Ray Charles is one of those performers who transcend categories and remain uniquely themselves. However unlikely it sounds, he has also come to represent the American Dream – that journey from extreme poverty, going blind when he was three and pulling himself up by his bootstraps by sheer talent. He survived racial prejudice, drug addiction and jail to become a national treasure, feted wherever he travels, and whose version of the unofficial national anthem, 'America the Beautiful', is the preferred version of millions. He is the musician he is because he's always made his own choices about material he plays and records, never bowing to fashion or commercial considerations. As a child he was just as likely to be listening to Hank Williams as Nat 'King' Cole.

Regarded by his record company as an r&b artist, they thought him ill advised to record *Modern Sounds in Country and Western Music* in 1963. His response was to say, 'you do the business, and I'll do the music'. The album contained 'I Can't Stop Loving You', and 'Take These Chains From My Heart', two classic interpretations of country standards. His influence on artists like Stevie Wonder and Van Morrison is there for all to hear.

He started writing in 1955 with 'I Gotta Woman' but it was not until **What'd I Say (parts 1 and 2)** in 1959 that he cracked the mainstream pop charts. Charles thought of it as straightforward r&b, but it became one of the first pop-soul classics to feature in the white dominated national charts. Drenched in the gospel sound of his youth, it broke new territory, a unique sound that helped make Tamla Motown possible. 'One night I couldn't think of nothing else to play, so I just told the guys in the band, I said you know, "you guys just follow me" and I said the same things to the girls, I said "whatever I say, you say, just repeat after me" and I just started and the people went wild, they just started dancing and going crazy. And if you listen to **"What'd I Say"**, if you look at the verses you can tell that there is nothing in it that's cohesive, they're just verses that I made up and put there, just thrown together, I mean there's no rhyme or reason and people were so wild over it I tried the same thing the next night and we got the same reaction.'

Those made-up-on-the-spot lyrics led to some radio stations banning the song for sounding too suggestive. But like so many banned songs it survived to be covered by King Curtis, The Beatles, Elvis Presley, Etta James, Bill Haley, Freddie King, Herbie Mann, John Mayall, Solomon Burke, Jerry Lee Lewis, Clarence Carter, Lightnin' Hopkins, Roy Orbison, Rare Earth, Hound Dog Taylor, Clyde McPhatter, Buddy Rich, Sammy Davis Jr, Bobby Darin, Johnny Cash, Jimmy Smith, Clifton Chenier, Nancy Sinatra, Duane Eddy...

Above Ray Charles

> " what'd I say (parts 1 and 2) became one of the first pop-soul classics to feature in the white-dominated national charts "

Above Jim Reeves

Words and **music** Joe and Audrey Allison **1960**

Right through to the 1980s, when CDs started to replace vinyl, you couldn't find a juke-box in the western world without Jim Reeves' version of **He'll Have to Go**.

Like most great country songs it's about love and loss, but it's the setting that makes the difference. You can shut your eyes and imagine the scene: there's 'Gentleman' Jim in the corner of a honky-tonk bar, drowning his sorrows, while everyone else is listening to the juke-box and enjoying themselves. His special lady has found a new friend and Jim is bereft. He just *has* to speak to her, so he moves over to the telephone booth in the corner and rings her up. Unfortunately, she's entertaining her new beau. And there we all are, stuck in this tiny telephone booth, while Jim pours out his deepest thoughts to his ex, asking her to put her lips closer to the phone.

The use of the phone call by the writers is a brilliant device for creating a sense of intimacy. The simplicity of the idea, the language and that loping, unobtrusive musical accompaniment, are such that the song stays with you. Forever.

He'll Have to Go was written by the then husband and wife team of Joe and Audrey Allison in 1959, but Reeves had a big hit with it the following year. Joe Allison recalls, 'My proudest moment in writing came when Jim Reeves decided to record my song **He'll Have to Go**'. Jim's album went platinum and the song was later recorded by Elvis Presley, Bing Crosby, Guy Lombardo, The Mills Brothers, Tom Jones, Eddy Arnold and over a hundred different artists worldwide. It is my wish that all writers will be blessed with, at least, one standard composition during his or her career.' The couple had had minor success with songs for country star Faron Young and Tex Ritter (who sang 'High Noon', see page 102). Joe Allison has had a life in country music, starting off as a radio DJ championing acts such as The Everly Brothers, and going on to be a record producer and executive for Liberty Records.

Hearing the song for the first time, Jim Reeves is alleged to have said, 'It was like a hot poker burning its way through my mind,' maybe not quite what you might want to hear if you'd just written the song.

Reeves' version was recorded in Nashville using the finest session musicians – Floyd Cramer on piano, Hank Garland on guitar and, unusually for a country track, a vibraphone player, Marvin Hughes. This was hardcore country music of the modern era. Reeves was not alone, Roy Orbison with 'Only the Lonely' and The Everly Brothers with 'Cathy's Clown', both hits in 1960, ploughed the same furrow. Like Elvis and Jerry Lee Lewis, Johnny Cash and Carl Perkins, they were all fully paid-up country artists making great country records with a hint of pop that penetrated the national and international charts.

Of course Jim, poor love, was never going to win her back. We all knew that really, but in case we had any doubts, Joe and Audrey Allison wrote a sequel called 'He'll Have To Stay'.

> you couldn't find a juke-box in the western world without jim reeves' version of **he'll have to go**

62 will you still love me tomorrow?

Words Gerry Goffin **Music** Carole King **1961**

A landmark song in several ways, **Will You Still Love Me Tomorrow?** was the first major hit for two young songwriters – Carole King and Jerry Goffin. It was also the first popular song to deal with emotional issues from a female perspective and the first record by a black girl group to top the national charts.

Goffin and King were two staff writers for Aldon Music in New York, working alongside (among others) Neil Sedaka and Howard Greenfield (who wrote 'Oh Carol' and 'Stupid Cupid'), Cynthia Weil and Barry Mann ('On Broadway', 'Walking in the Rain' and 'You've Lost That Lovin' Feelin'') and Jeff Barry and Ellie Greenwich ('Da Doo Ron Ron'). Together they represented a shiny, new, young generation of Tin Pan Alley writers with an intuitive feel for the newly established teen market. They worked in a building on the opposite side of Broadway's legendary Brill Building, which had housed generations of songwriters and publishers since the late 1920s. Such was the parish pump, small community feel of this handful of young talent, that Carole King had been the subject of Neil Sedaka's big hit 'Oh Carol' a couple of years earlier. He was clearly in love with her at the time.

Clearly less than impressed, King had replied with 'Oh Neil', whose sarcastic lyrics left one in no doubt of her feelings.

The song did nothing for her reputation and she had to wait till 1961 for her debut hit.

As King herself noted, **Will You Still Love Me Tomorrow?** articulated the universal dilemma of young women on the verge of taking a relationship to a new and physical level. In 1961 not only was that a bold idea for a lyric, but it can lay claim to be the first song to bring that discussion into the wider teen market, much to the disapproval of some the nation's moral guardians. The original performers, The Shirelles, were worried that the song's suggestive lyrics might reinforce the belief that pop music in general, and this song in particular, encouraged teenage promiscuity. There was the added issue of racial stereotyping at a time when the black Civil Rights Movement was gaining widespread credibility. But the song's virtues outweighed all those reservations. It became a massive hit around the world, and instantly achieved classic status. In reality, the lyrics were written by Gerry Goffin, 19-year-old King's new husband. King was responsible for the melody and the arrangement. She played piano and percussion of the original recording.

The song's yearning and sumptuous melody recalls Richard Rodgers in his Hammerstein phase (King was an admirer), but the most immediate influences were

Above Carole King and Gerry Goffin
Left The Shirelles

Jerry Lieber and Mike Stoller. They had written and produced for Elvis ('Jailhouse Rock', 'King Creole' and 'Hound Dog') and had great success in bringing a black r&b sound into mainstream pop with bands like The Drifters and The Coasters. Their dramatic orchestral arrangements had made them the benchmark of quality for the new generation of writers. Certainly King has acknowledged their influence in her orchestration of **Will You Still Love Me Tomorrow?**

63 stand by me

Words and **music** Jerry Leiber, Mike Stoller and Ben E. King **1962**

For some reason the title **Stand By Me** has been a popular one with 20th-century songwriters, and there are several in the song catalogues, the most recent by Noel Gallagher of Oasis. This song, by Jerry Leiber and Mike Stoller, bears comparison with the 1906 song of the same name (see page 20) in several ways.

Leiber and Stoller exemplify Tin Pan Alley rock 'n' roll. In the *Rolling Stone History of Rock and Roll* rock critic Greg Shaw said of them, 'They were the true architects of pop/rock... Their signal achievement was the marriage of rhythm & blues in its most primal form to the pop tradition.' It is true that they created early rock numbers that managed, by good and frequently witty writing and more importantly high-quality studio production, to take the raw edges from the r&b material from which they took their inspiration.

They themselves claimed they were just two guys who liked the blues and boogie-woogie and turned their passion into profit. In doing so they created a vast catalogue of songs across all the pop and rock genres. Their most notable successes (but not always their best songs) came out of an alliance with Elvis Presley that started with 'Hound Dog'. 'Hound Dog' was a key song in Elvis's transition from local hero to international icon, and they went on to write a further 20 songs for Elvis, including 'Jailhouse Rock' and 'King Creole'.

Prior to the Elvis connection most of their work was written for black artists like Big Mama Thornton, who first recorded 'Hound Dog', Ray Charles, Jimmy Witherspoon and Amos Milburn. In the early 1950s they were all regarded as 'race' artists whose sales did not figure in the national charts. What set Leiber and Stoller apart is that they didn't write songs at all, they wrote records, controlling every stage of the process from original idea to released disc.

By the late 1950s they were working near New York's celebrated Brill Building, influencing the next generation of young songwriters, like Carole King and Doc Pomus. Their contemporaries held Leiber and Stoller as state-of-the-art pop writers and producers who changed the sound of American popular music by their use of romantic strings and exotic percussion, foreshadowing the popularity of soul music. In this era they wrote **Stand By Me**, one of several songs written for Ben E. King and The Drifters.

Like its 1906 antecedent, **Stand By Me** is a gospel song, or rather a *secular* gospel song as are many early Tamla Motown songs. It uses the vocabulary of gospel and it sounds like gospel. But it is no more plagiarism than *West Side Story* is to *Romeo And Juliet*. But none of this stops it from being one of the great pop songs of all time and a massive hit as covered by Otis Redding, John Lennon and others.

However, nothing can beat the version by the majestic Ben E. King, recorded after he had left The Drifters to go solo following a string of successes for the group with Lieber And Stoller-produced songs, including 'Dance With Me', 'Up on the Roof' and 'On Broadway'.

Below Ben E. King

"I think we got zapped in the '60s. You know, I think him upstairs, he decided "The '60s are it, and this is the start of music, this is how it's gonna be from now on. All the good bits, the licks and the hooks, we're gonna give them to the '60s. And it'll last for ever." I think that's what happened. Lamont Dozier on the music of the 1960s.

Much to the distaste of the music establishment and adults in general, rock 'n' roll had taken a grip on the imagination of its teen audience by the late 1950s. A few years before, nobody had considered the teen market as a separate economic entity. In the wake of the Presley explosion, every self-respecting adolescent coveted the idolatry heaped on Elvis, more especially if their parents loathed him. Kids bought guitars and they formed groups. Songwriting was about to return to the people.

Guitars, Bass and Drums

Around the cusp of the 1960s, pop music was beginning to change. The first flush of rock 'n' roll in the mid-1950s gave us the giants of rock: Presley, Jerry Lee Lewis, Little Richard, Chuck Berry and Fats Domino; but by the end of the decade it was giving way to Tin Pan Alley cheesiness. Presley was outselling all the previous generations of pop singers, but, persuaded by Colonel Parker to head for the better-established pastures of family entertainment, all but a handful of his recorded material was second rate. Jerry Lee was out of favour with the moral majority, and black artists were still subjected to racial prejudice, both commercially and personally. During these years the charts were overrun by pretty boy singers called Bobbie, Ricky or Frankie. But through the mist a new young generation of writers loomed. Rather than being written in the old Tin Pan Alley discipline, music for the new era was now written on guitars, as often as not by the performers themselves. This was observably closer to the country and western, hand-me-down tradition, and conditional only on the availability of cheap guitars. Here was the first generation of writers who had spent their early adolescence exposed to rock, and whose taste for it was underpinned by the disapproval of their parents. This coincided with the first perception of a teen market with real purchasing power. They were the first age-gap kids, and they all 'believed in rock 'n' roll'.

'That'll Be the Day' by The Crickets was the first reference point of this change. The young Buddy Holly's three short years in the business, before his death in 1959, would influence not only his

Right Buddy Holly and The Crickets

immediate peer group, but all rock writers for the next 20 years. The configuration of two guitars, bass and drums (already a standard country band format) was clearly the model for the group sound of the 1960s.

Sweet Harmony

Holly had a great gift for melody, and just as Duke Ellington wrote with an orchestra in mind, Holly wrote for his group. With his Texan country roots, it would have been intuitive. While with The Crickets, Holly often overdubbed his melodies, and the harmonies became quite sophisticated. It seems fitting that Holly signed to Decca in 1955 after opening a show, in his hometown of Lubbock, Texas, for Elvis Presley. Beyond the solo pretty-boy records of the aforementioned Bobbies, Rickies and Frankies, there was a rekindling in the popularity of vocal harmonies. For example, with The Everly Brothers, the plaintive interplay between their two voices defines their music. This was the first era in the history of pop when the vocal group sound would dominate the charts. The group sound had come out of three quite distinct traditions: swing band vocal groups, like The Pied Pipers or The Tommy Dorsey Band; country and western groups, like the Carter Family; and gospel quartets, like Sam Cooke's Soul Stirrers.

Black pop vocal groups with a clear gospel influence, like The Platters, were mainly covering established back-catalogue songs, such as Jerome Kern's 'Smoke Gets In Your Eyes', right through to the early 1960s. The swing band vocal groups had mutated into jazzy, close harmony quartets like The Four Freshmen, who were a big influence on The Beach Boys, and The Four Seasons, who had hits with 'Sherry' and 'Big Girls Don't Cry', written by Bob Gaudio. Elaborate vocal harmonies also were the key to the success of The Marvelettes' 'Please Mr Postman', the first No.1 from the new Tamla Motown label and writer Brian Holland. The Beatles covered 'Please, Mr Postman' on their first LP and Lennon and McCartney started their writing career at the point when The Four Seasons, The Everly Brothers and The Marvelettes were having hits. The dual vocal lines of Lennon and McCartney in 'Love Me Do', 'Please Please Me' and 'She Loves You', fit more neatly into that category of pop hits than

February 3, 1959 is regarded by many as 'the day the music died'. This is because that day a plane carrying Buddy Holly, Richie Valens and the Big Bopper to a concert in Moorhead, North Dakota, crashed near Clear Lake, Iowa, killing everyone on board. Holly had decided to go on ahead of his band as the tour was behind schedule and he had some arrangements to make. The Big Bopper had decided to accompany him as he was a big man and didn't feel comfortable sitting on the tour bus for such a long time and because he had the flu. Valens was on board because it was his turn to do eveyone's washing.

into their better publicized passion for Little Richard and Chuck Berry. It was left to The Rolling Stones to champion the cause of black r&b. They didn't start writing for another couple of years (after noting how much money Lennon and McCartney were making with their own compositions), although the story goes that Mick Jagger and Keith Richard had to be locked in a room by their manager, Andrew Loog Oldham, before they came up with anything.

In America close harmony black girl groups were the thing; The Marvelettes, The Chiffons, The Crystals, The Dixie Cups, and The Supremes all appeared in the charts regularly. Two stables of writers were providing material for them: Tamla Motown and the staff writers in the Brill Building. At Motown, Eddie and Brian Holland and Lamont Dozier (second only to Lennon and McCartney in writing hit records in the 1960s) finally cracked the white writers' domination of the charts with a series of impeccable anthems of teen angst, such as 'Baby Love', 'Can I Get A Witness?', 'Heatwave', 'How Sweet It Is', 'Nowhere to Run' and 'You Can't Hurry Love'. Close behind them were Smokey Robinson and Stevie Wonder, both carrying the torch for secular gospel music. Tamla Motown's founder, Berry Gordy, determined to beat Tin Pan Alley at its own game, created a whole new nationwide industry selling black music to a white audience. Historically, this was of equal importance as The Beatles' impact on popular music.

Though Tamla Motown was central to the sweetening of gospel music, making it more palatable for white audiences, Gordy's label was not the only catalyst for this change. Sam Cooke left gospel behind when he left the Soul Stirrers in the late 1950s. His first secular single, 'You Send Me', was released in 1957 and topped both the r&b charts and the pop charts. And it was sweet – perhaps the first example of sweet soul music. Down in Atlanta, however, something else was stirring. The late 1950s and early 1960s saw a young James Brown working up his unique sound. Brown initially had trouble getting his material recorded, due to his insistence on working with his own band. He had so much trouble that he had to pay for the recording himself. The resulting LP, *Live at the Apollo*, released in 1962, shows why Brown was so insistent. A million sales later, Brown was in control of his career as one of the most influential soul artists ever. Combining elements of gospel, rock and r&b, with a collection of brilliant musicians, such as Pee Wee Ellis, Maceo Parker and Fred Wesley, and an exciting stage show, he created funk music – music which was as acceptable to white audiences as it was to black. Others followed, like Sly Stone and Curtis Mayfield, and the legend of 'the hardest working man in showbusiness' was born.

In New York, the gifted young Brill Building writers Leiber and Stoller, Greenwich and Barry, Pomus and Schumann and Goffin and King, although notionally Tin Pan Alley recruits, had rock 'n' roll as the only reference point in their writing careers. Not unlike their forebears in the 1920s and 1930s (Gershwin and Berlin), they produced well-crafted pastiches of black music, many of which subsequently became classics, 'Loco-Motion', 'Chains', 'He's A Rebel', 'Chapel of Love', 'Leader of the Pack' and 'You've Lost That Lovin' Feelin'' among them. Neil Sedaka and Burt Bacharach also

Right Rock 'n' rolling

were part of the Brill set-up, but with their classical training, they drew on a wider palate.

The Beatles and The Stones

On both sides of the Atlantic, the recording industry was completely re-energized by the British 'invasion' of the USA in 1964, and its championing of black music. Record sales grew without precedent in the period, and although black performers found themselves marginalized by the British groups in the short term, the Brits were at least partially responsible for kick-starting the revival of black music in the later 1960s.

It is important to remember that at this time groups were getting known for reasons other than for their music. In 1964 and 1965 The Beatles toured the world, causing havoc wherever they went. Wild scenes greeted them at airports everywhere, particularly in the United States. Their concerts were packed with screaming teenagers and no one could hear anything, particularly not the music. Their first appearance on American TV in February 1964, on the *Ed Sullivan Show*, was watched by an estimated audience of 73 million people. The Rolling Stones, too, were kicking up a storm. A series of police raids and arrests on drug charges, although they were eventually dropped, raised the profile (and popularity) of the band. The more they provoked outrage from the establishment, the more popular they became with their fans. Other British groups established themselves during the mid-1960s, The Kinks and The Who amongst them.

It's impossible to say that singers and songwriters in the States were unhappy with the British Invasion. The record companies, however, were obviously miffed, and the search was on to refill the American charts with American music. Over on the west coast The Beach Boys were also lifting black riffs and folding them into their utopian surfing songs. But in Brian Wilson, they had a writer of rare gifts whose capacity for melody and multi-layered harmony owed little to rock 'n' roll.

Right The marquee at the Paramount Theater, New York City

Fired up by the success of Lennon and McCartney, Wilson raised his game with songs that are often as musically inventive as The Beatles' (if sometimes let down by the lyrics), 'I Get Around', 'Help Me Rhonda' and 'Good Vibrations'. Wilson was aware that he had to work hard to equal his rivals' achievements, and was spurred on to create albums like *Pet Sounds* which featured songs such as 'God Only Knows', later described by Paul McCartney as 'the greatest pop song ever written'. Creative rivalry was at a premium, and that was good for business.

Pop's Reinvention

The collective effect of these artists was electric. Rock music suddenly had a respectable body of writer-performers who could sustain the market for teen pop. For the most part, they had entered the business out of passion, to be part of the enterprise, rather than in the expectation of making lots of money. Style was paramount. That set them apart from the traditional tenets of commercial popular song. Pop was reinventing itself and taking its place at the vanguard of popular culture. Its lyrics were still concerned with love, loss and attitude. There weren't too many poets around (the most notable exceptions being Chuck Berry and Smokey Robinson). That would be the next stage. But young people were now not only performing mass-market pop (it was ever thus); they were now largely its genesis. Whatever the reason, records began to sell even better than before, pop bands began to be the barometers of culture, and the 1960s began to swing.

Casting the beady eye of hindsight, for sheer creativity, verve, and listenability, the pop songs of this period from the mid-1950s to the end of the 1960s, bear comparison with that period in the late 1920s and early 1930s when George Gershwin, Cole Porter, Jerome Kern, Irving Berlin and Richard Rodgers were at the top of their game. So despite the distaste of its peers, rock, in its diverse forms, has proved to be the most enduring genre of the century, generating more money and influence than any other branch of the entertainment industry.

the top 100

songs 64-78

I want to hold your hand

Respect

Walk on by

You've lost that lovin' feelin'

Eight miles high/Good vibrations

Strawberry fields forever/

Penny lane

All along the watchtower

My way

ABC

Brown sugar

Superstition

Space oddity/Life on Mars

No woman no cry

Autobahn

Dancing queen

Hotel California

God save the queen

Words and **music** John Lennon and Paul McCartney
1963

By the time John Lennon and Paul McCartney wrote this song, The Beatles were established as a revolutionary force in British music – their previous single, 'She Loves You', having finally blown away the sad remnants of ersatz American pop which had dominated the UK music scene in the late 1950s and early 1960s.

But at this point in their career they meant nothing in the USA. Many industry figures regarded The Beatles' early recordings as sub-standard from a technical point of view, pointing to the thin bass, scratchy vocals and lack of stereo separation.

So Lennon and McCartney knew they had to come up with something special when they met to write together in the basement of Jane Asher's (McCartney's girlfriend of the period) parents' house in London's Wimpole Street. It was the first time they had enjoyed the luxury of specially set-aside time after a year of constant touring.

According to Lennon, **I Want To Hold Your Hand** was written specifically as a single, 'one to one, eyeball to eyeball', with both writers trying to surpass each other's contributions to the piece.

With this in mind it's not surprising that **I Want To Hold Your Hand** emerged as a piece of music designed to make maximum impact rather than last as a transcendent song. Stripped down to its bare components, the lyrics, for example, verge on the trite, but heard as a whole the song has extraordinary dynamism. The construction, full of strange twists and turns, marks the beginning of a real adventure in music that few would match.

It's since been said that the song typified The Beatles' cute phase, and that while The Stones were singing about sleeping with girls, the Fab Four were still at the holding hands stage. But that's really missing the point. The lyric is just one of many elements of the song and sits in balance with the music. In fact the song's sheer exuberant energy virtually reinvented teenage romance overnight.

With the added advantage of recording **I Want To Hold Your Hand** on Abbey Road's new four-track, complete with full stereo effects, The Beatles had their hottest single to date and a coveted spot on America's *Ed Sullivan Show*, and Epstein finally convinced Capitol to release it as a single in the States.

When it came out in Britain, bringing the group a Christmas No.1 and a residency at that spot for an incredible two months, the Americans held back. To coincide with the appearance of the Beatles on the legendary *Ed Sullivan Show* on 9 February 1964, Capitol decided to issue five Beatles singles at once.

Above The Beatles .

Their appearance was a huge success and many commentators recognized that this was a pivotal moment in the history of post-war culture. By April that year Capitol's bizarre marketing ploy had paid off. The Beatles held the first five positions in the US Top 10 with, in descending order, 'Can't Buy Me Love', 'Twist And Shout', 'She Loves You', **I Want To Hold Your Hand** and 'Please Please Me'.

There had been only two American No.1s by British artists before: Acker Bilk's 'Stranger on the Shore' and The Tornados' 'Telstar'. Literally overnight The Beatles had changed everything. Now it was American artists who wanted to know how the Brits did it. The Beatles had put British pop music on the map. During the period between 1964 and 1965 there were 52 weeks' of British No.1s.

Just as they totally changed the scene in Britain, The Beatles signalled the end of America's bland 'bobby sox' period of pop which had followed the castration of the original 1950s rock 'n' rollers. It seemed almost everybody loved them, including the young Bob Dylan. He had assumed that the song was written 'with a little help from their friends' when he mistook the line 'I can't hide' for 'I get high'.

The story goes that when Dylan got to meet The Beatles he congratulated them on the song and offered them a marijuana joint thinking it was their chosen drug. Ringo took it, assuming it was a cigarette, and started to smoke it on his own. It was in many ways the beginning of another story and part of the rich musical trade across the Atlantic which would do so much to enrich pop music during the next few years.

65 respect

Words and **music** Otis Redding **1964**

Above Otis Redding

The original recording of **Respect**, sung by its composer Otis Redding, fitted in perfectly with his image as one of the great men of soul. His strong and gritty style of singing gave this raw version of a gospel-type chorus song a particularly macho feel. Though he died in a plane crash aged 36 only two years after recording the song, his influence lived on much longer. His hoarse shout, vocal soaring and funky secular preaching oozed soul. It remains the perfect example of 1960s' black American, gospel-tinged, r&b soul. The original recording featured the great horn player Wayne Jackson – who later became one half of the Memphis Horns and graced hundreds of great pop songs – as well as the legendary Isaac Hayes on keyboards plus Booker T. Jones of Booker T. and the MGs.

But the best-known version of the song was very different. So different that its success in 1967 heralded a new political dawn, both for black Americans and for women's political and sexual liberation. The song became re-authored, showing respect for womankind, not asking but demanding it. And if somehow you didn't understand, Aretha Franklin, probably the greatest female soul singer of all time, helped when she spelt out the word 'respect' for you.

This lesson in spelling (and gender politics) was just one of many changes to the song apparently made by Franklin herself, which also included the great call-and-response vocal arrangement (the 'oohs' and 'sock it to me'), amply demonstrating her background as a gospel singer, and the increase in tempo which adds to the sense of urgency in her cry. Having had some success in the r&b charts, **Respect** became her first, and only, mainstream US No.1 as a solo artist, along the way catapulting her to becoming, at the time, the very symbol of black America itself.

Franklin's background was church. Her daddy really was a preacher man. But as with so many gospel artists, she had to leave the gospel genre to succeed in the mainstream music scene. After several moderate successes for Chess she was signed to Columbia Records by talent scout John Hammond.

White record executives at CBS were keen to exploit her obvious talent by marketing Franklin as an all-round entertainer, a black Barbra Streisand. After several largely unsuccessful albums, she signed to Atlantic Records, now forever synonymous with great black American music. There she teamed up with the production team of Jerry Wexler, Tom Dowd and Arif Marden, individually and collectively responsible for many of the funkiest soul records of this and subsequent eras. The rest, as they say, is definitely her story.

Where adulatory titles for artists are much debated the world over, her mantle as the 'Queen of Soul' is surely unquestioned. Having grown up under her father's ministry, where the likes of Mahalia Jackson, Sam Cooke, Art Tatum, Reverend James Cleveland and Smokey Robinson were fellow church-goers, in 1968 she became the first black woman to appear on the front cover of *Time* magazine. But the list of her achievements doesn't end there. She also eulogised at the funeral of Rev. Martin Luther King (from whom she'd earlier received an honorary award for **Respect**) and sang at both Jimmy Carter and Bill Clinton's presidential inaugurations. Along the way she picked up 17 Grammy awards, and, as with Ray Charles, Sam Cooke and Marvin Gaye, helped bring spiritual passion into mainstream popular music culture. And while God is always with her when she sings, so is that glorious mezzo-soprano voice with its swoops and dives, gospel growls, throaty howls, and a girly yet awesomely sexual tone. Where she may have sung better songs, **Respect** encompassed all these characteristics and allowed her to unleash them onto what was a much poorer world until she came along.

walk on by

Words Hal David **Music** Burt Bacharach **1964**

As a composer, Burt Bacharach had over 120 US chart hits to his name between 1957 and 1990. In the modern pop era, there may be a handful of composers who've matched the volume, but none who have matched the quality of his output. It now seems inconceivable that there was a period in the late 1970s when Bacharach songs were regarded as no better than elevator music. Fellow writer Elvis Costello, one of a growing number of Bacharach disciples, thinks the quality of the songs compares favourably with those of Richard Rodgers.

These days, if they were French wines you'd be investing in them for drinking in 10 or 20 years time. **Walk On By** fits into a list of the less mature vines, 20 or so hits in after 'Magic Moments', 'Make it Easy on Yourself', 'Don't Make Me Over', and 'Twenty-Four Hours From Tulsa', when his style was beginning to settle down and become discernible. Bacharach has never particularly been in the groove of what's current, though **Walk On By** resonates with the Tamla Motown influence of Holland, Dozier, Holland, which is underscored with that hypnotic South American rhythm. The elegiac Hal David lyric fits perfectly into that framework.

The key to understanding Bacharach is to note that he orchestrated his own material. He studied classical composition, and the influence of Debussy and Ravel's musical impressionism is evident in the arrangements of each of his songs. As is the West Coast cool jazz of players like Miles Davis. Tone and texture are of great importance in Bacharach songs, and only those vocalists who understand that their voice is just one part of the overall orchestration are able to carry them off successfully.

After he met backing singer Dionne Warwick at a Drifters session in 1962 she became and remained his preferred vocalist, her great technical skills and understated emotions being the perfect vehicle for his compositions. The next eight years yielded 20 hits and 15 million record sales for the collaboration, including the haunting **Walk On By**. But of equal importance to his success was the fact that he was a horn player as well as a pianist. He didn't come to composition simply via the piano or the guitar, as did the vast majority of his peers, so his songs are not simple chord progressions. Instead he takes a more holistic approach to a song. For Bacharach, '…it has to be heard in the head. Sitting at the piano and writing at the piano and finishing a song at the piano, is totally limiting because I don't hear the volume, the breadth, and the width of it. If you start doing that with synthesizers and midi keyboards, it'd sound great, but when you peel it all back, there'd better be a melody, or what are we talking about?'

Bacharach is most well known for his long-term collaboration with lyricist Hal David. David's ability to work with the melancholy of the melody and the often bizarre rhythms that Bacharach serves up is testament to his lyrical skills. Irving Berlin is said to have not been able to understand why it takes two grown men to write one song. In this instance, despite an often stormy relationship, Bacharach and David married words and music as well as anyone, in a century full of competition.

Left Burt Bacharach

Words and **music** Barry Mann, Cynthia Weill and Phil Spector **1965**

Classic pop at its most sublime, **You've Lost That Lovin' Feelin'** was truly a collaboration of talents. Writers Mann and Weill, artists The Righteous Brothers and the sonic architecture of producer Phil Spector all combined to ensure the song's lasting success. A white soul duo, The Righteous Brothers, comprising Bobby Hatfield and Bill Medley, hadn't had much luck in the charts before this record and found it difficult to match its long-term success afterwards. But they hit big with this one. As well as its worldwide chart success, some say that it tops the all-time radio playlist. It's certainly a song that's lost none of its original lustre and it's still getting regular play on the radio.

The words to **You've Lost That Lovin' Feelin'** were originally a dummy lyric that Barry Mann, who wrote the music, used to help him with the melody.

But Cynthia Weill picked up on the phrase, and from that constructed the song around it. Mann and Weill have since had the grace to credit Spector with adding drama to the original composition even before the song hit the studio and it was he who decided on the title. The song has a classic rising structure that draws the listener into its heightening emotions. The singers deserve some credit too, as it was Hatfield who later added the trilly bits to the melody and Medley who took the lower voice deeper and deeper. The autocratic Spector normally didn't approve of his singers improvising on a song, probably because it would

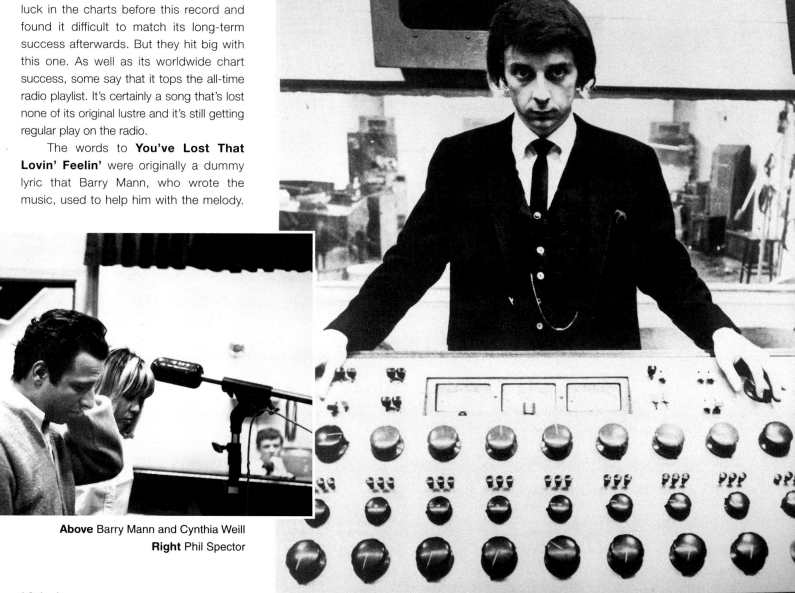

Above Barry Mann and Cynthia Weill
Right Phil Spector

distract the listener from the sound of the production. As his favoured session singer, Darlene Love, admitted, 'he wanted you to keep right in the pocket of the melody'.

The song was recorded in the Gold Star Studios on Santa Monica Boulevard in Hollywood. It was a small studio and much favoured by Spector, who liked to cram his musicians into a small space so that the sound of each separate musician spilled over into the next microphone. That, together with the duplication of each instrument: three drummers, three keyboard players, three bass players, numerous guitarists (often playing in unison), various horns and strings, and a cathedral-like echo, was the essence of his famous Wall of Sound.

Despite all that, none of the main players were confident of success. Spector was rather suspicious of the vocal improvisation, and Mann and Weill wondered about the range of the two male voices, with Medley's bass being chased by Hatfield's falsetto. But they needn't have worried, and the record went to No.1 on both sides of the Atlantic and is now widely regarded as one of Spector's finest productions.

Above The Righteous Brothers

trivia

★ The Righteous Brothers other biggest hit was 'Unchained Melody', also released in 1965.

★ 'Unchained Melody' was featured on the soundtrack of the film *Ghost* released in 1990. On the strength of this the single was re-released and reached No.1 in the UK charts. As a result of that success, their record company re-released **You've Lost That Lovin' Feelin'**, and that reached No.3.

★ Bill Medley also had a hit with his duet with Jennifer Warnes '(I've Had) The Time of My Life' which was featured in the movie *Dirty Dancing* in 1987.

Words and **music** Roger McGuinn, David Crosby and Gene Clark **1966**

So many American bands of the mid-1960s wanted to emulate The Beatles… and The Byrds were no exception. Inspired by the movie *A Hard Day's Night*, this LA-based band set out to make rock and pop music which was both creatively inspired and commercially successful. Both Roger McGuinn and David Crosby had graduated from the New York folk scene, while the band's other two writers, Gene Clark and Chris Hillman, emerged from the country and bluegrass scenes.

After the phenomenal impact of their first single, a jangling guitar version of Bob Dylan's 'Mr Tambourine Man', they were lauded as the harbingers of a whole new genre – folk-rock. McGuinn's distinctive 12-string Rickenbacker guitar combined with Crosby's folk harmonics and Hillman's mellifluous bass lines to shape a gorgeous new sound, which served them well as a springboard into many new forms.

In fact less than a year later, the band would come up with another song that was also heralded as a groundbreaking event. Late December 1966 The Byrds entered RCA Victor's studio in LA to cut the first version of **Eight Miles High**.

The song was developed in stages. It began with a skeletal structure devised by Gene Clark (the band's creative power house before fear of flying set in and led to his premature departure). They then added the free jazz-inspired harmonies of Crosby and an

explosive opening bass line from Hillman. The final piece of the jigsaw was McGuinn's extraordinary 12-string guitar runs – based on the tenor saxophone playing of John Coltrane. 'I wanted the guitar to sound like a saxophone solo,' McGuinn explained. It was a time when the most adventurous rock musicians were delving into more exotic musical styles than those normally associated with pop music. On a coast-to-coast tour of America Crosby had brought a couple of tapes to listen to on the tour bus – John Coltrane's *A Love Supreme* and an album of Ravi Shankar's sitar music.

The Byrds knew they had something unique, a sound which soared to breathtaking heights never reached before in popular music. But then the first setback hit them. The song had been cut using engineers at RCA, and so Columbia, their label, refused to let them release it. Very reluctantly the band went back into the studio and re-recorded the single in January 1966. When it was released it immediately gained widespread radio play which in turn attracted the attention of the Gavin Report, a radio tip sheet which suggested favoured tracks to play. **Eight Miles High** was certainly not one of them, in fact the Gavin Report urged stations *not* to play it because of its alleged drug references. It was a disaster for The Byrds as Middle America went into an anti-drugs frenzy. Several major stations banned it along with their earlier 'Mr Tambourine Man' (claiming that was about a drug dealer) and Dylan's 'Rainy Day Women Numbers 12 and 35', with its unambiguous chorus line 'everybody must get stoned'.

CBS ordered the B-side, 'Why', to be flipped to the A after the first week of release. And Roger McGuinn went to the media claiming the song was really about jet travel. But it was to no avail, sales of the single died away and it barely made the American Top 20. In later years McGuinn admitted the word high 'had a double meaning', and Crosby, who was to prove himself something of a drug connoisseur right through the 1960s and 1970s, said flatly, 'of course it was a drug song. We were stoned when we wrote it.'

Eight Miles High was among The Byrds' most influential songs. Critics talked of a new genre – psychedelic or acid rock – and the passing of time has proved it to be one of the most exceptional works in an exceptional time, predating both The Beatles' *Revolver* and *Sgt Pepper's Lonely Hearts Club Band*. 'For me it was the band at their peak,' McGuinn recalled later, 'it was my favourite period of all.'

Left The Byrds

good vibrations

Above The Beach Boys

Words and **music** Brian Wilson and Mike Love **1966**

The mid-1960s must rank as one of the most creative periods in modern pop music. The impetus of music in contemporary culture at that point was to scale ever more delirious heights and The Beach Boys' Brian Wilson was up there in every way.

With the album *Pet Sounds*, which included the heavenly 'God Only Knows', The Beach Boys had begun to throw off their striped shirt surfer image. Sadly though, the record sold relatively poorly, and while Paul McCartney would later admit it had influenced the making of *Sgt Pepper's Lonely Hearts Club Band*, it was little consolation at the time to Brian Wilson who was crushed by its failure. But, as if to prove a point both to the world and the more conservative members of the band, who thought Brian was taking them just too far out, he made plans to create another little masterpiece, greater than anything he'd done before. As he said later, 'The whole idea behind **Good Vibrations** was that we were setting out to create a record that everybody would spook to.'

Having withdrawn from touring following a series of nervous breakdowns, Brian had been using his time to explore the potential of the studio, and, following the lead of one his heroes, Phil Spector, he conceived a song which would work as a teenage symphony. In the end **Good Vibrations** took six months to record, took 17 sessions in four different studios and cost an extraordinary $50,000 dollars.

Made up of a series of sound collages mixed together, the record featured an array of exotic instruments including sleigh bells, Jews harp, wind chimes, harpsichord, flutes, organ and a theramin. And the song's structure was just as complex, with unexpected tempo changes, full on dynamics and classic Beach Boys close harmonies. Surprisingly all this loving care paid off. **Good Vibrations** sold over a million copies and became the band's best-selling single ever, hitting the No.1 spot on both sides of the Atlantic.

Subsequently, music critics have alluded to the song's slightly dated lyrics, which are very much of their time, and cited the majestic album *Surf's Up* as Brian Wilson's finest work. That's as maybe, but certainly at the time **Good Vibrations** seemed simply monumental. For a man notoriously riddled with self-doubt, the writer was for once assured, 'It was one of the heaviest records that we ever made, if not the heaviest.' Just to prove a point, in December 1966 The Beach Boys displaced The Beatles as the 'World's Best Group' in an *NME* readers' poll. Brian Wilson's wish had come true.

trivia

★ The Beach Boys original line-up was a family affair, and featured three brothers (Brian, Carl and Dennis Wilson), one cousin (Al Jardine) and a schoolfriend (Mike Love). Their first manager was Murray Wilson, father of the brothers.

★ Their compilation album *Endless Summer*, released in 1974, was the first 'oldies' album to top the charts.

★ When Brian Wilson decided to stop touring with the band in 1964, they replaced him for live performances with guitarist and singer Glen Campbell, better known for his hits, 'By the Time I Get to Phoenix', 'Wichita Lineman' and 'Galveston'.

68 strawberry fields forever/penny lane

Words and **music** John Lennon and
Paul McCartney **1967**

In August 1966 The Beatles released *Revolver*, their seventh chart-topping album; and for an increasingly affluent and liberated youth market it confirmed the group's stature as both the trailblazers and the embodiment of the times. The question for them then was how to follow *Revolver*?

In the winter of 1966–67 Lennon and McCartney began work on an album that, rather than just being a collection of possible hits, would have an over-arching theme: their hometown Liverpool. However, their contract required a new single in February 1967, and the first two completed tracks were duly purloined. The result was the double A-side **Strawberry Fields Forever** and **Penny Lane**.

Once again The Beatles had come up with something that seemed to be a quintessence of the time, which beckoned in the listener but which also pointed into an intriguing and unfamiliar world with a friendly avant-gardism. The two songs are both credited as Lennon/McCartney compositions but are individual creations from two very different and separate authors – one intuitive, rebellious, raw, scaldingly sarcastic, the other musically respectful of the past, methodical, polished.

Strawberry Fields was a girls' reform school in Liverpool, close to Lennon's childhood home, but the song has little to do with geographical reality and much more to do with a childlike state of mind suffused with awkward uncertainty and a sense of surreal detachment. The dreamy passivity is also an expression of Lennon's relationship with LSD, and in the recording of **Strawberry Fields Forever** he sought a sound that would be the aural equivalent of the alternative world he was experiencing with the drug. The Beatles had already been pushing at the limits of the recording process, abetted by their producer/collaborator George Martin. They were by now so successful that the Abbey Road studio was virtually at their disposal. Building on the experimentation that had gone into *Revolver*, **Strawberry Fields Forever** took things further with exotic instrumentation: cellos, marching drums, flutes, mellotron (a pre-cursor of the

Above The Beatles

synthesizer), harpsichord, trumpet, backward-recorded drum parts; all painstakingly layered, with two different versions deftly vari-speeded and spliced together. The result, with Lennon's distant dreaming voice, took the pop record into new worlds of sound imagery.

McCartney's song also took its title from a familiar childhood haunt in Liverpool. But whereas **Strawberry Fields Forever** is introspective, **Penny Lane** looks cheerfully outward into a world of observed curiosities: the banker who never wears a mac, a barber showing photographs, a pretty nurse selling poppies from a tray. As the music critic Ian Macdonald put it, 'Couched in the primary colours of a picture book, yet observed with the slyness of a gang of kids straggling home from school, **Penny Lane** is both alive and knowing – but above all thrilled to be alive.'

Like its companion song, **Penny Lane** employs a smorgasbord of instrumentation, with baroque trumpet lines, sound effects and so on, but whereas its counterpart slips and swims, even between keys, **Penny Lane** has the clear melodic leaps and falls and artful dancing rhythms that so clearly bear McCartney's stamp.

In spite of the purloining of **Strawberry Fields Forever** and **Penny Lane**, The Beatles were on an unstoppable creative roll. They carried straight on with work on the new, as yet untitled album with all the invention, wit and unorthodoxy that had gone into those songs, taking it a stage further. The result was *Sgt Pepper's Lonely Hearts Club Band*, an album that, three decades later, would be seen as the defining artistic moment of the 1960s.

Words and **music** Bob Dylan **1968**

The summer of 1967 is looked upon as a seminal time in the story of pop music: flower power, disillusionment with America's involvement in Vietnam, and psychedelic music was thrilling the young and dismaying the forces of propriety and order. This was the year of The Beatles' *Sgt Pepper's Lonely Hearts Club Band*. But from the figure regarded by many as the chief prophet and liberator of this cultural explosion there was silence.

In 1966, Bob Dylan had gone over the handlebars of his motorcycle and into semi-retirement. He had taken the opportunity his accident offered to step off the helter skelter and seek seclusion in a quiet corner of upstate New York.

Dylan's silence ended in January 1968 with *John Wesley Harding*, an album of unadorned songs recorded in Nashville, the heartland of country music.

The album's most enduring song, **All Along the Watchtower**, begins almost shyly with Dylan's familiar thin harmonica quietly backed with a simple country rhythm. There follow three short verses (no obligatory pop song chorus) shot through with biblical allusion (see Isaiah 21, on the fall of Babylon) and archaic idiom evoking a world of mystery and deep unease. And in the centre of this world a fragment of dialogue between two rootless characters, the joker and the thief.

Choosing not to refer to the turbulent contemporary world around him, Dylan creates allegorical fragments of a parallel world in which some serious spiritual questions about what matters in life and what doesn't press for an answer. And the question of an individual's spiritual salvation would become a recurrent theme for Dylan as he grew older.

As a youth, Dylan left his home in Hibbing, Minnesota, changed his surname from Zimmerman and arrived in New York in 1961 to be taken up by the Greenwich Village folk scene in spite of sounding, according to one commentator, 'like a dog with his leg caught in barbed wire'.

In the next five years Dylan's songs appeared on a succession of groundbreaking albums, releasing a swirling song-world of symbolist poetry, biblical allusions, acute details of American life, parades of rootless characters, scourged politicians, self deceivers and unmasked bourgeois materialists. And it spoke to people in droves.

Preceded by songs like 'Subterranean Homesick Blues' (1965), rock music was breaking out of its simple world of verse/chorus/middle-8 and adolescent love, and broadening its horizons by allowing its mass audience to relax with poetic expression. This liberation was Dylan's towering achievement. Dylan's songs have lent themselves to re-interpretation by other artists partly because Dylan's own recordings of them are so direct and unadorned.

This was especially true on Jimi Hendrix's hugely successful cover of **All Along the Watchtower**, where the ominous elements are elaborated in the howling guitar which overlays the song's mysterious scenario. Hendrix had been sent an acetate in advance of the release of *John Wesley Harding* and said, 'I felt like **All Along the Watchtower** was something I had written but could never quite get together... I often feel like that about Dylan.' Reciprocally, Dylan came to regard Hendrix's version as definitive, '...strange though how when I sing it I always feel like it's a tribute to him in some kind of way.'

Above Bob Dylan
Right Jimi Hendrix

Words Paul Anka **Music** Jacques Revaux and Claude Francois **1969**

My Way is nothing short of a phenomenon. It's a strange hybrid of Tin Pan Alley show tune and stadium rock anthem that has become the most popular song for playing at funerals in the UK. Frank Sinatra, whose version was in the UK charts for 108 weeks, is on record as not thinking much of it, and it's certainly not a song that plays to his strengths. It's essentially a love song, a song of self-celebration. One of the first of the 'Me, Me, Me' songs it's certainly the best known. Its maudlin, one size-fits-all lyric is a natural for bar room drunks, third-rate politicians, gangsters and karaoke performers the world over.

Originally a minor hit in France, recorded by Claude Francois, who with Gillis Thibault co-wrote the original (and completely different) lyrics, 'Comme, D'Habitude' is a rather subtle and low-key lament on how relationships gently disintegrate when they lose spontaneity and fall into a pattern. *'Et puis le jour s'en ira. Moi, je reviendra comme d'habitude. Toi, tu seras pas encore rentrée, comme d'habitude. Tout seul j'irai me coucher dans ce grand lit, comme d'habitude...'*

There's also a very early David Bowie version. Kenneth Pitt, his then manager, suggested he translate the original French lyric, and he called it 'Even A Fool Learns to Love'. It was never released, but a snippet of that version can be seen in the BBC's mischievous tribute programme to **My Way**.

The writer of the more famous English lyrics, Paul Anka, was on holiday in France when he heard the original version on the radio. He liked it so much, he bought the rights to the song in the hope of promoting it for the American market. Anka was a successful writer in his own right with 'Puppy Love', 'Lonely Boy' and 'Diana' to his credit. He started to rewrite the lyrics with Sinatra in mind. He claims Sinatra had been pestering him to write a song before he retired. He'd also had it in mind to write a song that reacted to the late 1960s 'Me' generation, the peace and love era, when any behaviour

Above Paul Anka
Left Frank Sinatra

was justifiable, as long as it made you feel good, 'I start playing the piano on that melody, then I go to the typewriter, away from the piano, I go, "and now the end is near and so I face the final curtain". He's retiring. My friend. And all I saw was Sinatra's image and the damn thing started to write itself.'

When he first heard **My Way**, Sinatra described the song as 'kooky'. It was his first recording of a pop song outside the classic American songbook material and certainly gave him an enormous new audience. It is now wheeled out and covered regularly whenever an artist is coming to the end of a career, or has been involved in some scandal and wishes to rebuild the public's affection, and there are now hundreds of versions and dozens of parodies. It was Elvis's first posthumous release when it became a hit all over again. The Sex Pistols recorded a version that treated the song with all the respect it so clearly deserves. There's an unexpected recording by Nina Simone that softens its hard, self-declamatory edges and gives it a gospel feel, but the greatest version, in terms of sales and by association, has to be Sinatra's.

Words and **music** The Corporation (Berry Gordy, Alphonso Mizell, Freddie Perren and Deke Richards) **1970**

The Jackson 5 exploded onto the music scene in 1970 when their first four singles all went to No.1 – the first time this had ever been achieved in the U.S. **ABC** was the third in this groundbreaking sequence, the song highlighting the very young and precocious Michael Jackson. Not since Little Stevie Wonder had Tamla Motown unveiled such a brilliant young talent. As with the two preceding hits, the song was written and produced by a hand-picked team known as The Corporation. Of course, it wasn't any old hand that picked this particular crop; it was Berry Gordy's, the same one that had been feeding the world on a constant diet of great pop songs from his Detroit-based record label. Already responsible for introducing The Supremes, The Temptations, Marvin Gaye and Stevie Wonder to record buyers, Tamla Motown were to have their greatest commercial success with The Jackson 5. Gordy had already worked with Deke Richards on several of The Supremes' hits, but it was Richards who invited two up-and-coming talents, Alphonso Mizell and Freddie Perren, to join The Corporation and complete this particular songwriting committee.

Once again Gordy's vision of how his acts should be showcased, proved inspired. He knew that the talented Jackson family had the potential for mass appeal and sure enough, under his stewardship and with his new team of writers, the five young brothers went on to conquer America, and then the world. Within a few years The Jackson 5 had a networked animated cartoon series based on their characters, were hosting a

musical variety show with another brother and three sisters, and were plastered all over every piece of merchandise imaginable – from posters to sandwich boxes – all leading up to their 1972 commendation from Congress for their 'contributions to American youth'.

Jackie, Jermaine, Marlon, Tito and the 11-year-old Michael (who reminded Gordy of a young Frankie Lymon of 'Why Do Fools Fool in Love' fame) proved to be the last of the superstars to graduate from the Gordy school of pop. Motown had been swinging throughout the 1960s and continued to so do for much of the 1970s, but the cracks were beginning to appear. Holland, Dozier, Holland, one of the greatest songwriting partnerships of all time, were suing Motown for millions of dollars in royalties. And later, the likes of Marvin Gaye, Stevie Wonder and indeed The Jackson 5 were to leave the label, seeking more control of their careers and a greater percentage of the sales.

Pop history really would be much the poorer without **ABC**, as it personifies all that is exciting about pop. It is energetic, catchy, youthful, funky, innocent, soulful and, of course, made to sound as simple as… ABC. Looking at the top-selling records in April 1970, this bubblegum-soul classic sits rather oddly at the tip of a Top 5 that also included The Beatles' 'Let It Be', Norman Greenbaum's one-hit-wonder 'Spirit in the Sky' and John Lennon's 'Instant Karma'. They would seem to be generations apart. But then again, pop's family tree has always been prone to throwing up these kinds of anomalies.

Right Jackie, Jermaine, Marlon, Tito and Michael Jackson

Words and **music** Mick Jagger and Keith Richards **1971**

In 1971 The Rolling Stones left London Records and set up their own label, Rolling Stone Records, with American distribution by Atlantic. It was the beginning of many changes for the band. Despite having generated $200 million during their seven-year run the group were looking at bankruptcy unless they became tax exiles. A new life in France beckoned. On top of this Keith Richards was suffering from a severe bout of band fatigue. Though he had once been the first to attack Brian Jones for missing sessions because of drug abuse it was now his turn to slack off.

As a result the group increasingly turned to other musicians to help them through the recording process. The making of the *Sticky Fingers* album, which featured **Brown Sugar**, was consequently something of a tense affair, with Jagger increasingly angry at Richards' lax attitude and the newfound music buddies he had started hanging out with. Gram Parsons, the wayward country-rock star, got particularly close to Keith in this period, and the song 'Wild Horses' was one of the more fruitful results of the relationship. A second figure in the frame was a 27-year-old Texan sax player, Bobby Keys, who was born on the same day as Keith and used to play with Buddy Holly. 'A lot of people overlooked the fact that it wasn't just Mick Taylor joining the band that changed our sound – it was the whole period when the horns joined too,' Richards commented.

Keys set to work with Richards on the arrangement of a song Jagger had written supposedly inspired by his girlfriend of the time, Marsha Hunt. **Brown Sugar** was a muscular rock song made special by Keys' and Richards' driving riffs and Jagger's steamy lyrics. Many rock critics have since debated the meaning of the song. Was it a tribute to raw heroin which often looks like brown sugar, was it about Mick's personal sexual proclivities, or was it simply part of The Stones' general obsession with America's deep south?

Whatever they meant the lyrics were regarded as some of Jagger's best.

The crude sexual imagery of **Brown Sugar** was further amplified by the *Sticky Fingers* cover. Jagger enlisted his friend Andy Warhol to come up with the infamous sleeve, which featured a male crotch in jeans with a working zip, under which was the red tongue logo that would become the Stones' insignia during the next few years.

The early 1970s may have seen the decline in Richards' health and sanity but for many observers it was one of the richest periods of The Stones' long and varied career. They followed the highly successful *Sticky Fingers* with the raw and ragged *Exile on Main Street* – often cited as their finest album.

Left The Rolling Stones

Words and **music** Stevie Wonder **1972**

Oh to be Jeff Beck! In 1972 Stevie Wonder started writing a song called **Superstition** for his newfound guitar-playing friend. But he liked it so much that he decided to include it on his own soon-to-be-released album *Talking Book*. Beck, as you would if you were given a song by Stevie Wonder, recorded it immediately, but Stevie Wonder's record label liked **Superstition** so much, they put it out as his own single, beating the guitar hero to it. The song went to No.1 in the US charts, Stevie's first in almost a decade.

The sheer maturity and confidence of this supreme artist is evident on **Superstition**. It opens with a simple but infectiously funky drum beat (played without a click track by Stevie Wonder). After a few bars we hear one of the most copied and influential riffs ever written, performed on the clavinet (played by Stevie Wonder) accompanied by a groovy synthesizer bass line (played by Stevie Wonder, naturally). Then the vocals come in – worldly-wise, authoritative, joyous and gospel-flavoured. It is evident by now that this song is going to move you – either physically (you have to really want to stay still if you don't want to dance to this tune), or emotionally – it is just so exhilarating. As soon as the brass section comes in (the only instruments not played by Stevie) you know that this must be what Heaven sounds like.

It just about makes sense that this gift of a groove could have been written, produced and performed by a single person when told that he has been successfully plying his trade for over a decade. What makes no sense at all, is that this person, Stevie Wonder, was still only 22 years old when he did it. Berry Gordy, the man behind Motown, got it spot on when he called Wonder's first album *Little Stevie Wonder Recorded Live – The 12-Year-Old Genius*. Stevie Wonder may no longer be little, but he is indeed still a genius.

Superstition was a by-product of the change in relationship between Stevie Wonder and Motown. Label-mate Marvin Gaye had recently fought, and won, a battle with Berry Gordy over the notion of releasing a themed album. His LP *What's Going On*, released in 1971, was seen by Gordy as being too serious for an audience brought up on pop singles. He was convinced it would be damaging, not only to sales, but to the whole image of the artist. However, it was a huge success, and Gaye, swiftly followed by Wonder, set about renegotiating their contracts ensuring higher royalties and, importantly, more artistic control. Wonder in fact, signed not only the most lucrative contract in the history of Motown, but one that guaranteed him total artistic control... at 21 years old!

Above Stevie Wonder

Music of My Mind came out in 1971 and with it a reasonably successful single in 'Superwoman (Where Were You When I Needed You)'. But it was *Talking Book* the following year that heralded the all-new improved Stevie, now the 22-Year-Old Genius. The album included not only **Superstition**, but also 'You Are The Sunshine of My Life' which also reached No.1 on the *Billboard* charts. A tour as support for The Rolling Stones that year meant that Stevie was able to break into the white audience and with it a place in music history.

The next album, *Innervisions*, reinforced the opinion that a serious talent was here to stay and for the rest of the decade he kept producing great album after great album, all the while expanding his musical horizons to include latin music, reggae and rap, as well as being at the forefront of technology, embracing and pushing the use of synthesizers and all the other advances in recorded sound.

Stevie Wonder's fusion of sophisticated Tin Pan Alley chord sequences with his natural r&b/gospel-influenced sound and energy was less evident in his previous incarnation as Little Stevie. Earlier in his career, he was marketed as more of an all-round entertainer, performing as he did on drums, harmonica and piano. At 21, the historical 'coming of age', this supreme artist did just that. While acknowledging the influence of Sly Stone, Jimi Hendrix and most definitely Curtis Mayfield, Stevie Wonder has carved a unique path for himself which perhaps only Prince has come close to following.

Words and **music** David Bowie **1973**

Although David Bowie's frequent changes of image, direction and career have been written about and discussed to the point of saturation, his songs are often overlooked. **Space Oddity**, released in 1969 to coincide with the US landing on the moon, was his first major hit. Producer Gus Dudgeon tells the story that because Major Tom clearly failed to return in the song, the BBC refused to play it until the real mission was successful. He and Bowie spent weeks willing the crew to return safely because, in those days, without the BBC's patronage there was no chance of the song being a hit. Well they did and it was.

The song has been re-recorded and re-released several times, but each incarnation includes the same opening lyrical gambit immediately setting the tone for what is to follow. It has a daring and unusual combination of music and lyrics with some eccentric scanning that puts the emphasis on the last syllable in the line, creating a rather uncomfortable tension.

Bowie's fascination with space figures frequently in his early career. After announcing to *Melody Maker* in 1972 that he was gay (the first of Bowie's personality makeovers) he reinvented himself from hippy singer-songwriter into Ziggy Stardust – full-on glam-rocker from another planet. Backed by his band, The Spiders From Mars, he carried on his quest to take over the Earth with the classic album *The Rise and Fall of Ziggy Stardust and the Spiders From Mars*. But by 1973 he had changed again, this time into Aladdin Sane, before releasing another of his finest albums of the same name.

In 1973 **Space Oddity** became Bowie's first US hit, while **Life on Mars**, taken from an earlier album *Hunky Dory*, continued his impressive sequence of UK chart success. Although his intriguing persona suggests otherwise, most of Bowie's best tunes are essentially love songs. But as with much of his material, his overt romanticism is toughened by smart lyric writing and an overriding sense of the dramatic. The tenderness of the piano playing on **Life on Mars**, with its big build towards the chorus, is testament to his all round musical abilities. Not only is he a fine singer with one of the most distinctive voices around, but he also plays keyboards, saxophone, guitar and drums.

While he may often pretend to play the James Dean-type, of arrogant anti-hero, Bowie has proven over many years that there is real substance behind his many styles. His savvy self-promotion combined with his great gift for melody and lyrical imagery has kept Bowie at the very top of pop's tree of inspiration.

Left David Bowie

> **space oddity** has a daring and unusual combination of music and lyrics

no woman no cry

Words and **music** Bob Marley **1974**

In 1975 *the* gig to be at in London was Bob Marley and the Wailers at the Lyceum. The crowd was different from the usual rock gig – half black and half white, and the marijuana smoke was denser than usual. The audience was also divided between the cognoscenti, who'd been following the still arcane world of reggae, and the curious, who'd been attracted by Island Record's packaging and promotion of three albums all released together the previous year. The first two, *Catch a Fire* and *Burnin'* are ascribed to The Wailers – Bob Marley, Peter Tosh and Bunny Livingstone – the third, however, *Natty Dread*, was ascribed to Marley alone with The Wailers listed as his band. Neither Tosh nor Livingstone was on the record and all the songs were credited to Marley. He was out on his own.

The song that emerged from the gig, recorded and released on *Live at the Lyceum*, and which became his first international hit was **No Woman No Cry**, one of the standout tracks. Although the song had already been included on *Natty Dread*, the live version created a new congregation of devotees who'd previously only had a passing interest in Jamaican music. To those who knew, reggae became the most misunderstood popular music, even more so than country.

Cashing in on the zeitgeist and with a stroke of marketing genius, Island printed Marley's lyrics on the album sleeves and used photographs that played up his image as a new breed of Third World rebel. The ploy worked and the world could no longer ignore the magnificence of Jamaican music.

Above Bob Marley

Marley became the leader of a musical assault that for a while made reggae the most influential music on the planet. He became more than a reggae star or a rock star. Like Nelson Mandela, his mere name became a byword for a critique of the way the world was run.

No Woman No Cry is the key song from the key album in reggae's history. The beauty of both the lyrics and the tune was an indication of Marley's ability to transcend a given musical form through a combination of passion and lightness of touch.

His yearning address to the woman and the song's faint air of nostalgia drew an audience that had never had and never would have any experience of sitting 'in the government yard in Trenchtown'. Its lyricism drew them into the subtext of Marley's politics and the puzzling but powerful message of Rastafari. To the outsider, the ideas of Rastafarianism are challenging to say the least, especially the proposition that Haile Selassie, the late Emperor of Ethiopia, was and is God. Rastafarianism developed in Jamaica in the 1950s as a spiritual quest that provided an alternative to the more established religious belief. Ras Tafari was the real name of Haile Selassie and he claimed direct lineage from the biblical King Solomon. Around the end of the 1960s many of Jamaica's leading musicians became Rastafarians. It was a life of rebellion and defiance and Marley became its prime ambassador.

Marley merges the personal, the political and the spiritual without any apparent effort: the woman cries for herself and for the people who preserve their integrity in the face of poverty and oppression with the simple apocalyptic message that such injustice cannot last. The result is something moving and sorrowful, politically motivating and spiritually uplifting all at the same time.

> " the world could no longer ignore the magnificence of jamaican music "

Words Hütter/Schneider/Schult **Music** Hütter/Schneider **1975**

Kraftwerk were a German art-house band who altered the way we listen to music. They were the catalyst for the significant change that the invention of electronically generated sound had on pop music. Unlike the previous generation, the kicks they got were not from Route 66. In Germany during the 1960s there was no form of pop music other than American and British imports, and Kraftwerk were influenced by technology and the sounds generated by industry. Armed with a classical training and the knowledge imparted to them while studying under avant garde composer Karlheinz Stockhausen, the two founder members of Kraftwerk, Ralf Hütter and Florian Schneider, set about revolutionizing pop.

Autobahn is a 22-minute sonic portrait of a car journey. We hear engines, horns and other cars passing by, and feel the monotony of such a journey. There are changes of speed and of surrounding landscape, all made solely by the use of synthesizers, drum machines and tape recorders. Kraftwerk (German for 'powerplant') were not writing songs in the traditional sense, they were recreating the sounds that nature and machinery make.

Lyrically **Autobahn** is not very challenging. This was their first foray into the world of text, and Kraftwerk had to have help from writer Emil Schult. Amusingly, the press accused Kraftwerk of stealing the song's main refrain 'fahr'n, fahr'n, fahr'n' ('drive, drive, drive'), from The Beach Boy's 'Fun, Fun, Fun', a claim that was subsequently denied. Overall though, the text continues the minimalist theme of the music – it is functional not decorative and does not suggest any form of emotion whatsoever. It ain't no love song.

Above Kraftwerk

trivia

★ In the late 1960s the band opened their own studio in Dusseldorf, called Kling Klang, recording their first work under the name Organisation.

★ The members of Kraftwerk try to remain isolated from the music business, and their studio allegedly has no fax and no phone, and they remain strictly without management of any kind.

It is hard to understate the importance of Kraftwerk on the pop music of the next 25 years. Their influence in the mid-1970s was felt in almost all aspects of pop. Firstly in the synth-pop of such bands as Joy Division, Ultravox, The Human League and Depeche Mode, all of whom were ardent admirers, and secondly in hip-hop and the whole spectre of modern dance music, as introduced by Grandmaster Flash and Afrika Bambaataa. The latter used a sample from Kraftwerk's 'Trans Europe Express' on his groundbreaking single 'Planet Rock'. But they were also influential in performance, where the likes of David Bowie, Talking Heads, Laurie Anderson and Peter Gabriel cited Kraftwerk's 1977 tour of the US when they dressed in mannequin outfits, as a big influence on their view of concert staging. Throughout Kraftwerk's career, the band, in whatever costume they were dressed, would remain pretty much static during their concerts, claiming that their fingers were doing all the necessary singing and dancing. This, as in all aspects of their make-up, forced audiences to use their own imagination, to create their own scenarios, be they joyous or sorrowful. Perhaps this is the reason that Kraftwerk remain so popular with artists of all genres: they created the ultimate blank canvas upon which everyone projected their own personal images.

Words and **music** Benny Andersson and Bjorn Ulvaeus **1976**

Abba took the world by storm in the mid-1970s and remained at the top until they disbanded in 1982. They are said to have shifted 280 million units in their career so far; in fact over 3,000 Abba albums are still sold throughout the world every day. Their career yielded 19 Top 10 hits in all. ABBA – Agnetha, Benny, Bjorn and Anni-Frida – burst onto the scene in 1974 with their Eurovision Song Contest-winning song 'Waterloo' which was No.1 in four countries, and became the first of their nine UK No.1s.

Dancing Queen was their biggest-selling single and has been covered countless times by, among others, squillions of karaoke-lovers around the world, by U2 during their ZooTV tour, by REM and more recently by Kylie Minogue during the closing ceremony of the 2000 Olympics in Sydney. Australia has a special affinity with Abba. It was there that they filmed *Abba – The Movie*, a behind-the-scenes look at their 1977 world tour; Abba songs are included in top Aussie movies *The Adventures of Priscilla – Queen of the Desert* and *Muriel's Wedding,* and Bjorn Again, the Abba tribute band, emanate from Down Under. But Abba were even bigger than that. Their official web site proudly proclaims that throughout the 1970s and 1980s they were the biggest thing, even in Bolivia! It is in such proud claims and trivia that we see what made the world love Abba. They were so uncool.

Dancing Queen was first performed at a gala concert honouring Silvia, the day before her wedding to Carl Gustav, the King of Sweden. In the summer of 1976 it topped the singles charts in the UK as well as in Australia, Austria, Belgium, Germany, New Zealand, Norway, Sweden and Switzerland, before going on to become their only US No.1. Lyrically, the song is typical of Abba – uncontroversial, aspirational and inclusive – relating a personal story to the listener.

Musically, Abba were very eclectic. Although all the songs have feel-good, 1970s' disco undertones, they mixed up-to-the-minute synthesizers with traditional horn sections, heavy rock guitar, luscious strings, accordions (of course), marimbas, various other assorted percussive instruments and their own unique clear-as-a-bell harmonies. **Dancing Queen** had all of this (except, inexplicably, the accordion) plus honky-tonk piano. Andersson and Ulvaeus wrote not just great tunes but great counter-melodies. Just as with all the really great pop songs from this era, you find yourself singing along, not just with the singer, but also the pianist, violinist and guitarist as they reply to the melody.

Abba truly were the kings of pop. Cheesy maybe, but every one of their hits was so tightly written and produced that listeners were swept up in their version of a wall of sound and enraptured by their mini fairy-stories, a world in which everything is rosy and love is just around the corner. Oh, almost forgot, the two guys married the two girls. Sweet! But it didn't last. And did you know that between 1974 and 1980 Abba were second only to Volvo as Sweden's biggest earning exports?

Left Abba

Words and **music** Glenn Frey, Don Henley and Don Felder **1977**

Taking their lead from bands like The Byrds (circa *Sweetheart of the Rodeo*) and The Flying Burrito Brothers, The Eagles made their name as a slick country-rock band. Their first single, 'Take It Easy', cleverly commercialized California's new style of mellow rock and introduced it to a much wider audience.

Whereas previous bands working in the country-rock genre had stumbled along the way through bad management or the kind of lifestyle excesses that prevailed at the time, The Eagles were determinedly professional. David Geffen, their label manager at Asylum, was even more ambitious, and together, armed with a pile of denim, cowboy boots and well-crafted songs, they set out to conquer the world – which is exactly what they did.

The band had been together for the best part of five years when they went into the Record Plant in LA in March 1976 to start recording the album that would become *Hotel California*. But by this stage in the group's history the first rush of creativity, which had carried them through their early career, had noticeably faded. In short, they didn't have a single finished song.

As a consequence the sessions were long and laboured. Added to this the group's principal writers were notorious for demanding endless retakes in search of that perfect sound. It was this obsession which led some critics to complain that their sound had become *too* polished, a criticism Henley always refuted. 'Yes, we strived for perfection, but what's wrong with that,' he complained in a later interview.

The album was finished a year later, the final sessions taking place in Florida after various members of the band got so paranoid they were convinced that LA was about to be consumed by another earthquake. The LP was released in January 1977, and went straight to the top of the American charts, staying there for 8 weeks, and remaining in the Top 50 for 63 weeks. The title track was released as

Above The Eagles

a single, and this also made the No.1 spot, further boosting the album's sales which went on to sell over twelve million copies – massive by anybody's standards.

As a song, **Hotel California** left something to be desired. Its ersatz reggae rhythms grated on many British ears which were more accustomed than the Americans to the real thing. But its lyrics, which depicted California as a dream gone bad, had more substance than most of the band's output. 'That song was about the demise of the '60s and the decadence and escapism of the '70s,' Henley explained. However, many people either misunderstood the song, thinking it was some kind of celebration of America (much as Springsteen's 'Born in the USA' was misconstrued) or felt The Eagles themselves were part of the decadence they claimed to be attacking. With punk and new wave breaking, suddenly The Eagles looked like another band of spoilt rock stars whingeing into their tequila sunrises.

With such success the band could easily afford to dismiss their critics and stick to their guns. 'We were using California as a microcosm for the rest of the world,' Frey maintained. 'California is merely an example that everybody holds up to the light because California is simply the last frontier.'

god save the queen

Words and **music** Steve Jones, Paul Cook, Glen Matlock and Johnny Rotten **1977**

For many, 1977 was a watershed year in rock music. A quick look at the No.1 singles that year, including 'Silver Lady' by David Soul, 'Chanson D'Amour' by Manhattan Transfer, 'Angelo' by Brotherhood of Man, 'Yes Sir I Can Boogie' by Baccara and 'Mull of Kintyre' by Wings, tells you why. Sick of the bombast of supergroups like Yes, the overindulgence of progressive rock bands like Pink Floyd, and the allegedly cocaine-fuelled nonsense of The Eagles, the youth of Britain rebelled. Along came the spitting, screaming and spiky Sex Pistols.

Their first single, 'Anarchy in the UK', was released in October 1976 and was a minor hit. But after a notorious 2-minute TV appearance on the BBC's *Nationwide*, in which they swore a lot, they became national celebrities. Crashing guitar chords and snarling lyrics gave their music energy and a freshness that people were crying out for. After a disastrous tour, huge publicity and several court appearances, the Sex Pistols released a second single, **God Save the Queen**, in June 1977 to coincide with the Queen's Silver Jubilee. Despite a radio ban and the fact that several chain stores refused to stock the record, it reached No.2 in the British charts.

Although its conventional guitar-driven framework was hardly revolutionary, **God Save the Queen** struck a massive chord. For many who lived on Thatcher's breadline Britain the Jubilee was a nonsense and an insult. They felt they had no part in it and this song seemed to sum up their feelings. The establishment was horrified, and in revenge for what was seen as a V-sign at the monarchy, several members of the band were attacked, both in the press and in the street.

Amid more controversy and lurid tabloid stories two further singles appeared, 'Pretty Vacant' and 'Holidays in the Sun', before the release of their legendary *Never Mind the Bollocks, Here's the Sex Pistols* album. Despite the fact that it is the quintessential punk record everything fell apart after that. Rotten left to form Public Image Ltd, and Sid Vicious, by that time on a murder charge, died of a heroin overdose in New York. The band soldiered on, but had become a parody of itself, and imploded in 1978.

Of course, any movement that claims that there's no future is doomed just as soon as it begins, and so it was with punk. But punk's real legacy was in sweeping away the old guard, bringing music back to the people, allowing even those who only knew three chords on the guitar to make records. Thousands of new groups appeared, some of them, like The Clash, The Stranglers and The Buzzcocks, going on to fame and fortune. Music hasn't been the same since.

Above Johnny Rotten

> **"** despite a radio ban and the fact that several chain stores refused to stock the record, it reached No.2 in the British charts **"**

> **Well, Dylan changed the rules. He fused a lyrical imagination with a beat. Some who followed his lead were not as talented as he was. And some were equally talented, but utterly different, like Joni Mitchell. I don't think they could have existed so comfortably, doing such original and forthright lyrical music, if Dylan hadn't been there first.**
>
> Elvis Costello on the debt owed by singer-songwriters to Bob Dylan.

Although many early pop vocalists – including rock 'n' rollers like Chuck Berry and Buddy Holly – sang their own songs, up to the 1960s the national hit parades in the US and the UK were largely supplied with songs written by the Tin Pan Alley professionals and sung by the Bobbies, Rickies and Frankies. Up to that point writers and performers were traditionally regarded as two different animals. In the early 1970s the term 'singer-songwriter' was coined, albeit by the record company marketing departments, and applied to the legions of performers that followed Bob Dylan. They were not doing anything new, of course – blues and country artists like Hank Williams and Chuck Berry had preceded them through the century. But what distinguished this new music genre was that the artists recorded albums rather than singles. Underscoring all this was the growth of FM radio, whose stations thrived on the new format.

Say You Want A Revolution

The 1960s had seen a revolution – a desire for freedom of thought and of expression – and this was reflected in a greater freedom in lyric writing. From 1964, groups – in particular British groups led by The Beatles – began to fill the charts spelling the end for the solo pop singers. Within a couple of years The Beatles moved on from 'She loves you, yeah, yeah, yeah' to more worldy concerns. Kennedy's assasination had signalled the end of the age of innocence and, with America embroiled in the Vietnam war, the sentiments of songs like 'It's My Party (And I'll Cry If I Want To)' seemed purile and inappropriate. Pop music was about to grow up and move to the next phase.

Out of the Greenwich Village coffee bar circuit in New York came a new generation of singers who showed that it was possible to write about more worldly concerns and without resorting to the cheesy gimmickry of Tin Pan Alley. Folk singers such as Bob Dylan, Joan Baez, Roger McGuinn, Tim Hardin, Phil Ochs and Judy Collins picked up where Woody Guthrie left off; many of their songs were based on traditional tunes with lyrics of protest and disillusionment.

Left Bob Dylan performing at Gerde's Folk City, Greenwich Village, NY

Their alignment with civil rights issues stimulated their growth as songwriters. Dylan's 'Blowin' in the Wind' was a barometer of the mood of pessimism among America's youth in the mid-1960s. One of the early signs that things had changed came with Dylan's back to the roots album *John Wesley Harding*, a clear recognition of his traditional folk roots after the controversy over his electric adventures.

The Singer-Songwriters

The late 1960s saw an escalation of popularity of singer-songwriters: Tom Paxton, Tom Rush, Jim Webb, James Taylor, Jackson Browne, Leonard Cohen, Joni Mitchell and Van Morrison all recorded influential albums during these years. Across the Atlantic, The Beatles, under the influence of Dylan, were turning out much more sophisticated songs by the late 1960s, and in turn were a major influence on folk-rock group The Byrds, who emulated Beatles' harmonies while recording covers of Bob Dylan songs. Former (unsuccessful) Brill Building writer Paul Simon was launched as a folk singer by English folkie Martin Carthy. For a couple of years, Simon became a staple figure on the British folk music. Carthy became a major figure in the British folk movement, working with Bert Jansch, Ashley Hutchins, Richard Thomson, Sandy Denny and John Martyn.

Back in the USA, Paul Simon reunited with his school friend Art Garfunkel. As Simon & Garfunkel they had huge worldwide success, and songs like 'Mrs Robinson', 'The Boxer' and 'Bridge Over Troubled Water' are now strong reminders of the era. Following in their wake were other folk-rock acts like Buffalo Springfield, out of which came Crosby, Stills & Nash, and eventually Neil Young.

The End of the Decade

Folk music was not the only music around at the end of the 1960s. True The Beatles had broken up, but The Rolling Stones had hit their purple patch with albums like *Beggars Banquet* and *Let It Bleed*. However, in general rock music, or progressive music as some people liked to call it, was going through a messy patch and had rather lost its way. Hendrix got everyone going, but no one, including

Hendrix himself, seemed to know which direction that was. Many artists were becoming a little self indulgent. Some were taking too many drugs and in the process taking their own lives – the likes of Jim Morrison, Janis Joplin, Brian Jones and even Hendrix himself. Others, like Eric Clapton, The Who and Pink Floyd, were losing themselves in 20-minute songs featuring 10-minute drum solos, rock operas or experiments in quadrophonic sounds. With the heavy metal of bands like Black Sabbath and Deep Purple also flying high, it seemed for a while as though the song had lost its place in popular music.

But these setbacks apart there was a sense that popular music had grown up after *Sgt Pepper's Lonely Hearts Club Band*, *Pet Sounds* and *Fifth Dimension*, and could now tackle more serious subjects.

Three events marked the end of the 1960s and the demise of psychedelia: Woodstock, the Altamont rock festival and the death of The Rolling Stones' Brian Jones, all taking place in 1969. Woodstock, though successful and for many a reminder of how things could be if 'peace, love and brotherhood' were a reality and not a fantasy, was musically reflective of the self-indulgent doodlings of bands like Santana and, increasingly, Jimi Hendrix. Altamont was a disaster. The Rolling Stones had misguidedly accepted an offer from the Hell's Angels San Francisco chapter to do the security for the event. It lacked both peace and love. Several bands, including Jefferson Airplane, were attacked by the so-called security guards. The event ended in turmoil when a man, who had allegedly brandished a hand gun, was battered to death by a number of Angels armed with pool cues. Brian Jones's death summed up the whole thing. Depressed through feeling increasingly sidelined by the rest of the band he co-founded, he was found drowned in his own swimming pool with high levels of narcotics in his blood. Within a year, The Beatles would split up and prime American bands, like The Beach Boys and The

Right Woodstock festival

Byrds, would start to atomize. The burn out from the 1960s took its toll and individuals began to turn to introspection in the big come down.

Album Time

Smelling the potential for making more money selling albums rather than singles, record companies went into overdrive marketing their artists and their product. One of the first major successes was *Tapestry*, the second album by (former Tin Pan Alley writer) Carole King. Released in 1970 this album went on to sell 15 million copies, starting a trend for commercial female singer-songwriters such as Linda Ronstadt, Carly Simon and Laura Nyro.

These artists, creating their own music with no one, not even other members of their band, to tell them what to do, were able to draw the subject matter of their songs from a wider palette. Lyrics became more personal, although they were often veiled by layers of metaphors and obscure imagery. Singer-songwriters drew primarily from folk and country music. Although certain writers, like Paul Simon, Randy Newman and Carole King, incorporated the song craft of Tin Pan Alley Pop, on many albums of the time the use of language and lores of poetry so evident in the work of lyricists like Cole Porter and Ira Gershwin, was thin on the ground. This is one of the reasons the older generations of lyric writers and performers disliked rock music so vehemently. Lyric writing became a more colloquial thing, incorporating the language of everyday speech with less concern for the old rules.

The main concern for many singer-songwriters was the song itself, and not necessarily the performance. In the 1970s many records by singer-songwriters sounded similar. Usually played solo on guitar or piano, their music, for the most part, is spare, direct and reflective, which places the emphasis on the song itself.

James Taylor, Jackson Browne, and Joni Mitchell were the quintessential singer-songwriters of the 1970s, best heard on albums like *Mud Slide Slim*, *The Pretender* and *Blue* respectively. Their influence on the songwriters that followed was matched only by Dylan's lasting legacy. Singer-songwriters were at the height of their popularity in the early 1970s, and although they faded away from the pop chart, they never disappeared altogether.

In the late 1970s, Rickie Lee Jones and Joan Armatrading crossed over into the pop charts, as did Suzanne Vega and Tracy

If there was an award for the longest-lasting singer-songwriter then surely Neil Young would win it. For almost 40 years he has written and sung great songs, about love, politics and life, covering country, rock 'n' roll and even punk and electronic styles to great acclaim. A superb guitarist, a gifted songwriter, it is his cussed insistence to go his own way that have earned Young a unique place in the history of rock, a world which would be considerably less bright without him in it.

Chapman in the late 1980s. More recently, a number of songwriters – like David Gray and P.J. Harvey – have kept the tradition alive.

The Black Experience

Following the success and critical acclaim of Marvin Gaye's highly politicized album *What's Going On*, black writers, like Bobby Womack, Ritchie Havens, Smokey Robinson and Curtis Mayfield, were now empowered to deal with issues from a black perspective. Isaac Hayes, son of a sharecropper from Covington, Texas, had carved a career as a staff writer for Stax Records in Memphis. He co-wrote a number of hits, most notably 'Soul Man' for Sam & Dave, and released a number of innovative albums under his own name. But in 1971 he hit paydirt. In writing the soundtrack to the film *Shaft*, Hayes got to No.1 in the US and UK charts, won himself an Oscar and set a trend for 'blaxploitation' movies that lasted for most of the 1970s.

Other artists were releasing high-quality, musically innovative albums during the 1970s, notably Stevie Wonder with *Talking Book*, John Martyn with *Solid Air*, and Van Morrison with *Astral Weeks* – all to become durable bestsellers. Californian cynics, like Randy Newman and Tom Waits, looked over their shoulders and bought a subverted notion of romance for a (probably non-existent) golden age. Lou Reed and David Bowie picked up where Velvet Underground ended with their dark excursions into gender and identity.

Only a few of the above would be making creditable records by the mid-1980s, but a handful, including Dylan, Stevie Wonder, Paul Simon, Lennon and McCartney, Joni Mitchell and Smokey Robinson, have ended up with a body of songs that will probably stand alongside the masters of American popular song of 40 years previously.

Right Joni Mitchell

the top 100

songs
79-90

Stayin' alive

Don't cry for me Argentina

Love will tear us apart

Don't you want me

The message

(Sexual) healing

Relax

Careless whisper

Sledgehammer

I still haven't found what I'm looking for

Never gonna give you up/

I should be so lucky

Back to life (however do you want me)

79 stayin' alive

Above The Bee Gees

Words and **music** Barry, Robin and Maurice Gibb **1978**

The soundtrack to the movie *Saturday Night Fever* must go down as one of the best ever. Not only did it include this particular Bee Gees hit as well as 'How Deep Is Your Love', 'Night Fever' and 'More Than A Woman', it was also home to 'If I Can't Have You' by Yvonne Elliman, 'Boogie Shoes' by KC and The Sunshine Band and 'Disco Inferno' by The Tramps. The film was so successful that the soundtrack album was the biggest selling record of all time until Michael Jackson's *Thriller* topped it. Incredibly, you could say 'Bee Gees' and 'disco' in the same sentence. For a few years this was a good thing – all that they did seemed to turn to gold (or rather double-platinum) – then suddenly disco sucked, and this high-voiced trinity of big-toothed brothers rapidly fell from grace. But these guys are the original 'comeback kids', reinventing themselves every few years, and have kept their undoubted talent at the forefront of pop for 33 years, and counting.

Strongly influenced by black American close-harmony group The Mills Brothers, the Gibb brothers, originally from Australia, found the lure of London's 'swinging '60s' just too much to ignore. One of their demo tapes found its way to Robert Stigwood, an associate of Brian Epstein, who immediately signed them up to a five-year management deal. Together they went on to produce a steady stream of hit records, perhaps most notably with 'New York Mining Disaster 1941' and 'Massachusetts'. However, after a few years, with the demise of the Fab Four, the Bee Gee's popularity waned. In 1974 the brothers flew to America to meet up with legendary Atlantic Records producer Arif Mardin. It was Mardin who pushed their music towards a much more r&b feel, and the Bee Gees, massive fans of Stevie Wonder and Ray Charles, had suddenly found the sound with which they are now most readily identified. Although Mardin was not involved in the *Saturday Night Fever* project, his influence was clear, and the Bee Gees became one of the few white acts to successfully exploit the 1970s' disco sound and come out with any credibility.

Stayin' Alive typified all that was cool in the late 1970s. The opening lyric says it all. Confident, cocky, streetwise and upbeat, the music directly complements Travolta's character from the film and indeed typifies the character of this, the last 'safe' era of sexual excess. The orchestration is as tight as expected from a Bee Gees offering, as is the accompanying band. Ultimately, as good though their high-pitched harmonies are, it is their finely honed songwriting skills that has made **Stayin' Alive** and their considerable songbook such a lasting success. As is well known, the Bee Gee's genuine talent turned them into one of the world's most successful recording groups. What is slightly less well known is that they were the talent behind such songs as Dionne Warwick's 'Heartbreaker', Diana Ross' 'Chain Reaction', the title track to the musical *Grease*, and Dolly Parton and Kenny Rogers' 'Islands in the Stream'. Barry Gibb's collaboration with Barbra Streisand, *Guilty*, remains her biggest selling album to date. Even when away from the full gaze of the public eye, their hands have always (sometimes unknowingly) reached out for more from three of pop's more enduring talents.

> " stayin' alive typified all that was cool in the late 1970s "

Words Tim Rice **Music** Andrew Lloyd Webber **1979**

The music of Andrew Lloyd Webber is both acclaimed and denounced with equal intensity. The public votes with its feet and Lloyd Webber has no peers when it comes to putting bums on seats. Yet the *Rolling Stone Record Guide* says of the original cast recording of the musical Evita '…wooden singing, horrid songwriting and a stupid concept… It's up to you to prevent it [from becoming a hit]'. Well the public signally ignored the book's advice and **Don't Cry For Me Argentina**, the big song from *Evita*, was a No.1 hit for Julie Covington in 1976. And Lloyd Webber's success didn't end there. 'You Must Love Me', also from *Evita*, won an Oscar 20 years later for the film version starring Madonna, and in *Cats* he has the longest running musical in the history of both the West End and Broadway. He became a knight, won numerous Grammy, Olivier and Tony Awards, and made an absolute fortune.

When compared to the great composers of 20th-century musical theatre – Gershwin, Kern, Porter, Berlin, Lerner and Loewe, Bernstein, and Rodgers and Hammerstein (Rice and Lloyd Webber's particular favourites) – Lloyd Webber doesn't make it to the top table. His talent, however (and it is a talent), is in judging the sort of story that will interest the theatre-going public. In creating his own brand of broad appeal, easy-listening pop music – albeit owing more to 'Puppy Love' than 'Night and Day' (see page 68) – Lloyd Webber has reinvented the vernacular of musical theatre and can very reasonably lay claim to having increased the numbers and widened the constituency of the theatre-going public. Once a middle-class occupation, it is now mass-market entertainment. Accessibility is very much his watchword and the key to his success.

Above Andrew Lloyd Webber and Tim Rice

Evita is a straightforward rags-to-riches story. Set in Argentina, it is based on the life-story of Eva, wife of Juan Peron, who was President during the 1940s and 1950s and very briefly in the 1970s. It tells of her humble beginnings, her romance with Juan, and her love affair with the Argentinian people, who, it appears, adored her even more than they adored her husband. It's a kind of South American Dream. Within months of her premature death from cancer at the age of 33, her husband was deposed in a military coup. It seems that she was, as the saying goes, the great woman behind a great man.

Tim Rice collaborated with Lloyd Webber on a couple of other projects prior to *Evita*. Their first hit was *Joseph and His Amazing Technicolour Dreamcoat*, though they were even more successful with *Jesus Christ Superstar*. *Evita*, of course, went global. Though many modern stage musicals rather lack the lightness of touch so prevalent in the golden age of the genre, Rice's literary approach to his lyrics suited the seriousness of the Webber style. What Lloyd Webber brought to the collaboration was the realization that the audience wanted more than just a few good tunes. They wanted the whole shooting match – rollerblading in *Starlight Express*, the mask and the dry ice in *Phantom of the Opera* and the revolving set from *Sunset*

Boulevard are all good examples. Of course, he could also deliver a good tune.

However, the relationship between composer and lyricist went the same way as that of other notable collaborations, such as Lerner and Loewe and Rodgers and Hart, and after *Evita*, Rice and Lloyd Webber fell out. Rice went on to write pop songs with varying degrees of success. He also collaborated with Abba's Bjorn Ulvaeus and Benny Andersson on the hit musical *Chess* and with Cliff Richard on *Heathcliff*. More recently he wrote music and songs for several Disney films, including *Aladdin*, *Beauty & The Beast* and *The Lion King*.

Whatever you think about the modern musical, the now Lord Lloyd Webber's positioning within the genre remains peerless. During the 1980s the West End survived only because of the popularity of his shows. His clever use of casting – recognizing the mass appeal of actors such as Michael Crawford, Elaine Paige and Jason Donovan, combined with his ability to exploit a good emotive melody, has succeeded in entertaining millions of theatre-goers throughout the world for more than thirty years. No mean feat.

Below Elaine Paige

Words and **music** Ian Curtis **1980**

Part of Manchester's post-punk scene, Joy Division emerged in 1978 playing their first show at a city club called Pip's. Their original name, Warsaw – after David Bowie's song 'Warszawa' on the LP *Low*, gave a strong clue about where they were coming from. Their music was gothic, dark and brooding, led by drums and the melodic bass of Peter Hook. But the lyrical and vocal focus was firmly on singer Ian Curtis whose neurotic stage presence dominated the group. Although the other members, Bernard Albrecht (later Sumner) and Steven Morris, would emerge later as significant forces in New Order, the band's second incarnation, it was Curtis who appeared to lead.

The band quickly attracted a devoted following and signed to Tony Wilson's Factory label, an organization based on Andy Warhol's notion of a total concept, the label coming complete with an in-house producer, Martin Hannet, and sleeve designer Peter Saville. Each had something to offer and Factory quickly established itself as a calling point for the moody young men of the early 1980s. Hannet's production skills gave anything he touched an air of dark, ambient mystery; Peter Saville's artwork was equally distinctive and unsettling; while TV presenter Tony Wilson provided the label with an inflated sense of purpose that was perfect for the times.

Joy Division cemented their early promise with a bleak first album, *Unknown Pleasures*, released in 1979. Shrugging off accusations of flirting with a kind of artistic neo-fascism, they assumed the mantle of the great white hopes in the British indie scene. A second album, *Closer*, followed in early 1980. Then on 18 May that year, on the eve of the band's first visit to America, Ian Curtis was found hanged at his home in Macclesfield. The coroner's verdict was suicide. The subsequent outpourings in the music press were gushing to say the least. It's one thing to be a rock star, but a dead rock star is something else. When it emerged that Curtis was wrestling in his mind over the two women in his life, his lover and wife, the myth was sealed.

Enter, **Love Will Tear Us Apart**, complete with a tombstone-style sleeve from Saville. The single was, in fact, vintage Joy Division – sombre, richly melancholic and dripping with circumstantial meaning. The lyrics seemed unbearably poignant.

It was almost inevitable that Curtis would be enshrined in the pantheon of rock's martyrs. The fact that the song did have great strength and Curtis's vocals were wonderfully atmospheric hardly mattered. **Love Will Tear Us Apart** reached No.8 in the UK charts, which for an independent single of the time was virtually unheard of.

Shortly afterwards the band evolved into New Order (the name taken from prostitutes in German concentration camps during the Second World War), a band who would go on to change the face of British pop after they embraced New York's hip-hop culture. That their talent had depth is not in doubt, but what Joy Division may have achieved had Ian Curtis survived is anybody's guess. It was his death that undoubtedly earned the band its place in musical history.

Left Ian Curtis and Peter Hook

Words and **music** Jo Callis, Philip Oakey and Philip Adrian Wright **1981**

For some reason, many pop historians file The Human League under the heading 'New Romantics'. Their dress sense may deserve its place in that particularly rickety old filing cabinet, but their music had little in common with the likes of Duran Duran, Culture Club and Adam Ant. The Human League's energy was much more post-punk and their reference points are more likely to be Kraftwerk, and somewhat bizarrely Emerson, Lake & Palmer, than anything else. Now that Duran Duran are turning themselves into a middle-aged grunge band, Boy George is reinventing himself as a hip DJ, and Adam Ant still trying to make it as a jobbing actor, Phil Oakey, one of pop's (somewhat reluctant) pioneers, has remained true to his core values. With his two original band members, Joanne Catherall and Susan Sulley, he still makes music from electronic sounds with vocals on top. He is a purist, and one who still adores Abba and Donna Summer.

Original band members Ian Craig Marsh and Martyn Ware left in 1981, just before the recording of the album *Dare* (they later set up Heaven 17). Their absence, an impending tour and recording session forced co-writer Philip Adrian Wright to take up the keyboards. Along with new recruit Jo Callis, The Human League created an album that built on the experimentation of the past, adhered to the strict policy of synth-only sounds and moved it on to create a much more commercially friendly sound. **Don't You Want Me** is what The Human League does best. The call-and-response interaction between Oakey and the

Above Phil Oakey and Joanne Catherall

girls is paramount to their sound, as is the emotion-free style of his singing. But it is the funky, melodic bass line that makes this song a classic.

The Human League came to define the mid-1980s, but quite why is a bit of a mystery, for Oakey and the girls are, by their own admission, not the most musical of pop stars. Perhaps it is the obvious imperfections in their music that has kept us on their side for 20 years. Or maybe it's because Oakey can write a damn good pop song. He also has a much better voice than he is given credit for, which often carries the efforts of the girls. But, of course, we don't mind because we know their background – Phil really did meet them in a cocktail bar, picked them out, shook them up and turned them into something new. Image has always been at the core of The Human League package, and Oakey knows that a huge part of the affection which the public feels for the band is based on the fact that everybody dreamed about being the waitress in that particular cocktail bar and becoming a pop star regardless of whether they had any talent. He knows that music is only a part of the pop fantasy, and that to lose the fairy-tale payoff would be to kill all of our dreams.

trivia

★ The Human League was one of the first bands to put out extended 12-inch remixes of their tunes. They even released an entire instrumental remix version of *Dare* by The League Unlimited Orchestra.

★ The Human League got a namecheck in The Undertones' 1980 hit 'My Perfect Cousin'.

★ Before joining The Human League, guitarist Jo Callis was in Scottish punk band The Rezillos.

★ **Don't You Want Me** was supposedly inspired by the hit movie *A Star is Born* starring Barbra Streisand and Kris Kristofferson.

Words and **music** Sylvia Robinson, Ed Fletcher, Melvin Glover and Nathaniel Chase **1982**

By the late 1970s the culture and music known as hip-hop had firmly taken hold of the street and club scene in New York's Bronx and Harlem. It was based on the cult of the DJ, whose emerging stars brought with them only a record box, a microphone for the rap and a dual mixing record deck for the music.

In the 1930s almost a quarter of Harlem's population were from the West Indies, and they imported with them not just a love of music, which was at the centre of most everything, but toasting – the early rap style by which the DJ, or master of ceremonies, would talk over the instrumental intro or break. The first DJ to adapt this to the modern age was Kool Herc, a Jamaican who dominated the scene simply by virtue of the size of his rig. Clumsy as his mixing was, he helped spawn a whole new breed of DJs who would basically remix records and beats to form a new kind of music altogether – hip-hop.

Grandmaster Flash was among this new wave and he was one of the best. Flash's parents were from Barbados, and right from an early age he'd risked a thrashing by borrowing his father's collection of classic American big band music which included '…everything from Benny Goodman to Artie Shaw' to play at his shows. But whereas Kool Herc had kept a crowd enthralled by the power of his system and the range of his record collection, Flash brought something else to the party. For a start his mixes were seamless, due to a customized deck and a natural musicality, but they also drew on everything from his dad's music to Kraftwerk and James Brown's horn breaks. In many ways it was the beginning of a post-modern music – the blending of forms, coupled with an ironic twist, which proved much more than the sum of its parts.

The year 1982 was to prove crucial for rap and hip-hop. Also out of the Bronx came Afrika Bambaataa, an ex-gang member turned cultural leader. His 'Planet Rock' single was a slow burner, but its mix of German electronica and computer-generated percussion was massively ahead its time and hugely influential. It didn't go unnoticed at Sugarhill Records either. Sugarhill was a small family business run by Joe and Sylvia Robinson, Sylvia a veteran from the music scene of the 1950s. Inspired by Bambaataa's hook-strewn 'Planet Rock', Robinson set Sugarhill mainman Melle Mel to work on a new track which would have both chart appeal and something more. There had been other 'message' raps before, Kurtis Blow's 'Hard Times' for example, but **The Message** turned it into a trend. Released in the late summer of 1982 it was a huge hit on both sides

Above Melle Mel

of the Atlantic. Despite its tough refrain of:

Don't push me 'cause I'm close to the edge,
I'm trying not to lose my head …
It's like a jungle out there
Sometimes I wonder how I keep from going under.

the record crossed rap into the mainstream for the first time.

Though the voice on this record belonged to Melle Mel, the creative force behind **The Message** was Grandmaster Flash, whose mixing recalled the super-tight rhythms of Chic, and put him on the world map. The notion of DJ as the star of the show was born.

(sexual) healing

Words Marvin Gaye and David Ritz **Music** Marvin Gaye and Odell Brown **1983**

(Sexual) Healing was in many ways Marvin Gaye's comeback song. The career of this most inspired of soul tenors had been in decline for many years. After initial phenomenal success with Berry Gordy's Motown, registering 39 Top 40 hits spanning much of the 1960s and 1970s, Gaye left the label, later leaving the US in an effort to avoid the tax man. In 1982, while living in Belgium, he recorded and released *Midnight Love*, his first album for Columbia Records. Not only was it a very good album, it included **(Sexual) Healing**, which earned him his first Grammy, and gave him 10 consecutive weeks at the top of the *Billboard* r&b chart, it was also Columbia's biggest hit of the decade.

Marvin Gaye was marketed during his Motown years as a ladies' man. Gordy, the label's founding father, decreed that all Gaye's singles were to be written in the first person, directly addressing his female audience – 'How Sweet it is to be Loved By You', 'I Heard it Through The Grapevine', 'You Are Everything', and 'Let's Get It On' all illustrate what a success that policy had been. Marvin Gaye played his part brilliantly, but although he was being given some of the best pop songs ever written, Gaye always yearned for a little more depth. His background as a gospel singer at his father's church and later as a jazz pianist and drummer perhaps explains his increasing discomfort with the shallowness of the Motown pop sound. In 1971 he composed, recorded and produced *What's Going On*. Gordy didn't want to release it because he considered the subject matter – ecological concerns, the Vietnam War and inner city troubles – to be too controversial for Motown. But Gaye insisted, and it went on to become one of the most influential records of all time – both musically and stylistically. However, it also signalled the end of Gaye's association with the Detroit-based label.

Co-written with David Ritz, Gaye's eventual biographer, and Hammond organ player, Odell Brown, **(Sexual) Healing** typifies everything about Marvin Gaye's music – soulful, smooth and sensuous, with a slight hint of sadness. With the exception of the funky guitar chops, Gaye performed all the instruments on the track, proving that as an all-round composer, musician and producer he was a first-rate talent. The lyrics were as sexy as they were sensuous and whereas previously it was his heart that had been on fire, now it was definitely his body. Sexier even than his 1973 album *Let's Get It On*, *Midnight Love* was completed despite Gaye's deteriorating mental state.

Battling with his addiction to cocaine, but finally with a hit single under his belt, Gaye decided it was time to return to the US. It was to be a tragic decision. Eighteen months after **(Sexual) Healing** was a hit, Gaye's preacher father shot him dead after yet another altercation. It was a sad end for a real talent, or as Berry Gordy called him, 'the truest artist I have ever known.'

Left Marvin Gaye

85 relax

Words and **music** Peter Gill, Holly Johnson, Brian Nash, Marc O'Toole and Paul Rutherford **1984**

Before we start, let's get a few things straight. Holly Johnson claims that the song is not about sex, gay or straight. And producer Trevor Horn did sign Frankie Goes to Hollywood to his new record label ZTT on the strength of seeing the band on the legendary British music TV show *The Tube*. But Horn didn't write the tune or the lyrics of **Relax** – it was, as with the majority of their first album *Welcome To the Pleasure Dome*, written by the band themselves. So, Frankie Goes to Hollywood were a proper band who sang, played and danced, not, as some would have it, an early form of the manufactured boy band, fresh from stage school.

The story of **Relax** takes many twists and turns. Written by the band in 1982, it took various forms on demos paid for by a variety of record companies, all of whom eventually turned it down. Luckily, one of the advances paid for a video as well, and, as the band had started to make waves on the live circuit in their hometown of Liverpool, *The Tube* decided to give the video an airing. And who should be watching that Friday night but Trevor Horn, formerly of The Buggles, soon to be in The Art of Noise, but at the time an up-and-coming record producer with a heavy influence in mechanical dance music. He signed them up to his new record label and set about recording this, their first single. After recording several different versions, including one with lead singer Holly Johnson backed by Ian Dury's band, The Blockheads, Horn announced that he didn't like any of the demos.

It was around this time that Horn had invested in a Fairlight, the earliest form of sampling machine. Greatly influenced by German art-house band Kraftwerk and the Giorgio Moroder-produced dance tracks of Donna Summer, he decided to strip back the song completely, send the band away and concentrate on creating a more mechanical, disco-based sound. Having taken such a long time in the studio, it was vital that this single, ZTT's second, was a hit. Alongside an aggressive marketing campaign headed up by ex-rock journalist Paul Morley, it was released in October 1983. Six weeks later it had started falling back down the charts having peaked at No.55. However, someone up there obviously liked them. More specifically, the producers of *The Tube* liked them, and they were invited to perform the song on the show's Christmas edition. It went down a storm, and by mid-January it had climbed to No.6.

The next part of the story has it that a prominent Radio 1 DJ, Mike Reid, who had been playing the record for some weeks, suddenly stumbled across the lyrics. Disgusted with what he saw, he took the record off halfway through, declaring it overtly obscene. The record was then banned by the BBC, both on radio and TV. It immediately climbed to the top of the charts where, to the embarrassment of TV executives, it stayed for five weeks. Urban myth or not, Frankie Goes to Hollywood had become a sensation. A few months later they released their follow-up single 'Two Tribes', which went straight in at No.1 and stayed there for nine weeks. On the back of this success, **Relax** started selling again and for the first time since The Beatles, one band occupied No.1 and No.2 in the charts at the same time.

Why such an unknown band, variously described as second-rate disco or the proponents of cock-rock, had captured the public imagination is a bit of a mystery. Never before had such an openly gay band been so popular. The video for **Relax** was set in a highly decadent gay s&m bar, the lyrics, whether by design or fault, were overtly suggestive, and the band members made a habit of baring their bottoms on stage. Not an obvious recipe for success, but it worked. And how! After subsequently taking America, where they had to tone down the s&m stuff, if not quite by storm then certainly pretty successfully, Frankie Goes to Hollywood could boast being No.1 in 11 countries and Top 10 in a further 11. The success was, however, to be short lived. Their third single, 'The Power of Love', repeated the achievements of the first two, and the band

Above Frankie Goes to Hollywood

became only the second ever to have their first three singles reach No.1 in the UK. Fellow Liverpudlians Gerry and the Pacemakers were the first (though they have subsequently been joined by The Spice Girls and Westlife). But from there on in, it was a slippery and pretty steep slope downhill and, after more moderate success with their second album, the band split up.

Oh yes, the song. Well, Trevor Horn really did a fantastic job with a pretty average melody. His pyrotechnic production, attainable because the Fairlight was polyphonic and therefore able to produce big, rich chords rather than single notes, was superb. With 'Two Tribes' the sound was even better, but **Relax** was the prototype. Phil Spector's notion of a Wall of Sound had been much imitated, but here it was dragged into the 1980s by using samples of, among other things, piano notes performed in a continuous sequence throughout the song. **Relax** is so dramatic (Horn claims that the band wanted to be a cross between Donna Summer and Kiss, which is a rather fitting description), and the curious mix of shameless camp combined with Liverpool laddishness created a perfect all-round, marketable

product. Frankie Goes to Hollywood marked the beginning of the super-producer revolution, and while pop music has always been about making money for record executives, the 1980s with its 'me, me, me' culture developed the theme to extremes. However, with Frankie Goes to Hollywood and Trevor Horn there was always a certain lightness and a sense of humour, and that is where the vast majority of the subsequent producer-led acts have so signally failed.

86 | careless whisper

Words and **music** George Michael and Andrew Ridgeley
1985

George Michael's first solo single, **Careless Whisper**, got to No.1 in 14 countries, including the UK, the US, Australia, Canada and Japan. It is typical of all that is George Michael, the heart of which is essentially good quality, white-boy soul. The sexy saxophone intro of the original recording, played by Steve Gregory, and reminiscent of Gerry Rafferty's 'Baker Street', instantly sets the scene as Michael leads us to the dancefloor on which his 'guilty feet have got no rhythm'.

Musically, **Careless Whisper** employs only four chords but it is a precursor to Michael's later flirtations with a more jazzy style in its use of minor ninths and major sevenths. The verse, chorus and middle eight all have the same chord sequence and so it is down to the well-crafted melody and Michael's production skills to ensure that the song moves along in a satisfying way. The guitar chops and use of the Fender Rhodes keyboard point towards Michael's musical influences as does his clever use of an instantly recognizable intro, reminiscent of Berry Gordy's Motown mantra of hooking the listener in within the first couple of bars.

In 1984, the year **Careless Whisper** was given its UK release, George Michael was in a pop duo called Wham!. He and Andrew Ridgeley, the duo's 'guitarist', were not yet at their peak. Although they'd achieved three UK Top 10 hits and were ever-present in the papers, in magazines and on television, the No.1 spot was proving elusive. Then in May, the brassy pop of 'Wake Me Up Before You Go-Go' went to the top of the charts. Despite the terrible dancing in the accompanying video, Wham! had officially arrived. Yet Michael, the musical one, was not really receiving the recognition that his obvious gifts deserved (teeny-pop music didn't garner critical broadsheet respect). Two months later **Careless Whisper** was released under the name of George Michael – a first dip into the pool of musical credibility as a solo artist. The critical response may have been only lukewarm, but the public thought it was hot, and Michael had a second No.1. Three months later Wham! were back at the top of the charts with 'Freedom'. But in the summer of 1986, after Michael had achieved solo success for a second time with 'A

trivia

Careless Whisper was Andrew Ridgeley's only number one as a composer.

Careless Whisper was released under the name Wham! in the US.

George Michael composed, performed and produced all the music on his first solo album *Faith*.

Above Wham!

Different Corner', Wham! split up. To date, George Michael and Wham! have sold over 67 million records worldwide, had 6 US and 11 UK No.1 singles.

Careless Whisper displays just about everything we now know about George Michael. He is a very gifted songwriter with a particular inclination for personalized, torturous and slightly paranoid ballads. Yet however self-obsessed his lyrics are, his musical ability, both in production and performance, shines through. A good vocalist with a confined range, George Michael's supreme talent is in the knowledge of his limitations. The sheer professionalism and dedication that runs through all his recordings is testament to his enduring popularity despite long absences from the scene due to legal wranglings both with his record companies and, somewhat embarrassingly, with the Los Angeles police force. **Careless Whisper** is no exception to this rule and in a poll of the London's pop radio listeners was voted their favourite ever song. But you'd think he could have learnt to dance by now.

87 sledgehammer

Words and **music** Peter Gabriel **1986**

Mention **Sledgehammer** and everyone will recall the groundbreaking video that accompanied its release. Mention Peter Gabriel and everyone has a different take. In the late 1960s and early 1970s, he was the face of Genesis, a prog-rock group who were just hitting the big time when Gabriel, a founder member, singer, co-writer and all-round creative impetus, left to begin a solo career. Throughout the remainder of the 1970s and early 1980s, he was an experimental pop artist. In 1982 he launched the World of Music, Arts & Dance (WOMAD), a festival designed to bring artists from all over the world to share their work in the UK. He also secured a role as a leading advocate of human rights by supporting Amnesty International at every opportunity and writing 'Biko', one of the first western pop songs to acknowledge and decry the tyranny of the racist regime in South Africa. Towards the end of the 1980s he composed the soundtrack to Martin Scorsese's movie *The Last Temptation of Christ*, and throughout the 1990s he developed his Real World empire which included recording facilities and a label dedicated to the promotion of indigenous music from around the world. Like Paul Simon and Talking Head's David Byrne, he also encouraged interaction between western pop and these new sources of inspiration.

In 1986 Peter Gabriel recorded **Sledgehammer** and the masterful album from which it came – *So*, easily to date his most commercially successfully recording, and the one that launched his international career. With more than a nod towards his love of southern soul, Gabriel used Memphis Horn maestro Wayne Jackson to lead and co-arrange the horn section. Jackson's experience in the house band for legendary record company Stax meant recording with the likes of Otis Redding and Sam & Dave, before becoming the most sought after 'horn-for-hire' of the last 30 years.

Gabriel had written and rewritten the tracks for *So* several times, before finally finding a sound with which he was satisfied. His approach to composition is analytical, rather than improvisational, patching together, bit by bit, various sounds and melodies, words and grooves, until it reaches its final destination. In **Sledgehammer**, he constructed a song which worked on many levels. It has a great groove, which when allied to the overall texture and strong hook, made for a very radio-friendly tune. Lyrically, it is pretty abstract for a song that reached the top of the US charts. Gabriel's ironic handling of its sexual theme allows him to get away with certain images that his contemporaries could not, and although in his Genesis days he had a tendency towards pomposity, the lyrics perfectly match the worldly-wise flavour of the music.

The video was a huge part of the success of this song. Combining live action with animation (produced by Aardman, the makers of *Wallace & Gromit*), Gabriel created a mini-masterpiece. Regarded by *Rolling Stone* magazine as the best-ever music video, it added to the abstract nature of the song by, among many other things, showing oven-ready chickens dancing to the beat, animated fruits whirling about, and a train set driving around a stop-action shot of Gabriel's head.

So is a great album of varied songs, diverse sounds and contrasting grooves. The common link is Gabriel's melancholic style which can be heard on even the most uptempo tunes. But **Sledgehammer** garners most acclaim as the soundtrack to a great music video. At the beginning of the MTV revolution, it was the perfect time to produce such a complete package.

Left Peter Gabriel

I still haven't found what I'm looking for

Words Bono **Music** Bono, The Edge, Adam Clayton and Larry Mullen **1987**

Released in 1987, **I Still Haven't Found What I'm Looking For** saw U2 moving on from the raw anger of their earlier work to a more sophisticated sound. Still relatively young, the band had yet to discover irony, but, as always, they feasted on their abundant capacity for soul-searching. Their album, *The Unforgettable Fire*, released in 1984 had helped their increasing reputation as the next name on the impossibly long list of 'Greatest Rock Band Ever', particularly in the US. The album illustrated their close affiliation with things American, soaked as it was with references ranging from Martin Luther King, to Elvis, to the declaration of independence. However, they were still bereft of that chart-topping single, on either side of the pond.

U2 had been propelled to international superstardom in 1985 when a billion viewers witnessed their jaw-dropping performance at Live Aid, and a year later they had toured the world headlining the Amnesty International 25th Anniversary tour, which also included Sting and Peter Gabriel. In 1987 they reigned supreme in the kingdom of huge stadium acts and achieved their ultimate goal with the release of their biggest selling album *The Joshua Tree*. The top-selling album was a heady mix of rock anthems and great musicianship, which not only featured memorable songs but also confronted the politics of the time when Thatcher and Reagan led the world. It included several chart-busting singles: 'Where The Streets Have No Name', 'With or Without You' and **I Still Haven't Found What I'm Looking For**.

Above Bono

I Still Haven't Found What I'm Looking For epitomizes all that is great about U2. Bono provides a classically epic and biblical lyric, is found believing in Kingdom Come, losing chains and carrying crosses, The Edge provides his trademark, ever-present, jangling and reverb-laden guitar sound, Clayton pumps his way through the song with a driving bass line that sticks only to the root notes, and Mullen Jr provides, as ever, a simple drumbeat that allows for the richness of the vocals and the guitar playing to shine through. It is in this simplicity that U2 are the world leaders. The sound is stripped down to its minimum. Like so many of rock 'n' roll's greatest songs, **I Still Haven't Found What I'm Looking For** uses only three chords. Heavily influenced by gospel music, the band make no bones about the importance of The Mighty Clouds of Joy, Rev. Cleveland and the Staple Singers to their musical education.

The success of *The Joshua Tree* and the singles it spawned heralded U2 as the biggest band on earth in the late 1980s. They were featured on the front cover of *Time* magazine (only The Beatles and The Who had ever been there before), and proclaimed by *Rolling Stone* magazine as 'the band of the '80s'. They produced a movie-documentary, *Rattle and Hum*, in which they paid tribute to a host of their musical heroes including Bob Dylan and B.B. King. The album version of **I Still**

Haven't Found What I'm Looking For features a full and glorious sounding gospel choir giving the song the feel of a church standard. The Chimes, a UK-based soul act, released a version in 1990, achieving a Top 10 spot, and Seal, Stevie Winwood and Booker T. & The MGs have all recorded versions. It is U2's most covered song.

Legend has it that in 1976 Larry Mullen Jr placed an advert on the bulletin board of his school looking for band members. A quarter of a century later, in a world of pop that sees change as always for the better, U2 constantly battle with transformations in fashion, recording technology, expectations, success and image. But one thing they keep at the heart of whatever they do is the fact that they started off as a group of young guys with a passion for rock 'n' roll. They kept things simple then because they didn't know any other way. Now they do so because they know that popular music is always at its best when least contrived.

Below U2

89 never gonna give you up/ I should be so lucky

Words and **music** Matt Stock, Mike Aitken and Pete Waterman **1988**

In the late 1980s and early 1990s, the UK charts belonged to three producer/writers – Matt Stock, Mike Aitken and Pete Waterman. Together they were responsible for over one hundred Top 40 hits from several dozen artists, and, despite their subsequent split, the magic touch has stayed with them all. Waterman, the older and more experienced of the three, had been in the music business for many years and had worked in various roles from DJ to producer to manager to record company executive. Stock and Aitken were two young session musicians who had made several recordings for various artists and had found themselves working in the same cabaret band. Together, and with early successes from the likes of Dead Or Alive, Mel & Kim and topless model Samantha Fox,

Above Rick Astley
Right Kylie Minogue

they developed a production line of artists and hit records.

Models, soap stars and comedians were all turned into pop stars by this formidable and relentless hit-factory. Even the tea-boy, Rick Astley, got in on the act. He proved that dreams really can come true when in the shortest possible time he climbed up the music industry ladder from the lowest rung, right to the top with **Never Gonna Give You Up**, which went to No.1 in the UK. The following year, the top of the ladder had to be extended as he topped the US charts, being hailed (rather prematurely) as the new Michael McDonald.

Unlike Astley, former Australian soap-star Kylie Minogue never really cracked the US. But in the UK between 1988 and 1990, she notched up 10 Top 5 hits including three No.1s. **I Should Be So Lucky** was her first, and like **Never Gonna Give You Up** it was a master class in hit making from Stock, Aitken and Waterman. As the saying goes, 'If it ain't broke, don't fix it' and the three super-producers churned out these winning hits all from the same basic recipe: Firstly take an uptempo soul/disco-lite beat, and be sure to use drums of the electronic variety. Add some bass, but none of those old-fashioned stringed bass instruments, a synthesized one will do just as well, and you don't have to worry about any loose notes along the way. Mix with some bouncy brass and string arrangements, vaguely reminiscent of the old 1960s and 1970s soul classics, but again trying to avoid actual saxophones or violins. Then add lots of repetition. Finally find an artist who can sing (but don't worry if they can't, a little longer in the recording studio's oven will soon fix it) and release to a now very suspecting public.

Repetition of words and phrases was their stock in trade, and the lyrics of **I Should Be So Lucky** include a phrase with the word 'lucky' repeated four times, a couplet that has, as Waterman has proudly pointed out, entered the language of common usage.

It is easy to deride many of their songs as being very formulaic and faintly vacuous, but these are two great pop songs and probably would have been hits in any era. The trio were masters of catchy hooks and bouncy melodies. The fact that they produced the songs as well, all in the same way and within weeks of the last one, definitely diluted what should have been much deserved industry praise. But with that kind of talent, they hardly needed the approval of their peers.

back to life
(however do you want me)

Words and **music** Beresford Romeo, Caron Wheeler, Simon Law and Nellee Hooper **1989**

A blend of r&b, soul, jazz, rap, reggae, dub, house and African percussion, **Back To Life (However Do You Want Me)** is widely regarded as being the first example of uniquely British, black music. It was Soul II Soul's only US No.1, but they have had several Top 10 hits, spanning a dozen years, and similar success worldwide (particularly in the US), selling over 7 million albums and 20 million singles in total.

Soul II Soul started life as a company selling sound equipment to DJs. Within a few years it had become an organization that housed an independent record label (Funki Dred Records), an artists' management, representation and development company, a publishing company, a commercial recording studio, a studio/holiday resort on the Caribbean island of Antigua, a highly successful fashion line and merchandising department, and an on-going comic strip. And, of course, the company also produced a successful band. Aside from the dub flavour that betrayed their Caribbean roots, the sound of Soul II Soul is really light soul in the Philadelphia mould, always featuring a joyful but relaxed beat with a crisp and prominent horn arrangement. While Jazzie B (Beresford Romeo), one half of the original equipment sales company and figurehead for all the current ventures, is known as the driving force behind Soul II Soul, it was vocalist Caron Wheeler and producer Nellee Hooper who deserve most credit for the band's success. For when both left, soon after the first album *Club Classics Volume One (Keep on Movin'* in the US), Soul II Soul badly missed Hooper's slick production and Wheeler's haunting vocals. The critical and commercial success of this first album has not been matched since.

Lyrically, **Back To Life (However Do You Want Me)** is not typical of a Soul II Soul song, which usually finds Jazzie B trying to represent a positive image of life – indeed the motto, 'A happy face and a thumpin' bass for a lovin' race', is often attributed to him. Here though, the song tells of a character questioning the nature of her relationship. The main hook – from the title '**(However Do You Want Me)**' – with its swinging rhythm and power singing, remains imprinted in the minds of anyone who has listened to pop radio over the last decade.

But Soul II Soul's main claim to fame was not any one of the many pies in which they placed their fingers, it was the whole package. It was the fact that the children of those who had emigrated from the Caribbean in the 1950s and 1960s had at long last broken through into mainstream British culture, and succeeded publicly. It was suddenly not just OK, but actually cool to be black. For this reason alone Soul II Soul influenced the music scene although they were cultural, rather than musical pioneers.

Structurally **Back To Life (However Do You Want Me)** is flawed, with the various sections sounding like they're from different songs. Given the sophisticated production techniques available today, particularly in the realms of sampling, this song also sounds rather dated. But the overall effect, with its large production, glorious feel, and the sheer excitement brought about by having a credible British r&b hit that also did well in the US (tea to China, snow to the Alaskans etc.) means that this song earned a place in pop history as the real face of black British music.

Left Jazzie B

> "One of the great things about a musical is that it can steal things emotionally, it can simplify the complicated aspects of our life into a single dream. In the world of musicals "All I want is a room somewhere" is the point of the piece, and, of course, life is more complicated than that.

Songwriter Alan Menken explaining the appeal of the stage musical.

From the moment Al Jolson uttered those immortal words, 'You ain't heard nothin' yet' in *The Jazz Singer*, movies and songs have been inseparable.

The link between Hollywood, Broadway and Tin Pan Alley has always been strong. Movies and stage shows have always been the songwriter's best marketing tools, and a hit song has often boosted the fortunes of a dull movie. But it's not always predictable. 'Over the Rainbow', bizarrely, was not perceived as a winning song when first written. Richard Rodgers, Jerome Kern and George Gershwin wrote exclusively for the stage in the early part of the century, quite simply because that was the best way to get their songs in front of an audience. Initially musicals had their roots in French and Viennese operettas. Light in tone, they were a type of variety entertainment, called burlesque and then vaudeville in the US and music hall in Britain. Perhaps the ultimate stage revue was Florenz Ziegfeld's series of *Follies* which were popular around the time of the First World War. By this time George M. Cohan and Victor Herbert were beginning to give a distinctive sound and style to Broadway shows. Jerome Kern, Guy Bolton and P.G. Wodehouse took things a stage further by putting believable characters into situations on the musical stage. However, *Showboat* changed everything, with a story brimming with difficult contemporary notions like interracial marriage, and boasting a proper three-act plot. The songs, therefore, needed to be part of the plot, which did not necessarily make them comprehensible outside the dramatic structure. But, of course, quality will always stand the test of time and the good songs, though written for shows, often lived on as stand-alone hits.

Its Got Legs

When Rodgers and Hart wrote 'My Funny Valentine' for the musical *Babes in Arms*, the simple expedient of giving the romantic lead the name Val (for Valentine) gave the song legs. It worked outside the show. In truth for most of the Astaire/Rogers vehicles any of the songs from any of the shows could probably have been changed for

Left A publicity shot for the first MGM musical, *Broadway Melody*

a different one on the list, and it would have made little difference to the show. What was important was that Fred Astaire sang the song. He could invest it with verve and style and a lightness of touch that hit the mark with theatre and later, cinema audiences. Of course, it helped that the music of Broadway became the popular music of the Western world, giving it glorious exposure, and aided by movies, radio and, later, TV.

The body of songs that survived these shows and gained popularity over and above the shows they came from became the basis of the canon, American popular song, endlessly revived throughout the century. These are the songs you will find on Ella Fitzgerald's *Songbook* albums and Sinatra's *Capitol Years*, both recorded in the 1950s, 20 or 30 years after most of them were written.

Movies had led to all the great Broadway composers decamping to Hollywood. Everybody knew great songs could change the fortunes of a movie. Harold Arlen and 'Yip' Harburg were commissioned to write the songs for *The Wizard of Oz*; they could hardly have known that 'Over the Rainbow' would become the great stand-alone song it is. Arlen was so insecure about the melody he had to run it past Ira Gershwin before he submitted it to the studio. And the studio was reluctant to allow the big song to be delivered by a little girl in a scruffy old farmyard. Of course, Judy Garland had the measure of the song and made it her own. It needed someone of her stature to upstage Toto the dog in that scene.

However good the songs were in *The Wizard of Oz*, they didn't move the narrative along in the way that musicals after Rodgers and Hammerstein's *Oklahoma!* did. That was the first integrated musical with great songs like 'Oh What A Beautiful Morning'. But that song apart, they were difficult to extract from the show and put into a cabaret set. You could say the same about *Carousel*, but 'You'll Never Walk Alone' has become one of the great anthemic secular hymns that clearly have a life outside the show.

Stephen Sondheim is less than enthusiastic about the lyrics he wrote to Bernstein's music for *West Side Story*, but the public rushed out to buy the album and pushed it into the charts. 'Somewhere', for which Sondheim reserves the most venom, has been successfully recorded many times. Clearly by the end of the 1960s the public taste was not only moving away from the professionals, but was more ready to accept material that was less conventionally a love song. While *Fiddler on the Roof* and *Hello Dolly* ploughed the same standard furrow, the rock musical *Hair* made people sit up and take notice, both on Broadway and on the London stage.

In the 1980s the musical had stagnated, and the public decided in favour of new-style mega-musicals, often emanating from Britain. *Cats*, *Les Miserables*, *Phantom of the Opera* and *Miss Saigon*, light on content and heavy on special effects, brought new names to the table. Everything that Andrew Lloyd Webber, Tim Rice and Cameron Macintosh touched seemed to turn to gold.

The future for musicals, however, looks bleak. There seems only one writer left who is capable of creating new material, and even he, Stephen Sondheim, is downhearted about the whole thing. In an article in the *New York Times* in March 2000, he said, 'You have two kinds of shows on Broadway, revivals and spectacles. You get your tickets for *The Lion King* a year in advance and the family comes as if it was a picnic. And they pass on to their children the idea that that's what the theatre is – a spectacular music that you see once a year, a stage version of a movie… it has nothing to do with the theatre at all.'

At the turn of the century it seems hard to imagine when Broadway will again play a significant role in the life of popular music.

Music from the Movies

The one-off movie theme song really got going in 1951 with 'High Noon'. Tex Ritter sang it on the soundtrack of the movie and Frankie Laine took it to the top of the charts, setting the path for all those Bond movie songs that charted through to the 1980s.

When Andrew Lloyd Webber and Tim Rice wrote *Jesus Christ Superstar* in 1969 they made a conscious decision not to obey the rather restrictive rules that their illustrious predecessors had laid down over the previous half-century. They didn't bother with stage show or movie. They wrote a song that they liked around a biblical theme, went straight to vinyl, and made a fortune, rendering the old guard apoplectic with rage and envy. So, no show and no movie: the next thought was why bother with narrative? Why not just write a

bunch of good stand-alone songs and put them on the soundtrack? Enter the Bee Gees, managed by Robert Stigwood, who also happened to be the producer of *Saturday Night Fever*. Great soundtrack. Made a fortune as an album (it became the best-selling soundtrack album of all time) and it promoted the movie. Who cares about the story? Think about the cross marketing.

There were, of course, exceptions to this rule. Composers like Bernard Herrmann, Jerry Goldsmith and John Barry wrote some memorable soundtracks, like *Psycho*, *Planet of the Apes* and *Goldfinger*, helped, of course, by great movies, but they rarely bothered the hit parade.

That was how it went through the 1970s and 1980s with movies like *Flashdance* and *Top Gun*, but by then it was finessed with the added value of rock star composers, such as Phil Collins and Elton John, writing for movies. Another trend began when movies featured a collection of songs already recorded and released for the regular pop and rock market. These compilation-style albums, starting with *Midnight Cowboy*, written by John Barry but featuring Harry Nilsson's version of a Fred Neil song 'Everybody's Talkin'', became huge sellers. Others followed, culminating in the 1990s when filmmakers like Quentin Tarantino used the music of 1970s, for example, to evoke a strong sense of time in which the films' stories were set. Other film soundtracks, like *The Crow* and *Trainspotting*, also sold millions. The biggest selling film soundtrack to this day, however, remains *The Bodyguard*, a box-office smash starring Kevin Costner and Whitney Houston. Houston also sang the theme song, 'I Will Always Love You', written by country singer Dolly Parton, and took it straight to No.1 all around the world.

The Disney Effect

Then suddenly in the mid-1990s, there was a return to core values with old-fashioned Tin Pan Alley composers like Alan Menken writing narrative songs which actually become hits, just like the old days. Who was the mysterious benefactor of this return to the past? It was the Walt Disney studios, with animated features like *The Little Mermaid* and *The Lion King*. The trend had begun in 1991 with

OK, so charts vary according to the criteria you use, etc. But, for arguments sake here are: The Top 10 Best-Loved Stage Musicals: 1 Oklahoma! 2 Showboat 3 Annie Get Your Gun 4 My Fair Lady 5 Pal Joey 6 Porgy and Bess 7 Gypsy 8 The King and I 9 Babes in Arms 10 Kiss Me Kate. The Billboard Top 10 Best-Selling Movie Soundtracks: 1 The Bodyguard (1992) 2 Saturday Night Fever (1977) 3 Purple Rain (1984) 4 Forrest Gump (1994) 5 Dirty Dancing (1987) 6 Titanic (1997) 7 The Lion King (1994) 8 Top Gun (1986) 9 Grease (1978) 10 Footloose (1984)

Right Ginger Rogers and Fred Astaire, dancing in *Swing Time*

Beauty and the Beast which won several Oscars, including Best Song. It continued for the rest of the decade with films like *Aladdin*, *Pocahontas* and *The Hunchback of Notre Dame*. Curious though that live action musicals had almost disappeared from the movie screens by then, and that musicals seemed to have become exclusively for kids, only *South Park* did anything to allay that fear, and that was not to everyone's taste at all.

Titanic Sales

No discussion of soundtracks would be complete, however, without a mention of the movie *Titanic*, released in 1997. With a spend reputed to be in the region of $200 million, the film and its music were rammed down the throats of the public as never before. A huge marketing campaign, for the film, the theme tune, the soundtrack, the video, and even a whole new range of make-up, were unprecedented. Of course, it was successful. The movie did well, the theme song, by Celine Dion, went to No.1 and stayed there for weeks. It must also be admitted that James Horner's soundtrack was remarkably successful in regenerating the emotional impact of the film. It seems likely that this cross-marketing of products from different fields is the way of the future.

In its own small way, the soundtrack to the Coen Brothers' film *Oh Brother Where Art Thou*, released in 2000 illustrates how things stand at the moment. The film is loosely (very loosely) based on Homer's *Odyssey*. The publishers of the *Odyssey*, sensing a marketing opportunity based on the quality of the film, which features an excellent collection of traditional country music, have republished the book with a film still on the cover.

Whatever will they think of next?

Left A scene from *Starlight Express*

the top 100

songs 91-100

Nothing compares 2 U

Smells like teen spirit

Unfinished sympathy

I'd do anything for love (but I won't do that)

Don't turn around

Gangsta paradise

Wannabe

Candle in the wind 97

My heart will go on

Baby one more time

91 nothing compares 2 U

Words and **music** Prince Rogers Nelson **1990**

Although he wrote the song in 1985 for Family, one of his many protégé acts, Prince has never actually released a studio recording of **Nothing Compares 2 U**. It was Sinead O'Connor who took the song to No.1 in January 1990. As well as being an excellent, typically Prince composition – dramatic, yearning, haunting and beautiful – the single did well partly because of the brilliant simplicity of O'Connor's promotional video. All we see is her face in close-up, her shaved head and big eyes set against a black background. And when the real tears appear, we're hooked.

Minneapolis-born Prince was a self-taught pianist, guitarist, bass player and drummer. As if that wasn't enough, he developed one of the most distinctive voices of all time. Among his musical influences are Earth, Wind & Fire, Sly & The Family Stone, Curtis Mayfield, Stevie Wonder and James Brown. His guitar playing is often compared to Jimi Hendrix, and while experimentally and energy-wise there is a similarity, Prince argues that his playing is influenced by the more lyrical style of the legendary Carlos Santana.

At the age of 19, Prince was given $100,000 by Warner Brothers to produce an album. He was given total artistic control with the promise of no record company interference. The album, titled *For You*, featuring Prince on every instrument, was released in 1978. Over the next five years he released a number of excellent and innovative albums to both public and critical acclaim. His sexually explicit lyrics and lewd performances, while occasionally earning him disapproval, only added to an air of intrigue and mystery that continues to this day.

In 1984 Prince was top of the US singles charts with 'When Doves Cry', top of the album charts with *Purple Rain* and, incredibly, top of the movie charts with the film of the same name. Only The Beatles and Elvis have achieved this. Warner Brothers believed they had found a black American musician with as much crossover appeal as Stevie Wonder and Michael Jackson. They were, however, to get increasingly concerned over the sheer volume of material that he produced over the next few years. Company executives saw a new album every year, sometimes a double album, as over-egging a very profitable pudding. While Prince was keen for his audience to hear his work, Warner Brothers knew that demand just couldn't keep up

Above Prince
Left Sinead O'Connor

with supply. Despite a $100 million, six-album deal signed in 1992, the notorious fall out between Prince and Warner Brothers was to last most of the decade. Prince became Symbol, Squiggle, The Artist Formerly Known as Prince or just plain bonkers, for several years but continued his prolific output. This period produced some of his best work but rarely within one album.

Not since Duke Ellington has there been a composer-arranger of such prodigious (and in Prince's case prodigal) talent. These two royal artists share an enviable knack of writing parts for their band members that take them into a completely different league, one which few are able to attain outside their leader's stewardship.

Words and **music** Kurt Cobain **1991**

This really was a song for a generation. Generation X, that is. Said by some commentators to be the '(I Can't Get No) Satisfaction' of the 1990s, **Smells Like Teen Spirit** certainly sums up the disaffected Beavis and Butt-head youth with all its inherent contradictions. A hugely political song without mentioning politics, **Smells Like Teen Spirit** was a massive commercial hit that denounced commercialism. In fact, in its short lyric, it denounces just about everything, yet is a very comprehensive statement about the kids who cry out that they can't get no satisfaction, but don't actually know whether they want it anyway.

Often cited as an attack on the apathy of the MTV generation, the song pays an unintentional reference to a cheap brand of deodorant. While discussing the teenage revolution with a friend, Cobain woke the next morning to find the words 'Kurt smells like teen spirit' daubed on his bedroom wall. Believing his friend was suggesting that he could incite teenage rebellion, Cobain was energized to write the song. Only later on did he claim that he found out the real meaning of the graffiti. Whatever the inspiration, this blistering four-chord anthem became the first ever song from a debutante band to get the much sought after 'world premier' slot on MTV's rock show *120 Minutes*. The fact that the video was then put on their A-list rotation meant that success was inevitable – for these were the lessons in which the MTV generation took most interest.

Smells Like Teen Spirit catapulted Nirvana to the forefront of pop music. Kurt Cobain – singer, guitarist, songwriter, lyricist and (dis)appointed spokesperson of a generation – became another of those famed overnight sensations who soon realized that they never wanted the limelight. In fact Cobain was one of those huge stars whose job

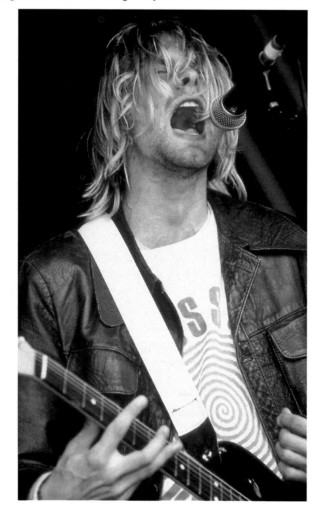

Right Curt Cobain

satisfaction diminished directly in proportion to the amount of contact he had with his fawning public. His career, curtailed by his suicide in April 1994 just three years after the song's first unveiling, was littered with cancelled shows, retirements from the band, from touring, from just about anything he could think up. It is widely believed that heroin was to blame for this constant indecision and paranoia, yet Cobain consistently denied addiction and put his health problems down to severe stomach pains which he claimed to have suffered since childhood. Whether his inspiration was drug or pain induced, it is hard not to acclaim this talent who has influenced not just a generation of kids, but also propelled and made credible a genre of music that was previously unheralded.

Nirvana are credited with inventing grunge, a music form which best describes their sound. While previously so-called alternative music was consigned to specialist sections of record shops, they were certainly most responsible for popularizing this fusion of punk, post-punk and indie-rock. Suddenly it was pop. To quote one Nirvana fan, 'Grunge is what happens when children of divorce get their hands on guitars.' *Nevermind* – the album that spawned this particular track – was originally expected to sell around 100,000 copies, a regular figure for this sort of band, yet the initial shipment of 50,000 sold out instantly. To date, the album has sold close to 10 million copies.

Words and **music** Grant Marshall, Andrew Vowles, Robert Del Naja and Shara Nelson **1992**

When first released, **Unfinished Sympathy** did not unduly trouble the singles chart compilers either in the UK or in the US. It was one of those word-of-mouth successes that over a period of time became many people's choice as the soundtrack of the 1990s. In fact, in 1998, Radio 1 listeners voted it their all-time favourite British anthem.

Massive Attack started as part of a loose collective of musicians, DJs and producers based in Bristol and known as the Wild Bunch. Together they formed a sound system. In the 1960s and 1970s a sound system was every teenager's dream present – a record player with cassette, radio, speakers and a volume control that was out of bounds for all grown-ups. But by the 1980s, a logical extension to this phenomena was born in the form of a group of people who toured local venues with a volume control that definitely went up as far as 11, often higher. What you got was a troupe of DJs, often with a very diverse range of discs to spin, a hired-in mega PA and loads of like-minded people. It was the beginnings of the current club-music scene that has swept up most of Europe and is now being transported across the pond to the US, a scene where the DJs don't just spin disks, but are themselves the new rock 'n' roll.

The album *Blue Lines* was their first and for many, it changed the world. Their fusion of American hip-hop, funk, soul and rap with Caribbean reggae and dub (perhaps the first purely electronic form of pop) gave birth to a new label for music journalists to bandy about, trip-hop. Although this new form of music, also promoted by Portishead and Tricky, was seen as hailing from Bristol, it was actually steeped in the consciousness of being a black Briton. Whereas previously, most black British music stars were playing either American r&b or Jamaican reggae, this new sound was about their experiences, not from the ghetto or the homeland, but from growing up in Britain. So it included classical music, 60s and 70s film and TV soundtracks, it embraced both punk and trance, all rolled up in a very British, introspective and rather polite form of angst.

Unfinished Sympathy, written by the band, has been variously described as lush, ravishing, windswept and atmospheric. Suckers for a pretty melody, Massive Attack want the listener to have to work a little, shown not only in the sometimes sparse arrangements, but also in the politicized lyrics. However, the music is perfect soundtrack material, both for ads and movies, as Shara Nelson's beautiful and melancholic vocals combine with the multi-layered backing to produce a haunting and very atmospheric song. To say that Massive Attack and their varied musical offspring produced the real Brit-pop of the 90s is rather a liberal, cliché. But it is certainly true that they were far more adventurous than the likes of Blur, Oasis and Pulp. As for the lyrics, you needed to be there.

Above Massive Attack

trivia

★ In 1990 the band dropped the word 'Attack' from their name to distance themselves from any involvement in UN Gulf War policy.

★ Tina Turner performs a cover of **Unfinished Sympathy** during her live appearances.

★ Reggae legend Horace Andy, Everything But the Girl's Tracey Thorn and The Cocteau Twins' Liz Fraser have all sung with Massive Attack.

> 66
> **unfinished sympathy** became many people's choice as the soundtrack of the 1990s
> 99

Words and **music** Jim Steinman **1993**

Quite what it is that Meatloaf won't do, in this song from the album *Bat Out of Hell II*, is open to debate, but what is undeniable is the phenomenal success that he and Jim Steinman share when they collaborate. The album, a follow up to their 17 million-selling *Bat Out of Hell* from 1977, was just like many a Hollywood blockbuster sequel, the same but more so. The Steinman power chords, the pseudo-classical piano sequences, the tearful verse followed by a triumphant chorus, is tremendously operatic. In fact, Steinman has referred to himself as a Little Richard Wagner. But then he has also claimed to be rock's Cecil B. de Mille, a Dr Frankenstein to Meatloaf's monster or, intriguingly, the Francis Ford Coppola to Meatloaf's Marlon Brando.

Whatever their relationship, when they work together, sparks fly. Neither has enjoyed quite as much success outside the partnership as they have within it, but that's not to say they can't exist without each other. They share a taste for the dramatic, both having started off in the theatre. In 1973 Meatloaf (the artist formerly known as Marvin Lee Aday) auditioned for a part in one of Steinman's musicals. He got the job and Steinman, as he was later to proclaim, had finally found his voice. A couple of years later, Steinman wrote a futuristic version of *Peter Pan*, called *Neverland*, and it was during the rehearsals for that show that *Bat Out of Hell* was conceived. Released in 1977, it stayed in the UK charts for an astonishing 400 weeks. No surprise then that these masters of excess repeated the formula some years later with *Bat Out of Hell II*, which included the same combination of vampires, fast cars, faster motorbikes, bad girls, obsessive love and countless references to their version of the American dream.

I'd Do Anything For Love (But I Won't Do That) is testament to Steinman's ability to create a mountain out of a molehill. He does write good uncomplicated melodies and is able to tell an epic story in a reasonably short timeframe – but master of the three-minute pop song he is not. **I'd Do Anything For Love (But I Won't Do That)** comes in at 12 minutes, and this is typical of the album. He has also written songs for Barry Manilow, Barbra Streisand and Celine Dion (no escape from the dramatic there), as well as Bonnie Tyler's 1983 hit 'Total Eclipse of the Heart'. Steinman is also famous for turning down Sir Andrew Lloyd Webber's invitation to provide the lyrics to his musical version of *Phantom of the Opera*, although they did finally collaborate on the recent *Whistle Down the Wind*.

While Steinman fans like to claw back as much credit as possible for his behind-the-scenes talent, Meatloaf's role in the collaboration shouldn't be underestimated. He is a pretty good singer with great energy and charisma, and in 1994 won a Grammy for the Best Solo Rock Vocal Performance on **I'd Do Anything For Love (But I Won't Do That)**. From the same blue-collar worker school of American rock stars as, say, Bruce Springsteen, Meat (as he likes to be known) has an added extra ingredient – humour. Despite all the dramatic themes and tragic situations that he brings to life in his songs, there aren't many people who can get away with delivering some of the lines that Steinman serves up for him. Meatloaf does it effortlessly.

Above Meatloaf

don't turn around

Words and **music** Diane Warren and Albert Hammond **1994**

It is the success of the songwriter that puts this song on the list of the best of the century. Diane Warren has written for such varied artists as Aerosmith, Alice Cooper, Aretha Franklin, Bette Midler, Boyzone, Johnny Mathis and Ricky Martin. But to confine the list to eight is to do her a real disservice; in fact her artist roster boasts over 100 of the biggest acts of the last 20 years. Co-writer Albert Hammond is also a seasoned veteran. Having written The Hollies' 'The Air That I Breathe', Leo Sayer's 'When I Need You' and Tina Turner's 'I Don't Wanna Lose You', there is nothing he doesn't know about the industry. But it is the sheer volume of Warren's compositions (apparently one of her creations is played on a radio station somewhere in the world every 20 seconds) that requires a mention. In this case, **Don't Turn Around** was a hit for Ace of Base, a Swedish band who very successfully exported their mid-tempo rock-pop to the world.

Warren is said to spend 12 hours a day, six days a week in her studio, writing her songs. Although she says there is no set structure to her songwriting, a quick flick through the Diane Warren songbook would show a definite pattern to her songs, particularly the power ballads for which she is most famous. Citing Carole King, Leiber & Stoller and Burt Bacharach as her idols, she has neither King's honesty, Leiber & Stoller's sense of fun nor Bacharach's artistry. Yet she has been responsible for shifting an estimated 125 million units during her 20-year career. Perhaps she unwittingly typifies the business-led pop scene of the late 1980s and 1990s, where the likes of Michael Bolton, Boyzone, Celine Dion and Britney Spears have become global superstars based on... well certainly

based on a lot less talent than Elvis, The Beatles and Michael Jackson, for example.

Warren is, however, supremely able at her craft. She has been Songwriter of the Year for ASCAP on six occasions, for *Billboard* four times, and twice for the BMI. Her own catalogue holds nearly 1,000 songs and her publishing company, Realsongs, is one of the top five of its ilk. Warren has also had songs in over 50 movies, including *Ghostbusters* and *Up Close and Personal*. Her fluent melodies, instinctive ability to build from verse to chorus and use of universal themes contribute to her incredible success. All of which amount to the fact that this Californian daughter of an insurance salesman, whose guitar teacher once told her that she was tone-deaf, has always made the most of her talents.

Don't Turn Around is a simple, melodic Euro-disco song, which incorporates a hint of dub. There is an obvious inclination to compare this band to fellow Swedes Abba: both quartets, both with two boys, two girls, one blonde, one brunette. But where Abba's music is quite rich and full sounding, with great session musicians creating a very accomplished feel to their songs, Ace of Base have a much more sparse sound, relying on a prominent drum loop and counter melodies played on rather cheap sounding synthesizers. Their vocal style is much sexier, the good times that these girls know are not from the tame disco floors of the 1970s, but from the more racy clubs of the 1980s and 1990s. But as with Abba, it is the quality of songwriting that shines through, and here, once again Diane Warren succeeds. Originally recorded as a B-side by Tina Turner, **Don't Turn Around** was yet another Top 10 triumph for the Diane Warren (and in this case Hammond) hit factory.

Right Ace of Base

gangsta's paradise

Words and **music** Artis Ivey Jr (Coolio), Larry Sanders (LV), Doug Rasheed and Stevie Wonder **1995**

This song propelled Coolio (the gangsta rapper you could just about take home to meet the parents) into the realm of international megastardom. Fueled to a large degree by massive MTV airplay and a place on the soundtrack of Michelle Pfeiffer's successful movie *Dangerous Minds*, **Gangsta's Paradise** was the title track of Coolio's second album. His debut album, *It Takes A Thief*, had been an instant hit, going platinum on the back of the single 'Fantastic Voyage', which seemed to capture the imagination of the American public. But **Gangsta's Paradise** went one better and placed Coolio as the top of pop's long list of bad-boys-made-good.

Coolio did all those crazy things that Hollywood says happens to the West Coast 'boyz from the hood'. Born in Compton, the notorious suburb of LA made famous by the mega-controversial Niggaz With Attitude, he joined gangs, had children with numerous women, spent time in jail and was addicted to crack cocaine. His deliverance from these difficulties took the form of enrolling as a Californian firefighter for 18 months. He claims it was his boot camp, easily the most physically demanding job he had ever undertaken, but, more importantly, one of the most fulfilling. The preachy lyrics of **Gangsta's Paradise** seem very heartfelt. But where some artists just talk the talk, Coolio really does walk the walk. He devotes a lot of his time to numerous charitable trusts, each of which revolve around youth, music and the concept of emancipation through education.

Gangsta's Paradise was one of the earliest gangsta rap tunes to be a global hit.

Right Coolio

It is not nearly as heavy a sound as the music of the pioneering Ice T, nor as aggressive or controversial as NWA, but it did pave the way for the likes of Puff Daddy and Tupac Shakur to make significant dents in charts the world over. It did so by fusing (or diluting, for those hardcore fans of genre) the political with the requirements of radio-friendly pop. The funkiness comes very definitely from the school of George Clinton and P-Funk although, again, not as heavily as Dr Dre or Snoop Doggy Dog.

The main hook of the song is a sample from Stevie Wonder's 'Pastime Paradise', yet another borrowing from his legendary album *Songs in the Key of Life* (hence Wonder's writing

credit). Both Coolio and LV, the gospel singer who co-wrote and performed on the track, recognized the infectious and ominous quality of the string arrangement and, along with in-demand producer Doug Rasheed, they set about updating the original song. The new lyrics provide a warning shot across the bows of those intoxicated with the lifestyle of the gangsta rappers, not least of which with the line where he questions whether, at the age of 23, he'll live to see 24.

Not long after the single was released, two fellow rappers, Tupac and Notorious B.I.G., were killed in drive-by shootings, starting an East Coast v. West Coast 'war', which represented the lowest ebb for gangsta rap.

The song also highlights the start of another 1990s' phenomena, the marriage of the movie and music industries. During this time, many companies were in merger talks, creating huge cross-platform, multi-national entertainment conglomerates, something previously limited to just one or two companies. One of the key differences this time around in the marketing of their products, was that the song led the film. Whereas previously films had kick-started the chartward bound journey of many a good pop song, now the song was being released long before the film, effectively creating hours and hours of free promotional spots on all stations that showed music videos. Of course, it also helps the song, as in the case of **Gangsta's Paradise**, which gets a sideways endorsement from a big Hollywood star like Michelle Pfeiffer.

> **"gangsta's paradise** was one of the earliest gangsta rap tunes to be a global hit**"**

Words and **music** Matt Rowe, Melanie Chisholm, Melanie Brown, Geri Halliwell, Victoria Adams, Emma Bunton and Richard Stannard **1996**

The summer of 1996 belonged to The Spice Girls. The five young wannabes finally saw two years of hard work turn out better than they could ever have dreamed, as they took the UK, then Europe and Japan, and eventually the US, by storm. None of the girls had great voices, but they exuded personality, energy and charisma. Added to that they created 'Girl Power', a tag that the media latched onto with such joyous abandon that the proverbial extra-terrestrial tourist could have been forgiven for mistaking it as a slogan for a political party. Armed with a bunch of immaculately crafted pop songs, they set about milking their 15 minutes under the celebrity lamppost for all it was worth.

The story goes that four of The Spice Girls responded to an advert in *The Stage* (a UK newspaper for the performing arts) for young energetic and ambitious girls who could sing and dance. Melanie Chisholm, Melanie Brown, Geri Halliwell and Victoria Adams got through the various auditions, along with another girl called Michelle, who was to leave the group at a time when success seemed too far away. Her replacement, Emma Bunton,

was plucked from one of London's leading stage schools to complete the quintet. After sacking Bob Herbert, who originally placed the advert, the girls were on the lookout for a new manager. Enter Simon Fuller, ex-manager of Annie Lennox and seasoned music industry man, who guided the girls through their phenomenal rise from obscurity to planet-wide megastardom.

Wannabe was the first single to come from their debut album *Spice*. It went straight in at No.1 in the UK, and then in 21 other countries, including the US the following year. It was perhaps the most confident debut by any artists in the history of pop. Even before their first hit these girls were already pop-stars, there was no 'growing into the role' period. They had nicknames already – Ginger, Scary, Posh, Baby and Sporty (apparently supplied by *Top of the Pops* magazine, which featured a photo-spread of them posing in a

spice rack), and they had an instant hit, staying at the top of the charts for seven weeks, and adding incredibly infectious and endlessly repeated phrases to the English language.

In a trick of repetition borrowed from masters of pop Stock, Aitken and Waterman, the Spice Girls told us what they wanted, really really wanted. In the summer of 1996, nobody could resist repeating this whenever somebody was putting in a request of any sort.

The song itself is a glorious mix of pop, r&b-lite with a hint of hip-hop… well… with a rather lame attempt at a rap actually. Written and produced by Richard Stannard and Matt Rowe (both of East 17 fame), with input from the girls, **Wannabe** is infectious. Perfectly produced, it seems no expense was spared on this song, nor indeed on the album as a whole, which includes several other top quality pop creations. The glorious cocktail of sass, contempt for authority and pure showbiz is reflected in the singing as each of the girls takes a turn. Effectively **Wannabe** works in much the same way as the opening number of a musical, it introduces the audience to the cast and gives them a little of each character. It also turned out to be somewhat prophetic for Ginger Spice, aka Geri, who sang that as for her, we'd see. And we did see. During the promotion of their second album *Spiceworld*, she left the band, just months after they had sacked their manager Simon Fuller.

As so often happens in the history of the boy/girl band, the handpicked young things get a taste for power, believing they can do better. The whole notion of such manufactured bands creates much debate. Normally, defenders of the genre will point to the Motown of the 1960s, where Berry Gordy created the Supremes and The Jackson 5 with huge success. This, however, is not a correct analogy. Gordy was the right man, in the right place, at the right time to harness a huge pool of talent that was aching to be discovered – that of black Americans. Not even the most ardent admirer of The Spice Girls, New Kids on the Block or Take That could surely say that within their midst lies a talent as great as Michael Jackson or Mary Wells. But just how long the remaining four Spice Girls will continue to peddle their particular brand of pop is not clear. It probably won't be too long though – their 15 minutes will shortly be up.

Left The Spice Girls

Words Bernie Taupin **Music** Elton John **1997**

Originally a track from Elton John's 1973 album *Goodbye Yellow Brick Road*, this tribute to screen legend Marilyn Monroe was updated in the wake of the death of Diana, Princess of Wales, for performance at her funeral. Written from the somewhat tragic viewpoint of a sentimental and obsessive young Monroe fan, the original version had pathos and a generalized emotional truth that underscored and informed Elton John's otherwise flamboyant and hugely camp character. But where the 1973 version was bittersweet, 1997's had lost the edge that had kept the song from being another saccharine-coated sycophantic tribute. However, **Candle in the Wind 97**, produced by Sir George Martin just a couple of days after the funeral, became the fastest selling single of all-time, shifting a whopping 3.4 million copies in its first week of release. So what do we know? The previous record holder, 'I Will Always Love You' by Whitney Houston, had sold a meagre 632,000. The next record it shattered was for the biggest selling single ever, previously Bing Crosby's version of 'White Christmas' (see page 84), but Elton John so captured the public mood during this period of global mourning, that his reworked eulogy won hands down, providing the soundtrack to endless hours of montages served up by TV stations throughout the world.

Left Elton John
Below Bernie Taupin

Elton John has been recording his brand of rock 'n' roll-flavoured pop since 1968 when he first started working with Bernie Taupin, the provider of the lyrics to his best songs. Today, 33 years on, Elton John is still going strong, one of a very small group of artists to bother the chart compilers across five decades. A turning point in his music came in the early 1980s when, having departed from the MCA label to join Geffen, he switched from a rock-pop feel to the more mellow adult contemporary sound so beloved of North American radio stations. This shift in musical style coincided with the start of a 15-year hiatus in his working relationship with Taupin. While the majority of Elton John's greatest hits are from the 1970s, he continued to garner great commercial success (despite some personally traumatic times) in the 1980s and throughout the 1990s when his soundtrack for Disney's *The Lion King* was nominated for three Oscars and five Grammies.

The original version of 'Candle in the Wind' shows off some of the best of Elton John's songwriting talents. Essentially a piano ballad rooted in a series of gospel-tinged chords, the song actually breaks away from the more traditional structure of a rock ballad but doesn't fail to include some typical John piano flourishes, the likes of which appear in many of his songs. A criticism levelled at the original song suggested that the rhythm of the lyrics didn't sit perfectly with the melody. However, Taupin and Elton obviously made the decision that the storytelling was more important than a perfect flow. And they were right. 'Candle in the Wind' from 1973 is a classic rock ballad, showing off Elton's talents to the full; however, the success of **Candle in the Wind 97** may well, in the eyes of the millions who associate it with Diana, Princess of Wales, relegate the original to that of a slightly inferior taste of what was to come later.

Words Will Jennings **Music** James Horner **1998**

When Leonardo Di Caprio slipped into his watery grave in that cold, cold sea in the movie *Titanic*, and Kate Winslett said, 'I'll never let go, I promise,' to the simple sound of a Celtic lament, pubescent girls all over the globe got their first whiff of the intoxicating affinity between sex and death, and then, as the credits rolled and the song kicked in, we were all in floods of tears. And for months and months, it seemed, you couldn't get it out of your head.

The story of **My Heart Will Go On** is an object lesson in writing songs for movies, should you ever be tempted. Composer James Horner and *Titanic* director James Cameron both cut their movie teeth working for the great junk film producer Roger Corman. They first met on the set of the movie *Aliens*. Horner was given two weeks to write the score and the pressure resulted in he and Cameron having a difficult working relationship. On *Titanic* the problems were the opposite, with extended deadlines and too much waiting around. The interesting thing is that there was no mention of a theme song during production, and Horner himself was the one to bring the subject up. At first, Cameron was not enthusiastic, which gave Horner an advantage. He maintains that if word had got out that Cameron was looking for a theme song, then every songwriter in the country would have submitted material and turned the thing into a three-ring circus.

The structure of **My Heart Will Go On** mirrors the structure of the film. It needed to transcend both the real drama of the ship going down and the angst of the two lovers about to be separated. Horner had a good working relationship with Celine Dion, who loved the song immediately. Fortunately Cameron did too. Working with lyricist Will Jennings, who relied on Horner's description of a film he had never seen, Horner chose to keep the song very simple in structure, but with a big range that few pop singers could manage. He based the Celtic element on the film's working-class characters and that gave him his basic idea for the big end song, '... it is supposed to sound vaguely Irish, and it does when Celine sings it in the film. When she sings it on radio, there's a lot more going on in it. This is the story of pop world, you get all kinds of people who haven't seen the movie who feel they have to put their stamp on it. I don't think I ever lost control, but I lost control of there only being one version. The version that's in the film is my version and it's very, very simple. The version that's out on the adult charts is her version and her producer's versions, over which I had really very little control... They basically took the song and did what they felt they needed to do for major radio play and I was accommodating up to a point, but at a certain point it was easier to deal with it without me.' Unlike in the film, the course of true love *did* run smoothly. And it was true love. It seemed as though the whole world went out and bought the soundtrack album, the single was No.1 for weeks and the film/album/video package was born. Is this the way of the future?

Above Celine Dion

> **❝** the story of **my heart will go on** is an object lesson in writing songs for movies **❞**

Words and **music** Max Martin **1999**

This is a great pop song, and Britney Spears makes the most of it. From the Abba school of song production, this world-wide mega-hit packs its first hefty punch by starting the song two beats early, catching the listener unawares, and guiding them in towards 'the one' – the first beat of the bar, upon which huge emphasis is made in all the funkiest tunes from James Brown's 'Sex Machine' onwards. But while all the accolades go to this young, sexy, overnight success story, if you take a look behind the scenes, failure was never an option. The House of Britney is built firmly upon such talented songwriting foundations as Diane Warren (see page 173), Eric Foster White (Whitney Houston's favoured producer) and for this song, the title track of Britney's debut album, Max Martin (who has also written for The Backstreet Boys, Ace of Base and Roxette).

Baby One More Time is The Backstreet Boys meets Abba. The chorus's epic arrangement with the pumping drum loop and thumping piano bass is in fact a direct lift from The Backstreet Boys' 'Everybody', but overall it is the layering of counter-melodies, both vocal and instrumental, that labels it as Euro-pop. In fact to say that is almost too general, in reality it is unmistakably Swedish. It is exceptionally well produced and Martin clearly has a knack for writing catchy hooks, absorbing melodies and engaging rhythms. But Britney proves that there is more to her than just another teenage girl who wears her lip-gloss with carefree abandon. She is a pretty good performer who, even if she is not totally in control of her talent, has enough natural nous, mixed with 10 years of showbiz schooling, to complete the all-round perfect pop package.

It was in the autumn of 1998, that this seemingly virtuous, coquettish young performer released her first single and took the world by storm. Surely she was no innocent? The song's refrain has her seemingly asking someone to hit her. But no, this wasn't a controversial reference to domestic violence; in fact it's a southern US colloquialism referring to getting a call from a mobile phone! The accompanying promotional video has her in class, dressed as a schoolgirl,

Right Britney Spears

dancing provocatively in stark contrast to the wholesome image she appears to covet. Is this a complex public image or what? The official publicity centres around her learning to sing in her local church in Kentwood, Louisiana (population 1200); that her first break was as a presenter on *The New Mickey Mouse Club*, a Disney TV children's show; that she is still a virgin; that she loves her mom and likes nothing more than hanging out, shopping, reading romance novels and, of course, singing. Yet Britney's video for 'Oops I Did It Again', the title track from the follow-up album, has her dressed up as Jane Fonda, *Barbarella*-style. And it was apparently all her idea. The innocent temptress image is, of course, not new, and Britney herself regularly cites that other pop queen Madonna as a major influence. But ultimately the world is buying into a character that goes further back even than that, for Britney is an all-singing, all-dancing Lolita.

There have already been a number of cover versions of this song, perhaps most notably by Scottish band Travis, who not only released it as a B-side, but regularly perform it live, including during their headline gig at Glastonbury 2000.

> " this is a great pop song, a world-wide mega-hit that packs a hefty punch "

> **A single is really a three-minute throw-away piece of plastic. Nothing greater than that. But it's entertainment, it's emotional. It can be heart-rending.**
>
> Matt Aitken.

In October 1966 The Beatles' album *Revolver* entered the American charts. With its elaborate harmonies, sophisticated themes – including the LSD-influenced 'Tomorrow Never Knows' – it was their most 'grown up' work to date. Less than three years earlier, The Beatles had arrived in the USA, their success seemingly bringing to an end American Tin Pan Alley pop which, with its teen angst-ridden messages such as 'It's My Party (And I'll Cry If I Want To)', suddenly seemed puerile, inappropriate and phoney. But one week after *Revolver* had taken up the No.1 album position, a single called 'Last Train To Clarksville' by a new band, The Monkees, hit No.1 in the *Billboard* singles chart.

It may have seemed like 'pop' was dead but, actually, it had only been sleeping. The story of popular music is nothing if not the story of survival. Modern pop, as we know it, was born in the 1950s with the advent of teen culture and, more importantly, a teen market. It had survived rock 'n' roll, it would survive the more sophisticated grown up world of The Beatles and Bob Dylan. It would live through psychedelia, progressive rock, punk and rap, to emerge victorious in the 1980s and 1990s in the global success of Wham!, Culture Club, Boyzone and The Spice Girls.

Within three years of The Beatles conquering America, Tin Pan Alley was back in business in the guise of the ultimate manufactured pop act The Monkees. Formed from unknowns (two former child actors and two musicians) to appear in a television show about a struggling band, The Monkees, managed by veteran songwiter and publisher Don Kirshner, went on to become a teen phenomenon. Singing Brill Building songs, like Neil Diamond's 'I'm A Believer' and Carole King's 'Pleasant Valley Sunday', they appealed to the younger sisters of the girls who had swooned over teen idols Bobby Darin, Paul Anka and Fabian – the very girls who had now moved on to Bob Dylan and The Beatles. The Monkees were America's Fab Four, rising to a crescendo of popularity that rivalled Beatlemania, at their height outselling both The Beatles and The Rolling Stones.

The Monkees' success, clearly helped by their network television series, proved there would always be a huge demand for good 'pop' music. They had access to some of the best contemporary Tin Pan

Left The Monkees

Alley tunesmiths in America. Their albums were filled with bright, fresh faced pop songs – perfect humable radio friendly fare. Despite stories that centred on the fact that they didn't play on their records, indeed that they couldn't even play their instruments, the four likeable lads – Davy Jones, Peter Tork, Mickey Dolenz and Mike Nesmith – became huge stars in America and in Europe.

But the inevitable happened. The band wanted more control, their fans grew up and moved on. The pop business was unfazed. They were already on the look out for the 'Next Big Thing'.

The Golden Age of Pop

The 1970s may have seen rock at its most overblown and pretentious, but it was an era that produced many songs of enduring quality, albeit an era rudely interrupted (but only briefly) by punk. As a backlash to the naval gazing of folk-rock and progressive stadium bands, pop music was alive and well in the plethora of teenie singles-oriented acts like The Osmonds, The Jackson 5, The Bay City Rollers and The Partridge Family (who followed directly in the footsteps of the manufactured-for-TV Monkees).

The Osmond family had been kicking around the American entertainment business for years, appearing on television shows as a safe, clean-cut family act. Pop producer Mike Curb recognized their potential, seeing them as a rival to The Jackson 5, then having great success at the original 'Hit Factory', Motown Records. With catchy, well-produced songs like 'One Bad Apple', 'Crazy Horses' and 'Love Me For A Reason' (revived 20 years later by 1990s' boy band Boyzone), the Osmonds became a national institution both in the USA and the UK, where 'Osmondmania' took hold in 1972.

The British seemed to have a particular love of 'teen sensation' pop. As David Cassidy's American hits dried up, he made his way to Britain where he was given the obligatory welcome by screaming crowds at London Airport. There was, of course, nothing new in this hopeless devotion. The mothers of Cassidy fans had probably screamed at The Beatles or The Rolling Stones 10 years earlier whereas their American grandmothers might have been fainting in the aisles at Frank Sinatra's shows in the early 1940s.

The British also seemed particularly good at producing music that tapped into and fed the teen (and now pre-teen) market. Mike

Chapman and Nicky Chinn became one of the most successful songwriting teams of the 1970s, writing and producing a string of hits for pops acts like Mud, Gary Glitter, Sweet, Suzie Quatro and Smokie. Mike Chapman went on to steer New York punk band Blondie in a pop direction and was responsible for worldwide hits like 'Heart of Glass', 'Atomic', 'Rapture', 'Sunday Girl' and 'The Tide is High'. The royalties from merely one of his songs, Tina Turner's 'The Best', endlessly used in television commercials, would provide a more than comfortable living for anyone. Chinn and Chapman's production line approach and their resulting success would only be matched 10 years later by Stock, Aitken and Waterman.

Chartbusters

In 1978 a new music magazine was launched in the UK. Unlike the big four – *NME*, *Melody Maker*, *Sounds* and *Record Mirror*, *Smash Hits* was concerned with pop (no articles or grainy pictures about recession era independent bands here!) and featured glossy colour pictures of glossy colourful new pop acts like Gary Numan, Toyah, Culture Club, Duran Duran and The Human League. Its concerns echoed those of the new post-punk pop stars who cared nothing for political commitment or artistic integrity, but everything for chart positions. These 1980s bands might have been seen as part of a 'New Wave/New Romantic' movement, but they were almost exclusively signed to major labels and they wanted hits, hits, hits. Phil Oakey, whose band The Human League was responsible for the archetypal 1980s pop/dance record 'Don't You Want Me' (see page 151) said he wanted to make records like Abba.

At their peak, Stock, Aitken and Waterman had seven records in the Top 20. In a six-year period during the 1980s, they clocked up over 100 hit singles. They claimed to make music for '… ordinary people with Woolworth ears'. It was music which was unashamedly commercial, upbeat, danceable, instant and disposable. It was pop music. It was also loathed by anyone of voting age. *NME* readers once voted Stock, Aitken and Waterman second in the 'Biggest Bastards' poll. Margaret Thatcher held the No.1 spot.

Pete Waterman used Motown Records as his role model, 'They were the people's label and that's what we were. We made records for people, not for critics. Motown gave me the greatest emotions of my life.' Pete Waterman, Mike Stock and Matt Aitken sat for hours pushing their names around, finally settling on 'Stock, Aitken and Waterman' because it sounded closest to their Motown gurus 'Holland, Dozier, Holland'.

Aitken explained their success by saying they were '… right about our attitude. A single is really a three-minute throw-away piece of plastic. Nothing greater than that. But it's entertainment, it's emotional. It can be heart-rending.' Like Motown, they found their own acts, nurturing from within in some cases (Rick Astley moved from making tea to making hit records – his 'Never Gonna Give You Up' is a 1980s' pop classic). They wrote their own

Right Take That

songs, 'chucking them out' at a rate of four a day and recorded in their own studio. They relaunched the careers of girl group Bananarama ('Love in the First Degree' and 'I Want You Back'), disco diva Donna Summer and the Peter Pan of pop, Cliff Richard.

The Boy Bands

Stock, Aitken and Waterman even had a hand in what has become the 1990s' phenomenon – the boy band – with acts like Big Fun. Their current successful act is Steps, whose every single sells, as Waterman might say, 'shedloads'. In the early 1980s, pop veteran Simon Napier-Bell took svengali-like control of pretty boys George Michael and Andrew Ridgeley. Before long, as Wham!, they were in the pop charts and on the bedroom walls of teenagers across the globe. The boy bands that followed in their successful footsteps – Take That, 911, East 17, New Edition, Boyzone and Westlife – are evidence of the ability of the pop business to constantly reinvent itself. When a 14-year-old Frankie Lymon made his debut with The Teenagers in 1955 singing 'Why Do Fools Fall in Love', it established a precedent of turning children, or very young teenagers, into pop stars.

Of all the boy bands, Take That came closest – in terms of commercial success and cross-generational appeal – to The Beatles. Like the Fab Four, they had a cuteness and a northern cheekiness and, more importantly, they could write songs. Although some of their greatest successes were with covers of earlier pop hits, such as Barry Manilow's 'Could It Be Magic', their lead singer Gary Barlow was responsible for composing much of their material including the ballad 'A Million Love Songs'. Just as they were beginning to be accepted by music critics (which had never been something that concerned their pre-pubescent fan base), the band split up. Robbie Williams went on to gain more rock 'n' roll credibility via a well publicized battle with drink and drugs before launching a successful solo career and seeing chart success with songs like 'Angels' and 'Let Me Entertain You'. But despite all the apparent success only one former incumbent of a boy band – Michael Jackson – managed to go on to international glory.

Girl Power

When Take That abdicated as monarchs of the UK teen band scene in February 1996, there were several pretenders lining up. But few could have predicted that a female quintet would have more success in the Smash Hits reading market than Boyzone or Bros. In true production line pop tradition, The Spice Girls were a group put together with the express purpose of setting the record charts alight, something they achieved with their first single. 'Wannabee' – an expression of their Girl Power philosophy – effortlessly made No.1 on both sides of the Atlantic. 'Wannabe', like its follow up, 'Say You'll Be

There', had all the glorious catchiness of Take That or Wham! at their commercial peak. Their success led to a rash of imitators.

Of course, as we have already seen, nothing is new in the world of popular music. The Spice Girls had their own heroes, and one of them, Madonna, was around before them and may well last longer than they do. A huge star in the 1980s, Madonna Ciccione couldn't decide whether she wanted to be a dancer, a singer or a film star. So she became all of them. She had her first hit in 1983 with 'Holiday'. Within two years she was a fixture in the charts throughout the world, starred in a hit movie, Desperately Seeking Susan, and was signed up by Pepsi Cola to market their hugely successful soft drink.

By the turn of the century Madonna had proved that she was around to stay. A successful record company owner, she released on her label Maverick her own material as well as product by Cleopatra and Me'shell Ndegé Ocello. A film star with roles in hit movies like Dick Tracy, A League of Their Own and Evita, a successful author with her controversial book Sex, and a new mother, Madonna had the temerity to make her best albums for years between 1998 and 2000. Always remaining at the cutting edge of production pop, she teamed up with William Orbit for her album Ray of Light. A single, from the soundtrack of Austin Powers: The Spy Who Shagged Me, followed and then in 2000 she released the album Music, to great acclaim from fans and music critics alike. No wonder The Spice Girls called their first single 'Wannabe', a term coined originally by La Ciccione as she is known in some circles, to describe fans who wanted to be like her. To complete the circle, during Madonna's live appearances in 2000 she took to wearing T-shirts with the names 'Kylie' and 'Britney' on them, proving that, as usual, she is one step ahead of the pack.

One hundred years on, the traditions of Tin Pan Alley are still present in the music business. In the early days, writers like Irving Berlin and Harry von Tilzer showed how to write to a brief with a specific market in mind. Their modern corollaries are the Stock, Aitken and Watermans who pride themselves on their ability to write to order, whether it be for The Spice Girls or Celine Dion. Whether they come up with songs that can endure is a matter for debate. The Spice Girls 'Wannabee' may, in 2050, say as much about its time as Gershwin's 'Our Love is Here To Stay' says about the 1920s. But the fact is that both were written with the same purpose – to be listened to and danced to, and to SELL!

Right Madonna

index

Song titles are in inverted commas. A bold page number indicates a main entry for a song. Album, show and film titles are in italics. Definite and indefinite articles (A, The) are inverted. For big bands and orchestras, see the bandleaders' names.

Copyright acknowledgements

Picture and Lyric Credits/Copyright © 2001

Alan Lewens and the Publishers wish to thank the undermentioned for permission to reproduce the following:

Photographs copyright © p8 Corbis; p10 Hulton Getty; p13 Hulton Getty; p14 Theatre Collection, Performing Arts Research Center, The New York Public Library at Lincoln Center, Astor, Lenox and Tilden Foundations; p15 Hulton Getty; p16 Hulton Getty; p17 Hulton Getty (top), Redferns Music Picture Library (bottom); p18 Redferns Music Picture Library; p20 Tindley Temple United Methodist Church, Philadelphia; p21 Hulton Getty; p22 Hulton Getty; p23 Redferns Music Picture Library; p24 Redferns Music Picture Library; p25 The Overtures Collection; p26 Redferns Music Picture Library; p27 Redferns Music Picture Library; p28 The Overtures Collection; p31 Hulton Getty; p32 Hulton Getty; p35 Courtesy of Stephen C. LaVere; p36 Hulton Getty; p37 The Overtures Collection; p38 Hulton Getty; p39 Hulton Getty; p40 The Overtures Collection (top, bottom); p41 Redferns Music Picture Library; p42 Hulton Getty; p43 Redferns Music Picture Library; p44 Redferns Music Picture Library; p45 Redferns Music Picture Library; p46 Hulton Getty; p48 Corbis; p49 Redferns Music Picture Library; p50 Hulton Getty; p51 Redferns Music Picture Library; p52 Hulton Getty; p54 Hulton Getty; p57 Hulton Getty; p59 Redferns Music Picture Library; p60 Hulton Getty; p61 Hulton Getty; p62 Hulton Getty; p63 Hulton Getty (top, bottom); p64 Redferns Music Picture Library; p65 Redferns Music Picture Library; p66 Hulton Getty; p67 The Overtures Collection (top), Redferns Music Picture Library (bottom); p68 Redferns Music Picture Library; p69 Redferns Music Picture Library (top), The Overtures Collection (bottom); p70 Redferns Music Picture Library; p71 Country Music Foundation; p72 Redferns Music Picture Library; p75 Hulton Getty; p76 Redferns Music Picture Library; p79 Redferns Music Picture Library; p81 The Overtures Collection; p82 The Overtures Collection (top), Redferns Music Picture Library (bottom); p83 Hulton Getty; p84 Redferns Music Picture Library; p85 Redferns Music Picture Library; p86 Hulton Getty; p87 Hulton Getty; p88 Redferns Music Picture Library (left and right); p90 Redferns Music Picture Library (top and bottom); p91 Redferns Music Picture Library (top and bottom); p92 Redferns Music Picture Library; p93 Courtesy of The British Archive of Country Music; p94 Redferns Music Picture Library; p97 Hulton Getty; p99 Hulton Getty; p101 Redferns Music Picture Library (left and right); p102 Hulton Getty; p103 Hulton Getty; p104 Redferns Music Picture Library (top and bottom); p105 Redferns Music Picture Library; p107 Redferns Music Picture Library; p108 Redferns Music Picture Library; p109 Redferns Music Picture Library; p110 Redferns Music Picture Library; p111 Redferns Music Picture Library; p112 Redferns Music Picture Library (top and bottom); p113 Redferns Music Picture Library; p114 Redferns Music Picture Library; p117 Hulton Getty; p118 Hulton Getty; p121 Hulton Getty; p122 Redferns Music Picture Library; p123 Redferns Music Picture Library; p124 Redferns Music Picture Library (left and right); p125 Redferns Music Picture Library; p126 Redferns Music Picture Library; p127 Redferns Music Picture Library; p128 Redferns Music Picture Library; p129 Redferns Music Picture Library (top and bottom); p130 Hulton Getty; p131 Hulton Getty; p132 Hulton Getty; p133 Hulton Getty; p134 Redferns Music Picture Library; p135 Redferns Music Picture Library; p136 Redferns Music Picture Library; p137 Redferns Music Picture Library; p138 Redferns Music Picture Library; p139 Redferns Music Picture Library; p140 Hulton Getty; p143 Redferns Music Picture Library; p145 Redferns Music Picture Library; p147 Redferns Music Picture Library; p148 Hulton Getty; p149 Hulton Getty; p150 Redferns Music Picture Library; p151 Redferns Music Picture Library; p152 Redferns Music Picture Library; p153 Redferns Music Picture Library; p154 Redferns Music Picture Library; p156 Redferns Music Picture Library; p157 Redferns Music Picture Library; p158 Redferns Music Picture Library; p159 Redferns Music Picture Library; p160 Redferns Music Picture Library (left and right); p161 Redferns Music Picture Library; p162 Hulton Getty; p165 *Swing Time*, RKO Pictures, Director George Stevens. Hulton Getty; p166 *Starlight Express*, Music: Andrew Loyd Webber, Lyrics: Richard Stilgoe, Director: Trevor Nunn. Redferns Music Picture Library; p169 Redferns Music Picture Library (top and bottom); p170 Redferns Music Picture Library; p171 Redferns Music Picture Library; p172 Redferns Music Picture Library; p173 Redferns Music Picture Library; p174 Redferns Music Picture Library; p176 Redferns Music Picture Library; p178 Redferns Music Picture Library (top and bottom); p179 Redferns Music Picture Library; p180 Redferns Music Picture Library; p182 Hulton Getty; p185 Redferns Music Picture Library; p187 PA Photos.

Lyrics copyright © All rights reserved. p39 Roses of Picardy. Words by Frederick Weatherly © 1916 Chappell Music Ltd, London W6 8BS. Reproduced by permission of International Music Publications Ltd. p42 Swanee. Words by Irving Caesar © 1919 Harms Inc, USA. (50%) Francis Day & Hunter Ltd, London WC2H OQY, (50%) Warner/Chappell Music Ltd, London W6 8BS. Reproduced by permission of International Music Publications Ltd. p50 Tea for Two. Words by Irving Caesar © 1920 Harms Inc, USA. Warner/Chappell Music Ltd, London W6 8BS. Reproduced by permission of International Music Publications Ltd. p64 But Not For Me. Words by Ira Gershwin © 1930 Chappell & Co Inc, USA. Warner/Chappell Music Ltd, London W6 8BS. Reproduced by permission of International Music Publications Ltd. p66 Brother Can You Spare a Dime. Words by E.Y. Harburg © 1932 Harms Inc, USA. Chappell Music Ltd, London W6 8BS. Reproduced by permission of International Music Publications Ltd. p68 Night and Day. Words by Cole Porter © 1932 Harms Inc, USA. Chappell Music Ltd, London W6 8BS. Reproduced by permission of International Music Publications Ltd. p82 Bewitched, Bothered and Bewildered. Words by Lorenz Hart © 1941 Chappell & Co Inc, USA. Warner/Chappell Music Ltd, London W6 8BS. Reproduced by permission of International Music Publications Ltd. p87 Ev'ry Time We Say Goodbye. Words by Cole Porter © 1944 Buxton Hill Music Corp, USA. Warner/Chappell Music Ltd, London W6 8BS. Reproduced by permission of International Music Publications Ltd. p103 Secret Love. Words by Paul Francis Webster © 1953 (renewed) Remick Music Corp, USA. Warner/Chappell North America Ltd, London W6 8BS. Reproduced by permission of International Music Publications Ltd. p152 The Message. Words by Edward G. Fletcher, Melvin Glover, Clifton Nathaniel Chase, Silvia Robinson © Four Hills Music Ltd/IQ Music Ltd.

The publishers have used their best endeavours to trace all copyright holders.